The GREEN LACE CORSET

Published June 19, 2018
Printed in the United States of America
Print ISBN: 978-1-63152-769-2
E-ISBN: 978-1-63152-770-8
Library of Congress Control Number: 2020907226

Book design by Stacey Aaronson

For information, address:
She Writes Press
1563 Solano Ave #546
Berkeley, CA 94707

She Writes Press is a division of SparkPoint Studio, LLC.

The Green Lace Corset

A Novel

JILL G. HALL

SHE WRITES PRESS

This book is dedicated to my dear friend Judy Reeves,
who made this and so much more possible.

1

Anne's boots clomped along the wooden sidewalk as she breathed in the clean, crisp air. April's sponge-painted clouds hung in the turquoise sky. Snow-capped peaks from the last storm of the season loomed above Flagstaff to the north.

Ever since her friend Sylvia had told her about the area's peaceful beauty, Anne had wanted to visit. She bet it hadn't changed much since Sylvia had been here in the 1960s. Long-standing downtown storefronts boasted Babbitt Brothers, Macy's European Coffeehouse, and the brick Monte Vista Hotel, with its original neon sign. The stone Nativity Church's steeple appeared as tall as the ponderosa pines that lined nearby Route 66.

Anne hadn't been certain Tweety, her yellow Karmann Ghia, would make it all the way from San Francisco, but it had chugged along the old route without so much as a cough. She'd spent the night in Needles, and this morning, after a good night's rest, she had traveled the short distance to Flagstaff. Tomorrow she'd cruise out to the Painted Desert and through the Navajo reservation, two places Sylvia had spoken of with fondness.

Anne wanted to feel close to her mentor, who'd been gone for more than two years now. She missed her wise guidance. Fortunately, Anne's boss, Priscilla, at the San Francisco Museum of Modern Art, where Anne taught, had found a substitute so she could go. Almost a year earlier, Anne had broken it off with her fiancé, Sergio, for the last time and still reeled from it. She'd been so certain he was the one. She hoped this journey would relieve some of her loneliness.

As she continued along the wooden sidewalk, the window of Really Resale Boutique's shop caught her attention. A mustached mannequin in full cowboy regalia—Stetson hat, checkered shirt with snaps, and suede-fringed chaps—was posed beside a rusty wagon wheel and a life-size plastic cow. Searching for found treasures was one of her passions. Sometimes she'd find a little something for herself, as well as objects for her artwork, still selling well at Gallery Noir.

Anne stepped inside to the tinkling of a bell. A straw aroma from the hay bales strewn around for ambience tickled her nose.

"Morning." From behind the counter, a girl looked up from her books with a smile. She wore a Northern Arizona University T-shirt; her blond braids hung down over it. "Can I help you?"

"Just looking." It was all in the hunt. Anne always let her intuition guide her.

"I'm Lola. Let me know if you need anything." The girl returned to her studies.

Anne looked through a basket of bandannas and flipped through a clothes rack. The 1950s tulle prom dress, the sequined Mexican shawl, and the faded gingham dress didn't do much for her, but she held her breath when she spotted a green corset.

Black lace trimmed the bodice's top edge and moved down its front. A short, flouncy skirt rested over it. Both pieces were the same color as her favorite cocktail dress, the one she'd had on the night she met Sergio.

The corset appeared to be from the 1800s, something Miss Kitty might have worn in that old TV show *Gunsmoke*—a true vintage piece. Rarely could something this old be discovered in a resale shop, especially in such good shape.

Anne pulled the hanger off the rack, held the corset up to the light, and checked for moth holes and tears. Some of the lace had become loose, but Anne could easily mend it. She ran her hand along the smooth satin and fingered the hooks that marched down the corset's center.

She fantasized about what it would feel like for Sergio to unlatch the hooks, one at a time, slowly. It had been months since she'd seen him. He called occasionally, but when he did, she felt sadder and lonelier than ever. She shook her head. She should be over him by now.

A country song played: "How Do I Live." She didn't remember the singer's name, but she liked the twang and the lyrics. Her eyes welled up. She never knew when a song would hit her.

"Want to try it on?" Lola asked from the counter.

Anne blinked away tears, shook off her emotions, and turned around. "How much for the set?" She searched for a price tag but found none.

Lola opened a ledger and scanned a page. "Don't know. I need to call the owner. Want to try it on in the meantime?"

"Sure." Anne couldn't pass up this opportunity.

Lola took the hanger from her, led her to the back of the shop, and hung the corset on a screen. "Just give a holler if you need help."

Behind the screen, Anne slipped out of her boots, jeans, and sweater. She unpinned the pieces, stepped into the skirt, and tied the side bows. She pulled the corset around her and reconnected the front metal hooks. Good thing she hadn't gained back the weight she'd lost last year after their breakup. Without all that yoga, the hooks would never have closed. She wished she had fishnet stockings to wear with the outfit.

As Anne slid back into her black boots, she heard Lola on the phone, asking, "How much for the green satin saloon number?"

"It's only one hundred dollars," Lola called. "Let me see."

Anne stepped out from behind the screen.

Lola's eyes lit up. "It's made for you."

"Here." Anne turned around. "Would you please tighten the back laces for me?"

Lola tugged on them until they were snug.

"Thanks." Anne leaned over and stuck her hand down the front twice, lifting each breast. "Gotta help the girls up."

Lola's eyes grew wide. "I've never seen that trick before."

"Read it on a blog somewhere." Anne studied her reflection in the standing mirror. Nice. A sexy hint of cleavage showed. She thrust out a hip and drawled, "What can I do for ya, fellas?"

Lola laughed. Anne handed Lola her phone, and Lola snapped a few photos.

Anne set her palms over the lace bows on the hips and slid her fingers down the satin below her belly button. A pale glow emanated within her and swirled slowly. The intoxicating aroma of sage filled the air. It had been so long since she'd been with Sergio.

She just had to get over him. Maybe they weren't meant to be, but she now longed for a connection with someone special. Someone who would appreciate a green lace corset like this.

"Do you take credit cards?" she asked.

2

Missouri, 1885

Sally Sue's heart felt as cold as the frozen river the train crossed over. Last night Mama had called her an old maid again. It wasn't her fault that at twenty-five, she'd never been proposed to. And here she was, with no prospects, on her way to Emporia to take care of her sick aunt Sarah for a week once again.

A hazy morning sun shone outside over the vast prairie. Nearly the end of March; the grasses would sprout again soon. Face reflected in the train window, she felt her cornflower-blue eyes holding back tears. She removed her bonnet, put it on the rack above, and ran a finger through a ringlet. Mama said her hair looked like the color of dirty dishwater: "Comes from your father's side of the family." Sally Sue grabbed her tatting from the basket.

A toddler sitting across from her started to cry. His mama picked him up, rocked him, and passed her hand over his peach-fuzzed head. "Hush, Sampson."

Sally Sue smiled at his ironic name. He soon quieted to a slow gurgle, grinned at her, and waved his tiny fingers. She put out her gloved hand, and he grasped it. Sadness clutched her heart. Without a husband, she'd never have a child of her own.

They both knew it was on account of her father's having left them that they had such troubles, but her ma always pinned it on Sally Sue. *Your father just didn't like having a child around. You were always underfoot. That's why he left. It's your fault I had to take in laundry to make ends meet. You can't sew worth beans; too bad your laugh is so loud; if you were prettier, you'd be married by now.*

Ma had told folks father had been killed in an accident while away on business selling anvils, but the whole town knew the truth. He had run off with a hootchy-cootchy girl from the big city of Chicago.

The train blew a forlorn whistle as it pulled into a depot and stopped. The woman got up with her son, nodded at Sally Sue, and exited, leaving her alone in the car.

As the train chugged out of the station again, a tall man ducked inside, placing his hat and a leather saddlebag on the rack behind him. He sat across from Sally Sue, set a boot over his knee, and opened a newspaper on his lap.

She tried to tat. The man flipped a page in his newspaper. Out of the corner of an eye, she noticed that the nails on his long, strong fingers were neatly trimmed. She examined his spotless white shirt. The cutaway jacket revealed a neat vest and gold watch chain, but the bottoms of his striped trousers and boots were mud splattered. She liked the smell of him, though—hay and horse—and he sure was handsome. Was he the marrying kind? The kind Mama wanted her to get hitched to? He might even be in the cattle business.

Right before she'd left for the train depot that morning, they'd had another spat.

"Now, don't talk to any strange men. You mind your p's and q's, girl." Her mama had straightened Sally Sue's bonnet.

"Mama, you know me better than that."

"We don't want neighbors' tongues wagging about you." Her mama always wagged her tongue about them with scowling gossip. If she despised them so much, why did she care what they thought, anyway?

In fact, since the robbery, Sally Sue hadn't spoken much to anyone. Her mama was always telling her how to behave, but she was a woman now and could take care of herself. She'd made it through that incident, hadn't she?

Whoo-whoo, the whistle warned, as the train careened around a bend, slamming her knee against the man's thigh. She took her time pulling away, tantalized by the firm feel of his strong muscles rubbing against her.

He chuckled and kept his eyes on the newspaper.

She had a hankering to slip off her gloves, put her thumb in his carved cleft chin, and run her hands along those clean-shaven cheeks.

"I'm Sally Sue Sullivan from Kansas City." She struggled to keep her voice from quivering. "What's your name?" Mama would have a conniption if she knew how forward Sally Sue was being and that she'd lied. They didn't really live in Kansas City proper; they were on the outskirts.

He didn't look at her. "Cliff. Cliff from nowhere." His gravelly voice sounded familiar.

"I've heard of that town but never been there." She grinned.

He peered at her and broke out into a belly laugh.

"Lived there long?" she teased.

"Forever."

"I'm on my way to check on Aunt Sarah, who suffers from a lung condition. She's real needy these days. Where're you going?"

"West."

"Where west?"

"Toward the Pacific."

She'd heard out West there was an ocean bigger than any lake she'd ever seen and that one could never get all the way across it.

"Maybe even San Francisco," he said.

She unwrapped her sandwich, ham on rye, and offered him half.

He closed his eyes, took large bites, and swallowed. "Thank you kindly." His eyes looked directly at her.

Her heart kicked like a bucking bronco's. She'd seen those steel-blue eyes before. That day in the bank. That day she'd never forget. It just couldn't be the same person. This was a gentleman. That bandit had been filthy, rough, and terrifying.

He blinked at her with what might be a flicker of recognition. She struggled to remain nonchalant and focused her eyes on her sandwich. What if it was he?

After the robbery, she had described what she could recall to the sketch artist. Because the robber had worn a kerchief, all she could recall were his brown Stetson and those eyes. The artist had been able to capture the coldness in them. Every time she saw one of the posters with those eyes above the kerchief in a post office, bank, or depot, her hands broke out in a sweat and her body shook. She could still hear that shot and smell gunpowder.

Now, as she glanced up, his eyes pierced hers and he grinned. A chill loped up her spine. She was sure it was him. Did he recognize her too?

3

Pleased to have made it back to San Francisco before dark, Anne crawled into the traffic moving into the city. After only two weeks away, she felt as rejuvenated as if she'd been gone for a year. As she chugged across the Bay Bridge, a sense of calm embraced her, despite the traffic.

The beautiful scenery reinforced that she'd made the right decision to stay in her chosen city, not to move home to Michigan when things had gotten tough or to move to New York with Sergio. This was where she belonged, near the Golden Gate Bridge; Coit Tower; Gallery Noir; SFMOMA; and her friends Paul, Fay, and George, who lived at Bay Breeze, Sylvia's old home.

As soon as Anne got settled back at home, she'd finish the artist-in-residence application for the museum. She'd promised herself she would work on it on her trip but hadn't. In addition to her teaching assignments, she'd have a working studio for four months there. Priscilla, her boss and the education director, had encouraged Anne to apply, saying she'd be perfect. She wasn't so sure, though—San Francisco claimed a lot of incredible local artists.

She pulled onto California Street, and a parking spot appeared miraculously in front of her apartment building. She squeezed Tweety into it and turned the wheels into the curb, facing downhill. She slipped on her backpack from the passenger seat and from the trunk grasped her box filled with found travel treasures, and the bag from the Really Resale Boutique.

In the restaurant window next to her apartment building, Tony tossed pizza and smiled hello. The aroma overtook her, and she realized how hungry she was. She lifted two fingers, her sign that she'd be down soon for two slices of her favorite pescatarian pizza with plenty of anchovies.

She set down her things, unlocked her building's door, and scrambled inside.

Mrs. Landenheim stepped out of her first-floor apartment. Thai, her Siamese cat, skittered out into the foyer, threaded through Anne's legs, and ran up the stairs.

Even though it was evening, the landlady still wore curlers. "Welcome home. I followed you on Instagram. Looked like a wonderful trip." Mrs. Landenheim dropped a stack of mail in the box Anne held up.

"Thanks." Exhausted, Anne didn't want to chat.

Mrs. Landenheim eyed the box of loot. "What did you find?"

Anne set her backpack, her boutique bag, and the box on the dingy carpet and pulled out a greasy hubcap. "Found this on Route 66."

Her head did a little dance as she sang, "Got my kicks on Route 66."

"What are you going to do with that?" Mrs. Landenheim managed a smile.

"Never know. It just called to me. Maybe a mosaic."

"What else you got there?" Mrs. Landenheim bent down, stuck her pink-polished nails into the box, and lifted out a turquoise-haired doll the size of a troll.

"Harrumph." She tossed it back and pulled out a lunch bag filled with colorful stones. To reward herself for following the law and not picking up rocks from the ground in the Painted Desert, Anne had bought the smooth stones in the park's gift shop. One at a time, Mrs. Landenheim picked out and studied the various items in Anne's box: a ceramic girl in a white apron and head scarf, a jar of marbles, an old washboard, a rusty horseshoe, a conch belt, and a baggie filled with flea-market silver charms.

Anne opened the baggie and held it out. "Close your eyes and pick one."

"What are they?" Mrs. Landenheim asked.

"*Milagros* means 'miracles' in Spanish. Each one symbolizes something different. Catholics pin them onto saint statues in churches."

Mrs. Landenheim dug her hand inside and selected a trinket in the shape of a skinny leg. "What's this?"

"It's a leg."

"What?" Mrs. Landenheim handed the tin curio back to Anne.

"It means it's time to step forward in your life, but you must go with care." Anne didn't know if that was what it meant, but she believed that was what Mrs. Landenheim needed to hear.

"Oh, my. Ray Ray proposed to me last week. Do you think the leg means I'm supposed to say yes? I've been hesitant to consent, after being widowed all these years. I don't want to give up my independence. What do you think? Is the leg giving me a message?"

Anne had never liked Mr. Block, former owner of Gallery Noir. He had called her collages "kindergarten cut-and-paste." She hadn't been surprised, and was even a little guiltily glad, when he had been forced to sell the business for financial reasons.

"I did say step forward with care. It's important to weigh the pros and cons. How's his retirement going?" Anne asked.

"He seems to be a changed man." Mrs. Landenheim took the *milagro* and pushed the leg to kick the foot. "I'll treasure it." She beamed and dropped it into the pocket of her pink bathrobe. "And in that bag of tricks?" She pointed toward the boutique bag on the floor next to the backpack.

Anne hesitated. She wasn't sure what Mrs. Landenheim would think or whether she wanted her opinion. Was her purchase too risqué? Maybe she shouldn't have bought it after all. Anne swallowed and then pulled out the corset with the skirt and held them up in front of her neighbor.

Mrs. Landenheim's droopy basset-hound eyes grew wide. "Oh, my. May I borrow it? I can't even imagine what Ray Ray might say."

"Maybe." Anne didn't even want to imagine Mrs. Landenheim wearing it. "See you later." She repacked her treasures and ran up the stairs.

Mrs. Landenheim's cat sat patiently on Anne's doorstep. Anne nudged Thai with a foot and whispered, "*Pssst.* Go away. Not now." If Mrs. Landenheim knew Anne had been feeding her scraps, she wouldn't be pleased.

The cat snarled and leaped down the stairs, crooked tail bouncing behind her.

Anne stepped inside her dark apartment, flipped on the lights, and put her stuff down on her carpet. It felt wonderful to be home. Her small studio was usually a mess—dirty dishes in the sink, bed unmade, canvases stacked on the floor, open bins of paints and found objects on every flat surface, knickknack shelf overflowing. Sergio had once accused her of being a hoarder. She defended herself by claiming it was impossible to keep a place neat when that place was your studio and your home too. Someday she wanted to have a big studio with plenty of space. In the meantime, for at least four months, if she got that residency, she'd have the museum studio to work in.

She'd recently read on the *Hoarder Comes Clean* blog that it was good feng shui to return home from a trip to a clean abode. So, before she'd left for Arizona, she had washed the dishes, put away all of her art supplies, and even made the daybed. Today, it felt so fantastic to return to a pristine home that she vowed to always keep it this way. She took a photo of the room, typed *home, sweet home* and posted it on Instagram.

"Alexa," she said, "play Enya."

The singer's voice magically filled the apartment. Sergio had bought her the Echo and hooked it up right before their breakup. Anne got a little thrill every time the bit of technology followed her commands.

"Alexa, turn on salt lamp." The light popped on.

She twirled around, took her lucky key from her jeans pocket and put it back on her artist altar in the corner, rubbed the Buddha's head, and fingered her father's dog tags. From the box of travel goodies, she located the pendant she'd bought at the Santa Fe Plaza, where local Native American artists lined up their wares under the veranda to sell. The Navajo she had bought it from had been patient as she'd picked up each of his pieces, until she'd finally chosen the one that called to her the most. The size of two quarters, the oval-shaped turquoise was inlaid in silver filigree and stamped on the back with the artist's initials. Turquoise signified creativity, good luck, and joy. Perfect for her. She kissed it and added it to the altar.

Val's vocalizations from downstairs floated up to her. *Ka-ke-kai-ko-koo. Ka-ke-kai-ko-koo.*

Anne sang down, echoing him. *Ka-ke-kai-ko-koo. Ka-ke-kai-ko-koo.* Some people would think these vocal warm-ups obnoxious, but she found them endearing.

Val performed in *Beach Blanket Babylon*, the campy satirical revue at Club Fugazi, in North Beach, that made fun of everything. She loved the humongous hats and cross-gender casting that constantly changed to reflect current politics and trends. Luckily, Val got her comp tickets whenever she wanted. But she'd recently heard that the show was going to be closed down. That would be so sad. It had been a San Francisco favorite since 1974. Where would Val ever find another job that was that much fun?

She pulled the corset and skirt out of the bag and held them up to her, looking in the full-length mirror on the back of her closet.

The light hit the outfit just so, and the sequins shone. Her belly tingled. She had made the right decision to buy it after all and couldn't wait to wear it with a special guy. She opened the door and hung it on the back.

Inside, she caressed the black velvet coat that had brought her to Sylvia and the friendship that meant so much to Anne. She fingered the snowflake pin and watched it sparkle in the light. She slipped it back on the rack.

She turned on the water in the farmhouse kitchen sink, added detergent, and stuck the oily hubcap in the suds to soak. She dried her hands and got her phone. There were several messages. Unlike many people, she never talked on the phone while driving. Hard enough to concentrate as it was. The first one was from her mom. Anne would call her later. The second message was from Sergio. Just seeing his number on her phone made her heart speed up.

"I see you're back. FaceTime me. It's been a long time since we talked."

He must be keeping close track of her. She had posted that Instagram photo not even half an hour earlier. He was right on time to break the silence. She was afraid to see him, though. It might let out all those feelings she'd been trying to shove into the cupboard of her heart and shut up tight for the past year. Since then, they'd occasionally texted and liked each other's posts but hadn't FaceTimed. She missed his sturdy body next to hers in bed, his warm hands and deep kisses. A fervent longing for him overtook her whole being. No, she wasn't ready to talk to him in person yet.

From her altar, she picked up the diamond ring that had been his *nonna*'s. He had insisted she keep it even after Anne broke off their engagement. She slipped it on and lolled on the daybed, remembering the romantic afternoon in Tuscany when he'd proposed.

Her phone broke her reverie with a text message from Tony: *Pizza's ready.*

She'd forgotten about it and the fact that she'd been starving, and she ran down the stairs. Outside the door, Anne almost bumped into Mata Hari, her homeless friend, who was walking down the sidewalk, wearing one of the pink pussy hats Anne had knitted for the women's shelter for the 2017 Women's March.

Mata's blue eyes lit up. "Hi, missy. Long time no seen you around-o."

"I went on a road trip to Arizon-o."

"I was there once. Thought I'd fry from the desert heat. Bad for beauty." Mata grinned.

"I was in northern Arizona; it's pretty nice this time of year. Hungry?"

"Am I ever."

Anne held up a finger. "Just a sec." She went inside Tony's, paid for the pizza, and gave one of the slices to Mata.

"Thanks." Mata took a bite. "Where's that handsome money-bags of yours?"

"We broke up ages ago." Anne had shared this with her several times before.

"I told you he was a keeper. You're not getting any younger."

Anne didn't need reminding of that. "I just couldn't live in New York."

"You're so right. Those hot Broadway lights dry out our skin, like Arizona deserts." Mata touched her wrinkled cheeks. "Not our misty San Francisco air and sultry moons."

After staying with Sergio in New York for a month, Anne had realized that even though they adored each other, it just wasn't going to work out. True love or not, home was here in San Francisco, and she planned never to leave it again. Still, she'd probably call him tomorrow. She hoped when she saw his face, she didn't fall in love with him all over again.

4

In the morning, Anne awoke from a Sergio kissing dream. His king-size New York bed was deep, sheets smooth. Wearing the green lace corset, she ran her fingers through the curly hair on the back of his neck. His hands explored the corset's bodice. His clean scent, honeysuckle mixed with sage, permeated the air.

Anne sat up. She certainly wasn't going to call him now. She eyed the corset hanging on the closet door. The dream was right: Sergio would like the outfit. She sighed. He'd never get to see it.

Who might have owned it before? What year could it be from? Maybe it was a costume from a movie or TV western. Many had been filmed out that way.

Out of coffee, she grabbed a Diet Coke from the fridge and poured it into the ARTISTS DO IT IN COLOR mug Sergio had given her for her birthday.

Anne remembered her mom telling her about someone in the family wearing a corset. Anne called her number.

"Hey, Mom."

"I followed your posts. Looked like you had a good trip. I'm sorry you couldn't come home to Michigan on your vacation. I understand that as an artist you need new experiences."

Anne appreciated that her mom really tried to be supportive. Most Michiganders didn't travel much. In fact, her mother had never even come out to visit in all the years Anne had lived in San Francisco.

Not even when she'd had her solo show at Gallery Noir. She'd accepted long ago that her mom didn't travel out of state, but it would be a whole lot easier if she would come to California, instead of depending on Anne to always make the trek.

"Find any treasures?"

"Plenty. The best find was a corset."

"What?"

"A corset. The most gorgeous green. Didn't you tell me your grandmother used to wear a corset?"

"Yes. An ugly old thing, dingy white cotton, with laces that crisscrossed down her spine. She wore it all the time, whalebones and all. She claimed the corset helped her bad back. I don't know how that could be. Grandma never left the house without hers on. She also wore all black, even though Grandpa had been gone for twenty years . . ."

Anne knew she had better hurry up this conversation, or she'd be on the phone all day. Anyway, she had to get that application finished to drop off before her afternoon class.

"Well, this one isn't ugly. I'll go now so I can send you a photo. Love you. Call you later."

Hard to believe women had worn corsets for so many years. All the time.

She scrolled through her photos, found a fun one of her posing for Lola in the boutique, and texted it to her mom. Sergio would like the picture, but she didn't send it. He might get the wrong idea.

Anne skimmed through more road-trip photos and forwarded a few to save to her computer. Some of her favorites were the whipped-cream clouds. On hot afternoons, they'd turn dark and thunder and lightning would ensue. She'd hurry back to the B and B before then so she could curl up in her room, listen to the rain pound on the gable roof, enjoy the show. That was what vacations were for.

How fun it will be to paint that sky. Even though she should really work on her application, it would take only a few minutes to start the background. She pulled out a new canvas and set it on the easel. "Nothing is truly white in the sky," she remembered her college professor telling the class.

Anne squished a dollop of Titanium White and a tad of Mars Black directly on the canvas, dunked her biggest brush in a jar of water, swirled the two paint colors together, and washed the mixture over the fabric. After having not painted for a few weeks, she felt the motion of spreading colors filling her whole body with sublime contentment. She'd never been a good dancer, but the rhythm of creating art was her dance. She swished the brush across the canvas a few more times and left it on the easel to dry.

She climbed out the kitchen door to inspect her rooftop garden, maybe find something for breakfast. She would go to the grocery store after work. Misty fog hung overhead, this sky so different from the giant Southwest sky. A blue jay pecking on a blackberry vine squawked at her and flew away. Anne watched it dart across California Street to the pitched roof of one of the pastel-colored Victorian row houses. They'd been painted two years before and still maintained their brilliant hues.

Mint had begun to march all over the other plants in her plot. She pulled up a handful, releasing the fresh aroma. With so much of it, she should research how to make mint tea, which was supposed to be very soothing.

Peeking from underneath the mint, vivid red strawberries emerged. She tugged one off and tossed it in her mouth, the sweet taste perfect.

"Choose delicious—that's nutritious." She quoted Sylvia, who'd had her own garden right outside her kitchen at Bay Breeze. She'd taught Anne so much about eating healthfully and the power of growing some of your own food staples.

She picked a dozen ripe strawberries and the few blackberries that smoothly came right off the vine. Inside, she tossed them in a colander on the counter beside the sink. Pushing aside the hubcap, she drained the dirty water, rinsed the berries, put them in her blender, and added water, chocolate protein powder, and a teaspoon of honey to make a smoothie. She scrubbed the hubcap; grease still clung to the inside edges, so she poured in more dish soap, turned on the hot water, and let the metal continue to soak.

As Anne sipped her smoothie, she climbed onto the daybed and began to read the application on her computer.

RESIDENCY DESCRIPTION

The artist-in-residence program will redefine the museum experience to make art more accessible and personally meaningful to guests. It will give them the opportunity to view the creative process firsthand and interact with local artists working in a studio environment. The interview panel will review proposals and choose an artist and project that have the strongest "wow" factor.

Provide a summary of the work you envision creating during the residency by answering the following questions:

1. *What is your project? How did the idea come to you?*
2. *In what ways is this project risk-taking or innovating?*
3. *How will you share your project with museum guests?*
4. *How much money will you need to complete the project?*

She read through the questions again, her mind blank. A shaky, panicky feeling hit her chest. She had no idea how to answer these questions. Maybe she wasn't supposed to apply after all. Many other local artists were more qualified. What chance did she have of getting it, anyway? She envisioned working in that big studio space and just had to suck it up and give it a go. Perhaps if she spread more paint on the sky canvas, the answers would come to her. Sometimes when she was blocked, she worked on something else and the problem was solved. This was different, though; now, she was just procrastinating—one of her downfalls.

She needed help. Fay would be at Gallery Noir now. Anne hated to bother her at work, but she had to get this done.

She texted Fay: *SOS!*

A few minutes later, Fay called. "Welcome back. What's up?"

"I'm stuck."

"Sorry, mate. Take deep breaths and follow your heart, like you always do."

Fay's British accent made Anne smile. "No, not my art. I've got lots to inspire me since my journey. I have to fill out this stupid museum residency application, and I don't know what to say."

"What's the difference between doing art and writing? Isn't writing an art too? As I said, take deep breaths and follow your heart, like you always do."

Anne thought for a moment. "You're brilliant. I owe you a coffee."

"Very soon. A customer just came in. Gotta go. Ta-ta."

Anne moved to the daybed, held her journal in her lap, closed her eyes, inhaled and exhaled a few times, relaxed into the zone, and started writing.

Magnificent Mosaic

I plan to create a life-size mosaic of a woodland creature. The idea came to me in dreams last year during the nearby wildfires, which killed many animals. This would be the first of a series to honor and remember lost fauna. It's risk-taking because this will be the largest piece I've ever made. Museum guests will be invited to adhere pieces to the mosaic so they can experience process versus product. Expenses will be minimal because most of the materials I use will be found and donated objects. I'll also approach local businesses about donating many supplies.

Anne reread her draft, typed it on her computer, printed it out, and kissed the application for luck. With only minutes to spare, she threw on some sweats, grabbed her backpack, and ran out the door to the museum.

5

Sally Sue broke the man's gaze to look at the rack above his head and saw his hat. A brown Stetson—exactly like the one he'd worn that day!

Her heart plunged, and she jumped up. "You're the bank robber! You held a gun to me."

He nodded and grinned. "Mighty fine to see you again. I've been keeping an eye out for you."

The whistle blew, and the train began to slow as they pulled into Emporia.

"This is my stop." She clutched her basket and stepped into the corridor.

He grasped her bustle from behind, pulled her toward him, and growled, "You're not going anywhere."

She tried to yank herself away. "Let me go!"

"No." He held her tight around the waist, as he'd done the prior month in the National Bank, though this time he didn't hold a gun to her chest. Her heart beat rapidly, and her mind revived that horrible day.

"Please," she pleaded.

He pulled her beside him on the seat next to the window, held open his jacket, and showed her the pistol resting in a holster on his hip.

Her shoulders slumped, and she looked down at her hands.

"Glad you see it my way."

"Do I really have any choice?"

The train whistle sounded again. The locomotive creaked, its bottom scraped along the tracks, and it rumbled out of the station.

Fear rippled in her chest as she relived that horrible day for the hundredth time. She had just stepped into the bank as the guard shot a bandit, who fell to the ground with a blood-wrenching scream. This man—the man beside her now on the train, the man who'd laughed at her joke—blasted the guard, who also collapsed to the floor.

This man had seized her shoulders, held her tight, with his pistol to her chest, and yelled, as he pulled her backward toward the door, "Nobody move!"

God, please save me, she'd silently prayed.

And, as if in answer to her prayer, the man had released her and run out of the bank with that bag of money—a fortune, she later learned: $10,000.

The conductor entered the car and stood beside them. "Tickets, please."

Sally Sue opened her mouth to speak. Cliff patted his jacket above the gun. "Yes, sir." He handed the conductor his ticket. "Honey, give him yours."

Her hands juddered while she searched through the basket. She handed it to the conductor, who didn't notice as she tried to catch his eye.

He studied the ticket with a frown. "This was only good to the last town."

Sally Sue tried to stand, but Cliff put an arm tightly around her shoulders, as if they were lovers. "You don't say. See, here's my ticket."

The conductor inspected it. "Must be some kind of mistake. I apologize. Have a nice ride." He left the car.

Cliff leaned back and closed his eyes. When he seemed to have nodded off, Sally Sue stealthily rose, gathered her things, and headed toward the corridor. He pulled her back down and grumbled, "You're going nowhere without me, pretty lady."

Was he making fun of her? "Pretty"—ha. "Wallflower" was more like it, her mother would have said. Sally Sue scowled back at him. "Why won't you let me go?"

"You'll tell the authorities where I am."

"No, I won't. I promise. I have to go to my aunt. She shouldn't die alone."

"All of us die alone sooner or later."

Sally Sue cried, "Where're you taking me?"

"West. Toward the Pacific." He handed her a white handkerchief from his front pocket. "Better get used to the idea."

"Isn't it wild out there?" She dabbed at her tears.

"That's why I want to go there."

She just couldn't look at him any longer, so she took her tatting from her basket, but she was shaking so hard, she couldn't work the needles. She considered jabbing him with one and running away, but it would only poke him, and he'd shoot her for sure. She put the needles back in her basket and folded her arms across her chest.

Why would a man rob a bank? Did he have hungry children to feed, or a sick parent, or was he just greedy?

"Why'd you do it?" she asked.

"Do what?"

"Rob that bank."

"I had my reasons."

"What could ever justify killing a man?"

"That was never part of the plan. I'll say no more about it."

She looked out the window. A line of five covered wagons crossed the desolate plain.

"Look at those prairie schooners," Cliff said.

"What?"

"Those wagons seem like ships sailing out to sea."

"Why don't those people just take the train?"

"They're moving all their possessions west. Now that trains go all the way across to the Pacific, we'll probably see fewer prairie schooners."

Up ahead, a dozen shaggy beasts roamed the tall grasses near the tracks, their horned heads bowed, as if in prayer. Their skinny legs didn't look like they could hold up their immense bodies. As the train slowed with a squeal, the bison began to scatter.

"Peculiar-looking things," Cliff said. "Used to be millions of them. I heard there are fewer than a thousand left now."

"What happened to them?"

She'd heard stories of engines slowing down for hunters to shoot bison from open windows. "Did hunters really kill bison from trains?"

"Yes."

"Why would anyone shoot them? They're not hurting anything. Was it Indians?"

"No, they only kill what they planned to eat. White hunters mostly shot bison for sport. Sometimes railroad companies paid hunters to keep bison off the tracks."

"Did you ever do it?"

"Do what?"

"Shoot bison from a train?"

He just stared at her and didn't say a word.

She shivered. As the train continued along, she searched for peaceful animal sightings to dispel the gruesome image of bison shootings and counted each new group she saw: flocks of geese, rafters of wild turkey, herds of elk, bands of wild horses.

It began to grow dark. She took a shawl from her basket and wrapped it around her shoulders.

"Are you cold?" Cliff put an arm around her.

She pulled away. "Don't touch me." Memories of the robbery flowed into her senses.

"Sorry." He closed his eyes.

Darkness fell. The train rumbled rhythmically beneath her. After a while, she heard Cliff's soft breathing. Quietly, she picked up her basket and crept into the corridor again.

She heard Cliff's gun cock against the small of her back.

"Like I said, you're not going anywhere without me."

She returned to the seat and stared out into the blackness. How would she ever get away from him? Wouldn't he have killed her already if he was going to do so? Even though she was exhausted, she would never be able to sleep.

Cliff nudged Sally Sue's shoulder. "Morning, glory."

She opened her eyes, stretched, and yawned. She must have fallen asleep. The train continued to chug along the winding tracks. Outside the window, as the sun rose, a vast, sandy landscape glowed rose pink. The train passed lofty, flat mesas striped with bands of color. Maybe that was what the moon looked like.

Cliff handed her his canteen.

Her heart lurched as the realization of this nightmare journey flooded back into her. She shook her head no, but he pushed it toward her again, with force. She took a sip but refused the biscuit he offered.

He eyed her.

"What are you looking at?" she asked, with a scowl.

"Your beauty."

"Stop teasing." For an outlaw, he sure was a sweet-talker. If she was going to escape him, she'd need to stay alert.

The train slowed but didn't stop as it passed a few buildings beside a wooden sign that said ADAMA.

Frothy, scalloped clouds with navy-blue undersides floated above. That was probably what ocean waves looked like. She didn't know for certain, because she'd never seen them before. Since Cliff said they were going to the Pacific, she'd find out soon enough. To her chagrin, even though he was a thief, she still thought he was handsome.

A line of pines taller than any church steeples she'd ever seen passed by. Misty rain wafted sideways, hovered, then disappeared from sight. The train curved around a bend, and her heart opened at the awe-inspiring vista. She'd never seen such massive snowcapped mountains. She wished she could reach up and touch the peaks with her white-gloved hand. They resembled Mount Olympus, like she'd seen in the mythology book at the library, as if gods really could live up there.

As the train began to slow, she spied a real church steeple and a smattering of buildings up ahead. Beside them, a cowboy lassoed a roan mare and led her into a corral. The whistle blew, and a crowd of folks looked up expectantly at the windows as the train rolled to a stop beside a row of rusted-out boxcars.

Cliff stood and handed her bonnet to her. "Let's get out."

"Are we at the Pacific?" She tied the bow beneath her chin.

"No. We're gonna get off here for a while." He grabbed his saddlebag and tilted his head toward the corridor. Sally Sue followed him, holding her basket tightly.

6

Anne knocked on Priscilla's door and stepped inside. An abstract painting, maybe even an original Rothko, hung behind her desk. Diplomas up the yin-yang covered another wall: BA in art history from Vanderbilt, MA from the Rhode Island School of Design, PhD from Yale.

From behind her desk, Priscilla peered at Anne through thick-rimmed glasses. "Welcome back. Have a seat. You look rested."

Anne held the application with shaky hands. "Thanks again for letting me go. I really appreciate it, Dr. Preston."

"No problem." Priscilla removed a pen from her gray, schoolmarm-ish bun and spanked it on the desk as if it were a paddle. "Artists need rejuvenation. Are you feeling fresh?"

"Yes. How did my classes go?"

"One of our new volunteers did a fine job covering for you."

"Glad to hear it. Speaking of rejuvenation, I've come up with a project I think the kids will enjoy."

"You mean young artists."

Oh, brother. "Yes, young artists will enjoy. Do you happen to know anyone who has horses?"

Priscilla hesitated. "In fact, I do. One of our board members has a ranch out near Los Olivos. What do you need?"

"Used horseshoes."

"Really?" Priscilla tapped the pen on her desk again. "Why?"

"We're going to mosaic them using found objects. You've encouraged me to be more innovative with my lessons."

Priscilla shrugged. Her big, shoulder-padded jacket looked like something out of the 1980s. She was probably about Anne's mom's age, but it was hard to tell. At least her mom tried to stay stylish for her Avon business.

"I'm sure he can help with that. I'll introduce you by e-mail."

Anne stood up. "I'd better get ready for class. Here's my application." She put it on the desk.

"Oh, that's right—you're applying for the residency. It's going to be hard work. You'll be on your feet all day and interacting with museum guests."

Strange. Priscilla had told her to apply. She'd always been warm to Anne; today, though, she was downright chilly.

"I know. Thank you for the support and encouragement."

Anne made her way down the hall to the classroom, went inside, and opened the blinds for the natural light. Even though she'd been gone only two weeks, everything looked different. The space was neater than usual; a new shelving unit had been added, and many of the bins had been rearranged. She hoped she'd be able to find her materials. Adorable tinfoil sculptures were displayed on a top shelf.

"Hi, Anne. You're looking gorgeous."

Stunned at the sight of her old boyfriend, she stepped back. It had ended very badly. "Karl, what are you doing here?"

"I covered for you while you were gone." He closed the space between them, gave her a hug, and kissed her on the cheek.

His cinnamon scent used to entice her but now made her want to throw up. She pulled away. "But you aren't even an artist."

"I am now. I left the hardware business and studied sculpture at the community college."

She pictured him whittling with a Swiss Army knife, scraping a twig into a marshmallow skewer. An artist, he must have been kidding. When they were together, he hadn't understood her creativity and hadn't been supportive of her artwork at all, had even called it a hobby.

She eyed his handsome, chiseled face, with its steep cheekbones and cleft chin. "You were always handy."

That was for sure. He was handy in bed. Their sex life had been incredible, and she had fallen for him right away. The jerk. After she'd finally broken up with him, he'd kept texting and calling until she'd decided to block him.

Anne looked at the clock. Her students would be arriving any moment. She spread collage paper on the tables. She'd been seeing Karl for a year when she'd broached the commitment subject and he'd been forced to make a confession. He'd said he was married but that he and his wife slept in separate rooms—as if Anne would ever believe that.

"How's your wife?" she asked now.

"I don't know. We're not living together anymore. I haven't seen her for a year."

"What about your son?" Anne asked. Karl had wanted to move in with Anne while his divorce was being finalized and she could help him with his one-year old baby boy on weekends.

"I haven't seen him for a while, either."

"Why ever not?" She grabbed a pile of magazines and tossed them in the middle of the tables.

"Let's just say it's complicated."

"I'm sure it is."

Fortunately, Perky Penelope, Anne's favorite student, bounded in the door. She knew she shouldn't have a favorite, but she couldn't help herself.

"Hi, Penny. I missed you." Anne opened her arms wide.

"Oh. Are you back?" Penny barely glanced at her as she ran into Karl's arms and gazed up at him. "Mr. Karl is so cool."

Anne felt like she'd been kicked in the stomach by a horse. Penny used to say Anne was cool too.

Then the Tromble twins bounded in. Each grabbed one of Penny's elbows and lifted her off the ground. She shrieked.

"Find a penny, pick it up. All day long, we'll have good luck," they said simultaneously, with loud laughs.

"Boys, stop!" Karl stood between them. "Sit down."

"Sorry, Mr. Karl." They made their way to their seats, while Penny found a chair as far away from them as possible.

Anne could never tell the twins apart.

"Mr. Karl is so cool," one of them said.

"So I've heard." She tried not to feel jealous.

One of the boys pointed at a tinfoil sculpture. "There's the piece I made."

"And there's mine." His twin aimed his finger at another and looked at the paper on the table. "Not collage again!"

"I thought you liked collage." Anne felt her face redden in front of Karl.

"I'd rather do sculpture."

Karl looked at Anne and shrugged.

Before long, ten more students darted into the room, all screeching and running around the tables.

"Sit down!" Karl hollered.

The students rushed to find seats.

"Sorry, Mr. Karl." Rhonda popped a wad of gum.

"Would you like me to stay and help out?" he asked Anne.

"No, thanks."

"I've gotta turn in my residency application now anyway."

He was applying for the residency too. How could he be infringing on her territory like this?

"Want to have coffee after you get off?"

"I have plans." She passed out some scissors.

He whispered in her ear, “Let’s take up where we left off.”

She thought she might gag.

“See you kids later,” Karl called, and started out the door.

She wanted to throw the scissors at his back.

7

The next morning, Anne woke up with a yawn. The night before, she'd tossed and turned, trying to expel the bad memories of Karl from her mind, along with the fact that he was now applying for the residency. She couldn't let him get to her.

She googled him. He didn't even have a website, or any art photos posted on Facebook or Instagram that she could find. He wouldn't be any competition for the residency. On the other hand, she had no trouble locating plenty of pictures of him posing next to women wearing lots of makeup and low-cut tops. What a pants man!

She loved Sundays without anything scheduled. She had the whole day to do her art, and she didn't want to waste it. So many ideas from her trip were buzzing in her head, she didn't know where to start.

The apartment still dark from the fog outside, she yawned, tempted to go back to sleep. Instead, she said, "Alexa, play disco music." That always got her going.

"Stayin' Alive" came on, and in her sweats and old T-shirt, she flipped on the lights, boogied to the sink, scrubbed the hubcap as best she could, and set it on a dish towel to dry, then made coffee.

She decided to start with her lesson sample. She covered the kitchenette table with newspaper, grabbed a paper plate, and placed on it the horseshoe she'd brought back from her trip. She poured the baggie filled with small found objects onto a silver tray. She selected possible focal-point options; a plastic pony, a rose pendant, and a red heart called to her. She placed each, one at a time, in the middle of the horseshoe. The heart looked best, and she glued it down.

When she had bought it at the flea market, the man had said, "Anyone who owns one will have good luck. Be sure the arch is at the bottom, or the luck will pour out."

Uh-oh. She'd glued the heart on the wrong way. She quickly pulled it off, reset it, and flipped the horseshoe around. She squeezed out more glue; placed three blue marbles, white buttons, and other objects from her grab bag on it; and sprinkled seed beads over the entire surface, then set the whole thing aside to dry. She couldn't wait to see how it turned out.

She began to mix more paint to add to her sky canvas when her phone chimed. She should have put it on silent mode. She hated to be interrupted when doing her art. Staying in the zone took practice.

Sergio again: *Call me.*

She finished mixing the paint and quickly washed it over the canvas. She wanted to call him later, but she knew she wouldn't be able to focus on her art because she'd keep thinking about talking to him. In the bathroom, she brushed her teeth, put up her messy hair in a scrunchie, and added lipstick.

She commanded Alexa to turn off the music and FaceTimed Sergio. She held her phone tight.

"Amore mio."

She loved it when he spoke Italian to her. Just hearing his voice made her heart chakra feel like it might explode. She adjusted her phone so she could see his whole, handsome face: deep-set brown eyes; curly, dark hair bouncing on his shoulders; bright smile.

"How are you?" she asked, trying to keep her voice even.

"I miss you," he said.

A siren screamed outside, and she paused. "I miss you too."

"Looked like you had a good trip."

"Yes. Incredible. What have you been up to?" She was tempted to ask if he was seeing anyone, but she didn't really want to know. "How's work going?"

"There's no business like shoe business," he sang.

"Hardy-har-har."

"How's the museum?"

"My Saturday kids are adorable, even though they're sometimes a little rambunctious. A lot of my adults are more accomplished artists than I'll ever be."

"I doubt that."

"Many are stuck in traditional genres, like painting, ceramics, or sculpture, and are trying to break out. I've been able to help them there. I've connected them with Fay, and she's even putting some of their pieces in Gallery Noir's next group show."

"When's the reception?"

"I'm not sure. I'll let you know. I also applied for that artist-in-residence program."

"*Splendido.* I'm sure you're a shoe-in. Get it?"

"That's enough with the shoe jokes for one call."

"Tell me more about your trip."

"I can't believe how beautiful it is there. And the sky! The sky is to die for. Brilliant blue, with fluffy clouds. And the stars. Did you know Flagstaff was the first International Dark Sky Community, with regulations limiting lights so you can see the stars? I saw the Milky Way every night. And all that other nature, and arts and culture. Wouldn't it be great to go there together someday?" She put her hand to her chest. She couldn't believe she'd just said that.

"I'd really love that." His dark brown eyes softened. "Discover any found treasures?"

She glanced at the corset, still hanging on the back of the closet. Like magic, it sparkled in the overhead light, and she swore the scent of sage filled the room. She wanted to show it to Sergio, but he might think she was being suggestive. They were broken up this time for good.

Oh, what the heck. She turned her phone toward the closet and pointed it at the corset. "Only this."

He raised his voice. "*Oh là là!* I can't wait to see it on you."

How could she flirt with him like this? Anne flipped the phone back to her face. "Sergio, I'm sorry—I didn't mean to tease you like that. We're broken up. We have to be broken up."

He sighed. "I know. Can we get together, though? I'm coming out really soon on business. I want to see you in person."

She hesitated. "I guess so. Check in with me then. But I won't wear the corset."

He laughed. "Are you sure?"

"Bye." Once she hung up, she silenced her ringer. After talking to him, she missed him all the more. It would be wonderful to see him in person, but she really needed to move on.

How would she ever meet someone new? Some of her friends had had luck with sites like Zoosk, Match.com, and even Tinder, but she didn't see herself as the online-dating type. What she wanted was a serious relationship and to find her real soul mate. She'd thought Sergio was hers, but, sadly, he wasn't.

Anne needed to get back to her art. "Alexa, play Enya."

Enya's ethereal voice filled the apartment. Anne closed her eyes, breathed in and out, and felt her heart open as she returned to her mosaic. She centered an old-fashioned ceramic farm girl in an antique tray and placed an Irish setter beside her. She put a chipped, blue-and-white Wedgwood plate in a paper bag on a cutting board and smashed it with a hammer. She dumped out the shards and used the smooth-rimmed edges along the tray's border.

From the baggie of found objects, she selected a key, an old watch, and a gold sun charm and placed them around the girl. She added gray, blue, and green stones from the Painted Desert Museum, and multicolored seed beads for grout.

She thought wistfully about her conversation with Sergio again. She needed some serious mojo to help her move on. The horseshoe dry, she shook the loose seed beads off it, made sure to hang it the correct way, and nailed it to the wall in the relationship corner of her apartment, which also happened to be her bathroom. She kissed her pointer finger and touched the heart on the horseshoe. She'd take it down to use as a sample at the museum when she got the other horseshoes and was ready to introduce the lesson. But for now, she'd let the chi flow toward a new man.

Back in the kitchenette, she brushed loose beads off the tray piece and grinned as the ceramic girl emerged. Anne called it *A Time to Cast Away Stones*, after Ecclesiastes. With it, she was casting Sergio away and, she hoped, gathering another lover soon.

As if on cue, Howard, her old friend from her valet-parking days, sent her a text: *Rhinestone Ruby's tonight?*

That would be the perfect place to meet a new man.

8

A burly man in a long leather coat studied them as they exited the train. Cliff tugged his hat low over his eyes, took Sally Sue's arm in his, and drew her in the opposite direction. Her instincts told her to scream, kick him in the shins, and run away, but she feared he'd pull out his gun and shoot her.

A sign attached to the front of a rusted-out boxcar facing her said FLAGSTAFF. A cold wind hit her. Under a cloudy sky, nearby pine trees were covered with snow, and to the north, white-peaked mountains rose high above. She wondered what it would feel like to be way up there. A hawk flew overhead. She wished she was free like it was.

They crossed a wide road away from the tracks, and she stumbled into a puddle of melting snow. The muddy ground sopped her skirt's hem and soaked her favorite shoes clear through to the toes. Cliff led her down a street filled with ramshackle buildings that looked like they'd been put up really fast. Most were wooden, but others were even made of tent canvas. They passed the white-painted church with the tall steeple she'd seen from afar.

At McMillan's Mercantile, a pair of dungarees, bolts of fabric, and tools were expertly arranged in the window. Sally Sue's spirits soared when she spotted Cliff's WANTED poster, with its $500 reward, displayed prominently on the glass in front of the items. She felt certain someone would capture him soon. But then Cliff tilted his head toward the poster and grinned at her and she realized nobody would ever recognize him, because in the drawing only his eyes were visible, peeking out from between his hat and his kerchief.

As they walked farther down the street, at Berry's Saloon, a man flew out of the swinging doors into the mire right in front of her. She yelped as her heart jumped. Another man dove on top of him, pounding on the other man's back. Cliff drew her out of the way just in time, or she might have been caught in the melee.

A crowd of folks rushed out of the saloon, cheering on the fighters.

"Go for his gut, Charlie!"

"Kick 'im in the head!"

"Get him!"

The man in the leather coat sauntered over to the crowd, raised his pistol, and shot it into the air. "Okay, boys, that's enough," he bellowed. He slid the gun back into his holster, gripped each man by an ear, and headed them down the street. "I told you I'm putting order in this town."

"S-s-sorry, Sheriff, but he was mockin' me," whined the smaller of the two.

"He wouldn't let me dance with that dame," the scrawny one hiccupped.

"No excuses, you young whippersnappers. I'm keepin' you till you've slept it off."

As the sheriff escorted the two men down the street to the jail, the crowd hooted and hollered. Big-hatted, long-mustached, kerchief-wearing, gun-toting cowboys. Other men, in plaid flannel shirts. Three women in risqué, wildflower-colored getups laughed. Kohl-eyed and red-lipped, without bonnets, they had tendrils of hair piled high atop their heads.

A redhead in a green silk outfit gave a shrill whistle. "Go get 'em, Sheriff."

He threw the men inside the jail, locked the door, and waved to the crowd.

Cliff escorted Sally Sue across the street to a hotel. The poster hung in a window there too.

"Set here." He pushed her down into a rocker on the porch and went inside.

Her stomach felt as if it had been turned inside out. She had to get away from him.

The sheriff dragged a chair from his office beside the jail, sat in the chair, put his rifle on his lap, and lit a cigar. He reminded Sally Sue of her father, taller than most men, strongly built and fine-looking.

Her father had also had a forceful voice when he'd needed it. "Wife, leave the girl alone," he'd say. "She's not hurting anyone."

It was darn cold. She pulled her shawl tightly around her shoulders. But her father had also been soft-spoken, like the last time she'd seen him: "My sweet Sal, don't cry. I'll be back in no time." And he was right—he never returned and was back no time.

She glanced at the hotel door and hurried down the steps to alert the sheriff.

"Hey, darling! Where're you off to?" Cliff's voice called from behind her.

Her shoulders slumped, and she turned around. "Just stretching my legs is all."

A man holding a broom stood in the hotel doorway, staring at her.

Cliff took her arm and escorted her back to the rocker. "Rest here awhile. I'll be right back. This here's Mr. Bjork, the hotel's proprietor." He tilted his head at the man with the broom and walked up the street.

She sat down.

Mr. Bjork leaned on the broom. "Your husband says he's thinking of settling here. Would be a prudent decision."

She watched as Cliff entered a shop. She stood up and pointed at the poster. "Help me! He's not really my husband but this bank robber."

The man chuckled. "Mr. Cliff told me you might say that. He asked me to keep an eye on you. Said you were dealing with some kind of condition."

"What?"

"Said you'd been suffering a nervous collapse."

"That's not true." She jumped up and started down the steps again, waving her arms toward the jail.

The man took his broom handle and pulled her back onto the porch. "I promised Mr. Cliff I'd take care of you while he checked out the town. Come on back. I don't want to take out my gun."

Afraid of what Cliff might do to this man, she acquiesced.

"There's a good girl." Mr. Bjork patted her shoulder.

"Won't you at least go get the sheriff and tell him what I told you?" she pleaded.

"Sheriff Mack? He was a Texas Ranger. Knows how to deal with all kinds a' rascality: cow rustlers, horse thieves, scallywags, stagecoach robbers, desperadoes, and other human transgressors. If Mr. Cliff really was a bandit, the sheriff would have spotted him right away."

Sheriff Mack looked up the street toward them, as if he knew they were talking about him. For an experienced lawman like that, it would be only a matter of time before he recognized Cliff, rustled him up, and arrested him, or maybe even killed him. After all, the poster did say "dead or alive."

An Indian with a red-and-black woven blanket around his shoulders rode by on a pinto. A woman in a gingham dress and a large straw hat walked by, holding her identical twin boys' hands.

"Morning," she said to Sally Sue, and kept going.

"Like I was saying, this here Flagstaff New Town's booming, especially since fire last year ravaged Old Town, out near the sawmill," Mr. Bjork continued.

"That's horrible. What happened?" Sally Sue asked.

He looked toward the saloon. "Word is, one of them dance hall girls kicked over a lantern. Old Town burned to the ground. Yep, thirty buildings destroyed in thirty minutes. They rebuilt some homes, but the businesses relocated here, to New Town, closer to the railroad stop. I know the depot is just a bunch of old boxcars now, but someday we'll erect a real one. We're the largest city between Albuquerque and the West Coast. Santa Fe Railroad Company sells lots here for twenty-five dollars each. We now have a post office, seven saloons, three restaurants, two general stores, two laundries, a newsstand, a boot shop, a livery, a brewery, and this here hotel."

He pointed kitty-corner across the street to the wooden structure. "And the McMillans have a fine building there. They even live upstairs. Fine folks, they are. And look at that limestone building farther down the street, past the church. Brannen's. Isn't it grand?"

"May I have a drink of water, please?" she asked Mr. Bjork, to get him to stop yapping.

"Sure thing. How about some lemonade? I'll be just a moment. Don't do anything foolish."

This mud-forsaken place didn't even compare to Kansas City, with its mighty three-story constructions, commerce, and population. Flagstaff folks moved at a slower pace, just moseyed along in the dirt. In Kansas City, the hustle-bustle of jam-packed streets, horse-drawn carriages, and streetcars kept a lively pace. They were even getting ready to switch from horsepower to electric streetcars.

She stood up to run down to Sheriff Mack, but a woman hurried up the steps toward Sally Sue. "Herbs for sale."

Sally Sue shook her head.

The woman's skin was the color of cocoa. Between that and her raven hair, if she hadn't been dressed in a yellow frock with a calico bonnet, Sally Sue would have thought she was a squaw, or maybe a Mexican.

The peculiar women grasped Sally Sue's hand. "I've something to tell you."

Sally Sue's impulse told her to pull away, but the woman's hand felt warm and comforting. Her deep-set eyes seemed to reflect that she understood what Sally Sue was going through.

"Find the honey in every heart." The woman's voice sounded as smooth as that liquid itself.

Spellbound, Sally Sue replied, "But what if the person is evil?"

"Evil? No one is entirely evil. Actions can be deceiving. Look further, for the goodness within." The woman's hand fiddled for something in her basket; then, finding it, she handed a silk pouch to Sally Sue.

It fit perfectly in the palm of her hand. "What is it?"

"Just a little sweet tea to help you see. No sugar needed."

"But I haven't any money to pay you."

"A smile will do."

Sally Sue's lips felt rusted into a frown. With difficulty, she forced the edges up. The woman smiled back and patted Sally Sue's hand. "That's better, now."

Sally Sue's smile softened and became genuine. Her heart felt full and open. A trickle of hope poured through. She glanced at the hotel and across at the mercantile and whispered, "I need help."

"Elvira. I told you to stay away." Mr. Bjork came out of the hotel and swept his broom toward the woman, as if she were a piece of dirt.

"I'm not hurtin' anybody, Mr. Bjork." She blinked at him, dashed down the stairs, and started up the road out of town.

"Don't go talking to that evil one." He handed Sally Sue her lemonade. "Here comes your husband now."

Cliff started down the street toward the hotel.

The redhead came out of the saloon and stood on the porch. "Yoo-hoo!" she called to him in a Southern drawl.

He changed direction and walked toward the woman, who fluttered her eyes at him and put her hands on the black lace on her hips.

Was that what Sally Sue's ma had meant by a harlot, the kind of woman Sally Sue's father had left them for? Sally Sue glared at Cliff, sat, and crossed her arms. Did men do offensive things with them, like the Bible said? Sally Sue should have been appalled, but instead she was mesmerized.

She imagined what it would feel like to be dressed in something so sinful and parade in front of men, the feel of lace on her chest and thighs, the smoothness of the satin. The green one, her favorite, was a low-cut corset with a skirt and a giant bustle in back. What would Mama say if she knew Sally Sue had these thoughts? What would Johnny Jones and his mother back home think if she sauntered into the church hall for a dance dressed in that? She smiled. Would he ask her to dance? Certainly, Pastor Grimes would grab a coat, cover her up, and whisk her home to Mama.

It was no fun being a persona non grata on account of her father. Like the time Johnny Jones had sat next to her at that church potluck. He had been so charming. But when his mother arrived, she had given him the evil eye and spoiled all the joy. Johnny had gotten up and moved next to her.

Sally Sue had never even been kissed. Charlie Flanders had tried to once. But as soon as he'd gotten close, with his smelly, hay-like beard, she had pulled away. He'd ended up marrying Gladys Goodings, anyway. Last time Sally Sue had seen them in church, the poor girl's cheeks had been rubbed red raw.

Sally Sue stood. While Cliff was occupied, she should get down there to the sheriff and tell him who the outlaw really was. But Cliff turned around, stared at her, and patted his holster again. Did he have eyes in the back of his head and peepholes in his hat? How was she ever going to get away from him?

9

"Let's go," Cliff called, and waved at Sally Sue as he walked down the street. She deposited the pouch in her basket and joined him reluctantly. What other choice did she have?

As Cliff opened the door at McMillan's Mercantile, a butterscotch tabby sprang out, zigzagged around Sally Sue's ankles, purred loudly, and skittered away. It reminded her of the Rowlings' cat next door at home. Sally Sue had tried to get her ma to let her have one too, but she said they were dirty.

Sally Sue's and Cliff's shoes tracked mud into the mercantile. The wooden floors were already dirty, so it didn't matter much. Burning pine scent filled the air from the potbellied stove. The shop had shelving on every wall, and the floors were crammed with boxes, barrels, crates, and tables holding crockery and dishes. A bed, a rocker, and even a casket sat in a corner.

A tall woman with blond braids pinned on top of her head sorted buttons. "I'll be with you in a moment."

The twins Sally Sue had seen earlier knelt at the candy displayed in wooden cartons beneath the counter.

Their mother in the gingham dress said, "Decide, boys. There are customers waiting."

One of the boys finally yelled, "I'll have a peppermint." He paused. "Please."

"Please. I want a licorice," his brother said.

The woman behind the counter handed them each their candy with a smile, and their mother gave her two cents.

"Thank you, Mrs. McMillan!" the boys yelled, as they stuck the candy in their mouths and ran out the door behind their mother.

Cliff and Sally Sue stepped up to the counter.

"Can I help you?" Mrs. McMillan looked at Cliff.

He glanced at the WANTED poster displayed on the wall behind the counter and gave the woman a big, phony smile. "Sure can. First off, we'd like some of that cheese and crackers you've got there."

"Certainly, sir." Mrs. McMillan sliced a hunk of cheese for each of them from the wheel on the counter and handed the pieces to them on napkins. "Help yourself to the crackers."

Even though she was starving, Sally Sue nibbled slowly on the food.

"What else, sir?" Mrs. McMillan asked.

"I need some articles for myself and my little lady."

"I'm not your—"

He situated his hand on Sally Sue's shoulder. "She's spunky as all get-out. Small as an acorn but mighty as an oak."

She tried to tug away, but he held tight as he gave the woman a slip of paper from his coat pocket.

Sally Sue tried to read the list. She couldn't make out the words but could tell the letters were precise.

"We've got plenty of goods to choose from. New shipments arrived from Prescott just yesterday, and another on this morning's train." The woman set the list on the counter, put on her pince-nez, and studied it.

"Darrel," she hollered. "Darrel McMillan!"

From the back of the store, a bald man with a beard crawled down off a ladder and strode toward them. "Howdy."

She handed him the list.

"New in town?" Darrel asked Cliff.

"Yes, sir." He shook the man's hand; arm garters bound back the sleeves of his white shirt.

"I'm Clifford Canyon, and this is my missus, Sally Sue. You must be Darrel McMillan."

"Yes'm, and this is my wife, Danica."

Danica tipped her head.

Darrel read the list. He looked at Sally Sue's feet. "We'll get you fixed up right away. Take a seat."

She sat in a chair beside the stove. The heat sure felt good. Cliff wandered over, perused the guns and ammunition nearby, chose a few items, and put them on the counter.

Darrel ran his hand along a shelf, grabbed a pair of boots, and handed them to his wife. "Give these a try." He took the list and walked to the back of the shop.

Sally Sue slipped off her thin shoes, embarrassed by their filth and her dirty stockinged feet.

Danica helped her get the boots on and tied them for her. "Stand, please." She pressed her finger in front of the toes. "Perfect fit. Walk a bit."

Sally Sue clomped along the wooden floor. Ugh. They looked like something a forty-niner would wear. She'd never get away with something so ugly at home.

"They might feel tight now, but the leather will soon give way." Danica picked up Sally Sue's filthy shoes and looked at Cliff.

"Throw them away." Cliff nodded and gave her a crooked smile.

Sally Sue put her hand on her chest. Her beautiful favorite shoes.

Danica looked at her sympathetically. "They must have been really pretty before they got all muddy."

I want to keep them, Sally Sue wanted to yell, but it was no use. The celery-green peau de soie would never come clean anyway.

"Mrs. McMillan, would you help her pick material for a new frock?" Cliff asked.

Danica extended an arm to Sally Sue. "Certainly. Right this way, Mrs. Canyon."

Mrs. Canyon—for goodness' sake. Sally Sue clomped over to the fabric bolts. The boots might be clunky, but they were comfortable to walk in and would keep her feet dry. In her fancy suit, she must appear ridiculous.

Darrel continued to collect and pile more items on the list—coffee, sugar, flour, oatmeal, dried beans—on the counter, filling in a ledger as he worked. Cliff placed a packet of tobacco beside the other supplies.

"You're not from around these parts, are you?" Danica asked.

"No, Missouri." Sally Sue wanted to say more, but Cliff peered at her as he leaned on the counter.

"I think that's everything on the list. Is there anything else?" Darrel asked.

"I'm in need of a quiet place for us to settle down for a while. Might do a little farming. Know of any land I can procure?"

"Yes, sir. I certainly do. There's a homestead out yonder, way past the lumberyard, at the base of the peaks."

"Do you mean the Ivrys' place?" Danica piped up. "They're lookin' to sell?"

"No." He paused and exchanged glances with Cliff. "They've up and left."

"Where'd they go?" Sally Sue asked.

"No one knows for certain." Darrel shrugged.

She had a feeling he wasn't telling the truth.

Danica said, "It's rough living out there. Sometimes folks just up and leave."

"Need anything else, Mr. Canyon?"

"Cliff. Call me Cliff. Which livery do you suggest for a wagon and horses?"

"Might need to pick them up out of town, but Rutledges would be best."

"Do you want to go with me to make arrangements?"

"Sure. And I'll draw you a map on how to get to the Ivrys' place. There's probably tack in the barn and hay left in the loft."

"Be right back." Cliff glanced at Sally Sue, patted his hip, and walked out the door.

"This would be lovely on you." Danica held up a bolt of dusty green.

This was Sally Sue's chance to get help. "Danica, I'm—"

Cliff stuck his head back in the door. "Pick out anything you want, sweetheart."

Sally Sue sat in the chair by the fire. Who did he think he was, calling her "sweetheart"? Was he trying to trick her? She'd better wait until he was down the road before asking for help.

"What about this green?" Danica wiggled the bolt in front of Sally Sue.

It had a washed-out look to it. To bide her time, she might as well look at the material. Sally Sue walked over to the shelf and scanned the other fabrics. Her eyes landed on a green satin similar to that of the saloon girl's outfit, but Sally Sue wouldn't dare wear such a decadent, bright color.

She ran her hand along a blue, yellow, and red posy print. "How about this one?"

Danica pulled it from the stack and carried it to the counter. "You have good taste. It's very pretty, and practical, too, because it won't show the dirt as much."

Oh, for heaven's sake.

"How much do you want?"

"Five yards." Sally Sue made her way to the door and watched Cliff and Darrel stop in front of the saloon. Cliff held open the swinging doors for Darrel, but he shook his head and they continued on.

"Where's the livery?" Sally Sue asked. Perhaps she could make it to the sheriff while they were there.

"Down the road a spell."

"Past the jail?"

"Just on the other side."

Sally Sue would need to wait before she could hurry to the sheriff.

10

A blond little one dashed across the room and stopped in front of her. "Hellooo."

"Aren't you a big boy?" Sally Sue smiled.

His bright eyes stared at her. "Pitty."

"Do you mean 'pretty'? Thank you kindly." Her heart melted, and she wanted to gather him in her arms.

"How old are you?" she asked.

"I's three." He propped a thumb on top of his pinky finger and held up his hand.

"Isaiah, don't bother Mrs. Canyon." Danica shook her head.

"Oh, he's fine."

Isaiah rummaged in his overall pockets and pulled out his hand.

"What have you got there?" Sally Sue knelt down.

"Marblie." He handed it to her.

She studied it—"It's a beautiful blue marble"—and tried to give it back to him.

He pushed her hand away. "You keep. Blue like sky."

Danica nodded and grinned.

He pointed to her head.

"My hat?" Sally Sue untied the ribbon, removed her bonnet, and held it out to him.

He patted the silk flowers. "Isaiah wear?"

Sally Sue set it on the boy's head, tilted it back, and tied the bow. She smiled as he ran in a circle, halted at the mirror, and giggled at his reflection. The bonnet toppled off his head.

"Oopsy-daisy." She picked it up off the floor.

"Oopsy-daisy." He giggled again, cocked his head, and ran out the door.

In her new boots, Sally Sue followed him down the steps as a stagecoach created ruts in the mud and the snorting horse pulled up and stopped in front of the hotel. A cowboy lurched out of the coach and made his way across to the saloon. Sally Sue ran back inside the mercantile, snatched her basket, hurried down the steps, and stopped.

Mr. Bjork unloaded a trunk off the top of the coach and carried it into the hotel. She scanned the street to make certain Cliff wasn't nearby. As quickly as possible, despite her tight skirt, she made a beeline to the stagecoach.

The driver, with a scraggly mustache and a floppy hat, held the door open for her. "Ma'am, where's your luggage?"

She held up her basket and handed him a few coins. "I travel light."

"Runnin' away, are you?" He chortled.

"Maybe." She feigned a flirtatious giggle.

He blushed and closed the door.

She breathed more easily and sat back in the empty coach, offering a silent prayer of thanks to God. It seemed to take forever before the stagecoach began to roll down the street.

From outside a man yelled, "Hold the coach!"

It slowed down and stopped, and the door flew open. Mr. Bjork pointed a rifle at her. "Here she is," he called.

"Where're you off to?" Cliff, out of breath, said from behind Mr. Bjork.

Her heart flip-flopped in her chest. "I need to get back to Ma and Auntie."

Cliff glowered. "This coach is going west, not east, darling."

"Oh, my stars and garters." Even though her heart was beating fast, she forced a laugh. "Silly me. I meant west."

Cliff gently pushed Mr. Bjork's gun down and spoke to him. "Thank you kindly. I'll take care of her from here."

Mr. Bjork stepped back. She heard Darrel's voice outside the stagecoach. "Can you take Mr. and Mrs. Canyon and their supplies to Sven's place to pick up their wagon and horses?"

"Be happy to."

Cliff settled in beside her, and they rode up the street to the mercantile. As he got out, Sally Sue followed him, but he lightly pushed her back inside.

"Let me go," she squealed.

"I can't do that, darling." He slammed the door and closed the leather curtains.

She crossed her arms. She had no option but to wait while Cliff helped load their goods on top of the coach. Everyone in town by now believed she had suffered some kind of breakdown.

Cliff piled in a few crates, then climbed in and sat across from her.

Darrel handed him one filled with apples. "These are complimentary. Good luck."

Cliff put the crate beside him on the seat and shook Darrel's hand. "Thanks. I'll pay up at the end of the month."

"Sure thing." Darrel closed the door and hit the side of the coach.

Sally Sue sat back as they pulled out of town. "Let me go. I'll just be a burden to you. I won't tell anybody who you are." She folded her hands under her chin.

"We're going to the homestead."

Her eyes opened wide. "But that's out in the middle of nowhere."

"That's the point."

She sat back with a groan. The dark, stuffy coach smelled of musty leather, sweat, and grime. It picked up speed and began to rock back and forth.

Cliff put his saddlebag on top of a mail pouch, picked up her feet, and slid them over it. "This should make you more comfortable. It might be a rough ride."

"I'll be fine." She stared at the saddlebags. Was the money in there?

He pulled an apple from the crate and offered her one. Even though she was hungry, she shook her head. She wouldn't give him the satisfaction of taking anything from him.

"Suit yourself." He shined the apple on his thigh, took a big bite, chewed, swallowed slowly, and licked his lips, then pulled his Stetson over his eyes.

Famished, she grabbed an apple from the bin and munched it down fast. Soon, the stagecoach picked up speed. Sally Sue closed her eyes, but the rocking and intermittent jolts jarred her body, and her belly began to roil. She shouldn't have eaten that apple.

She wanted to knock on the ceiling and ask the driver to slow down, but instead she held back the leather curtain and gasped for air. The sun shone from behind billowy clouds. Muddy ruts from previous travelers made the road rugged. To help settle her stomach, she tried to count the pines as they passed. When the coach rounded a bend, mud splashed up from a wheel and flew into her face. She closed the curtain with a scream.

Cliff laughed. She had to get out now. She put her fingers on the door handle. Cliff removed his hat. If she jumped out, she'd probably be killed, but it would be better than being in this stagecoach with a murderer.

11

That evening, Anne donned the corset, skirt, cowgirl boots, and black coat. Bushy hair updoed, she applied plenty of makeup and false eyelashes. She checked herself out in the full-length mirror on the back of her closet door, put a hand behind her head, wiggled her hips, and said aloud, "I am lovable, gorgeous, and sexy."

She wrote it on a sticky note with a Sharpie and attached it to the top of the mirror. If this didn't do the trick, she didn't know what would.

Stars glittered in the sky as she rode a Lyft to Sockshop on Haight Street. She asked the driver to wait while she ran in and purchased a pair of fishnet stockings. She pulled them on in the Lyft's back seat and texted Howard: *On my way.*

As they drove into Hayes Valley, the shops were just starting to close. Warning foghorns hooted from the bay. That eerie sound always made her feel as if danger were ahead; she shivered in her coat.

The driver dropped her off in front of Ruby's. Country music beat a rhythm as she stepped inside the foyer and waited for her eyes to adjust to the darkness. Along the side walls hung framed antique posters. Small art lights illuminated each.

One poster had a sketch of a bandit, but because of his hat and the kerchief over his mouth, only his beady eyes showed. Anne wondered how the drawing could have helped find the bandit. The poster read:

WANTED

DEAD OR ALIVE

$1,000 REWARD

CLIFFORD CLIFTON, ALIAS CLIFF CLABOURN

SHOULD BE CONSIDERED DANGEROUS

BANK ROBBER, MURDERER

KANSAS CITY, 1885

"Cool." She took a photo with her phone. The poster might work in one of her collages.

"Boot Scootin' Boogie," one of her favorite songs, began to play, and she entered the jam-packed space. Howard waved at her from a high bar. To the beat of the music, she strutted around the dance floor and wound her way through the tables, toward the back. She gave Howard a hug and hung her coat on the stool.

"Girlfriend, look at you." Howard touched the sequins on her waist.

"Arizona vintage." She wiggled her hips.

"Yeehaw! You look plum purty.'" He spoke in an exaggerated country drawl.

"You're looking dapper yourself."

His blond hair slicked back, he walked in a circle to show off his sequined vest and fitted jeans. "Yes'm. I'm always ready. Never know who I might meet."

"I guess so." He was such a character.

"I ordered us some ale."

A waitress swung by and dropped off their beers.

Howard held up his stein. "To vintage shopping."

Anne clicked her glass with his, took a sip. She leaned in and said, "I had the best time."

"It's too loud to talk," he yelled. "Show me more pics."

She handed him her phone, and Howard started scrolling through while she watched the crowd on the dance floor.

They finished their beers, and he ordered another round. The band switched to "Electric Boogie."

Anne and Howard gazed into each other's eyes and mouthed the lyrics. *Ready? Let's do this.*

He took her hand, and she followed him onto the dance floor, lights flashing above. Step-touch, step-touch, she then shimmied her shoulders, feeling sexy dancing in the corset. But when it came time to turn, she missed the beat, her feet got all tangled up, and she bumped into the guy beside her.

"Sorry." How embarrassing.

The guy shrugged, jumped in front of her, and pointed at his feet for her to copy his exaggerated moves.

Dancing had never been her forte, but she thought she'd be able to follow along to this one. When she still couldn't get the hang of it, she returned to her chair but continued to sing along.

"You do know what the words are about, don't you?" Howard yelled over the music as he sat back beside her.

She shook her head. "No. What?"

"Listen."

She listened closely: *electric*, *shakin'*, *pumpin'*.

"A sex toy? Oh my God. No way." She couldn't stop laughing.

"I've heard the composer denies it, but you've gotta wonder." Howard slapped his knee.

They finished their beer. When their server passed by, Howard ordered another round.

The music switched to Brooks & Dunn's "Brand New Man." Anne loved the song and watched the guy she had run into move smoothly around the dance floor, doing the cowboy cha-cha. Thumbs tucked into his front jean pockets, he rocked back and forth and did the turns perfectly. The buckle on his belt, big as a rodeo star's, gleamed in the light. Anne imagined what he'd look like with his shirt off. He reminded her of one of the Thunder from Down Under dancers she'd taken Fay to see for her bachelorette party.

Maybe he really was a cowboy, sexy in his rust suede chaps and Stetson. Maybe he owned a horse or even a ranch out in Los Olivos, Napa, or Sonoma. They could ride from his property to go wine tasting. He'd sit real tall on a big palomino like Trigger, and she'd wear her green lace corset on a paint. An artist should always ride a colorful horse. Maybe he even played a guitar and sang like Roy Rogers.

A cowboy was exactly the kind of man she needed. He'd be much more down to earth and grounded than a jet-setting foodie like Sergio.

The guy caught her staring at him, touched the brim of his hat, and continued to dance.

"Isn't he a hottie?" Anne leaned over and asked Howard.

"He's not my type."

When "Man! I Feel Like a Woman" came on, Howard jumped up and hollered, "They're playing my song!" and ran onto the dance floor.

The hottie sauntered over to her, straightening his hat, and said something to her.

"What?" She couldn't hear him.

He raised his voice. "Buy you a drink?"

"Sure." Anne leaned forward and moved to the music, showing a little cleavage, her flirt-o-matic machine on. "I'm drinking beer on tap."

Hottie sat in Howard's seat and tried to wave over a waitress, but the place was so packed, it seemed impossible. "Shall I go up to the bar?" he asked.

"No, that'll be even worse. Sorry I bumped into you during the Electric Slide."

"No problem. It just takes a little practice." His eyes grazed her body, and he put his warm hand on her shoulder. "You'll soon get the hang of it."

Little did he know, she'd been trying to learn that dance for years now. "Do you understand what the . . ." She stopped herself just in time.

"What?"

"Nothing." It would be too embarrassing to ask if he knew about the lyrics.

"Do you mean about the words?" He laughed.

She felt herself turn red.

"You naughty thing, you." He leaned toward her and rubbed his hand on her thigh over the fishnet stocking.

Her insides tingled. She liked the look of him. Tall, smoothly shaven, big grin. His eyes under his hat didn't reveal their color. She sure wished he'd take it off so she could see his face more clearly.

A waitress finally came by, and he ordered their beer.

"You from around here?" he asked Anne.

She held up her left hand. "This is Michigan, shaped like a mitten. I'm from Oscoda, a little town on Lake Huron." She indicated the place on the outer edge of her pointer finger.

"No, I mean where do you live in San Francisco?"

Anne giggled. "California and Polk. What about you?"

"I live just up the hill." He peered at her suggestively, and she began to feel juicy. Was he already inviting her over? Maybe he had a view home besides his ranch. She wanted to know everything about him.

"Excuse me. Let me get my drink." Howard reached his hand between Anne and Hottie and gulped down the dregs of his beer.

Hottie stood up. "Hello, Howard."

Howard ignored him, ran his fingers through his blond locks, and returned to the dance floor.

That was weird. "Do you know him?" Anne asked.

"Kinda."

"How?"

"It's a long story." Hottie shrugged, grabbed a handful of pretzels from the bowl, and stuffed them into his mouth.

The waitress delivered their beers and a fresh bowl of pretzels.

"I'm sure thirsty." Hottie gulped down his beer.

Anne took a sip of hers too.

"Tell me."

"Another time." He turned his gaze to the dance floor.

What was that all about? She felt like there might be bad blood between Hottie and Howard, but he would have mentioned earlier if there was anything she needed to worry about.

Howard was two-stepping with a muscular man in a tummy shirt and Daisy Dukes. Yes, that one was more his type.

She wanted to keep the conversation going. "What do you do for work?"

"I'm in hospitality."

"You are? I used to be too. I parked cars at the St. Francis."

"No way."

"Way."

"What do you do now?" he asked.

"I'm an artist."

Hottie put his hand on her leg again. "Really? I've never met a real one before."

"Yes, I make collages and mosaics using found objects."

He didn't say anything else; he just moved his hand up her thigh.

Clint Black's "A Good Run of Bad Luck" began to play. "Let's dance." Hottie pulled her up.

"I'm not good at the slow stuff."

"Don't worry. It's a two-step anyway. I can lead any klutz." He escorted her onto the dance floor, put her left hand on his shoulder, and held her right hand in his left.

At first she felt awkward and had a hard time following. She stepped hard on his foot, and he counted, "Quick, quick, slow, slow. Quick, quick, slow, slow."

She concentrated, and soon they were in a rhythmic flow. For the first time in her life, she was getting it. As the disco ball circled overhead, she savored the power of being so close to a man like this, guiding and gliding her around the floor.

The song ended, and she started back to the table, but he grasped her hand. "Come on. I'm going to teach you how to line dance if it kills me."

He danced in front of her so she could copy him. Every time the group changed directions, he jumped in front of her so she could still follow his feet. After a while, she actually had the hang of it.

She continued to rotate between dancing with him and drinking beer all evening. After last call, they danced the last dance and sang the refrain to each other. She liked the idea that riding a cowboy could save a horse.

Back at their table after all those beers and adrenaline, she couldn't focus. His voice was muffled, his face a blur. He pulled her to him and kissed her. She liked the salty taste of him and kissed him back.

"I'm Barn, by the way. As in Barnaby." He put out his hand.

She shook it. "Pleased to meet you. I'm Anne."

"Let's go to my place," he whispered in her ear.

She knew her head should shake no, except it nodded yes.

12

Anne and Barn staggered out of the bar into the dense fog. The streetlights glowed in the mist. She snuggled into her coat. Linden Street was usually busy, but this time of night—or should she say morning?—it was deserted.

He took her hand and walked a block, and she stopped to look in the window of a new shop. "Dark Garden. What a fantastic name." Her words slurred. She shouldn't have had so much to drink.

She stared at the multitude of rainbow-colored lingerie. Leave it to San Francisco to have a corset shop. "Which one do you like best?"

"I don't know. Come on." He grabbed her hand.

She let it go. "Wait a minute." She kept looking in the window.

Sergio would have wanted to choose a favorite. He loved lingerie. She made a note to go back and visit when they were open. Maybe next time he came to town. No. Drop that thought. She was getting over him now.

"Okay." She took Barn's hand and kissed him on the cheek. "I'm ready."

They walked ten blocks. Getting to his place seemed to take forever. Heated, she removed her coat and put it over her arm. Her feet had begun to ache. "How much farther?"

"Not far," Barn said.

They walked another two blocks, down three more, and around

a block. They climbed down a few dark steps into Barn's apartment, which reeked of skunk weed. The stench reminded her of her old best friend, Dottie's, New York loft. Dottie claimed getting high helped her do her art. In college, Anne had smoked marijuana a few times to fit in, but it had always put her right to sleep. She already had a difficult enough time staying focused when she was sober.

Barn threw her coat on the floor as she stepped inside. He didn't turn on the lights. He pulled her toward a couch, pushed her onto it, and kissed her.

She sat up. "May I have some water, please?"

"Sure." He got up and went into the kitchen.

Her eyes had begun to adjust to the darkness. Still dizzy and tanked from all those drinks, she managed to make out mirrored beer logos: Budweiser, Coors, Schlitz Malt Liquor. A big-screen TV filled an entire wall. A plant resembling corn stalks sat in a corner.

When he returned with her water, she took a sip and put it on the coffee table. "Thanks."

"You're so gorgeous." He kissed her again.

Leather couch beneath her, he cupped his hands over the corset's satin and lace on top of her boobs, the sensations driving her crazy. He ran his fingers down her fishnet-stockinged thighs and moved his hand upward. She grasped his biceps. She needed him to slow down. He got the message and put his arms around her.

Finally, they drew apart. "Let's go in the bedroom," he said.

"May I use the bathroom?" she asked.

He pointed down the hall.

She studied herself in the mirror. Her makeup smeared, she took down her updo and shook her head upside down. Sexy. What a lush. How could she even consider jumping into bed with someone she'd just met? But it had been months and months since she'd been with Sergio. This guy was hot, and it would help her get over Sergio. Wouldn't it?

She should probably take a shower, but she didn't want Barn to fall asleep, so she rinsed her underarms in the sink. She squished toothpaste on her finger and ran it over her teeth. Shimmying, she braced herself for a fulfilling time.

She found him in a bedroom. By the light of a lamp with a kerchief over it, Anne saw him pull back the blankets on his single bed. She climbed in beside him. He tried unsuccessfully to unlatch the hooks on the front of the corset, and, without much foreplay, it was over as fast as it had begun.

In the morning, she woke with a splitting headache. Her new lover was bald and smelled of stale beer. His roommate snored in a bed across the room.

Naked, she gathered up her clothes, ran into the bathroom, and turned on the shower. About to step in, she noticed a hospital gown–green fungus growing between broken tiles. Gross. She'd wait until she got home. Why hadn't she noticed it the night before? She wasn't the neatest person in the world, but at least her place was sanitary.

She dressed and wanted to get out of there before the unhottie awoke. She passed by the kitchen and noted the counters, covered in filthy pots and pans, and dirty dishes piled in the sink. No way would this guy ever offer to cook her a breakfast frittata like Sergio always did.

Carrying her coat, she escaped up to the sidewalk. A truck drove by and honked. In broad daylight, she felt ridiculous in her saloon outfit. She put on her coat and booked a Lyft.

Howard had left a text on her phone: *What happened to you last night?*

Anne: *Nothing*. She'd be too embarrassed to tell him what happened. In fact, she'd never tell anyone.

Howard: *I wanted to get you home safely, but you'd already gone.*

Anne: *Your friend dropped me off.*

Howard: *Not Barnaby. He's no friend of mine. He's the kind to use a counterfeit one-hundred-dollar bill to buy Girl Scout cookies.*

At home, she looked in the full-length mirror, outfit askew, hair a frizzy mess. She said to herself, "Getting drunk and having a one-night stand is no way to find your soul mate."

How could she have done something so disgusting? She'd been so wasted, she couldn't even recall if they'd used protection. She could only hope Barn hadn't given her some kind of disease.

She stepped out of the skirt, unhooked the corset, and left them on the floor. Her head pounded so much that all she wanted to do was go to sleep, but she couldn't stand her stench. Climbing into the shower, she washed her hair and scrubbed her body with a loofah. She still felt dirty, so she filled the tub, tossed in a honey bath bomb, and settled in for a soak.

God, this was the worst hangover she'd ever had. Perhaps she should text Fay and see if she'd meet her for a Bloody Mary. Fay would take one look at her, though, and start asking bawdy questions. Anne couldn't tell her the details of the disastrous night.

Wrapped in a towel, Anne checked the cupboard to see if she had any Snap E Tom, tomato juice, and vodka. She didn't. She swallowed two Advil, crawled onto her daybed, and fell asleep.

A little while later, her phone pinged with a text. Not him, not now.

Sergio: *Hi Bigfoot.*

Anne smiled at his nickname for her, his way of teasing about her size 9 shoes.

Anne: *Hi.*

Sergio: *I'm flying in tomorrow. Want to hang out?*

What? Just yesterday she'd agreed to see him the next time he came to town.

She wrote: *That was fast.*

Sergio: *I was so happy you said you'd see me that I couldn't wait.*

Her heart tingled. She'd thought being with someone else might take care of her feelings for Sergio, but after last night's disaster, she wanted him back in her life more than ever. She needed to resist that urge, though.

She lied: *I have to work.*

Sergio: *How about happy hour?*

After her behavior last night, she imagined she'd be able to see Sergio without being tempted to jump back into bed with him. Even though they were broken up, would she feel guilty when she saw him?

Anne: *Okay.*

Sergio: *I'll come by.*

Anne: *No, no. I'll meet you somewhere.*

Sergio: *How about Top of the Mark?*

That romantic. He knew the Mark. It had the best sunset views in town. They'd tried to eat there when they were still together, but the line had been too long, and, as usual, Sergio had been hungry and didn't want to wait. The restaurant didn't take reservations for dinner, but since tomorrow was a weeknight, it should be easy to get a table.

Anne: *Perfecto.*

She set her alarm for two hours, turned off her phone, and fell asleep again.

At noon, her alarm woke her. She still felt groggy from her headache and continued to loll in bed. The sky painting on the easel called to her, but she had no energy to create any art. What a waste of a day.

She made coffee, ate a few saltines, took more Advil, and climbed back into bed. Her phone had no messages. All was quiet on the western front.

Scrolling through her photos, she ran across a selfie of her and Barn that she didn't remember taking. Fortunately, the bar had been dark, and no one could tell who she was, so it wasn't really evidence of last night's fiasco. But she deleted it anyway.

She checked out the wanted poster from Ruby's. The bandit's name was Clifford Clifton, alias Cliff Clabourn. Was it a print of an authentic poster, or had someone created it just for decor? Was this Clifford a real outlaw?

She pulled up the picture on her laptop and zoomed in on the small print at the bottom of the poster. She typed "Kansas City" and "1885" into Google, and several interesting historical snippets appeared on a website called Missouri Outlaw History.

Southwest City, Missouri

On May 20, 1895, the Bill Doolin Gang attempt to rob the bank but are thwarted. State auditor J. C. Seaborn is killed, and Bill Doolin receives a head wound.

La Grange, Missouri

February 27, 1887: Bank is robbed of $21,000.
Melvin E. Baughn, 1836–68, b. Virginia, moved to Missouri
He was a pony express rider, guerrilla raider, jayhawker, horse thief, robber, and killer. Before he was hanged in Kansas, he requested to be buried in Doniphan, Missouri.

A really great guy.

Clay Wilson and Conrad W. Caddigan, July 1, 1884, were caught with gambling implements and bunco material in their possession. They are well known to western detectives as smart confidence men and thieves.

Anne googled "confidence man."

noun: confidence man; plural noun: confidence men

1. *old-fashioned term for con man.*

That's hysterical. The opposite of what you'd think it would mean. Howard would have called Barnaby that. Anne kept scrolling through the outlaw information, and a chill traveled up her spine as she read the next entry:

Kansas City, Missouri, September 8, 1885:

BANK ROBBED!

The spirit of Jesse James is still rampant in Missouri. The National Bank was robbed in the old Missouri way today. Shortly after one o'clock, two men wearing slouch hats and kerchiefs over their faces entered the bank, drew revolvers, and pointed them at the two customers, cashier, and guard. The prisoners were told that if they made an outcry, they would be shot dead. Cashier Hunt was marched behind the counter with a pistol at his head and forced to open the safe.

Anne held her breath and kept reading.

One of the thieves tossed $10,000 in a bag and demanded more. The cashier said that was all the cash in the bank. He was then marched back

> to the other prisoners. The guard pulled out his gun and shot one of the robbers, and the other robber shot the guard, grabbed a female customer, pointed a gun to her chest, and warned the prisoners to stay back or he'd kill her. He then told them to remain in the bank for ten minutes, on pain of death. He let the woman go and ran out the door with the money. The cashier did not wait for the limit of time to expire but gave the alarm as soon as the robber was out of the building. The authorities were too late, as the robber had mounted and left town. A posse was sent out, but so far, the thief has not been captured. The directors of the bank offer a $1,000 reward for him. This is the second robbery that has taken place in the vicinity in the past month.

Oh my God. Could this Clifford be the real robber? She typed in his names and "Kansas City," but nothing came up. Maybe he got on a train, rode it west, and ended up in an Arizona saloon with a girl in a green corset. Anne laughed at herself as her wild imagination exploded again.

13

The next morning, headache gone, Anne rolled over, trying to remember her strange dream about standing in a meadow, wearing the green corset. The sky reminded her of the beautiful ones she'd seen in the Southwest.

A scratching sound came from the other side of her door. Anne got up and opened it. "Good morning, Thai."

Purring, the cat ran in. Anne gave him a cracker and made coffee.

Images of her dream still floated in her mind. She'd read that if you wrote dreams down soon after waking up, you remembered them more clearly. And if you got in the habit of doing so, you'd remember more in the future.

Thai ran to the door, and Anne let him out. At least she didn't have to go to the museum until tomorrow and had the day to herself. She poured herself some coffee, crawled back into bed, and wrote in her journal: *In my dream, a small blond girl filled with guilt had on the corset.*

Anne could relate to that guilt. The dream pictures in her mind were blurry, but she jotted them down:

Lake, cabin, oaks, meadow = like that place up above Flagstaff where I saw the deer.

That was all she could recall. She scrolled through her travel pictures for the deer photo. As soon as she'd snapped it, the doe had bounded away. It had large eyes, tall, pointy ears, and a white-tufted tail. Anne made a mental note to print the photo out to use in a collage later.

After Sylvia had seen a deer on her first trip to Arizona, she'd said to Anne, "Those big eyes were healing. I felt as if the doe knew what a hard time I was going through."

To honor Sylvia, Anne had been determined to see one on her own trip. There must have been a lot more wildlife in the 1960s, because Anne had to hike out into the mountains for an hour before she spotted one. The doe had stopped and gazed into Anne's eyes, as if posing for the photo, and she understood what Sylvia had meant. Perhaps deer were Sylvia's spirit animals.

Anne pulled her copy of *Animal-Speak*, by Ted Andrews, from her bookshelf and read: *A spirit animal helps guide or protect a person on a journey and whose characteristics that person shares or embodies.*

Anne flipped to the index, found the page for deer, and read:

Meanings associated with the deer:

Gentleness

Move through life and obstacles with grace

In touch with inner child, innocence

Sensitive and intuitive

Vigilance, ability to change directions quickly

In touch with life's mysteries

That sounded like Sylvia. Even though she probably hadn't been aware of the spirit-animal concept, she could still have had one without naming it. But then, Sylvia had always talked about how much she loved her beagle-basset, Lucy—maybe Lucy had been Sylvia's spirit animal too. You could have more than one, couldn't you?

Anne was certain the great blue heron was her spirit animal. Every time she saw one in Michigan, her heart soared. At the lake, she always watched and waited for one to fly over, or maybe even land and preen nearby. Perhaps Thai was another of Anne's spirit animals, and that was why the cat kept trying to hang out with her. Or it could be because Anne kept feeding it?

She reread the information about the dream again and pretended the girl lived in Arizona in 1885. Anne googled "Arizona 1885" and wrote notes in her journal:

What would life have been like in 1885 in Arizona?

It wasn't even a state until 1912. The city of Flagstaff was founded in 1881. In 1882, the Atlantic and Pacific Railroad (later the Santa Fe) arrived and assured the community's growth.

Main population: lumber, ranching, railroad workers.

She kept going down the rabbit hole, discovering more information about Flagstaff life in the olden days. This sparked a big question, and she brainstormed in her journal:

What would life have been like in Flagstaff about the time trains came through?

No running water—pumps, windmills, outhouses

No cars or airplanes; no bicoastal romances

No electricity

No computers

No TV

No telephones—texting, Facebook, Instagram, cell phone cameras

No cell phone camera! That had become her favorite form of technology.

Anne imagined going under a black hood to take photographs

with the big-box camera on a tripod. In college, she had learned how to develop pictures in a darkroom, using harsh chemicals, and her boyfriend had kissed her in there.

On the other hand, life would have been a lot simpler in 1885. What would the advantages have been?

No air, water, noise, or light pollution

No GMOs or pesticides

More time with friends and loved ones

She scrolled through Pinterest photos and pictured herself in a bonnet, modest long dress, and lace-up boots. Perhaps she could do a series incorporating her Southwest experiences, personal pics, and vintage photo inspirations.

Late that afternoon, she lounged in a hot bath, fantasizing about her upcoming date with Sergio. She thought about his honeysuckle scent, his deep, dark eyes when he looked at her, his long, curly hair. Uh-oh. Maybe she needed to cancel. No, she was an adult and could resist him. Besides, her remorse about her disgusting behavior two nights before would keep her from jumping into bed with someone else so soon.

She dried off, wrapped herself in her kimono, and tried to decide what to wear. She picked up the corset and skirt from the floor and considered wearing them again tonight. That would be over the top, especially for the Top of the Mark. The corset would look cool with a pair of black jeans and boots. But she didn't want Sergio to get the wrong idea. Plus, the outfit smelled of bar and sweat, and it would take forever to get the odor out. She folded the outfit into a bag to drop off at the dry cleaner later.

She slipped on her favorite green lace dress, her silver shoes, and her black coat. She certainly wouldn't be inviting Sergio back to her place afterward, but she straightened up her apartment anyway.

14

At four o'clock, Anne rode a cable car up California Street to the Mark Hopkins. A few feathery clouds draped the sky. She hoped a beautiful sunset was in store. At the hotel, the man at reception said hello. As she crossed the lobby, heading toward the elevators, the thought of seeing Sergio again filled her with trepidation. Maybe this was a bad idea. She turned around and started back toward the lobby door, but there he was.

He removed his fedora with a smile. "How nice of you to greet me here, *amore mio*."

Anne's heart chakra permeated with heat. She was still deeply in love with him. "Hi" was all she could eke out.

He walked toward her, kissed her cheeks, and led her across the lobby to the bank of elevators. As the doors closed, she stood as far away from him as possible. The spark between them was impossible to ignore, and they stared at each other all the way to the nineteenth floor.

The Top of the Mark hostess led them to a table overlooking the bay. Sergio pulled out a chair overlooking Grace Cathedral and gestured for Anne to sit. He always gave her the seat with the best view.

He removed his jacket, draped it carefully on the back of his chair, and sat down across from her. His shoulders looked as if he'd been doing extra workouts. Darn it. Why did he have to be so sexy?

She wished they could still be together. But his life was in New York and hers was here, and there was no way to make it work. Their early long-distance relationship had been tantalizing and fun, but then, after a year, it had become unrealistic.

A waitress carrying a tray came by. "Hot mango margaritas are our specialty tonight."

"Want one?" Sergio asked Anne.

"Sounds delish." After the other night, she'd thought she'd never drink again, but she felt fine now.

"Okay, we'll each have one."

"Yes, sir." The waitress sashayed away toward the bar.

He redid his ponytail. "It's good to see you. You look healthy."

To some women, that might not have sounded like a compliment, but he knew Anne struggled to stay in shape and had been the one who'd gotten her started doing yoga. "Thanks. I've been trying to eat well and practicing a lot of yoga."

"That makes me happy. It's all really paying off." He smiled. "I'm excited about your artist-in-residence opportunity. When will they decide?"

"I don't know. They haven't even scheduled the interviews yet." She considered telling him about Karl but didn't want to ruin the evening with negative thoughts.

The waitress dropped off their drinks. Sergio held up his margarita to Anne. "To us."

What was that supposed to mean? She clinked her glass with his anyway. "There's no more us," she blurted out. So much for not ruining the evening.

He leaned toward her. "That's not true. We still have our history. No one can ever take that away."

"I guess you're right. Sorry."

"I'm taking a ski vacation early next year. I'd love it if you'd join me."

"We're broken up. How can we go on a trip together?"

"Separate rooms?" He smiled sheepishly.

"Oh, yeah. That would work really well."

"Just think about it."

She had always wanted to go skiing. Her klutziness shouldn't be a problem. He could ride the lifts to the top peaks, and she could take lessons on the bunny slope. When she got tired, she'd hang out in the lodge by the fire, drinking hot toddies in a cute après-ski outfit. Sergio would meet her and think she looked really sexy in it. She considered where she might find a vintage one, then caught herself.

"As nice as it sounds, I'll probably need to work." She took another sip of her margarita.

The tables had filled up with guests by now. They hovered at the windows, taking photos of the bay and the Golden Gate Bridge as a pink sunset ignited above San Francisco's skyline and fairy-tale lights began to blink below. Grace Cathedral's rose window glowed with color.

A waitress lit the candle on their table, and Sergio studied the menu.

"Careful." He pointed to Anne's menu as it dipped toward the flame. He handed her his phone, with the flashlight app on. "Here, use this. Remember Rome?"

How could she forget the night she had caught a restaurant on fire? She'd never been so embarrassed in her life. As they'd planned their scooter trip for the next day, the map had fallen into the candle, smoke filled the air, and the map caught fire. Sergio grabbed it from her, tossed in on the floor, and stomped on it. The maître d' had rushed over and sprayed it out with an extinguisher.

"I'm a-gonna lose a whole night's business," the restaurant owner yelled, as the fire alarm shrieked and the guests evacuated.

"*Spiacente.*" Sergio gave him a handful of euros as they headed out the door.

Now, Sergio said, "I've never understood why you can't use GPS, like everyone else."

"I like to use the real thing, and besides, I repurpose my used maps in collages."

"You sure weren't able to use that one for art."

They both laughed. It hadn't been funny then. She had been even more embarrassed than she had the time her cell phone went off at the Metropolitan Opera. He'd been pretty pissed about that too.

She finished her margarita, the color of the sun that had just gone down.

He reached his hands across the table to take hers, and his eyes softened. "I've missed you so much."

"Me too."

"I'm so glad to see you."

"Me too." She pulled her hands away. "Aren't you hungry? You're usually starved."

Sergio waved over the waitress. "What do you want?" he asked Anne.

"No, you go right ahead." She always had him do it because he was a foodie. "Remember, I'm a pescatarian."

"I'd never forget that about you."

He looked at the waitress. "We'll have the olives and baked Camembert." Sergio pronounced the name of the cheese perfectly—another reason she always wanted him to order.

"We'll also have Dungeness crab quesadillas and truffles for dessert, and another round of margaritas."

"Not for me, thanks." Anne handed her glass to the waitress. That one drink had made her dizzy, and she needed to stay sober.

"Another one won't hurt. Please join me."

"I don't think so."

"Please. For old times' sake."

She acquiesced. "Okay."

The waitress repeated the order and left. Dishes clinked and voices murmured around them. The people at the next table laughed loudly. The waitress dropped off the olives, and Anne and Sergio each popped one into their mouth.

After they'd finished the quesadillas, the waitress cleared the table and brought over the dessert. Anne closed her eyes and ate a chocolate truffle. The decadence tasted like passion.

She opened her eyes. There were two more on the plate.

"Finish them." Sergio pointed and grinned.

She knew that he knew chocolate this rich turned her on. She knew she shouldn't, but she couldn't resist and ate every bite.

He moved to a chair beside her, swiped a chocolate drip from her bottom lip, and kissed her. "Let's go to your place," he whispered. She inhaled the scent of him, wanted to hold on, melt into his arms, and never let go. One night together couldn't hurt. Tomorrow he'd get on a plane, and she'd return to being an independent woman. She stared into his deep-brown eyes and nodded.

When they reached her apartment, Thai greeted them at her door.

"Not tonight." Anne pushed him away with a foot, and he skittered down the stairs.

Sergio stepped inside and commanded, "Alexa, play *La Traviata*."

"Here's *La Traviata*, act one," Alexa said, and the opera began.

"*Grazie*," Sergio said to Alexa, as he filled two wine goblets.

They clinked glasses, then sat on the daybed, drank the wine, and kissed again. Then Anne pushed the coffee table aside tipsily and stood facing Sergio. "Alexa," she said seductively, and raised her eyebrows at him, "play 'Do Ya Think I'm Sexy,' by Rod Stewart."

The music started. She raised her arms and starting dancing for Sergio. This was something she'd always wanted to do. She'd really show him how healthy she was. Even though she could be a klutz, she could do this.

She slowly took off her black velvet coat, walked to the corner, and let it drop to the floor. Sergio's eyes lit up as she began to strut around the room in her silver shoes, singing the words to the song.

She stopped, raised her arms, and rotated her hips. Then she leaned over, pulled off her dress, swung it in the air, and tossed it across the room. In her black lace push-up bra and matching panties, she continued to dance. On the next chorus, she unhooked the bra, twirled it over her head, and threw it at Sergio. He caught it with a smile. As the song ended, she pushed him down, climbed on top of him, and kissed him deeply.

A few hot-and-heavy minutes later, he fumbled in her night-stand drawer.

"Where are they?" he asked.

She didn't want to tell him that in her grief about their breakup, she'd thrown out their condoms. "Their expiration date had passed, so I tossed them."

He sat up and stared at her. "But it was a new package."

She shrugged and pulled him to her.

"Are you sure you didn't use them all?"

Her one-night stand with Barn was a fuzzy, nightmarish memory that she still wanted to erase.

"How can you even think that?"

"You never know."

She pulled him onto her and continued kissing him.

"But . . ." he started.

She wanted him so much. "It'll be fine."

15

Before dusk, just when Sally Sue was certain she couldn't abide the bumpy ride one more minute, the stagecoach stopped at a ramshackle property. Two mangy horses stood in a corral. The cistern was full of bullet holes, fence railings hung off their posts, and a prairie schooner with a torn canvas top tilted on its side. Piles of snow still dotted the soil underneath the oaks.

Sally Sue hobbled to a tree stump and perched on it. Her body would be sore for ages. The driver and Cliff moved the crates, eight in all, to the back of a wagon. Cliff loaded his saddlebags on the floor in front and handed the man some cash.

The driver waved as he pulled back down the road. Sally Sue was tempted to run after him, but Cliff wouldn't let her get far. Her shoulders slumped at the realization that she was now all alone with Cliff.

He wandered over to the corral, holding out an apple in each hand, and the horses trotted toward him.

"You pretty girl," he said to the red one. "We're gonna get to know each other quite well." With his hand flat, he offered an apple to her. She swiped it and began chewing.

With his big head, the spotted horse nudged Cliff, who opened his other hand. "Aren't you a handsome pinto."

The animals' open mouths revealed huge teeth. Obviously starving, the horses gobbled the fruit, including the core.

Cliff must really be daft. He talked to horses as if they understood what he was saying.

Cliff grabbed halters from the back of the wagon, put them on the horses, led them to the wagon, and hitched them up with ease. He took a blanket from a crate, folded it neatly, and laid it on the wooden seat in front. "Milady." He held out a hand to Sally Sue as if she were the queen of England.

"No, thanks." She brushed past him, and on her third try she hoisted herself successfully onto the wagon's wood seat. He chuckled and climbed in beside her.

Although the chances were slim, she listened for the sound of horses' hooves that would signal Sheriff Mack and his posse coming to save her before Cliff carried her even farther away.

Cliff clicked the reins, and the horses started down the road away from town. She clung to the basket on her lap. Where was he taking her? How far was this homestead? Would he kill her there? Her mind bounced along with the wagon on the rocky path, jumping to all sorts of possible situations. Fear overtook her senses. She could scarcely breathe. For a fleeting moment, she considered leaping off the wagon and rolling down the embankment away from Cliff, but she knew she'd never get far.

Without another person or even another homestead in sight, they plodded along the lonely road for what seemed like miles. The temperature continued to drop as they rode higher and higher up into the mountains.

Hoo. Hoo. Hooooo, an owl called. Tall tree shadows shifted, and while the darkness should have made Sally Sue more afraid, the horses' cadence began to soothe her. She was breathing more easily by the time Cliff turned off the road and onto a trail that ascended steeply.

"How do you know where to go?" she asked. "Have you been here before?"

"You'd be surprised what I learned in town."

The sun set in an explosion of fire colors that waned to darkness. A few stars sprinkled the sky. Will he ravage her body, kill her, and dump it into a ravine?

The sky grew pitch black, and she shivered.

"Use those mittens and hat from the floor in front of you," Cliff said quietly.

She leaned over and picked up the items. She pulled the mittens on over her gloves, removed her bonnet, and pulled the wool cap on her head. He must have bought these at the mercantile. She didn't want to admit it had been thoughtful of him.

"Now, hand me the blanket."

She did, and Cliff threw it over their legs.

The trail crisscrossed here and there. Once they arrived at the homestead, she'd have no way of finding her way back to town.

She watched the horses' rears as they clopped along. She hadn't spent much time around animals. Some folks at home had horses that they rode all over town. Her ma had never let her ride, saying, "It's undignified for a lady to do so. Those beasts are for pulling carts and carriages and herding cattle." Sally Sue had to admit she was afraid of horses. Her mother had always pulled her away when she got too close. "Never walk behind one, or it'll kick you."

Perhaps if Sally Sue pretended to go along with Cliff and gained his trust, he'd go easy on her.

"How do the horses see in the dark?" she asked.

"I think they instinctively know the way." He slid a bottle from his pocket, pulled out the cork, and offered her a swig.

"No, thanks."

"It'll help keep you warm."

It smelled like the rum her father used to drink. Before he left them, she'd seen her ma hide it many times and heard them argue about it.

"Lips that touch liquor shall never touch mine." Sally Sue put her hand over her mouth. She couldn't believe she'd blurted that out.

Cliff guffawed. "Suit yourself."

The moonless sky donned a plethora of stars. Sally Sue's hands and feet and even her nose grew cold, and she regretted not having taken a sip. Cliff put his arm around her shoulders and pulled her close. She flashed back to when he had grabbed her at the bank, and she tried to pull away, but he held her tightly now too.

"Don't fight me." His silver-blue eyes shone in the dark. "You're with me now. Don't worry—I'll take care of you."

What did he mean, take care of her? Here she was, nestled under a blanket with a murderer.

A cold wind blew. She shivered again and let her body lean into his for warmth but not for pleasure. She closed her eyes and silently prayed, *Please save me.*

She prayed to God all the time but hated church. Every Sunday her whole life, her ma had made her dress up and go. When Sally Sue was young, she'd fidget on the hard pew and her ma would pinch her hands or hit them with her fan and whisper, "God hates you when you don't sit still in his house."

Sally Sue never understood why, if God was everywhere, he had to live in a house. Wasn't he living in their home too, in the petunia beds and maple tree out back? Besides at church, they prayed to him at supper, and at bedtime too. Actually, Sally Sue talked to him all the time without anyone else knowing. Not out loud, only to him, through her heart, like she had just now. It came in handy, especially that day at the bank when he had held the gun to her chest and had his arm around her—the same arm that was now around her in the wagon.

In fact, maybe the Good Lord was her best friend. Not like the girls in school who were sometimes her friends and other times not.

She could sense their parents had told them to steer clear of her because she came from a broken home.

The wagon jolted, and Cliff's arm pushed hard against her.

She screamed.

"Sorry, just hit a big rock is all."

With a chuckle, he began to sing "She'll Be Coming 'Round the Mountain." His deep voice echoed across the canyon.

What a surprise that he knew all the words to the song. She did, too, but resisted the urge to join in. He held the last note for a long time, until it faded into the sky.

How could a bank-robbing murderer know how to sing like that? Sally Sue wanted to ask, but she didn't dare. He might get angry at her, and there was no telling what he'd do.

16

The buckboard carried them along. Sally Sue's eyes began to droop again. Needing to stay sharp, she shook herself awake and looked up at the sky. A shooting star streaked down from the heavens. She hadn't seen one in years, and her mind hurtled back to a night long ago, as she remembered her father saying, "Make a wish." At that time, she had wished her parents would stop arguing. Now she wished to get away from Cliff.

The next star, she'd fill her mind with good thoughts—good wishes—for after she got away from Cliff. She kept watch until another shooting star graced the sky, and on that one, she wished to see the ocean someday. Another star flew from the sky, and she put her hand on her belly. She wished to someday have a child to hold and call her own. A boy as sweet as that Isaiah McMillan. These were all chimerical wishes, though, things that she hoped for but that were impossible to achieve.

As they crossed a wooden bridge, dimly outlined buildings up ahead became visible. The horses picked up speed and trotted along, bouncing Sally Sue's sore body. In front of a towering barn, Cliff stopped them with a pull on the reins and a "whoa."

An owl hooted in the distance, and then another answered. A chill prickled Sally Sue's spine. She had never been anywhere so desolate in her whole life. How would she ever be able to get away?

Cliff climbed down off the wagon. As he swung open the barn

doors, the rusty hinges squealed and he led the horses inside. They neighed and stomped the dusty ground. Still sitting on the wagon, blind in the cavernous space, Sally Sue felt squeaking sounds vibrate and shadows swoop down toward her.

She screeched, bent over, and threw her hands above her head.

"It's just bats." Cliff laughed. "They won't hurt you."

Her heart slowed, and she strained to see the bats escape from the barn and fly toward the moonlight. She'd read Bram Stoker's terrifying book and thought of the count, wild horses' hooves, and bloody fangs. She touched her neck.

Cliff reached for one of her mittened hands. Too tired to refuse, she let him help her to the ground. Legs wobbly, she fell off-balance.

He caught her elbows. "You okay, little lady?"

She stood up straight. "Certainly."

He lit the lantern he found on a nail near the door and handed it to her. The barn was filled with gloomy silhouettes: tools, an anvil, a plow.

"Darrel said there should still be hay somewhere." Cliff removed the halters, climbed the ladder up to the loft, and tossed down fodder for the horses. Then he took the lantern from her and they trudged outside, into the deep chill. Piles of snow on the ground reflected the lantern light.

"You'll be wanting to use the privy. There's gotta be one."

They walked behind the cabin, and Cliff peered into an armoire-size building, brushed back a spongy cobweb, and held the door open for her. "All's clear."

He put the lantern on the hook inside and stepped back. She hoped there weren't any spiders inside. She didn't like them at all. Their outhouse at home was painted a cheerful yellow. This one wasn't painted at all. It sure stank to high heaven. At home, Ma had insisted upon using powdered lime to help with that.

Cliff waited beside a large tree while she finished her business.

She handed him the lantern, and they walked around to the cabin's door. He held the lantern aloft while he pushed the door open and they stepped inside. The tang of earth and stone filled the air. Dust motes caught in the lamplight and drifted down to reveal a hooked rug splayed across the dirt floor; busted-out windows; a crystal chandelier, with dried, dripping candle wax, hung over a rough-hewn table; and chairs pulled back, one even thrown to the ground, as if someone had left in a hurry. How odd to have a crystal chandelier all the way out here. More luxurious than any she'd seen in Kansas City—must be worth a fortune.

Cliff put his saddlebag on the table. She wandered over to the potbellied stove, where a cast-iron skillet had hardened and reeked of mold.

"Uncivilized," Cliff said, carrying the skillet outside.

That's a peculiar thing for a kidnapper to say. She sat in a rocker. Cliff returned with firewood from the porch. He handed her a hunk of cheese and crackers from his pocket and ate some himself.

"What do you think happened to the folks who lived here?"

"Don't know." He just looked at her and kept his jaw clamped shut. "There's more food in the wagon. Want me to get you something else?"

"That's fine. I'm not hungry."

"Okay. We'll unload the supplies tomorrow." Cliff turned his back to set the fire in the stone hearth, and she gobbled down the food ravenously.

He lit the fire, sat across from her, and lit his pipe. Soon the cabin began to warm and the scents of pine and pipe tobacco filled the air.

Sally Sue yawned.

"You must be bone tired." He tilted his head toward the brass bed.

The white eyelet quilt looked as inviting as a cloud. She glanced at Cliff. Did he plan on sharing the bed with her?

Mama had always told her never to be alone with a man, because they wanted only one thing. Sally Sue felt herself blush, even though she didn't understand what her mama had meant. She peeked at Cliff. Would he try to do that one thing to her? Her mama had told her that after she was married, she'd have to do it—whatever "it" was—as a wifely duty.

Cliff walked toward the bed. At the foot of it, he leaned down, opened the trunk, and pulled out another blanket.

Her body, which had been weary for sleep, now quaked with anxiety. "I'll just sleep here, in the rocker."

"Oh, no, you won't. I'll bunk down in the barn."

"But it's freezing out there."

"No matter. The horses will keep me warm."

Would he really sleep with the horses?

"Sleep tight." He slung his saddlebag over an arm, grasped the lantern, trod out the door, and closed it behind him.

Sleep tight? That's what he thought. She planned to stay awake, give him plenty of time to fall asleep, and then scurry away. Alone for the first time in days, she fell onto the bed and crawled under the covers, boots and all—only to warm up, she told herself. On the mantel, a woven bowl, a clay pot, and a carved, hand-painted Indian doll cast eerie shadows on the firelit wall. Her eyelids fluttered closed, but they popped open and her heart picked up when she heard him coming back up the steps.

The door flung open, and he said, "You'll be wanting this." He yawned, set her basket on the table, and left again.

For heaven's sake. She should escape tonight, but she knew by the time he was asleep, and with the cold and her weary body, she'd never get far. And where would she go, anyhow? She had no idea where she was. He was probably too tired to harm her tonight anyway. Tomorrow, with a good night's rest and warm clothes, she'd go. She untied her boots and dropped them on the floor.

Exhaustion overpowered her. She closed her eyes, but no matter how hard she tried, sleep wouldn't find her, wouldn't bless her fearful thoughts shut. Sally Sue pulled the eyelet quilt up under her chin.

She tried to forget, but her mind kept replaying the robbery. The sound of the gunshot, the man falling, his dead eyes staring at her, Cliff's arms around her, the cold gun pointed at her chest, fear pounding there. She wanted to harness and then let go of her fear, but despite her attempts, sleep wouldn't come. It would be a long winter's night.

17

At dawn, mourning doves cooed a sorrowful refrain outside. Sally Sue rolled over, ready to fall back to sleep, but then remembered where she was and sat up with a start. Through the window, dark clouds hovered in the sky.

The relit fire sent a soft glow throughout the cabin, and she smelled coffee. Her rumpled clothes were piled next to her boots on the floor. She must have escaped her corset, blouse, and bustled skirt and tossed them there sometime in the night. At home, much to her ma's dismay, Sally Sue slept bare. She'd go to bed in her nightgown, but it would twist around her body and she'd end up pulling it off. Ma told her sleeping without nightclothes was a sin, but Sally Sue knew it wasn't one of Moses's Ten Commandments, and she couldn't find a Bible passage that said so either. She had been too embarrassed to ask Pastor Grimes if there was any truth to it.

She quickly pulled the quilt around her and stared at the door.

Invisible the night before, a silver-spindled spiderweb hung above her, between the beams. A fly buzzed in it. She knew how it felt. Just like that fly, she was stuck in the middle of nowhere, without a way to break free. The insect quieted to a low hum and grew silent. She could die like that too.

A baby's crib stood in a corner. On the wall, a framed piece of embroidery said TO THINE OWN SELF BE TRUE. Blue-and-white willow plates like her ma's were displayed on shelves above the sideboard. Sally Sue remembered the star-crossed lovers' story that the plates' pattern depicted. The two had tried to elope, but the girl's father didn't want her to marry a commoner. He was about to kill them, but instead the gods transformed the lovers into a pair of doves. On the plate, they were stretching their wings and flying toward heaven, where the lovers' spirits lived together happily for eternity.

Sally Sue realized now that she'd never have an eternal love like she'd dreamed of. This ruffian would kill her before that could ever happen. But wait—if he had planned to kill her, wouldn't he have done it by now, before they'd journeyed all this way? Out here, though, covering up the crime would be easier.

"Morning glory." Cliff stomped into the cabin. "Rise and shine."

She curled up like the fly and tugged the quilt over her head. If she played dead, would he leave her alone? She wished it could be that simple.

He tossed some garments on the foot of the bed. "Sleep well?"

She peeked out from under the covers and sat up, pulling the quilt up to her chin. Her hands went to her scalp. She must look a fright with her squished bouffant and quickly braided strands on either side of her head, like she'd worn when she was a girl. But how could she be worried about her appearance when she was in such a dire situation?

"Breakfast?" He handed her an apple from a bowl he'd filled and placed on the table.

She was hungry but wouldn't give him the satisfaction of seeing her eat.

He poured coffee from a pot into a willow cup and carried it to her. "Do you take cream or sugar?"

She accepted the cup. "Nothing."

He picked up an apple and bit it. "I'll be in the barn."

She listened for the squeal of the barn door's hinges before she shimmied out of bed, the quilt still around her, and devoured the apple.

What in the world? She examined the clothes he'd brought her: long johns, a plaid flannel shirt, dungarees, and clean socks. They were so big, she'd swim in them.

She scrambled into the long johns, slid on the shirt, buttoned it, and rolled up the sleeves. She stepped into the pants and rolled up the legs also. For goodness' sake.

If only Mama could see her now: "Tighten that corset"; "button your top button"; "floof those bows." In spite of it all, Sally Sue had to smile. She'd never liked all those clothing-etiquette constraints anyway.

She put on her boots, made her way out to the porch, and sat on the swing. The silent beauty made her heart tremble. Snow-covered peaks soared in the distance. Oaks dotted the meadow. A frozen pond the size of a rodeo roundup ring glistened in the morning sunlight through a smattering of clouds.

A solo doe wandered across the meadow, stopped, and stared at Sally Sue. What a beauty. She didn't see many in Kansas City, only sometimes in the park. The hustle and bustle probably scared them away.

Dark clouds began to roll in from behind the mountain peaks, and the air grew cold. She went inside and got her mittens and shawl, wishing she had a coat too. She made her way to the side of the cabin, toward the privy. As she exited, a sharp noise emanated and she spied Cliff using a pickax to dig a hole under a giant oak. She put her hand on her chest. He must be planning to hide the money—or maybe he was going to kill her and bury her body there.

Heart banging against her ribs, she tiptoed back to the cabin. Through a window, she watched him struggle to break the frozen ground. After a while, he leaned on the pickax, wiped the sweat from his brow with a bandanna, and glanced at the cabin. She stepped aside. He grinned and waved hello to her, as if trying to dig a hole behind the house under an oak was the most natural thing in the world.

She needed to find the cash and escape soon, before he killed her.

A few minutes later, he came in, carrying a crate full of supplies from the barn. "Here, you'll need this." He handed her a men's coat.

"Thanks." She took it from him. Even though it was too big, it would keep her warm.

Then, lo and behold, he cooked her flapjacks for breakfast, garnished with melted butter and honey. Imagine a man cooking like that.

"That was delicious." She pretended all was fine with her. She didn't want him to suspect she planned to slip away.

While he washed the dishes, as if she planned to stay, she unpacked her basket, putting her brush, Bible, and nightgown on top of the trunk at the foot of the bed.

He drew the buckboard out in front of the cabin, and she helped him unpack the goods. They placed their perishables in a box on the porch. "Always keep the lid on tight so animals don't help themselves," he told her.

They put in the cupboard a coffee grinder, spices, dried beans, and many other items. She was amazed by all he'd been able to buy. He must have robbed a bank. She put a hand over her mouth to conceal her smile at her own joke.

Right when they'd finished their work, snow fell and continued all afternoon. They sat by the fire. She tatted, and he smoked his pipe. They didn't say much.

That night, certain Cliff had fallen asleep in the barn, she lit the lantern. The loot was probably with him, but it would be worth a try to search high and low in the cabin for the money: every shelf in the cabin cupboards, under her bed; she even rolled up the carpet and checked for a hole. But she found nothing. She'd have to go ahead and leave without it.

Bundled up in the clothes he'd given her, Sally Sue held her basket and stepped out onto the porch. Darkness contrasted with the white snow below. The frozen pond shimmered as if candlelight shone across it. Sally Sue's eyes drifted above. The lights were only the reflection of pinprick stars in the dark sky. The moon hadn't risen yet.

She wished she could reach up, pull down a star, and toss it into the barn, explode it like a Civil War cannon. Way out here, no one would know if she killed Cliff while he slept inside the barn and set it on fire in a burst of hot flames. Then she'd be free to go home.

She paused. As frightening as he was, had he really harmed her? He had given her clothes and food. Did he deserve to die? Would God forgive her?

Her feet crunched in the snow, and she searched for the horse trail that the buckboard had made the day before, but the evening snow had covered it. She shivered with cold.

On their way in, she hadn't seen any other cabins for miles. It didn't matter. She just had to get away. She hoped she could find her way back to town. There, she'd go straight to Sheriff Mack and convince him Cliff was the wanted man. The sheriff would come out and capture him, and she'd be safe.

They could contact her ma, and she'd send money for a ticket. Or the McMillans at the mercantile might hire Sally Sue until she made enough. She was good with figures. She'd never had a real job. Plus, she'd be able to see that delightful young Isaiah again. She'd like that.

Wisps of clouds escaped from her mouth. She tightened the shawl over her head, wrapped her arms around her chest, and kept pace to warm herself and let her imagination keep her company while she slogged along.

Perhaps she'd become a saloon girl and wear a colorful outfit like the women she'd seen. How hard could it be? She could carry a tune and do dance steps. She'd seen the way that one girl in the green corset had flirted with Cliff, blinking her eyelashes and smiling. Sally Sue could do that too.

She'd had such a crush on Johnny Jones, and he'd smiled at her in a special way—at least, when his ma wasn't around. It would be a challenge, though, to be a coquette with the dirty men she'd seen in town. Maybe if she pretended the men were Johnny, she could do it—wiggle her shoulders forward and back, tilt her head, and laugh at their jokes, maybe even touch a hand.

She'd observe what the other women did and follow their lead. God wouldn't think she was a sinner. It didn't count, because she was in a desperate situation and she really had no choice if she was going to survive.

Sally Sue remembered the way that girl had looked at Cliff. Possibly, he had known her before, or maybe she just considered him appealing. Sally Sue couldn't blame her. On the train, before Sally Sue realized he was the man who'd held a gun to her chest, she'd also thought he was handsome.

Even though she was uncertain of her destination, she kept putting one boot in front of the other. As she crossed the hoarfrost-sprinkled bridge, she had to concentrate in order not to slide and fall. On the other side, her body began to warm, and her tension eased. Maybe she really could get away.

She could see the path more clearly as a crescent moon began to rise, but soon dark clouds covered the sky. In the afterglow, snowflakes began to fall and sparkled like sequins. Within minutes, the snow fell more fiercely. Her clothes were soaked through, and her teeth chattered. She wanted to take shelter beside a boulder under a pine, but if she stopped, she could freeze to death.

At least that would be better than being killed by Cliff. Her body ached; she imagined crawling onto the ground and letting the snow cover her. She'd just stay there until she died. But she kept trudging along, until finally her knees buckled.

18

Collapsed on the ground, shivering to the bone, covered in snow, Sally Sue was sure she was going to die. She might as well. She had nothing to live for anyway.

As she lost track of time and space, the world smelled of cold. Her mind slashed through blurred childhood memories: her father's kind face smiling at her, Kansas City folks' disparaging glances and sneering faces, Ma's twisted grimace and echoing rebukes—"Sally Sue, our miserable life is all your fault."

Snow continued to fall. Had God really chosen this time to take her? Was he punishing her for wanting to kill Cliff, or for some earlier transgression, and that was why she was the one Cliff had held at gunpoint in the bank?

Preparing to die, she silently began to recite the 23rd Psalm: *The Lord is my shepherd . . .*

She started to lose consciousness.

The sound of slushing snow moved toward her. She hunkered down to meet her maker. A horse neighed. A hand touched her back.

"Are you a lunatic? You could have died out here!" Cliff hollered. He bundled Sally Sue in a blanket, rubbed her body to rekindle the warmth within it, and loaded her onto the horse, then climbed behind her and put his arms around her. She leaned her body into him and saw black.

As her eyes fluttered open, deep, unrememberable dreams enshrouded her mind in cobwebs. Dim light entered through the windows. How long had she been asleep? Why was she so weak? Recollections of snow falling on her back stirred the edges of her consciousness.

She shivered despite the mile of blankets piled atop her and the fire roaring in the hearth. His back to her, Cliff stirred a pot on the stove. He rummaged through the shelf of supplies, sprinkled in this and that. The smell of baking sweetness filled the air. He turned. She quickly closed her eyes and soon fell back to sleep.

Later, his hand touched her shoulder. "Welcome back to the living."

As hard as she tried, her tongue wouldn't form words. She blinked at him and attempted to sit up, but she collapsed back underneath the covers. She tried to wiggle her fingers, but they wouldn't budge. He grabbed her hands, rubbing, and blew his hot breath on them. She laid her head back and felt sensation begin to return. An "ah" escaped her lips.

He let go of her hands. "Here. Give me your feet."

They were numb. She slid her legs to the side, realized she was stark naked under the covers, and stared at him. She felt herself blush.

"Don't worry—it's nothing I haven't seen before." He picked up the nightgown lying on the floor and handed it to her.

She crawled deep under the blankets and slid it on.

At the hearth, from a cauldron on a swinging arm, he filled a teacup with his cooking concoction and came at her with a spoon.

Even though it smelled delicious, she shook her head. "I'm not hungry." Maybe she should just starve herself to death.

"For goodness' sake, girl. You're as stubborn as a mule. Eat up—you need your strength."

"For what?" She'd found her voice.

His eyes turned stormy blue. He approached her with the spoon again and said softly, "For whatever cotton-picking thing destiny has in store for you."

She'd better not make him angry. There was no telling what he might do. She opened her mouth, let him slide the spoon inside, and held the deliciousness on her tongue. She closed her eyes: apples, cinnamon, nutmeg, molasses. What was that last ingredient?

She paused. She opened her eyes and glared at him. Rum. How could he? Even so, the apple concoction was the best darn thing she'd ever tasted. She accepted the cup, dipped the spoon in, and took another bite. It sure did warm her. Cliff filled her cup again, and she had to force herself not to gobble it down.

"Aren't you gonna thank me?" He put his hands on his hips and smiled.

"What for?" she squeaked out.

"For saving your life."

She glowered. "I wish you'd just let me die out there."

"You fool!" His voice was as hard-edged as his knife. He stomped out the door, slammed it, and left her alone in the cabin.

He was right—she was a fool. She should have put more effort into escaping when they were in town, or should have told someone there that he'd kidnapped her. Feeling hopeless, she drifted in and out of sleep all afternoon, sensing his dark presence as he added logs to the fire.

She was too frail to get out of bed; it took all day for her body to thaw out. She'd lost track of time and presence and didn't even know what day it was. It didn't matter, because she had nowhere to go. Her leaden heart rusted within her chest as her last hope of escape perished. She raised her hand to brush away tears.

She jolted when Cliff's hand touched her shoulder again, rousing her. It was light outside now. "Is it morning?" she asked.

"Yes. You need to get your strength back. Eat again."

He must have hunted down a varmint, because the aroma of cooking meat filled the cabin. He handed her a bowl and spoon. She ate a few bites of the tasty stew and fell back to sleep again.

She awoke in the night. Darkness hovered as wind screamed down the peaks and circled the rough-hewn cabin walls. Hunched in bed, she felt waves of sorrow, loneliness, and fear sweep over her. She couldn't get up to stoke the dying fire. She missed the blanket her grandmother had crocheted for her the year before she passed, longed for the soft feel of the yarn on her chin.

Why was Cliff being so kind—feeding her, keeping her alive? Maybe he wanted her healthy so he could have that one thing Ma said men wanted. Cliff might be not really asleep in the barn but waiting outside to pounce on her at any moment. Every creak made her heart race.

How would she find the courage to go on, a captive in a strange land with a strange man who could at any moment enter the cabin and ravish her? It truly would have been better if he had just let her die.

Sally Sue had no choice but to accept the situation and resigned herself to abide by Cliff. She'd wait until spring before she tried to escape again. Even then, he'd probably track her down. She'd have to look over her shoulder wherever she went.

19

Anne slid the last photograph into her portfolio sleeve with a smile. It had taken six weeks for the museum to schedule the interviews, and finally tomorrow was the day. She considered taking a small original piece or two with her as well but thought it might be overkill.

She had continued to teach at the museum. The board member's horseshoes had been delivered the other day, and Anne planned to teach the mosaic lesson to her students next week. At home, the sky painting was really coming along, she let go of perfectionism, and remembered not to be a slave to the photo.

Her phone buzzed with a text from Sergio. It was a cute emoji of a guy who looked just like him, pointing and saying, *You got this!*

She sent Sergio back a thanks and a smiley-face emoji. He called often, but she still tried to keep her distance.

The morning after their Top of the Mark night, he had kissed her goodbye and said, "*Amore mio, grazie* for *una notte meravigliosa*."

She'd kissed him back. "Remember, this doesn't mean we're back together."

He'd whispered in her ear, "I know. I'll keep in touch anyway."

She yawned. She'd been so tired lately. She searched through her closet. Should she dress like an artist? She tried on her blue dress, sighed, and texted Fay.

Anne: *I'm nervous about the interview tomorrow.*

Fay: *Don't worry, you'll wow the nickers off them.*

Anne: *What should I wear?*

Fay: *New blue dress is smashing.*

Anne: *It's a little snug today.* Why had she been feeling so bloated lately? She had been going to yoga and drinking a lot of smoothies. Maybe it was her time of the month. She thought back; she was a little late.

Fay: *Put on some Spanx.*

Anne: *Lol. You know I'm not that kind of girl. Thanks again for that glowing reference.*

Fay: *It's all true.*

Anne: *I don't feel qualified.*

Fay: *Rubbish!*

Anne: *What do you think they'll ask me?*

Fay: *Fredricka's on the panel. Want me to check with her?*

Anne: *No! That would feel like cheating?*

Fay: *Not really. Maybe write out sample questions and practice answers.*

Anne: *Great idea.*

Fredricka, Fay's boss and the Gallery Noir owner, collected Anne's work and was always supportive to her. It was wonderful that she was sitting on the panel.

Fay: *Keep your answers short and to the point. Don't ramble.*

Anne: *Do I ramble?*

Fay: *Sometimes when you're gobsmacked about a project, you get carried away. Keep in mind not all committee members are artists, so don't overwhelm them with lingo. Want me to come over and practice with you? I could leave work early.*

Anne: *No, that's okay.*

Fay: *I know you'll wow them.*

Anne really hoped so.

She dialed her mom. "Hi. I've got the museum residency interview tomorrow; what do you think I should wear?"

"You can't go wrong with a power outfit: white blouse under a navy jacket."

"Are pants okay?"

"Wear something comfortable, but not sweats." Her mom laughed. "Fitted slacks are fine. And accessorize with a colorful scarf. I don't want to be critical, dear, but please leave your backpack at home."

"Why?"

"It's not professional. It doesn't say, 'I can do this.'"

Anne returned to her closet and saw the corset outfit. She should just wear that. It would wow them for sure. Dry-cleaning it had cost a pretty penny, but if she'd washed it by hand, it might have lost some of its shape. Even after she'd brought it home and tried it on, the memory of her gross mistake with Barn lingered, so she'd lit some white sage and cleansed the green silk.

She considered her black velvet coat for luck, but that would be too much. Instead, she pulled out an old navy-blue jacket. She tried on three blouses and chose the white one that fit best, even though it had underarm stains. Thrift-shop, elastic-waist polyester pants and wingtips from her valet-parking days would do. She chose a flamingo-pink vintage scarf and an old lady–style leather purse her mother had sent for Anne's birthday. She laid the ensemble over the kitchenette so it would be ready for the morning.

Anne curled on the daybed with her journal to brainstorm questions and answers:

Tell us about your artistic path.

1. *BA in studio art*
2. *Sold canvases at farmers' markets*
3. *Group show at Gallery Noir*
4. *Solo show at Gallery Noir*
5. *Teaching position at SFMOMA*

Why are you the best candidate for this residency?

1. *Love SFMOMA*
2. *Have teaching experience*
3. *Am creative*
4. *Can interact well with people*

She was so much more qualified than Karl. He probably hadn't even passed the paper screening. She'd seen him around. He had been volunteering in the museum gift shop. He used to come in and bug her in the classroom until she told him to leave her alone or she'd tell Priscilla. Anne hadn't seen him for a while.

She'd do another sample question. She closed her eyes, breathed in and out. Pen in hand, she wrote:

What is your artist statement?
I'm an intuitive artist who is inspired to work from my heart and not my mind. As I create I breathe, get into the zone, and lose myself in the process. My collages are inspired by nature, architecture, and cityscapes. I use found objects to make my mosaics. I believe everyone is an artist and can be guided to achieve a sense of fulfillment through the process of creating art.

At two o'clock in the morning, Anne awoke feeling queasy, and her chest burned like bitter rain. She hoped she was just nervous about the interview and hadn't caught Penny's flu. She fluffed her pillow and tried to go back to sleep but couldn't.

She dumped two tablespoons of apple cider vinegar in a glass, added water, and stirred. That usually did the trick after she'd eaten too much pizza or greasy food. She put the glass to her lips, but the stench made her rush to the bathroom and throw up. She'd always been sensitive to smells, but vinegar had never done this to her before.

She made herself a cup of chamomile tea and added a little honey. She felt rotten.

At sunrise, she finally fell back to sleep.

20

Anne overslept by an hour. She'd planned to walk but now would have to take a Lyft. She threw on the clothes, clutched her portfolio and nerdy purse.

Mrs. Landenheim stepped out her door. "Look!"

"Sorry, I'm running late." Anne glanced at the cupped hands her landlady held toward her.

Anne paused and fingered the soft black back of the furry kitten. "How cute!"

"Just got her last night."

Anne pulled herself away. "Bye. I've gotta go!"

In the car she ate a PowerBar, worked on her hair, and applied lipstick. She sprinted down the museum halls, but when she arrived at the conference room out of breath and ten minutes past her time slot, the door was closed. They must be running late too. She could hear voices coming from inside, but she couldn't make out what they were saying.

She plopped heavily in the chair placed across from the door and slid her portfolio underneath. She drummed her hands on her knees, squirmed, and folded her hands. Why hadn't she brought her lucky key from the altar? She closed her eyes and visualized a white light of success surrounding her. *I am beautiful, I am strong, I am happy. I am the best artist in San Francisco. I am the best person for the residency.*

What was taking so long? She read over her interview questions and answers again, then looked down at her wingtips. Since she'd taken a Lyft, she could have worn her Ferragamos after all.

She picked up her portfolio and flipped through the pages. The door opened, and she snapped the portfolio shut. Karl stepped out of the room, his back to Anne, and bowed. "Thank you all so very much."

The panelists applauded as if he had just sung an operatic aria. Anne gritted her teeth. The jerk actually bowed.

"Please, shut the door," Priscilla called.

Karl turned with a grin that clouded over when he saw Anne.

"Seems like that went well for you." She forced herself to smile.

"May the best artist win." He smirked and sauntered down the hall.

His foul cinnamon scent made her stomach roil. Even though she didn't want to leave her seat in case they came out to get her, she rushed to the bathroom anyway. She got sick, cleaned herself up, and stuck a piece of peppermint gum in her mouth to mask the odor. Feeling better, she hurried back.

Luckily, she had sat back down when Fredricka came out into the hallway.

"Hi." Anne beamed at her.

Fredricka had a rare frown on her face and toyed with her silver necklace. "I have to recuse myself because of a conflict of interest."

"Close the door," Priscilla called.

Fredricka closed it.

"What's going on?"

"The committee asked me to step down because I sell your work in my gallery." Fredricka put her hand on Anne's shoulder and raised her brows. "Sorry."

"Me too." Anne watched Fredricka walk down the hall. With her on the committee Anne had hoped she might have a chance.

Priscilla opened the door with a sober face. "Come on in."

Anne realized she was still chewing her gum. It would be unprofessional for her to have gum in her mouth during an interview. She didn't see a trash can, so, in a panic, she swallowed it instead and stepped inside the room.

Priscilla and a stocky, square-jawed man with a wispy comb-over sat at the long conference table. Anne had assumed the interview committee would be larger. Karl's cinnamon scent lingered in the room, and she tried not to inhale. Her portfolio slipped out of her hands and dropped on the floor in front of her. She picked it up, put it on the table, and tried to hang her purse on a chair back, but the strap kept slipping off.

She sat down across from Priscilla and the man, then, remembering her practice, stood and held out her hand to him. "Hello. I'm Anne McFarland."

"Yes, I know. I'm Jessie Willingsby." He shook her hand with his own; it was twice the size of hers, and hers were big.

"I'm so glad to meet you. I just got the horseshoes. Thanks for them, and for pulling out the nails."

"No problem." He had a kind face. In his dark corporate suit, he didn't seem like a typical cowboy. She was tempted to look under the table and see if he wore boots. His tie did have horseshoes on it, though.

He pulled his hand away, and she realized she'd still been holding it.

"I look forward to seeing what you do with them."

"I can't wait to show you." Anne sat down and untied her portfolio. "Do you want to see my work?"

"Not yet." Priscilla's hair had been dyed blond and styled in a Marilyn Monroe fashion. It looked better that way. "First off, is it true you're having problems controlling our little artists?"

That jerk. He had been trying to throw her under the bus.

"Not really. No."

"Karl has graciously offered to help you."

"That's okay. Everything's under control." Why would Priscilla bring this up in an interview? Anne had thought Priscilla liked her.

"It better be. I'll be stopping by more often to see how you're doing." Priscilla paused. "And the last time I was in there, the classroom was a mess."

"I'm sorry. I'll work on that." Anne began to perspire. Not only had Priscilla thrown her under the bus, but now she was backing up over her.

Anne folded her hands on her lap. Good thing they weren't meeting in the classroom now. She hadn't cleaned up very well after the last session.

"Okay, let's start with the official interview questions." Priscilla looked at Mr. Willingsby.

He cleared his throat and read from the paper in front of him: "Why are you the right person for the residency?"

Perfect—she could answer this one. "First of all, I love the museum." She ticked off the other three points on her fingers as she nailed the question.

Mr. Willingsby jotted notes while she talked.

Priscilla asked, "Being an artist can be very challenging. How do you keep balance in your life?"

Anne froze for a moment. She hadn't thought of this question. Priscilla tapped her pen on the table edge. Mr. Willingsby frowned at her, and she stopped.

"Sorry. Would you please repeat the question?" Anne felt like a third grader at a spelling bee.

"How do you maintain work-life balance?"

Anne swallowed. "Even though art is my life, I practice yoga, walk the San Francisco hills, and spend time with friends."

Mr. Willingsby jotted more on his paper and asked the next question. "Tell us about your artistic path."

She had anticipated this one too. However, the fan twirling overhead cast shadows on the table in front of her, and she couldn't concentrate. Her body felt like an overheating Karmann Ghia. The air conditioner must not be working. She wanted to take off her jacket, but she didn't want the underarm stains on her blouse to show. Suddenly, a wave of nausea hit her again.

"Excuse me. I need some air." She stood, and her chair fell over. She darted out of the room, down the hall, and into the bathroom.

21

That night, Anne stared at the stick resting on the sink. She felt faint, put the toilet seat down, and sat. It just couldn't be. But those two blue lines didn't lie. Oh my God! What was she going to do?

She counted on her calendar again, backward and forward. It had been seven weeks since she'd been with Sergio and, oh God, that guy from Ruby's. She just couldn't be pregnant. Not now. Not when her career had been going so well. She loved her work at the museum. She had the residency opportunity. The museum hadn't contacted her yet about its decision. After her fiasco of an interview, she probably wouldn't get it, but at least she had a chance.

How could she have let this happen? What a hussy. Sure, she'd been a bit down and lonely, but that was no excuse. Yes, she wanted a baby someday, but with a committed partner.

God, how could you be so mean as to put me in this predicament? Deep in Anne's heart, she acknowledged she was the only one at fault. How could she have had sex with two guys within forty-eight hours? Both dalliances had taken her by surprise and caught her unprepared. Obviously.

She touched the lucky horseshoe she'd hung in the relationship corner above the shower. "You worked too well. I meant for you to get me a new man, not get me pregnant."

She grabbed the hammer, ripped the horseshoe off the wall, pulling some plaster with it, and dropped the art piece in the trash can, then pulled it back out. She had to use it as a sample with her students. She carried it to the box of materials for the museum and placed the horseshoe inside, then lay on her daybed.

What was his name, that creepy wannabe cowboy from Rhinestone Ruby's? Barnaby. What a name. She'd thought he was so sexy in his Stetson and tight chaps. How cliché. Just like in the movies, she'd been the girl who woke up in the morning with regret beside a guy in a raunchy apartment. She couldn't blame it on the beers, Electric Slide endorphins, or even the green lace corset.

The day after their tryst (if she could call it that), he'd sent her a Facebook friend request, but she'd deleted it. Was he the guy who'd continued to like her Instagram posts?

How could Sergio have shown up in town so soon afterward?

Yes, they'd jumped right back into bed as if no time had elapsed. And because of their absence from each other, their lovemaking had been even more intense.

She looked down, put her hand on her stomach, and asked, "Who's your daddy? I wish that little stick could tell us."

She imagined DNA tests, lawyers, court orders. Sergio had always told her he wanted lots of children.

She closed her eyes and thought about her last visit to Michigan. As she'd held little Brian, her cousin Pootie's son, Anne's maternal instincts had kicked in. His blond peach-fuzz head, blinking blue eyes, and tiny, soft hands holding on to her fingers had made her wish she had one of her own.

What was she going to do? She should make an appointment at Planned Parenthood and consider her options. But she needed someone to talk to. She picked up her phone and dialed her mom.

"Hello." A loudspeaker echoed in the background.

"Mom, what's all that noise?"

"I'm in Detroit, at an Avon convention. They've got so many new wonderful products. I'll send you some."

Anne visualized her mom rubbing overly scented lotion on her hands. "Fine."

"Did you hear Sue Garner is getting married?"

"Who's that?"

"You remember—she's Gloria Garner's daughter. You used to babysit her. Called her Susie Q."

"Oh, yeah."

"It seems she's in the family way. Gloria is so excited. How's your love life?"

Anne swallowed. She so wanted to tell her mom she was pregnant and ask for advice, but under these circumstances, she couldn't share that. Anne couldn't call Pootie, either. She'd tell Anne's mom and Aunt Tootie, and then everyone in Oscoda would know. They'd all ask if Sergio was the father. Then they'd all get their hopes up that she was going to keep it.

"Annie, I've gotta go! The awards are starting. I'm getting a Mrs. Albee Award for being one of Michigan's best-selling representatives."

"That's great, Mom. Bye." If Anne decided to have an abortion she wouldn't tell her family anything about it. Ever.

Fay would understand and help her make a decision. But could Anne confess the whole truth? She'd never told anyone about Barnaby.

I had a one-night stand, and we got drunk, and then Sergio came for an unexpected visit, we got carried away, and, well, oops.

She could hear Fay now: blimey this and blimey that.

The next morning, Anne walked into the Coffee Cup Café. Taylor Swift's "Lover" played softly. Anne waved at Stan the Barista Man and looked around. Even though the place was packed, Fay had managed to snag their favorite, bay-window table. Anne hoped she'd have the courage to confide in Fay about her predicament. If not, she would need to make a decision on her own.

Fay stood and gave Anne a quick squeeze. "Sorry, I don't have much time. I've an install."

She handed Anne a cup. "Here, I've ordered for you."

Anne licked the whipped cream off the top of the mocha and sat down.

Fay sat, ran her hand through her smashing turquoise bob, and gave Anne an envelope. "And here's your check from the gallery. Five of your small heart pieces sold. Everyone is bonkers over them."

"Sweet." Outside the window, summer breezes blew ornamental pear-tree branches.

"We sold the hearts for one hundred dollars apiece, so the check is for two fifty, since the gallery's cut is fifty percent. Will you make some more for me?" Fay dunked her tea bag.

"I'll try. I'm still working on my Southwest inspirations."

"Okay." Fay nibbled a bite of scone. "Ooh, scrummy." She pushed it toward Anne. "Have some."

The thought of taking a bite nauseated her. She'd already been sick once that morning. She felt better now but didn't want to chance it. "I didn't get much sleep. This mocha will help." She took a sip.

"You do look tired."

A group of teenage girls sat at a nearby table, drinking coffee and scrolling through their cell phones. Their bra straps showed beneath their sundresses.

Fay leaned toward Anne. "Blimey. Me mum would have killed me if I'd tried to wear something like that out of the house."

"Mine too. Fashionista Fay, why don't you say something to them?"

"They have no class. But it's not my job to tell them so. They wouldn't appreciate it anyway."

"My mom didn't let me drink coffee at that age, either. Did yours?"

"No. How'd the interview go? I heard Fredricka had to sit out."

Anne filled her in about Karl's bow. "I think Mr. Willingsby liked me, but Priscilla was very businesslike. In fact, she was downright icy." Anne told Fay about Priscilla's snarky comments. "What a disaster." She didn't mention the part when she ran out to the bathroom and discovered that Priscilla and Mr. Willingsby were gone when she returned. "I really wanted it."

"Don't worry—I'm sure you'll get it!" Fay pulled off another piece of scone.

Anne drank some mocha. "What do you know about Priscilla? What kind of art did she do?"

"I've never seen her work." Fay pulled out her phone and googled her. "Nothing here about her genre. Degrees up the wazoo, though."

"I know. Maybe she's a shadow artist."

"What's that?"

"It's from Julia Cameron's book *The Artist's Way*—someone who hangs out with artists but never does any work herself."

Fay stuck out her lower lip and ran her hand through her hair.

"I didn't mean you." Anne put her hand on Fay's arm. "You're a professional. You do more than just hang out. You encourage. You curate. You sell." Anne held up the check with a grin.

"Maybe someday your workaholic friend will try to do some art."

Anne leaned forward. "Maybe you can take my adult class at the museum. I do all sorts of lessons for artists at all levels."

"Maybe. You never know what life will bring." Fay raised her eyebrows.

"That's true." Anne held on to the edges of her chair, took a deep breath, and let it out. "I've got news."

"So do I. You go first."

"No, you."

Fay smiled and raised her voice. "I've got a bun in the oven."

Confused, Anne glanced at the scone, at the barista behind the counter, and back at her friend. Face aglow, Fay put a hand on her stomach.

Anne's hands flew to her cheeks as the realization set in. "What? You're pregnant." Her plans blew up in flames. No way could she tell Fay now what she was considering.

Fay guffawed. "Abso-bloody-lutely. Isn't it a miracle?"

Anne forced a smile. It had been more than a year since Fay had moved into Bay Breeze with George and subsequently married him.

Anne swallowed. "Congratulations. How far along are you?"

"Four months. We waited to share the news until the coast was clear." She continued, in her bawdy English accent, "I know. I thought I was going through the change. When the doctor told me, I said, "Blimey. I'm no spring chickadee! Isn't it dangerous? I'm almost forty-seven." She reassured me geriatric pregnancies are commonplace now and easy to monitor. I'm a geriatric! How do you like that?"

Anne didn't know what to say. She just stared at her friend.

"I know what you're thinking. We're kind of old, but George is deliriously happy. When we were first engaged, we considered adoption, but then we decided we were too old. This is all meant to be!"

Feeling queasy, Anne eked out, "What a blessing."

"Yes, it sure is. It was soooo hard not to tell you, but I promised George I'd wait until after we got all our geriatric test results back. Paul was ecstatic; he insisted we all continue to live together at Bay Breeze and take care of him. He said he'd be delighted to hear the pitter-patter of little feet besides just Lucky's, his beagle-basset. There's plenty of room there for all of us."

Anne sipped her mocha, trying to listen with an open heart as Fay bubbled on. "Because of my age, they've done a bunch of tests, and there's every indication she—yes, it's a she—will be healthy. We're going to name her Diana. After Lady Princess Diana."

Anne couldn't help but smile.

Fay glanced at her phone and stood. "I've got to get to work. But wait." She sat back down. "What's your big news?"

Anne was afraid she might throw up. "I'm not feeling well."

"Sorry. You do look green around the gills."

Anne needed air. "Nothing important. I've got to get to work too. I'll tell you another time." She ran out of the café.

22

How could Fay be pregnant too? At least she knew who the father was. Late that afternoon, Anne crawled into her daybed, picked up her journal, and began to jot:

Pros	*Cons*
a cutie in my life	*no partner*
clock is ticking	*family would be mortified*
	loss of freedom
	not enough money

Even though the cons side tipped the balance way over, thinking about ending the pregnancy grieved her. She'd never wanted a white picket fence or to be a stay-at-home mom. She'd always wanted to have children, though, hoped to get married and after a while have a child or two. But now, without a partner in her midst and as her thirtysomething clock ticked, she knew this might be her only chance. Maybe God's plan was for her to have this baby.

It was probably the biggest decision she'd ever make. She needed some kind of grounded spiritual connection. She wasn't religious, never went to church services, except when she visited her family in Michigan. She felt closest to God when in nature: walking on a beach or a park path, or even fishing on a lake. Doing her art was a form of worship for her too. When she let her heart guide her and created intuitively, she could feel God's divine love within her.

She felt too ruffled to make art right now, though, and it would be dark soon, so walking in nature was out of the question. Going up to Grace Cathedral, Sylvia's church, might help. She always felt close to her old friend there. Sometimes Anne walked the cathedral's labyrinth or did Tuesday night yoga.

She glanced at her phone. Yoga started in forty-five minutes. Even though she was pretty wiped out, she decided to go anyway. For cleansing and balance, she rolled eucalyptus balm on her hands, rubbed them together, and inhaled three times. Then she added some balm to the bottoms of her feet and rubbed them together. She swore eucalyptus helped her do the tree and other balancing poses.

She'd better hurry now; the space filled up fast. Plus, it was bad manners to show up late. She gathered her mat, huddled in her black coat, and hiked up the hill. As she followed a few other stragglers carrying mats into the cathedral, early-evening light streamed in through the rose window, reflecting colors on the floor and yogis.

A musician played live new-age rhythms. Hundreds of colorful mats covered the black-and-white mosaic labyrinth in a circular fashion, up the aisles and even around the altar. Yogis of all ages, shapes, sizes, genders, and colors had gathered. A young woman lit votives.

Anne dropped a few dollars in the donation basket and zigzagged quietly around the supine bodies until she found a spot. She slipped off her sneakers, rolled out her mat, and sat down with a thud.

Her body had been changing rapidly: bigger boobs, puffy stomach. Her balance felt way off. After practicing yoga regularly the past two years, she'd begun to master the tree and dancer poses. Soon her whole body would be off-kilter again. That was the least of her worries, though.

The instructor's soothing voice began, and Anne rolled down, one vertebra at a time, until she was flat on the mat and closed her eyes. Hands on her stomach, she thought of the baby growing inside her and inhaled and exhaled. The music began to trill within her, and tears leaked out the sides of her eyes. She couldn't raise a child alone. If she had that simple procedure at the clinic, all those cons would disappear. Her life could go back to normal again. But would it ever really return to normal after what she'd done?

What she had really always wanted was to start a family with her soul mate. She hoped he was out there somewhere. She'd thought Sergio was the one, but he'd turned out not to be. As much as she tried to deny it, though, she still loved him. With his fun, outgoing, loving personality and generous spirit, he would be a great father. Maybe with a baby, she'd feel differently about living in New York with him and wouldn't get so lonely when he worked late or traveled, because she'd have a cutie-patootie with her. Wasn't home where the love was?

Anne rolled onto her hands and knees, did cat and cow, pushed up to downward-facing dog, and stepped forward. Reaching her arms up into warrior-one pose, she swayed to the left and had to catch herself. This had always been so easy for her.

Their passionate sex life would probably be nonexistent, or at least interrupted by the baby's cries and exhaustion. Sergio also insisted on a pristine condo. How would that be possible with a child? The last time Anne had visited Michigan, Pootie's house toys had been scattered everywhere, sticky sippy cups had lined the counter, and the high chair had had food scraps underneath it. When Anne had stayed with Sergio and left even a Coke can on the kitchen island, he never yelled, just gave her the disappointed puppy-dog look that made her feel so bad.

The really scary thing was that there was a good chance it was Barnaby's baby. She'd gotten tipsy several times before with Sergio, skipped the condoms, and never gotten pregnant. She didn't even want to think about how the baby might have Barnaby's genes and how gross it would be to live with that one-night stand. No, if it was his and she kept it, she'd need to raise it alone.

"Come down to the ground and pull your legs up to your chest," the instructor said, and the musician began to play a rendition of Anne's favorite hymn, "All Things Bright and Beautiful."

Anne followed the lyrics she knew by heart: *All creatures great and small / All things wise and wonderful / the Lord God made them all.*

Maybe this was a sign. How could she eliminate the small creature growing inside her? Did God love it already?

But, again, she didn't want to raise a child alone. She'd watched Pootie and Brian support each other by passing their little doll back and forth. Plus, Aunt Tootie and Anne's own mom were there to help them at a moment's notice.

If she kept the baby, Anne was sure her mom would welcome her home with open arms. That was, after she got over the shock that Anne was going to be an unwed mother. Anne had considered moving back there a few years ago but had decided against it. Maybe that would be best now, though—small-town Oscoda was a good place to raise kids. But she really didn't want to do that. San Francisco was her home, her soul place. She couldn't even move to New York with Sergio—how could she ever go back to Michigan? And what about her art?

If she stayed here and had the baby in San Francisco, she'd need to pack away most of her art materials to make way for a crib in the apartment. She didn't need a man or her mother. Anne could do it. She'd get by. How hard could it be? Streetlamps cast a halo in the dewy air. Usually yoga rejuvenated her, but tonight it made her more exhausted than ever.

She spied Mata Hari curled up in a doorway. "Hi, Mata."

Mata looked up. "Missy, looks like you've been crying."

"I'm fine." Anne grabbed for a tissue in her backpack. "Allergies is all. Did you eat at the shelter tonight?"

"Sure did. The spaghetti was tasty. Here, do you want a ginger snap?" Mata pulled a cookie from her pocket and held it out.

"No, thanks. You eat it." Anne felt a pang in her heart. The kitchen used Sylvia's special recipes. Anne thought back to learning to make spaghetti and cookies with her dear friend in Sylvia's kitchen at Bay Breeze before the shelter had been endowed its own. What Anne wouldn't give to have Sylvia to go to now.

"Okeydoke, Annie Oakley!" Mata took a bite.

Anne remembered something about Mata saying she preferred to live on the streets than with family. "Didn't you tell me you have a daughter you hated?" Anne asked.

"I said I couldn't stand living with her, not that I hated her. She's still the most important person in my life."

Firsthand, Anne understood how important the mother-daughter connection was. Even though she didn't want to live with her own mom anymore, they were still close.

At home, she crawled into bed and tried to sleep, but she was suddenly wired. She couldn't get used to these strange things happening in her body. Might as well do some art. She got up, rang her Tibetan chimes, and lit a gardenia candle.

"Alexa, play Enya, please."

"Okay. Here's some assorted music by Enya."

"Thank you." Anne picked up the washboard from her trip. The rectangular top measured three by nine inches. She ruffled through her remnants, found a crocheted oval that fit in the space, and adhered it to the wood. Next, she placed a blue-and-white chipped plate in a paper bag, broke it with a hammer, and filled in the spaces around the remnant with the shards. She dumped out a baggie filled with a random assortment of found objects: old jewelry, Polly Pocket paraphernalia, and tiny toys. She closed her eyes, stuck her hand in the pile, and picked up a piece. The teddy bear fit perfectly in the washboard's one-inch groove. She breathed in and out as she got into the zone and randomly tried other pieces to find ones that fit: a pearl earring with gold trim, a blue button, a baby bottle, a boot, a cameo pin, a heart button, a pony, a Road Runner pin, marbles, XOXO tic-tac-toe game pieces, a diaper pin, a star.

On her found-object shelf, she spied a tiny plastic baby doll. Voilà! It fit on top of the crocheted piece nicely. She glued turquoise and cobalt lace trim along the edge. She stepped back and examined the finished mosaic, filled with love and baby themes. Was this another sign?

23

Hazy morning sunshine sent light through the window. Sally Sue tried to sit up but fell back onto the pillow, still light-headed. At least she felt better than yesterday—she was thinking clearly and well rested. For good or bad, she'd made it safely through another night.

Cliff hummed softly, stoked the fire and stirred a cauldron, and went back outside. Her face reddened, and she lifted her hands to her cheeks. Yesterday, she'd been too drowsy to even be embarrassed when he carried the bedpan outside and brought it back to her all clean.

The room grew dark as clouds formed outside. She'd better get to the outhouse before it snowed again. Forcing herself up onto her elbows, she spotted her men's clothes folded neatly at the foot of the bed. She snatched them, pulled them under the covers, and put on the shirt. It smelled of oak and something else heavenly. Was it lavender?

She finished dressing; put on her hat, gloves, and coat; and made her way to the outhouse. As she returned to the cabin, it began to snow and she hurried inside.

Cliff was setting two plates on the table. "I'm glad to see you're up and at 'em."

"I'm glad too." Winded, she sat.

"We're miles from any neighbors or town. There's no way you could have made it anywhere on foot in this inclement weather."

She took off her hat and redid her braids. She could barely stand her dirty hair; it smelled of caked mud. "I wanted to get away from you."

"You mustn't stray far. There are worse things than freezing to death. You never know what's out there."

"Like what?" She crossed her arms.

He raised his voice. "Wolves, bears, Injuns, bandits."

She tried to laugh, but her voice quivered. "You don't say. Bandits?"

"This is not a joke." He turned his back to her and put another log on the fire. "Whether you like it or not, you're gonna be here awhile. Now that you're regaining your vigor, you need to pitch in and help."

"What do you want me to do?"

He turned around. "What are you good at?"

"I can read and do figures."

He eyed her. "That's not much use out here. How's your cooking?"

"Not good." She sighed. There was no way she could make anything as good as his flapjacks, apple crisp, or rabbit stew.

"Anyone can clean house. I've seen you with your needles, making doilies. I bet you can sew."

"A bit."

"Maybe mend clothes, do laundry, make us some curtains." She hated to do laundry. The floral fabric from McMillan's would make pretty curtains. No need for a lovely dress out here.

The snow continued. Cliff sat by the fire all afternoon, doing leatherwork, while she curled up in bed and worked on memorizing psalms in her Bible.

The next day, Cliff carried in a vat of snow and placed it in the cauldron. He handed her a washboard that the previous owners had left, a box of Sunlight soap that he had bought at the mercantile, and a pile of dirty clothes, then left. She held her nose as she placed his soiled long johns and holey socks in the water. She also added in her green traveling suit but then paused. The thought of mixing her own undergarments with his made her body shiver. But she wouldn't want to ask Cliff to bring in another vat of water, so she tossed in her chemise, drawers, corset, petticoat, and bustle.

Her father had been gone a year when Mrs. Rowling from next door had her fifth baby and Sally Sue's ma took in the woman's laundry. Ma said it was the neighborly thing to do. Even though Sally Sue was only seven, she knew the reason was to help make ends meet. She'd seen her ma frown on Saturdays as she counted out the dwindling pile of money on the table. She also noticed her ma had stopped putting a dollar in the Sunday offering basket at church and instead cupped a penny in her palm and put it in. Gradually, word seemed to spread, as more folks in town needed neighborly help with their laundry too.

When she grew older, she pitched in to help; however, people complained about how their clothes were scratchy from soap residue, poorly ironed, and awkwardly folded. Sally Sue wasn't disappointed when her ma took over those tasks again.

Sally Sue did continue to collect the money and do the deliveries. Afterward, her ma pumped her for the local gossip. She never repeated any of the rumors she'd heard. She knew others had talked about them when her father had left, and she didn't want to speak ill of anyone else who'd fallen on hard times.

And now here she was, doing this washing. The fire kept the cabin warm. She rolled up her sleeves and scrubbed Cliff's socks on the washboard, but no matter how much elbow grease she used, they still felt gritty. She glanced up. No wonder—she'd forgotten to use the soap. From the box, instead of bars, white flakes drifted out like snow. This was much easier than what her ma used, and smelled much nicer. Sally Sue rubbed the socks on the washboard, squeezed out the excess water, and laid them on the mantel to dry. She made a note to darn the holes in the toes.

Even though she rubbed her suit skirt on the washboard, the mud stains wouldn't come out of the hem. She sighed as her green shoes came to mind. She had to admit her boots were much more practical.

Next, she worked on the bustle. No matter how much she fluffed it, it just wouldn't pouf back up—squished forever. She draped the skirt and bustle over the crib to dry and ran her hand over the smooth wood. Did the people who lived here have a baby? Who were they? What happened to them?

She finished the laundry and surveyed the cabin. What a filthy mess. Dust and soot covered everything. She tried to sweep the floor, but since it was dirt, that didn't do much good. Her things sitting on the trunk were covered in dust.

She opened the trunk lid. On top of a Mexican serape sat a handful of yarn scraps, other remnants, and a wooden egg darner. She put it in her shirt pocket. As she lifted up the serape, her eyes spotted bright red fabric underneath. She picked it up and fingered the scoop-necked dress with lace trim and puffed sleeves, more beautiful than anything she'd ever seen before. Who had worn something so lovely? Looking in the mirror, she held it up and turned this way and that with a smile. Her ma would call the red color shameful. When Cliff came through the door, Sally Sue quickly slid the dress back into the trunk.

"How're you doing?" he asked.

"Laundry's all done. Just trying my best to clean, as you asked."

He grunted and went back outside.

Cobwebs and dried candle wax clung to the crystal chandelier. Cleaned, this would be more luxurious than any she'd seen in a mansion while delivering laundry. The folks who'd lived here must have been rich. Had they brought the chandelier all the way here in a covered wagon?

Dustrag in hand, she climbed up onto a chair and then to the tabletop and started picking off the candle wax. She lost her balance and wobbled.

"Careful!" Cliff came in, ran toward her, and caught her in his arms. "Take a break."

So close to him, inhaling his musky scent, she felt a bit weak and sat in a kitchen chair. "Okay."

He heated up last night's stew, ladled some into cups, and handed one to her, along with a spoon. "Eat up, now," he said.

She'd decided to quit arguing with him about eating and swallowed a bite. The stew was even tastier than it had been the day before.

He sat across from her, holding his own cup. "Been snowing all day."

She took another bite. They each had a second helping and continued to eat in silence. Darkness began to hover as the storm brewed, and he lit the lamp. When they finished their food, she yawned, picked up her cup, and tried to take his, but he held it tight. "I'll do the cleanup. After all that laundry, you must be tuckered out."

"I'm not really that tired."

He smiled at her, his brown hair slicked back, blue eyes reflecting the firelight, cleft chin a wonder. "Close your eyes, and soon you'll be in the arms of Morpheus." With that, he washed the dishes, and left her alone in the cabin, taking the lantern with him.

She climbed into bed. How could he stand it out there in the cold? Did he sleep up in the hayloft or down with the horses? Did he have plenty of blankets? Her eyes soon drooped, and before she knew it, she was asleep.

The sound of rattling dishes in the cupboard woke her in the night, and a scratching noise ensued. The fire had gone out, and the room was pitch black. She was too cold and afraid to investigate. Even if she got out of bed, she wouldn't be able to see anything. The noise continued off and on all night. She didn't get another wink of sleep.

At daybreak she followed the dark droppings, probably mice, to the cupboard. Darn it. She knew how they could take over. She'd had them in Missouri too.

Inside the cupboard, a nest of straw and thread had been made in the bottom shelf. She reached for it, and a mouse skittered out and across the dirt floor. Sally Sue jumped back with a scream and grabbed the broom. She shouldn't be afraid of a little mouse.

Cliff came running in. "What is it?"

She stood up with the nest in hand. "Just a little mouse is all." She kept her voice even; leaned over to make sure there weren't any more; and checked the flour, cornstarch, and other supplies.

"That's to be expected." He opened all the cupboard doors, and together they took everything out. "Fortunately, no more droppings here. I'll see what we've got in the barn to take care of it," he said.

She swept up the droppings from the floor, poured water and soap flakes in a bowl, dunked a rag, and cleaned out the cupboard.

Cliff carried a small bottle inside, pulled out the cork, and shook some powder along the bottom of the cupboard. "This should do the trick. A little bit goes a long way."

"Let's hope so," Sally Sue said.

He put the bottle on the cupboard's top shelf and climbed up to finish cleaning the chandelier.

"I'll do that." Sally Sue reached out to pull him back but quickly felt her face turn red and sat down.

"No, I'll do it. I don't want you falling and breaking a leg. Then you'd be no help to me."

She couldn't help but laugh. She knew she wasn't much help to him anyway.

24

The next morning, the weather had warmed. Outside, as she filled a bucket with snow before it all melted, Sally Sue's spirits lifted and she waved when she spied a wagon coming down the trail toward the cabin. This might be her chance to escape.

She glanced over at the barn. The door was open, but there was no sign of Cliff. She hadn't seen him yet that morning.

Pots and pans clanged on the makeshift shed in the wagon's back. The man's nag made his way toward her and stopped.

"Yes, girlie!" The driver doffed his bowler hat, revealing dark hair speckled with gray. His voice was high and squeaky. "I've got anything you could ever want. I've got ribbons and laces to set off faces of pretty young sweethearts and wives." He held up a handful of brightly colored remnants.

What an odd little man. Sally Sue tried not to laugh as she recognized the lyrics from Gilbert and Sullivan's *H.M.S. Pinafore*, which she'd seen in Kansas City with her aunt. "Sir, I—"

He interrupted her and held up a jar. "Yes, I have Dr. Pierce's Pleasant Purgative Pellets."

"Sir." She waved him farther away from the barn.

He followed her and jumped down out of the wagon. His patchwork jacket hung loosely on his shoulders, and his pants had holes in the knees.

Speaking fast, he said, "Cures bilious headaches, dizziness, constipation, indigestion."

She shook her head. "Sir."

He eyed her and held up some lace. "You could sure use something pretty."

She looked around for Cliff.

"How about Blackwell's Durham Smoking Tobacco for your husband?" He held up a pouch with a bull on its side.

Sally Sue waved her arms above her head, but the peddler just kept on talking.

He showed her a small vial. "Price's Special Flavoring Extract? Great for that home cooking of yours. Or perhaps this potion to cure what ails you?" Sally Sue recognized the medicine she'd had to give her aunt, along with strict directions not to give her too much or it could kill her.

He finally stopped to catch his breath.

"Sir, I'm ever so glad to see you." She finally got some words in edgewise. "I've been kidnapped by an outlaw."

"You have, have you?" He raised his bushy eyebrows and grinned. She could tell he didn't believe her.

"Please take me to town."

The man's smile fell. "You're not gonna buy some of my goods?"

"I told you, I'm captive here. I don't have any money. This man is wanted. You could collect the bounty."

"Ma'am, I've heard that one before. Your man's not taking care of you the way you'd like." He tightened the rope belt around his waist. "I can't get mixed up in any domestic disputes."

She clenched her fists beside her and stamped her boot. "It's not a dispute, I say. There's a one-thousand-dollar reward out for him, dead or alive. Please, take me to Flagstaff!" She folded her hands under her chin.

His dark eyes shifted. "I'm not headed that way."

"How about down to Prescott?"

"I need to keep from towns these days."

Sally Sue understood what he meant. Flimflam men like him had come through her neighborhood in Kansas City all the time. What they said was always too good to be true. The last one had sold a tonic that gave folks diarrhea, including her ma. Sally Sue hadn't been able to enter the outhouse for a week, the stench had been so bad.

"If I write a quick note, will you post it for me? I'd really appreciate it."

"Be happy to." He beamed. "I'll wait right here."

Sally Sue ran in the cabin, grabbed her writing materials out of her basket, set them on the table, and sat. Dipping the pen in ink, she started writing:

Dear Mama,
I'm okay.

That was a lie. Sally Sue scratched it out and started again:

Ma,
I've been kidnapped by the bank robber and taken to a homestead outside Flagstaff. Please send help.
Your daughter,
Sally Sue

She hurriedly wrote another:

Sheriff Mack,
I'm out at the Ivrys' place with Clifford the outlaw. Please bring a posse.
Sally Sue Sullivan

She folded the notes in half, slid them into her last two envelopes, addressed each, grabbed some coins for stamps, and ran back outside. But the wagon was way up on top of the knoll. Darn it!

She stomped her foot, ran out onto the meadow, and opened her mouth to yell.

"Who's that?" Cliff came around the side of the cabin on the mare.

She froze, hid the letters behind her, and started backing up toward the cabin. "Nobody. Just a flimflam man. I sent him away."

"Really? What've you got there?" Cliff asked.

"Uh, just a little poetry I'm writing."

"I didn't know you wrote poetry."

"You don't know everything about me."

"I suppose not." He rode toward the barn, a fowl swinging from the back of his saddle. He stopped and turned around. "Do you want to learn how to pluck a turkey?"

"Not really." She averted her eyes away from the disgusting dead bird. She couldn't imagine touching it, let alone plucking it. At home, they got their meat ready to cook from a butcher. Next, Cliff would be asking her to muck the horse manure.

"Clean out the fireplace, why don't you?"

Sally Sue saw some things lying in the mud. She stooped down, picked them up, and brushed them off on her trousers: black lace and red ribbon remnants. Had the man left them for her because he felt guilty about running off, or had he dropped them by accident? Didn't really matter. She'd keep them anyway.

She hid the letters and the remnants in the trunk under the red dress. Was there anything more she could have done to get that man to take her with him? She set to work cleaning out the fireplace ashes, now that they had cooled.

After a supper of flapjacks and eggs, she rinsed the dishes while Cliff reset and started the fire. She checked his holey socks to make sure they were dry on the hearth. From the trunk, she pulled out the darning egg and sat in the rocker. She inserted the egg into the sock under the hole and stretched it slightly, examining it.

His tall body stood before her, and when she looked up, he was smiling. "This is just cozy."

"What?"

"Nothing." Cliff knocked his pipe on the mantel and sat across from her. He added tobacco to the pipe, lit it, took a puff, and blew out the smoke. The aromas of anisette and chocolate filled the air.

She put her basket on her lap and searched her sewing kit for a needle.

"Darn it!" She jumped up. "Mouse droppings. They're all over in here."

"I'm sorry. Let me take care of it for you." He began to stand.

"No, you set." She waved her hand at him. "I'll be right back."

She shook out all her supplies off the porch, waggled the basket upside down, and stomped back inside.

"That darned powder didn't work."

"It hasn't been long. You gotta give it some time." She could tell Cliff was trying not to laugh.

She held up her metal tatting shuttle. The collar she'd been making had been nibbled through. "How much time?"

He shrugged.

At least her Bible hadn't been eaten. She was glad she had put it in her basket. She'd planned to read it to her bedridden aunt. Had she died? What did Ma think now that it was long past time for Sally Sue to return home?

Sally Sue found her biggest needle and pulled the egg and some yarn scraps from her pocket. She chose indigo blue, to match his eyes. She paused. She shouldn't be thinking like that. Instead, she chose blue to match the sky and threaded it through the needle.

"How did the turkey cleaning go?" she asked.

"Fine, fine. We'll be eating some tomorrow." He took another puff on his pipe.

"Did you get all the buckshot out of it?" One time, she had broken a back tooth on some the butcher hadn't found.

"No buckshot. I use a bow and arrow. It's cleaner that way."

"Really? Like an Indian? Wouldn't you be able to get more turkeys with a gun?" She leaned toward the lantern hanging nearby and carefully began to weave the needle around the hole, making sure it lay flat. If it didn't, he could get a blister on his foot—though why she should care about that, she didn't know.

He put down his pipe on the end table next to him, stoked the fire, and sat again. "I only kill what I'm gonna eat."

That made sense. She began to create the warp over the sock hole. She looked up to say something, but his eyes had drooped closed.

Loneliness gnawed at her chest. She began to give up on the notion of ever going home again. She missed Rusty the mutt. Did he still wait by the door for her return with sad eyes and whining lonesomeness? She missed her favorite dress, sky blue and white checkers, with the blue satin bow she'd worn to the potluck the night Johnny Jones sat next to her.

She missed her favorite books, which lined the shelf in her bedroom: Walt Whitman, Jane Austen, the Brontë sisters. Main Street, with the café, bank, and courthouse. The giant pine in the town square. She didn't miss Pastor Grimes's guilt-ridden sermons but longed to sing hymns with the congregation. She even had begun to miss her ma.

Weaving the last loose ends, she made sure her sewing was secure. If she used knots, Cliff would get blisters for sure. There she went again, worrying about his blisters. She folded the socks and put them on her lap to give to him to take to the barn. The fire crackled.

She looked up, and he was staring at her, his eyes bright in the firelight. "Sally Sue, read me one of your poems."

She flushed and put a hand to her cheek. He probably thought she was embarrassed. How imprudent she was to have told him she wrote poetry. "They're private."

"Please." He paused and leaned toward her. "When I was growing up, my ma used to read to us every night."

"Us?" He'd never mentioned anything personal about his life before.

He lit his pipe again. "Ma, Pa, three brothers, me, and my little sister, Lula. She was cute as a button. Kind of reminds me of you."

Sally Sue felt herself blush again, for real this time. "Where was that?"

"Buffalo."

"New York?"

The fire snapped.

"How long since you've seen them?" she asked.

"Nigh on many years. They're all gone now." He sighed.

"I'm sorry."

"Pa and my brothers died in the Civil War. I'm the only one who survived."

"You must have been only a boy."

"Fourteen. Lied about my age to enlist. When I finally returned home, Ma and Lula had passed from consumption." He unwrapped the kerchief from around his neck and wiped tears from his eyes.

Sally Sue had a hankering to put her arms around him. She got up the nerve to finally ask him the big question again: "Why'd you do it? Why'd you rob that bank?"

He scowled at her. "I had my reasons."

"What reasons?"

He shrugged sadly. "Please read me a poem. It would feel ever so good to hear you."

Her shoulders fell. "Maybe some other time."

"Please."

"I could read you something from the Bible." She picked it out of her basket. "What's your favorite?"

"The Psalms."

She couldn't believe it. "They're my favorite also." She opened to the first verse and began, "Blessed is the man . . ."

25

The next day, early in the morning, without even eating breakfast, Cliff took off again without telling Sally Sue where he was going or when he'd be back. What did he do all day? Was he hunting again?

Most of the snow had melted, but dark clouds still hung overhead. She put another log on the fire. She sure needed a bath. She untied her braids. The matted mess, which hung down to her waist, itched like the dickens, as if it had a mouse nest in it. She tried to untangle the snarls but couldn't get her brush through them.

It had been two weeks since she'd last bathed. Saturdays at home were bath days. Early in the morning, she'd heat water, fill the tub, climb in, and wash her hair. After she got out, Ma would brush it out, and by the end of the day, it would be dry, ready to put up for the church potluck.

The water basins in the cabin were all too small. If she told Cliff she wanted a bath, he'd probably throw her in the horse trough. How had the woman who lived here before, the one with the beautiful dress, bathed?

Rain tapped on the window and soon battered the tin roof. She scooped a handful of soap flakes from the box and ran outside. Shivering in her nightgown, gritting her teeth, she stood in the downpour, letting the cold water douse her body.

Her fingers massaged the soap flakes into her scalp for a few minutes and rubbed the rain along her shoulders, underarms, arms, stomach, back, and legs. Her feet were muddy, so she'd need to deal with them inside later. When she couldn't take the cold anymore, she threw back her head and let the rain rinse out her locks. She rushed back inside, slipped out of her clean nightgown, laid it on the crib to dry, wrapped a blanket around her, and warmed herself by the fire. It felt wonderful to be clean.

She gripped her brush but couldn't even begin to get it through the snarls. At that moment, she missed her ma. This would never do. Sally Sue really needed help, but there was only one other person on the ranch, and she'd never ask him for any favors.

Rain continued to pound on the roof. She found her sewing scissors in her basket, and tightened the blanket around her chest. She grabbed a knotted tendril resting on her shoulder, but her small scissors wouldn't go through it.

"What are you up to now?" Cliff stood in the doorway with a grin on his face.

She shrugged. Bare shouldered, she wrapped the blanket more tightly around her.

"Let me help." He pulled a chair over near the fire. "Sit here." He found a pair of larger scissors in a drawer and put a hand on her head. "How short do you want it?"

"Get rid of it all!"

"Are you sure?"

"Yes."

He began to snip, dropping handfuls of hair on the floor.

Sally Sue kept her head still, closed her eyes, and listened to the sound of the scissors. She pictured a nice shoulder-length style, easy to braid.

He could be so kind and caring. She tried to imagine what it would be like to be married to someone like that. Sleeping next to a warm body every night. Marriage—it was expected, but after what her ma and pa had gone through, she didn't think she would ever want it.

Cliff hummed softly and continued to cut away at her hair.

But she did have a yearning for a child. Too bad you couldn't raise one without a husband. Well, you could if your husband died or ran off. But you couldn't get a child without being married at some point. Then you could have a baby and it wouldn't be a sin.

Cliff dropped another clump to the ground, walked around in front of her, lifted a handful of hair, and snipped away until he could see her face.

He stepped back and raised his brows. "Not bad."

"Can I see?" she asked.

"Not until I'm done." He started cutting again. "Ready to start learning to cook yet?"

"Maybe."

"How about tomorrow?"

She hoped she wouldn't make a fool of herself by burning up the meal. "Sure thing."

"What do you want me to teach you first?"

She knew right away. "Apple stew."

He grinned at her.

His offspring might have his blue eyes and a cleft chin too. What kind of father would he be?

He had the bluest eyes, eyes that changed color with the weather. On stormy days they were steely gray; misty days, dove gray; snowy days, powder blue. In sunny weather, they seemed azure, like the sky. They also changed with his moods. Happy: bright blue; sad: pale; angry, like during the robbery: steel gray. After he drank his rum, they turned murky, like a dirty pond.

Recently, his eyes had been mostly bright. She knew now that he'd never harm her. In fact, he acted like he was even sweet on her, grinning and flattering. He could just be pretending, though. No, he wasn't. Maybe she could let down her guard a little. He wouldn't turn back into the fiend who'd robbed the bank and kidnapped her six weeks earlier.

The rain had stopped; the only sound was the scissors, still snipping.

After a few more minutes, he said, "All done! Take a look." He pointed toward the mirror.

She wandered over and stared at her reflection. "Eek! I look like a drowned mouse."

"No, you don't. It's much more practical."

She ran her fingers through it. He was right about that.

"It shows off your face more."

"What do you mean?" she asked.

"Pretty enough to marry."

What an odd thing to say. "Are you proposing?" How could she have just said that?

"Maybe." He ruffled his hand over her hair and went out the door.

She looked in the mirror. Was she really pretty, like Cliff had said? She tossed her head back and forth and brushed her hair, marvelously lighter. She wouldn't even need to braid it; she could just run her hands through it. It would be easier to keep clean too. She glanced at the door, let the towel drop, and inspected her body. Her breasts weren't as voluptuous as that hussy's in the green corset, but Sally Sue's small waist and petite frame might be just as appealing to a man.

Now that she was clean, she wanted to put on something more feminine. She opened the trunk and held up the dress, but then decided against it and donned her men's clothes. She lifted the washbowl onto the floor, cleaned her dirty feet, and put on socks and boots.

A racket came from the barn. She wanted to see what Cliff was up to, so she wandered out there and opened the door.

"I told you never to come in here!" he yelled at her.

"Sorry!" She jumped back outside, but not before she saw him sharpening a large knife on a whetstone. She ran back to the cabin. Her idea of waiting until spring to try to get away was too far off. She needed to come up with another plan.

26

Anne dragged herself to work. It had been only a few days since she'd found out she was pregnant, but it felt like an eternity. Worried about the pregnancy, exhausted and queasy, she decided to do a collage lesson instead of the horseshoe project with the kiddos. She'd save that for when she felt better.

When she arrived, a note was taped to the classroom door: *See me after your class today unless I drop by first. Priscilla*

Anne's heart revved up. They must have made a decision about the residency. Teaching would be a challenge; she'd spend the whole time wondering whether she'd been selected or not. But Priscilla had insisted Anne ramp up her lessons, so she'd better go ahead and present the horseshoe project anyway.

She pulled off the note, unlocked the room, turned on some Enya, and covered the six tables with newspapers, then lined up the horseshoes along the counter. She dumped plastic containers of found objects onto silver trays and placed them on the middles of the tables.

As the students began to arrive, she instructed, "Pick a horseshoe and take a seat."

One of the twins hit Penny on the shoulder. "Hello, Fart Face."

"Be nice," Anne said.

The twins each grabbed a horseshoe and sat down, banging them on the table as if they were Ringo Starr.

Penny picked up a horseshoe. "This one's too big." She grasped another. "This one's too small." She must have just read "Goldilocks and the Three Bears." She held one over her head. "And this one's just right."

One of the twins snatched it from her.

Penny howled.

Anne put an arm around Penny and scowled at the boy. "How could you be so mean?" Anne looked over at the door, frightened that Priscilla might be watching.

Instead, Karl stood in the doorway. What the heck was he doing here?

He squinted his eyes at the twin and yelled, "Sit down, sir. You've already picked one."

"But . . ." the boy protested, then acquiesced. "Yes, Mr. Karl." He handed Penny the horseshoe she'd chosen and, sulking, put his head on the table.

Hugh, a cute, freckle-faced kid, came in and hugged Karl. "We've missed you."

"I know. Me too. I've come in for a meeting with Priscilla." Karl smirked at Anne.

Why was he smirking at her? Maybe they'd decided on the residency. But he wouldn't have been chosen. He wasn't even a professional artist.

"Pick a horseshoe and sit for Anne," he told more students as they came in.

He looked at her. "Need help?"

From you? Never. "No, thank you."

He watched while she pulled out her sample from her backpack and waited for the rest of the class—twelve students, ages six to ten, all shapes and sizes—to get settled.

"May the best artist win!" Karl whispered in her ear, and left.

Anne froze. She didn't think she had gotten the residency, but the thought of his getting it stuck in her craw. However, Anne knew firsthand how charming he could be.

Hugh tugged on the bottom of Anne's sweatshirt. "What are we doing?"

As the cacophony of voices overpowered her, she turned off the music and clapped her hands three times. Penny and her tablemate Cindy echoed Anne's gesture. She clapped again until all her students copied her and fell silent. She'd learned this simple trick online. It worked like magic.

She held up her sample. "This is a lucky horseshoe. Yours aren't lucky yet, but they will be after you mosaic them."

Penny raised her hand. "Really? Will they really be lucky?"

"Of course not, dingbat," one of the twins scoffed.

"Don't name-call," Anne continued, and put her hand on Penny's shoulder. "Yes! It'll be lucky if you put your heart into making it and if you believe. Mine brought me luck big-time."

The twins rolled their eyes at each other.

Anne ignored them and continued, "Hold up your horseshoes like this." She demonstrated. "Now, turn them that way. Make sure you have the points at the top. If you make it this way, all the luck will fall out." She tilted her horseshoe over.

"Carefully put yours down in front of you, facing the lucky way." She passed out paper plates to each of the students. "Choose found objects from the trays on the table that appeal to you, and put them on your plates."

Anne turned on Enya again.

"Can't we listen to something else?" Hugh asked.

Anne switched to Bruno Mars.

Heads down, the students started digging through the trays. Hugh chose a purple earring, Cindy a tiny plastic snake, and the twins picked up handfuls of objects and tossed them on their plates.

Anne placed a glue bottle next to each student. When all the plates were filled, she put on her sunglasses, waved her hands in the air, and sang the lyrics to "Uptown Funk" with a pouty expression on her face. At the end of the song, she turned off the music and posed, her arms across her chest. The students applauded, even the twins.

Anne bowed. "Now, spread glue on your horseshoes. It comes out white but turns invisible when it dries. Then go over to the counter, scoop up seed beads, and sprinkle them over your horseshoes. When you finish, leave them here on their plates to dry," she instructed, and turned Bruno Mars back on.

The students began to glue objects to their horseshoes. Penny, Hugh, Cindy, and many of the others seemed lost in deep concentration. Anne felt her spirits lift; she was grateful she had decided to go ahead and do this lesson today. The twins finished their horseshoes right away and left them on the counter. Back at their seats, they covered their palms with glue. Anne shrugged. At least they were sitting nicely. All the other students besides Penny lined up and took turns sprinkling seed beads.

Anne put her hand on Penny's shoulder. "You'd better get a wiggle on and finish up. It will be time to go soon."

"Okay. I just can't decide on this one or that one." Penny held up a white button and a red one. "What do you think?"

"Which color do you like best?"

"Pink. But you don't have any pink buttons."

"What's your next-favorite color?" Anne asked.

"Red."

"Go for it!" Anne suggested.

Penny glued on the red one, and Anne escorted her to the counter. Penny began to sprinkle seed beads on her piece, but then she dropped the whole container. As the beads flew across the floor, she started crying.

Anne put her hand on Penny's shoulder. "Don't worry—accidents happen."

"Yes, doofus." One of the twins laughed. The boys were holding their hands up, letting the glue dry.

"Can't I take mine home now?" Penny whined.

Anne stooped and put her arms around Penny. "They'll have more magic if we give them a week."

Something hit Anne on the head, and she jumped up.

The twins were flinging faux pearls at Penny.

Anne couldn't believe her eyes. "You guys, stop!"

Priscilla swept into the room with a shriek: "Sit down!"

The students obliged quickly.

Priscilla continued, "Fold your hands, and there'll be one minute of silence before you go." She set the timer on her phone. "Anne, turn off that atrocious music."

Anne did as she was told, then sat impulsively in an empty seat and folded her hands too. She'd never been so embarrassed in all her life. She wouldn't keep her job now, let alone get the residency.

Priscilla's timer went off. "Okay, you are dismissed," she said. "Walk single-file out the door."

The little artists followed Priscilla's directions. The twins kept their hands, now stuck together with glue, folded.

"Bye, everyone. See you next week," Anne called after them.

The room looked like a cyclone had hit it: beads and pearls all over the floor, found objects strewn about, glue stuck to the tables. She'd recently read an article about the positive correlation between creativity and messy studios. Chaos was part of the creative process, but Priscilla probably didn't understand that.

Priscilla eyed Anne. "Clean up, and I'll see you in my office."

Half an hour later, as Anne walked down the hallway, Karl came toward her. Why was he still here? He shot her a big grin as he passed her but didn't say a word. He must have gotten the residency.

Priscilla's door was open when she arrived. Anne knocked on the doorjamb, her heart beating against her chest.

Priscilla tapped her pen on the edge of her desk. "About the residency."

Here it was. Karl got it.

"The panel wasn't able to come to a consensus. We're going to do second interviews. It's down to you and Karl. Come back Monday at one o'clock, and bring student work samples with you."

27

Early June roses bloomed, and a blue jay fluttered in the birdbath as Anne pulled Tweety into Bay Breeze's circular drive. What was Fay going to say when Anne told her she was pregnant too? Fay would probably at least try to convince her to find out who the father was. Maybe she should tell Fay only about the one-night stand. In that case, she might be more supportive if Anne decided to have an abortion. Fay wouldn't want her to be connected to someone that gross for the rest of her days.

Anne opened the car door, hiked up the mansion's steps, and paused to take in the sparkling bay view below. Lucky barked a greeting behind the door. George opened it, holding back the beagle-basset.

"Hi, George." Anne leaned down and pulled a bacon bit from her pocket. The odor made her queasy. "Lucky, how you've grown. Sit," she commanded the dog.

Lucky put down his behind. Anne opened her hand, and he gobbled the treat.

"Good boy." She stroked him behind the ears and stood up.

George grinned. "You've sure got that covered. Come on in."

She stepped inside. "Congratulations on the baby."

He rubbed his bald head. "Geriatric parents."

Anne laughed.

"You haven't been over in ages."

"I know; it's great to be here." She paused in the foyer. The crystal chandelier still sparkled overhead, and the marble floors still shone below her feet, but she sensed a change and held back tears. Even though it had been a few years since Sylvia's passing, Anne missed the gardenia scent that had accompanied her friend's every move in this house.

"Where is everyone?" she asked. Usually the whole gang met her at the door.

"Paul's still asleep. We recently had to move him to the downstairs bedroom. The stairs were getting to be too much for him."

"What about that knee surgery?" Anne asked.

"He still refuses to have it."

At least he'd agreed to cataract surgery. She thought about Sylvia's husband and how much he'd aged since her passing. They walked through the kitchen and peeked in at Paul, still asleep. How sad—it was nearly ten o'clock. He used to be such an early riser. One of his favorite sayings had been "The early bird catches the caterpillar."

George closed the door and whispered, "Ever since Sylvia's been gone, he's lost his stamina. You can't blame him. Losing a soul mate must be devastating."

Anne sighed.

"May I get you a drink? Lemonade? Iced tea?" George kept his voice low.

"No, thanks. Where's Fay?"

"Upstairs. Go on up."

Anne hurried up the steps two at a time and found Fay sitting up in the canopy bed in the master bedroom with an open laptop.

Fay honked. "Hello, mate."

Anne hugged her. "Why are you in bed? Is the baby okay?"

"Everything's hunky-dory. I'm just having a bit of a lie-in is all."

"You've moved into Sylvia's room?" Anne's eyes clouded over.

She remembered the many times she'd been up here, helping Sylvia. The sunlit room hadn't changed at all: same hydrangea wallpaper, same antique dresser and vanity, same brocade curtains.

"Paul insisted. He said with the baby on the way, we'd need the larger space." Fay touched the pink velvet turban on her head. She had on a colorful silk blouse too.

"You're awful fancy. Let me see."

Fay closed her computer, put it on the nightstand, and stood up to model her outfit. "They're by Jennafer Grace, a designer out of San Diego. Paglamas—glamorous pajamas."

Anne smiled. "They sure are."

"Won't fit me much longer." Fay pulled out the elastic waistband to show the inch she had left and climbed back into bed. "Fortunately Jennafer makes kimonos too. What's up? Did you get the residency?"

"Not really." Anne explained the situation. "At least by Monday, the horseshoes should be dry and I'll be able to show those as samples."

"I'm sure you'll get it.

"Now, I have an important question to ask." Fay reached out and took Anne's hand. "Will you be the godmother?"

"You know I'm not religious."

"Neither are we. It would be nice to know you're someone special to our daughter and part of the family."

That was so sweet. "How about if I'm her arts godmother?"

"Bloody good idea." Fay continued, "We're making that room next to us into a nursery." She pulled paint chips from her purse and spread them on the table. "I'm thinking of going with this color for the walls." She pointed to a bright square and handed it to Anne.

Anne studied the swatch and read the name: "Fiery Fuchsia. That's not very calming for a nursery."

She ran her finger down toward the pale hues and read, "Satin

Ribbon, Fairy Wings, Piglet. I always pick one with a good name."

"Fairy Wings it is." Fay drew a smiley face by the square.

"Paint large patches on the wall to make sure before you decide."

"I hope you'll create a mural for us."

This was all too much. Anne had better get it over with. She took a step back. "Fay, I'm pregnant."

"Blimey." Fay looked Anne up and down. "You're kidding, right?"

Anne forced a smile. "No."

"Why didn't you tell me you had a new boyfriend?"

"I don't." Anne shrugged.

"You're back with Sergio, then?"

Anne swallowed. "Not really."

"Come on, spill it. Who's the father? It's not Sergio?"

Anne paused, embarrassed to share the sordid details of the situation. "I'm not sure."

Fay raised her voice. "What do you mean?"

"I had a one-night fling."

"With who?" Fay lifted her arms.

Anne couldn't even look at Fay as words tumbled out. "I met him at Rhinestone Ruby's. Howard knew him. I believed if I had sex with someone else, it would help me get over Sergio. The guy was a really good dancer, and I thought he was a hottie. I'd had a lot to drink."

Mouth agape, Fay listened.

Anne sheepishly looked at her friend and shrugged. "I know that's no excuse, but I went home with him, and, to make a long, awful story short, the next morning I realized he wasn't as charming as I thought. My whole plan backfired on me."

"How?" Fay prompted.

"It made me miss Sergio all the more. Two days later, he came to town, and, well . . ." She paused. "You know."

Fay guffawed. "You tart, you!"

"It's not funny," Anne said, and began to cry.

"I'm sorry. Come here." Fay handed her a tissue, opened her arms, and put them around Anne while she sobbed.

Finally, Anne pulled away and dried her eyes. "What am I going to do?"

"How far along are you?"

"Almost eight weeks."

"This is marvelous. Our babies will be like cousins."

"But I haven't decided whether I'm keeping it or not," Anne blurted out.

"Don't be daft. Of course you're keeping it." Fay scrunched up her lips.

Anne blubbered, "But my life was just getting back on track."

"Maybe this is part of that track?" Fay's voice was soft as she handed Anne another tissue. "Have you been to the doctor yet?"

"I have an appointment at Planned Parenthood tomorrow, after my interview." Anne blew her nose.

"Good. I'm ordering you a book." Fay grabbed her computer and started typing. "I'd loan you mine, but it's my bible. *What to Expect When You're Expecting*. Next step is to find out who the father is."

"But I can't learn that for another seven months. Don't I need to wait until the baby's born?"

Fay paused her typing and looked at Anne. "Not anymore. I've heard there's new technology that makes it possible to find out in utero. Come sit here." Fay patted the bed beside her.

Anne sat next to Fay and looked at the screen while she typed, *How early can you get a paternity test?*

Several articles popped up.

Anne pointed at the screen. "Let's see that *TIME* article."

Fay clicked it and read aloud: "It's from 2011. 'DDC, a privately held company, now offers various genetic tests and has the exclusive

US license to market the clunkily named noninvasive prenatal paternity test, which analyzes what's known as circulating cell-free fetal DNA in the mother's blood to suss out Daddy's identity.'"

"It doesn't really say that." Anne leaned over. "'Suss out'?"

Fay continued, "Yes, it does. DDC says it receives 'four hundred thousand calls annually from people inquiring about paternity tests. Until now, only amniocentesis or chorionic villus sampling could determine paternity in utero, and both carry a slight risk of miscarriage.' Blimey, that's all hard to pronounce.

"'Barring those options, couples had to wait until a baby was born. The new test is able to separate fetal DNA from that of the mother and father.' Who knew?"

Anne shrugged. "I didn't. How much does it cost?"

Fay scrolled down. "One thousand, six hundred twenty-five dollars."

"That's pretty pricey." Anne didn't even have half that in savings.

"I'll loan you money if need be." Fay clicked and found a more recent post. "Yes, you can get a paternity test while pregnant, and the safest way to do so is with a noninvasive prenatal paternity test (NIPP). This test requires only a blood sample from the mother and a simple cheek swab from the possible father and can be performed as early as eight weeks into pregnancy."

"Wow." Anne was relieved she would be able to learn who the father was soon.

Fay scrolled down the list of companies. "Here's one: Who's Your Daddy? It says here it's the holy grail of paternity tests."

Anne and Fay both laughed.

"Doesn't sound very scientific. Let's try another," Anne said.

Fay read, "'Home DNA paternity test starting at one hundred ninety-nine dollars. Order online today.'"

Now Anne really felt relieved. "Thank God the price has come down."

Quietly, they read more reviews.

"Looks like a good one."

"Let's get it." Anne pulled her credit card from her backpack and handed it to Fay.

"Now all you need to do is tell one of the guys you're up the duff and get a sample."

"I don't ever want to see that unhottie again."

"What's his name, by the way?" Fay asked.

"Barnaby."

Fay laughed.

"Yes, I know."

"You'll need to ask Sergio, then."

Anne groaned. "But I don't have the heart to tell him I've been with someone else and he might not be the father."

"Girl, you've just gotta do it."

"Also, if he finds out he's the father, he might bring up marriage again, when I'm just getting over him."

Fay raised her arms. "You aren't over him. You just slept with him two months ago."

28

Good morning!" Anne slipped into the conference room and sat across the table from the three committee members—Mr. Willingsby, Fredricka, and Priscilla—hoping they hadn't noticed she was a few minutes late. She set her old-lady purse on the floor beside her and put the box of horseshoes on the table.

"Morning," Mr. Willingsby said. He wore a bolo tie with his gray suit.

Fredricka smiled and fingered her necklace, filled with colorful Zuni animal fetishes. Fay had told Anne Fredricka had pledged another donation toward the program if she could sit in on the panel now.

Priscilla had a bored expression on her face, tapped her pen on the table, pursed her red lips. She didn't have on those big glasses. Maybe she'd gotten contacts.

No one said anything, so Anne twisted the lucky key in her pants pocket and sat quietly, waiting for Priscilla to begin. Today, Anne had on the same outfit she'd worn to the previous interview but had looped a turquoise scarf around her neck instead of the pink. She felt woozy and put her hand on her stomach. The mint tea and saltines she'd had for breakfast didn't seem to have worked.

Mr. Willingsby and Fredricka glared at Priscilla. She stopped tapping the table but didn't say anything.

Let's get this show on the road. Anne took the horseshoes from her box and lined them up in front of her. "My young artists created these using found objects. Mr. Willingsby, you'll recognize the horseshoes."

"It's fun to see what the students have done with these."

"Feel free to pass them around."

Mr. Willingsby and Fredricka reached for them.

Priscilla pushed out her hands. "Stop."

Everyone froze.

"Let's wait until everyone's here."

Who the heck else was coming? Have they found more committee members?

Three minutes later, Karl sauntered in, sat beside her, and placed a shoebox of tinfoil sculptures on the table. Anne couldn't believe he was here.

Priscilla began, "We're interviewing you together for simplicity's sake. For a straight playing field."

Oh, for gosh sakes, this wasn't a football game.

"Karl. Show us your samples first." Priscilla smiled at him.

"When I subbed for Anne, the students made these self-portraits." He held up each of the sculptures one at a time and placed them on the table.

To Anne, they resembled RoboCops, not children.

Fredricka squinted, leaned to the side, and examined the sculptures at eye level. Mr. Willingsby picked up one by its head and rotated the piece.

Anne couldn't tell whether they were impressed or not.

Karl placed one on Priscilla's open palm. She gazed at it as if it were a stunning Degas ballerina. "Very nice." She raised her brows at Karl. "How did you come up with the idea for these?"

He paused. "I use this technique to create preliminary drafts of my own sculptures."

"What foundry casts your work? What galleries represent you?" Fredricka asked, holding up one of the pieces.

Karl grinned at her. "I work only in wood, so I don't need a foundry. Right now, I'm saving my pieces for a solo exhibit. Do you have any interest in showing them at the Noir?" He laughed as if he was teasing, but Anne could tell he was serious.

"I don't think they'd fit our profile." Fredricka put down the piece and played with her necklace again.

"What are the three most important things you'd like to get out of the residency?" Priscilla asked.

The pants man shot the committee his biggest smile. "I'm going to demonstrate to museum guests the beauty of sculpture and how difficult it is to create. Perhaps sell some pieces and even receive some new commissions. I'm looking forward to having a large studio to work in. I need a lot of space."

He talked as if he already had the position. That was more than three things, buster.

"Any other questions?" Priscilla asked.

Mr. Willingsby asked, "Karl, do you have any thoughts about improving our arts programming?"

"Yes: a bigger budget."

Priscilla laughed. What was going on with those two?

Mr. Willingsby and Fredricka sat stone-faced.

"It's your turn. Show us the shoes." Priscilla tilted her head at Anne.

Anne's heart sped up, and she slid the horseshoes toward the panel.

As Mr. Willingsby picked up Penny's horseshoe, the button popped off onto the table and some seed beads sprinkled on the floor.

"Oops! Sorry," he said.

"No problem. That happens all the time." Anne couldn't believe she'd just said that. She should have shaken them upside down in the classroom to make sure all the loose materials had fallen off.

"What adhesives do you use?" Fredricka asked, as she ran her finger gently over Hugh's purple earring.

"Weldbond. Like Tacky Glue, but stronger. Mosaic artists use it these days. For the bigger objects, like that metal rose there, we used E6000." Anne pointed at Cindy's horseshoe.

"Isn't that toxic?" Karl asked.

Oh. Karl gets to ask questions? If Anne had known that, she would have asked him a few. "We used only a tad, under my supervision."

Priscilla sat back and crossed her arms. "Anne. How about you? What are three things you hope to get out of the residency?"

Anne took a breath and began. She'd practiced this one. "I'd like to welcome museum guests not just as observers but as artists. I believe the best way for patrons to appreciate and learn about art is by doing it themselves. I'll provide hands-on materials so they can do that."

She paused. Was that three things?

"Go on," Fredricka encouraged.

Anne heard her voice strengthen as she went on, "For instance, I'll be bringing in a large mosaic. Guests will put chipped plates and tiles in a paper bag and break them with a hammer."

"Isn't that dangerous?" Karl asked.

Anne wanted to kick him under the table. "I've used this technique for years and will make sure they're safe."

"You'd better make sure you have plenty of Band-Aids available." He laughed, and so did Priscilla.

Anne continued, "I'll encourage guests to choose pieces that appeal to them and adhere those pieces to the mosaics themselves."

Priscilla stood. "Yes, well. Thank you both for coming."

Everyone else stood also.

They hadn't asked Anne about ideas for improving the program, and she had so many. "Wait. I have something else to add."

Mr. Willingsby and Fredricka sat down again. "Go on," Fredricka said.

Anne began again: "I'd like to see us offer classes to children whose families can't afford to pay for them. Maybe do some outreach in the community with seniors or even the homeless."

Mr. Willingsby nodded, and Fredricka smiled. Priscilla just stared. What was wrong with that woman?

"We'll make a decision within a few days," Priscilla said.

Feeling like a broken plate herself, Anne shook hands with the committee members and left the room as Karl continued to chat it up with his smarmy grin.

Too tired, queasy, and depressed to walk to Planned Parenthood, Anne ordered a Lyft. She checked in at reception and sat in the waiting room among other women of all shapes and sizes. Anne wondered which other ones were pregnant.

She skimmed an article in *Natural Parent* magazine about the dangers of good child syndrome until she was called fifteen minutes later.

Lying on the exam table in the paper gown and drape, she was freezing. Why did they have the air conditioner up so high? Didn't they know naked women were in these rooms? And the decor . . . If it were up to her, she'd repaint these sickly green walls Fairy Wings pink.

The door opened, and a large woman with wavy red hair entered and shook Anne's hand. "I'm the midwife, Lori. How are you feeling today?"

"Nauseated." Anne yawned.

Lori looked at the chart. "Yes, your urine test confirms you're pregnant. Almost nine weeks." She looked at Anne with large, kind eyes. "You should start to feel better soon."

"I sure hope so."

"Me too. Do you want a prescription?"

"No, it's not that bad. I'll be fine." Anne hated to take meds. They couldn't be good for the baby anyway.

"Let's hear what we've got." Lori lifted the paper gown, put her stethoscope to Anne's bloated stomach, and listened. "I can hear a healthy, steady heartbeat. Do you want to hear?"

If she heard it, she might be swayed to make a bad decision. "What if . . . What if . . ."

"What if what?" Lori looked at her sympathetically.

Anne couldn't ask about ending the pregnancy. She wished her mom were here. Maybe she should have let Fay come with her.

"I'm going to draw some blood to make sure you're healthy." Lori put the drape back over Anne and picked up a syringe. "This might prick."

Anne felt the pinch and turned her head. "Can you tell the sex of the baby?" she asked, feeling faint as she watched Lori put the vial on the table.

"Not yet. We can when you have your eighteen-week ultrasound. Any more questions?"

"Is there a way I can have some of that blood?"

"What? Why?"

Anne swallowed. "I ordered a paternity kit online."

Lori didn't even flinch. "I see. You'll need the form for that. Make an appointment, and we'll be happy to draw blood for you then."

She handed Anne some prescriptions and brochures, including one about terminations. "Read these over and e-mail me if you have any additional questions."

29

Even though it had been only two days since she'd ordered it, Anne opened her mailbox, hoping the kit had arrived. Thai purred like a motor and zigzagged around her feet as she flipped through the junk mail, then bent down and petted the cat's silver-gray fur coat.

"What happened to that little-ball-of-sweetness sister of yours?" Anne asked Thai, and looked over at Mrs. Landenheim's door. Thai hissed and sprinted away.

She hoped the kit would fit in her thin mailbox. If it had to go in the open bin below, someone might see it. She had once caught Mrs. Landenheim picking up packages and looking at labels. Anne hoped the DNA company would be discreet.

She ran up the stairs, Thai on her heels. Anne's phone rang. Priscilla. That was fast. The interview had been only a few hours earlier. Anne sat on the daybed and braced herself, with a sinking feeling in her stomach. Thai curled up in a corner of the apartment and looked at her with crossed eyes.

"Anne, I have good news and bad news." Priscilla's shrill voice was grating. "Against my better judgment, we'd like to offer you the residency. The bad news is, you and Karl will both be residents."

Anne's heart plummeted. "What does that mean?"

"The stipend will be split in half. You'll be sharing the studio space with him."

"That's not a good idea."

"I know it's not what you were hoping for, but many artists collaborate."

"It's not that." Anne paused a few seconds to gather her next words. "We just aren't very good friends."

No way was she going to tell Priscilla that a few years earlier, she'd dated him without realizing he was married. Anne didn't want to throw him under the bus like he had with her. Karma and all that.

Priscilla's pen clicked on her desk. "I'm not asking you to be beasties."

"Do you mean besties?" Anne held back a snicker.

"Whatever."

"Would I need to be in the studio at the same time he's there?"

"Yes, the committee felt it would be more interesting for the museum guests to observe two artists working instead of just one."

"Just like monkeys at the zoo?" Anne couldn't believe she'd blurted that out.

"It isn't like that at all. Think about it, and let me know by the end of the week." Priscilla sounded like she didn't want Anne to take it. Why had she turned against her?

"When would the residency begin?"

"In a month."

A month. Well, by then Anne should have made a decision about the baby. Her gut instinct told her to say no to Priscilla, but she decided to wait. "I'll let you know." She tried to keep the sarcasm out of her voice when she said thank you.

"And you need to get your little artists under control and keep the work spaces neat."

"Alexa, play The Pretenders," Anne ordered after she hung up. She seized a plate from her stack on an art-supply shelf, put it in a paper bag, broke it with a hammer, and shook the shards into a box. Thai skittered across the room and hid under the bed.

Anne seized another plate, put it in a paper bag, broke it with a hammer, and shook it into the box. Repeat, repeat, repeat, repeat.

She sang along to "Precious" with Chrissie Hynde.

The music and smashing worked their magic. Anne considered the hubcap leaning on the floor but instead chose a wide white wooden bowl and laid it on her kitchenette table. She pranced over to her found objects lined up on the shelf, selected a Goodwill Our Lady of Guadalupe statue, and glued it in the bowl's center. There, that felt good.

She dumped a Tupperware of found objects on the table, chose pieces that called to her, and adhered them around the statue.

Out of breath, Anne lay on the bed. "Alexa, off." She tried to get Thai to come out from under the bed, but to no avail, and soon Anne fell asleep.

It was dark by the time Thai's nails scratching on the door woke Anne. She let the cat out and studied the piece she'd made. Not bad, if she said so herself.

In her journal, she listed the assortment of earrings, pins, and other found objects she'd used and what they might signify.

Silver spoon = born with riches
Sun = good weather
Umbrella = rain
Airplane pin = safe travels
Heart = love
"Mother" charm = a mom
Chicken and grapes = food
A watch = more time
Assorted coins = money
Caesar's Palace chit = win big in Vegas
Flowers = environment
Fish = clean ocean
Lamppost = to see the light

She closed her eyes and took several deep breaths, in and out. What did all these objects have in common? After a few moments, it came to her.

She wrote, *Things People Pray For.*

That was the mosaic's title. Anne loved that she didn't need to think about titles for her pieces but let her intuition tell her. She studied the piece again. No baby. No baby symbols. Where's the baby? Don't people pray for babies? She put her hand on her stomach. She certainly hadn't. Maybe she wasn't supposed to have this one. Or maybe she should start praying for a healthy baby.

She searched the tray of objects until she found it. She glued the tiny pink rattle onto the mosaic. With a paintbrush, she spread glue in the crevices between the objects and sprinkled safety glass from a broken windshield for grout.

She looked around her cramped, crowded, messy apartment and thought about having access to half that big museum studio and the giant project she had always dreamed of making. Come on. She was a professional. Even if she had to share the space with a jerk, and pregnant or not, she could do it. She'd show them!

Anne googled "discipline for art teachers." She followed the list to a blog called Creatubbles and read:

Art Room Discipline

> Whether it's roughhousing, using crayons as missiles, not cleaning up, or general back talk, there's not a teacher on Earth who doesn't have issues with discipline. If you're looking for ways to handle an unruly class, read on. . . .

She felt like the writer knew what she was up against. Anne continued reading:

> Don't take it personally, scold, or raise your voice when the class is misbehaving. Kids have an inherent sense of fairness, and most of your class will welcome your restoring an atmosphere of calm. Develop a plan with rules and consequences.

The students deserved a peaceful atmosphere that was conducive to creativity, and so did she. She continued to read the blog and write down notes, then adapted some into positive affirmations for herself:

I will keep my voice calm.
I will be consistent.
I will stop early enough that students can help clean up.

She copied them onto an index card and put it in her backpack. Editing examples of rules and consequences from the blog, she composed four simple rules and three consequences, from warnings to parental notifications, appropriate for her class. She wrote them down neatly on a poster board with markers and couldn't wait until Saturday to give it all a try.

30

Another night had passed. Sally Sue had been on pins and needles since Cliff had yelled at her yesterday while honing that knife. She prayed her plan would work. Ma harped that most women could use their womanly wiles to get a man to do anything, like that fallen woman her father had left them for. Maybe if Sally Sue used her own womanly wiles, she could entice Cliff to take her back to the train and let her go.

Her first step was to get him off guard and thinking everything was copacetic. "What are you making in there?"

He sat down at the table, she served him, and he tasted a bite. "This oatmeal is delicious, Sally Sue. What a surprise. I thought you couldn't cook."

"I'm full of surprises." Her aunt had taught her. Sally Sue sat across from him and smiled slyly, with a hint of flirtatiousness.

"I bet you are." He didn't seem to notice as he added the honey she handed him and took another bite.

After they finished the oatmeal, he taught her how to make his special apple dish.

"Now you can bake it anytime you want." He served her some to taste on a spoon, but it dropped on the ground, and he picked it up and wiped the spoon on a cloth. "Aren't you getting tired of these dirt floors? I'm gonna start splicing that wood to cover them today."

"You'd do that for me?" She clapped her hands. "You're so thoughtful." She shot him that look again.

Before sunset and before he came in, Sally Sue undressed, removed the red dress from the trunk, slipped it on over her head, and looked in the mirror. The dress fit perfectly, showing off her tiny waist. The woman who had lived here must also have been small.

Sally Sue sighed. Mama, if you were stuck out here in the middle of nowhere with a dangerous man, you might put on a red dress and do something shameful too.

Sally Sue tugged the scooped neck down around her shoulders and pulled them back, pretending her breasts were two roses in full bloom. She found the flimflam man's ribbon, strung it through her hair, and tied it underneath like a forest sprite might have done. The short cut was freeing.

Did Sally Sue have the courage to give this a try? She'd never attempted to use her "womanly wiles" before. She put her hands behind her head and circled her hips. Was that how those saloon women did it?

She climbed a chair, lit the candles Cliff had put in the sparkling chandelier, and got back down, ready to receive him. She heard Cliff stomping snow from his boots, and then the door opened. Heart galloping, she felt her legs go weak, and she quickly sat at the table.

He came in, removed his coat, and hung it on a hook.

She took a deep breath, stood, and strolled toward him.

At the sight of her, his eyes lit up. "Why, Sally Sue, aren't you just the prettiest girl I've ever seen?" His face was handsome in the candlelight.

She batted her eyelashes, wiggled her shoulders, and leaned over, showing him a bit of cleavage, just like the girl in the green corset had done.

She drawled, "You rascal, you. Aren't you just the *complimentinest* man I've ever known?"

His smile faded, and he looked away.

She sauntered closer to him. "Come on, Cliffie. Don't you find me appealing?"

His eyes widened, and he backed up, with his palms toward her. "Of course, Sally Sue. You're a vision of beauty, but . . ."

"Do you really think so?" She continued to sway toward him.

"Of course. Look at yourself in the mirror."

If he thought she was so pretty, why wasn't this working? She'd better take it up a notch.

She put her hand on his elbow and tilted her head up. "Wanna have amorous congress?" She'd learned that term from her aunt too.

He moved her hand to her side with a laugh and stepped back. "You don't know what you're proposing. Why would a nice girl like you say something like that?"

Embarrassed, she sat with a thud at the kitchen table, put her head on her arms, and wept.

He was right—she had no idea what it all meant. How could she have acted like such a hussy? She didn't know the first thing about cajoling a man to do her bidding.

He sat across from her and said slowly, "A gentleman doesn't take advantage of a fine lady like you." He blew out the chandelier candles, lit a lamp for her, put on his coat, and left for the night, without so much as a good night. She cried herself to sleep.

The next morning, he carried strips of wood inside and laid them on the floor. With droopy eyes, she collected pails full of snow and dumped them in the cauldron. Mortified about the night before, she refused to meet his eyes.

At the breakfast table, he rambled on cheerily as if nothing had happened. "We'll wait until chances of frost are over, then prepare the ground and plant the garden."

Outside the window, sleet flew sideways in icy strips. "What would grow out here in this godforsaken place?"

"Lots. Corn, squash, and beans. Haven't you noticed the plot laid out on the side of the cabin? Might even get us some goats, sheep, or cattle to graze. That'd make you happy, wouldn't it?"

It didn't matter to her, because come spring, she wouldn't even still be there. She changed the subject. "How about teaching me to shoot a gun?"

He paused. "In this weather?"

"How about just showing me how to hold one?"

He stared at her with those eyes. No smile, no frown.

She tried to gauge Cliff's emotions, usually evident in his facial expressions. But it seemed like he hid a secret, just like he'd hidden that money somewhere. What was he thinking? Did he want to teach her to shoot, or didn't he? Maybe his emotions were mixed, like when meadow colors shifted as clouds passed overhead, first blocking the sun and then opening up.

"I'm going out to slice more wood." He put on his coat and stomped out the door.

She spied a clump of gray yarn on the floor. Something must have dropped from her basket. She leaned down to pick up the clump. It was a dead mouse! The poor dear. Sally Sue squinted, grasped the thin tail between her thumb and forefinger, and avoided looking at the teeny buckteeth and closed eyes. The little critter was one of God's creatures. Was it right to poison them just because they made a mess? Was there a way to pack everything away more carefully? After all, the mice had been here before she was.

She hurried outside, shivering in the cold, and called to Cliff, sawing in the barn.

He poked his head out the door. "What have you got there?"

She held up the mouse. "A dead mouse."

"That's good. Just throw it out and the birds will get it."

"But won't the birds eat it and get poisoned too?" Sally Sue blinked back a tear.

"Never thought of that. Just a minute." He went into the barn and got a shovel.

"Come on." He motioned for her to follow him to the big oak, broke the ice, and dug a deep hole. Sally Sue laid the mouse in it and said a silent prayer while Cliff covered the poor soul with dirt.

That evening, Cliff came into the cabin with a sideways grin on his face. "I've got something that'll be a surefire way to keep the mice away."

"Not another poison?"

"Nope." Cliff stuck his fingers in his front shirt pocket, pulled out a squeaky ball of fur, and handed it to her.

It fit in the palm of her hand. She stroked the kitten's soft ears. Its eyes were still clamped shut. "This is the most precious thing I've ever seen. Wherever did you find him?"

He took the kitten back from Sally Sue, tilted it onto its back, and pointed at the smooth mound. "He's a she."

"Oh." She felt herself redden.

He guffawed. "It's just nature, Sally Sue. I found her mewing in the hayloft."

"What about her mama?" Sally Sue was in awe of the fur's sleek blackness.

"There was a feral hussy slinking around. But I haven't seen her for nigh on five days."

The kitten mewed loudly. It had a white chest, paws, and tail tip.

"If we don't do something to help, this little one won't make it."

He held the kitten in one hand, grabbed a rag, and went out to the front. "Open up the chest and a fresh milk container."

Sally Sue followed his instructions. He dipped the rag in the milk pot and let the liquid drip into the kitten's mouth; she quickly sucked it up.

He handed her back to Sally Sue. "Try it."

She couldn't believe how the kitten wouldn't let go of the rag.

"You'll need to feed her every few hours like this. Are you up to the task?"

"Of course." Every time the neighbors' Butterscotch had kittens, there were a slew of them. "Were there others?"

He shook his head. His eyes didn't meet hers. "Keep her inside."

"I know it's dangerous out there." She wanted to thank him but didn't quite know what to say.

"I guarantee we won't see any mice for a while."

She pictured the kitten grown big and fat, with blood dripping from a mouse in its jaw. "The poor mice."

"Don't worry, darling. Once they know there's a cat living here, the mice'll tell each other and stay out."

Sally Sue liked that he had called her "darling." "Is that really true?"

"Cross my heart." He waved a finger over his chest.

She sure hoped so.

He brought in a box filled with dirt and set it in the corner of the room.

"I'm gonna name her Socks." Sally Sue petted the kitten's soft white paws.

31

A week later, the skies had cleared to a cerulean blue and the temperature had warmed. Ducks swam in the thawed pond. The horses grazed in the grass that seemed to have sprung up overnight.

Hope flowered in Sally Sue's chest as a horseman appeared on the horizon above the ranch. *God, please let this be the answer to my prayers.*

She glanced at the barn. Cliff was in there, sanding away on the last of the floor slats. She shielded her eyes from the sun and waved as the lofty horseman loped on his cream-colored palomino down the pasture toward her. He raised a leather-gloved hand and drew near her, and she recognized the town sheriff.

She couldn't contain her exhilaration and shouted, "I'm ever so happy to—"

"Hold it right there." Cliff dashed out of the barn with his rifle pointed at the sheriff.

The sheriff pulled out his pistol, raised it at Cliff, and dragged out his words. "Put your gun down, son. I'm Sheriff Mack. Come out here to welcome you to my territory."

Sally Sue tried not to grin at Cliff.

He lowered his rifle and put on that whopping smile of his. "Sheriff. Good of you to come all this way."

"Settling in well?" the sheriff asked, and replaced his gun in his holster.

"Yes, sir." Cliff paused.

"Come on in." Sally Sue motioned toward the door.

Cliff lost his smile and glared at Sally Sue. "Now, darling, I'm sure the sheriff's too busy."

"Plenty of time." Mack set his tree trunk of a body on the ground. He was at least two heads taller than Cliff, and broader also. "Brought you supplies you might be needing." He handed Cliff a gunnysack.

"That's kind of you, Sheriff." She hoped he'd brought milk. With the kitten, they'd run out, and she had resorted to feeding Socks sugar water instead.

Mack removed the palomino's tooled saddle, hung it over the round pen's railing, and slapped the horse's flank. "Okay, Dusty." Dusty skidded off toward the pond.

As they stepped inside, Sally Sue asked, "Would you care for tea?"

"I'm sure he can't stay long." Cliff kept his voice light, set the gunnysack on the table, and rested his rifle in his arms.

"I could visit for a spell after riding all this way." Sheriff Mack removed his hat and coat and put them on hooks by the door. "I brought you some of my missus's muffins." He sat at the kitchen table, ran his hands through his tawny-colored hair, opened the gunnysack, and pulled out a tin. Cliff sat too, laid his rifle on the table, and rested his hand on it. With the other, he selected a muffin from the tin Mack offered.

Mack began to take out other items one at a time. "Here's some of her blackberry preserves. Jalapeños—she chops them up real small and adds them to sauce. Butter, milk . . ." He grinned at Cliff and pulled out a jug. "And rum."

She eyed it. Just what we needed, more liquor.

"You are ever so thoughtful." Sally Sue put the kettle on and busied herself with the cups. She picked up the tin and placed the muffins on a plate from the shelf, glad for the fancy blue-and-white dishes to use with their guest.

"Have another?" she offered Sheriff Mack. How was she going to get a message to him?

He picked one up, took a bite, and said, "Yes, you got some prime land here."

"I plan to do some planting." Cliff tapped a rhythm on his rifle. Was he fixing to pick it up and shoot the sheriff, and maybe her too?

"Farm if you like, but I recommend cattle to make your fortune. Sheep can be profitable also."

Cliff grimaced. "I've heard they get covered in worms and insects."

"You dip 'em in creosote to kill the vermin."

Sally Sue didn't like the sound of that. She gathered up Socks, sleeping in a ball on the carpet, and a rag and handed them to Cliff. He put Socks on his lap, opened the milk bottle, and fed her.

Mack leaned over and petted Socks. Sally Sue wandered to the trunk, lifted the lid, and reached for the letters.

Cliff turned. "Honey pie, come on over and set with us." He shook his head at the sheriff. "A woman's work is never done."

She closed the lid and sat at the table.

Mack looked around, and then at Sally Sue. "I like how you've cleaned up the place."

"Thank you, sir." She tilted her head toward the mantel, the array of artifacts there. "Where did those come from? Did savages bring gifts to the Ivrys?"

"Hell, no. Sorry for my cursin', ma'am. Injuns probably traded those things for food. That doll there's a Hopi kachina; the basket's Navajo. Both tribes live out in the nearby desert."

"What happened to the Ivrys?" she asked.

"About six months ago, they just up and left." He shrugged. "Coulda been the rough weather, a family matter, a yearning for gold farther west, or maybe even those damn Apaches. No one knows for sure." He exchanged glances with Cliff.

The kettle whistled. Sally Sue jumped up, put a hand on her beating chest, and made the tea. She set the pot and cups around the table and sat back down.

Cliff grinned. "I've told her not to stray far. Injuns, wolves, and bandits prowl hereabout."

Mack eyed Cliff's rifle. "Don't worry, little lady. Seems you're well protected. Careful, though. I hate to scare you, but there might even be a murdering bank robber hiding out somewhere nearby." He lit a long cigar, handed one to Cliff, and said, "I'm putting together a posse. Wanna join?"

Cliff didn't even flinch. "Don't think I should. We're still trying to settle in here. I'm cleaning up the barn, putting in these wood floors, and plan to build a front porch and another room on the cabin."

Sally Sue wondered if he really meant all that. She poured the tea from the pot and pushed over the honey and milk for them to use.

"Mighty handy of you." Mack blew on his tea, sniffed it, and eyed the jug he'd brought. "Got anything stronger?"

Cliff grasped the jug and poured some rum into Mack's teacup and his own. He tilted it toward Sally Sue, but she shook her head.

"I understand." Mack handed Cliff the wanted poster. "Keep an eye out. They say he's mighty crafty. Big hat, beady eyes, maybe a beard too. It's hard to tell with that bandanna over his mouth."

Cliff surreptitiously put his hand on the kerchief on his neck.

Standing behind him, Sally Sue tried to catch Mack's eyes, tilted her head toward Cliff and down at the poster. Cliff turned around and shot her a dagger look.

"Yes. He looks terrifying. I hope never to meet him." She wanted to scream, *It's him!*, hide behind the sheriff, and ask for his protection, but with Cliff's rifle so nearby, she didn't dare. Instead, she sat down and picked up her cup, but her hands were shaking, so she put it back down.

Cliff stood and kept his tone light. "You must be pretty busy. We don't mean to keep you."

"It's fine." Mack ate another muffin from the plate. "Yes, you'll like Arizona. Spring's here, summer weather is delightful, and come fall the aspen leaves change color." He drank from his cup.

"Lots of nearby natural sights too. Up north of here, there's a canyon deeper and wider than anyone has ever seen. East of here, giant buttes and bluffs decorate the desert. If you want to go further over into New Mexico, there's the strangest darn church. Señors and señoritas walk on their knees for miles to get to it. They scrape dirt that's supposed to have healing powers from a hole in the ground to get over what ails them."

"You don't say," Cliff said.

Sally Sue thought it all sounded far-fetched but fascinating.

Cigar smoke filled the cabin, more rum got poured, and the men chatted. Cliff acted as if Mack was his new best friend. Sally Sue took Socks from Cliff and moved to the rocker. The kitten opened her blue eyes and blinked at Sally Sue. How was she going to get Mack alone and tell him who Cliff really was?

She leaned over and picked up her tatting, now a tangled heap.

"Darn Socks!" Sally Sue scolded.

Cliff looked at her and chuckled. "That's a knee-slapper. Darn Socks!"

At first, she didn't get the inadvertent joke, but then she started laughing also.

Cliff explained the hilarity to Mack, and he joined in.

"I know you have big plans, but it's hard to get started out here. If you need to make money, there's a ranch farther up the mountain that might need some help," Mack said.

"I'll be just fine."

"May I use your privy?" Mack stood.

This was her chance. She hopped up. "I'll show you."

"No need, darling. I'll do it." Cliff stood and threw a friendly arm around Mack's shoulder. "I want to show him the barn, anyway."

The men staggered outside. She reached for Cliff's gun, still sitting on the table, but he hurried back inside and grabbed it first.

"Forgot my rifle, honey. Don't know what dangers might be about." He chuckled and left.

"Darn it to hell." She got the letters from the trunk, slid them into her pocket, put the empty muffin tin in the washbasin, and scrubbed it harshly.

The men soon returned and recommenced drinking and smoking. When the jug was empty and the sun faded over the horizon, Mack finally rode off, taking with him all her hopes for a rescue.

Cliff had passed out on the table. Angry at herself for not having the courage to confront him in front of Mack or at least get the letter to the sheriff, she stomped outside and into the meadow. The silver crescent moon, an empty cradle suspended in the dark sky, glittered above. She longed to fly up to it, curl up, and stay there, hidden from Cliff's view, rocking back and forth for comfort, her shawl a blanket.

Cliff's snoring woke her. Sally Sue must have dozed off in the rocker. She shook her shoulders. Cigar stench permeated the cabin, and she couldn't abide it.

Crickets chirped in cadence with her heartbeat as she stepped outside. Ripe loam and horse scent filled her senses. Oaks shifted in the light breeze, and she pulled her shawl tightly around her shoulders. Her body, just a small dot in the universe, rested under the inky sky filled with shimmering stars. The canopy's grandness soothed her soul, and she began to relax.

"What're you doin' out here?" Cliff yelled, and ambled toward her. "Come on back inside."

"I'm getting air is all."

Far off, a howl filled the air and a shiver went up her spine. Mother of God, here it was the "I told you so."

"Listen to that. Even Mack said it's dangerous to be out here alone."

Another wail, this time louder and more insistent. Sally Sue tried not to shudder noticeably. "What is it?" she asked.

He held up a finger for her to be quiet as another sound echoed.

"A wolf, or maybe an Injun pretending to be a wolf. It's hard to tell."

Cliff's eyes shone in the darkness as a bark from another direction answered the others. "Probably a coyote. They shift their sounds to mimic the prey they plan to capture. It might have been a feral cat, a bobcat, or even a fight to the death with a cougar. I've heard it called natural selection or survival of the fittest."

This also referred to humans, including her. Sally Sue needed to learn to protect herself. Cliff led her back to the house and trudged out to the barn. She slipped on her nightgown, climbed into bed, and fell asleep, but then a yip and a howl from outside woke her. Her heart beating rapidly, she sat up straight and stared into the darkness.

Back in the meadow, her nightdress wafted around in the cool zephyr. Smoky fog had rolled in, so dense she could barely see the trees through the pallid air. From behind a ponderosa, a towering figure lurched out and staggered toward her. His white face gleamed. Tough grin on red-painted lips, black lines drawn on his cheeks, stringy raven hair. He continued toward her with outstretched, muscular arms.

Trapped in a tepee of fear, she tried to run, but her feet were frozen in place. More strong-bodied men stepped out from between the trees and lumbered toward her. She opened her mouth to scream, but nothing came out.

A firm hand grasped her shoulder. "Sal. Wake up. You're having a nightmare."

She opened her eyes and clutched Cliff tightly. "There were Injuns. They seemed so real."

"None here. You're safe." He gently ran his hand over her hair.

Within his arms, she felt protected, but then, suddenly realizing where she was, she shoved him away. How did he know about her nightmare? Why was he inside the cabin? He went outside and closed the door. Fear gripped her soul. She'd need to come up with a firm plan to get away from this dangerous place and this dangerous man.

32

In the morning, a strong breeze blew and Sally Sue had a brilliant idea. If Annie Oakley had learned to shoot like an expert at fifteen, Sally Sue could do it too. In Kansas City, she'd seen the cowgirl in a traveling show. At five feet tall, they happened to be the same height. When Annie rode on the horse's back, she seemed much taller than that.

To gain Cliff's trust, Sally Sue needed to make him think she was a helpless female, content to stay.

When he came in for breakfast, she said, "Cliff, thank you for these beautiful floors. It's ever so much easier to keep the cabin clean." She stirred oatmeal in the cauldron, filled bowls, and sat at the table with him.

"I did it for me as much as you. I should be done this afternoon."

"Were you serious about adding another room?"

"Sure am." He picked up his spoon, and dug it into his oatmeal.

"That'll be nice. As Sheriff Mack said, you sure are handy."

"Thanks."

"I know Mama said it's not ladylike, but I want to learn how to shoot a gun."

He harrumphed.

"Cliff, please, teach me. Sometimes I'm scared being alone out here." She stuck out her lower lip. "If you can't trust me, who can you trust?"

He flinched, then exploded into a giant belly laugh. "Oh, Sally

Sue, you slay me. Of course I can trust you. You wouldn't ever hurt a flea. If you killed me, what would you do out here all alone in this wilderness?"

Plenty! She feigned a laugh. "You're right, Cliff. I'm so weak, I need a man to take care of me." She considered batting her lashes at him, but that would be overkill; plus, she'd tried that tactic before and it had backfired on her.

Overkill. Ha. Backfired. Ha. She held back a giggle.

Her mama used to say a man didn't have much horse sense. If Cliff did, he'd know Sally Sue couldn't be trusted, because she'd shoot him dead as soon as she'd learned how to release a bullet. She'd shoot to kill, not to injure, because then he'd go after her like a wounded bear and that would be the end of her.

He raised his voice. "I said, let me think about it. Besides, it's too windy anyway."

She gave him her biggest smile. "How about just showing me how to hold it?"

He sighed. "I guess that wouldn't hurt anything." He picked up the rifle leaning on the fireplace. "This one's pretty big for a little gal like you, but it'll do."

She stood next to him.

"Put it in your arm like this, as if you're cradling a baby." He rocked the gun back and forth and demonstrated. "One finger goes here, on the stock; the other rests there, on the trigger."

Seemed easy enough.

He handed the gun to her. "Now you try."

"Like this?" It was heavier than she'd thought it would be. She closed one eye, swung around, and aimed at his chest.

He jumped and ducked to the side and bellowed, "Never point a gun unless you're planning to use it." He gently pushed the point away.

Nervous, she giggled.

"It's no laughing matter. You mighta killed me."

"Maybe." She raised an eyebrow at him.

"Except it's not even loaded." He took the gun and laid it against the fireplace.

"Thanks for breakfast. I'll be out finishing the rest of the planks." He walked out the door, shaking his head. "I'm not ever gonna teach you to shoot. No telling what you'll do."

Now she sighed. That plan wasn't going to work. Just in case, though, she practiced holding the gun for a while, then leaned it back against the hearth.

That night, before she crawled into bed, she prayed, *God, how will I ever get away from Cliff?*

The following morning just before sunrise, the winds had died and the sound of crooning frogs woke her. She threw her nightgown back on, tossed her shawl over it, and laced up her boots. Lantern in hand, she stepped outside, inhaling the crisp air. A quarter moon and smattering of stars still hung in the sky.

She followed the frog song down to the thawed pond. In the lamplight, the muddy banks teemed with shimmery sea-green reptiles. Their mesmerizing cadence reverberated along the shore. Were they talking to each other or to her?

She closed her eyes, breathed deeply, and listened.

Do it! Do it! Do it!

Her eyes popped open.

Do it! Do it! Do it!

What were they telling her to do? Run away? She'd tried that before, and it hadn't worked.

Do it!

Were they encouraging her to kill Cliff? The thought had crossed her mind, but she'd never seriously considered it. Could she kill him? It was the worst sin of all. Because of her dire situation, would God forgive her? Would she ever be able to forgive herself? She didn't know the first thing about doing it. If she tried to smother him in his sleep, he'd probably wake up and kill her instead. Shooting him would be violent but quick, but after yesterday, he wasn't going to teach her how to use a gun anyway. Poison might be the answer.

A blood-orange sunrise filled the sky. No way would she be able to do it.

Tiny frogs climbed over Sally Sue's boots. She jumped back, stared at them, and listened to their message again.

Do it! Do it! Do it!

She ran back to the cabin as Cliff came out of the barn. "What's going on?" he asked.

"I went to the pond to see the frogs. There must be a million of them."

"Mmm. Makes for good eatin'. I'll go get us some for breakfast. Wanna help?"

Even though they'd been living out here together all this time, she still couldn't tell when he was teasing. "No, thanks."

By the time he returned from his collecting, she'd gotten dressed and was feeding Socks. Cliff put a pailful of frogs on the sideboard. They slithered up and over each other, trying to crawl out. Cliff was just trying to scare her, but she showed him. She picked one up and petted its bumpy back, slimy as a wet cucumber.

Do it! Do it! Do it! the frog croaked.

Sally Sue glanced at Cliff, fearful he'd heard the frog's message too, but he just had that silly grin on his face that he sometimes got and placed a china plate atop the bucket.

"Wait for them to suffocate, then cook 'em up good and greasy." He licked his lips and went out to do his chores.

She picked up the plate and peeked in again at the hopping little monsters.

Do it! Do it! they teased.

"Oh, be quiet!" Sally Sue hollered at the frogs. Then she clasped her hand over her mouth and put the plate back on the pail.

Cliff came running in. "You okay?"

She looked up innocently. "What?"

"I thought I heard you call."

"Not me."

"Okay, darlin'. Let me know if you need anything." He left her alone again.

Cliff did show his sweet side sometimes, but at any moment he could snap, and there was no telling what he would do then.

Do it! Do it!

Maybe she should. She wished she had some of that potion she'd seen on the tinker man's wagon. Some berries could heal, and others could kill. Some of the killing kind would probably be growing on the hill nearby come spring, and by summer they'd ripen. She could test a tiny bite of each until she discovered which one was potent. No, that wouldn't work—she might taste one that could kill a person with one lick.

The frogs had grown silent. She pulled off the plate and peeked inside. One frog squirmed slowly, but the rest seemed dead.

Out front in the larder, she got the butter and scooped some into the iron skillet on the stove. While collecting flour and cornstarch, she spotted the bottle of white powder Cliff used to kill mice.

She checked to make sure he wasn't coming, reached for the bottle, shook her head, changed her mind. It probably wouldn't work on a big man anyway.

As the butter melted in the skillet, she stirred in flour and cornstarch and held the spoon aloft.

Do it! Do it! her mind sang. She'd need to be careful. Quickly, she grabbed the powder and laced a trace amount into the batter. If she wasn't careful, Cliff might taste the bitterness and grow suspicious. What if he didn't die and realized what she'd done? Would it be better to stir in more, in hopes he'd die right away? She sprinkled additional powder into the mixture.

Her squeamish stomach roiled as she picked up a dead frog with her fingers, rolled it in the batter, tossed it into another skillet, and fried the corpse to a crispy texture. Cliff might die right there at the kitchen table, keel over onto the new wooden floor planks, or stumble out to upchuck and fall down dead on the dusty ground. Would he call her to help him?

But soon she'd be free, and with this break in the weather, she could take off right away. No way did she have the strength to dig a hole, move him, and give him a good Christian burial.

Would she go to hell? Thou shalt not kill. Was breaking that commandment ever justified? After all, he was wanted dead or alive. Either way, she'd never try to collect the reward; they might suspect she'd killed him.

Cliff poked his head in the door. "What's taking you so darn long? I'm a hungry man, woman."

"I had to wait until they conked out." She smiled at him innocently. "It'll be ready soon."

"I'll be back in a few minutes. Smells good." The blue of his eyes brightened to match the color of the day's sky.

Would he really harm her? She finished cooking, opened the door to call him in, and watched his strong and graceful body as he twirled a lasso in graceful circles around his feet, then over his head, singing at the top of his lungs, "Oh, my daaarlin' Clementine."

No, she couldn't justify killing him. Who was she kidding? She couldn't even kill a mouse. She sighed, tossed the entire concoction into an empty jar, and began the process over again, this time without the powder.

That night, in the twilight, frogs sang her a lullaby to sleep. She hoped she'd made the right decision, and might as well give in and accept the fact that she'd be here for a very long time.

33

Early the next morning, mist seeped over the ranch, thick as an eider quilt. Socks curled up in Sally Sue's lap while she tried to write a poem. Cliff had been begging to hear one, and she needed to at least pretend she wrote. She picked up the pen, dipped it in ink, and carefully used her best cursive:

Snowed In

The ranch house sits in the valley
filled with blue-and-white dishes,
wooden antiques, and crackling fire.

Isn't a poem supposed to rhyme?

Someone rapped on the cabin door. She jumped up. Maybe it was Sheriff Mack. Cliff never knocked.

"Coming," she called, and held Socks in her arms. Sally Sue cracked open the door and peeked out. A scrawny fellow with a mangy mustache and beard stood on the porch. He stunk to high heaven, as if he hadn't had a bath in years. Gnats flew around his sideways hat. His beaded and fringed suede jacket matched his soiled pants.

He looked like a sinful man, tipped-up nose like a coyote. "Kin you spare a poor man somethin' to eat?" he asked. A mule and a sled filled with what appeared to be beaver furs stood behind him.

At least she had on the men's clothing. "Wait here. I'll see what I have." She closed the door, but he pushed it open and followed her inside.

"Yer purty. I ain't seen a gurl nigh on a year." The man grinned at her.

She put Socks on the bed, glanced at the door, and raised her voice so Cliff might hear: "Smells like you haven't seen a bath in that long, either, you scallywag!"

"But I've been up in them peaks," he whined, and kept walking toward her.

Heart pounding, she kept backing up. "Don't they have streams up there?"

"Aren't you the alley cat?" The man lunged toward her with a high-pitched titter.

She reached out and slapped him. "Stay away."

Tears in his eyes, he put a hand to his cheek. "Why'd you go and do that?"

She tried to keep her hands from shaking as she pulled out a chair. "You set while I make you some fixins. In the meantime, here's an apple." She picked a rotten one from the horse stash, handed it to the man, and put the stationery and ink on the mantel.

He pulled out a knife, cut up the apple, and chowed it down quickly. "Mmm. Tasty." He growled like a wolf, leered at her. What was he going to do?

He rose, scurried around the table, and grasped her wrists with sweaty fingers that wiggled like snakes.

She pulled away with a roiling grimace, grabbed the gun from the hearth, and aimed it at his chest. "Git out." she hollered.

"You ain't the shootin' kind," he snickered, with a toothy grin.

"Wanna try me?" she asked. "I've never shot a man before but have always wanted to." She cocked the gun.

He winced, backed up toward the door, and opened it.

"Thanks for the apple," he said, hurrying down the porch steps and out to his mule.

Sally Sue followed and pulled the trigger, and, to her shock, a bullet whizzed out over the man's head. She was sure Cliff had said the gun wasn't loaded. The mountain man yelped and hightailed on his mule up to the hills.

"Don't you ever come back!" she yelled.

Cliff came running from the barn in his long johns. "What in the Sam Hill blazes . . ." He followed Sally Sue's gaze as the man continued on the path off the ranch.

"You told me it wasn't loaded." She'd liked the power of shooting a gun.

"Just a white lie. I wasn't sure what you would do with it."

"Are you cockeyed? I could've killed him. Besides, I'm no scaredy-cat," she said, even though she was still shaking in her boots.

Cliff put his hand on her shoulder. "Did he hurt you?"

"No, but he's gonna be hurting soon."

"Why?"

"I gave him one of those rotten apples."

"You're as wise as an owl."

"Thank you for the compliment. Now, put your clothes on and teach me how to actually shoot before I really kill somebody."

He paused and walked with her to the cabin and looked around inside. "Not today. I've got something else I wanna do."

"So, you'll teach me?" She couldn't believe it.

"I suppose I might." He picked up the crib from the corner and carried it toward the door.

"Where're you going with that?" Sally Sue asked.

"You'll see."

"But I use it to dry laundry."

"You're wise—figure out something else."

Her chest prickled; she was sorry to see the crib go. It had reminded her to have hope that she'd escape and have a child of her own to put in one someday. They were foolish desires, but she couldn't help herself.

As she began to sew the curtains again, a loud sawing exploded from the barn.

What was he up to? For an hour she tried to ignore the noise, but eventually she tiptoed out and peeked through the slats.

"Go away, or I'll tar and feather you!" he hollered.

She skittered back to the cabin. What in the world was he making?

Around noon, he came in for a bite to eat.

"What're you making?" Sally Sue asked.

"A surprise." He raised an eyebrow.

"What is it?"

"If I told you, it wouldn't be a surprise."

He finished eating and returned to the barn. Soon a pounding racket ensued.

As the sun set and she was fixing supper, Cliff carried in under his arm an odd-looking leather-and-wood folded contraption and placed it near the corner where the crib had been. He set blankets and a small satchel atop it.

"What's going on here?" she asked.

He took out a hammer and a small mirror and nailed the mirror above the washbasin.

"A blizzard's coming." He eyed her and sat at the table.

She served up supper and sat across from him. "But it's warmed up considerably. I thought spring was on the way." They'd even let the fire die out. There hadn't been a cloud in the sky all day. "What makes you say that?"

"My right knee tells me."

"Tells you what?" This man didn't make any sense.

"Aren't you listening? It's gonna snow."

"But winter has passed."

"I know, but my knee aches when a snowstorm is on its way."

They ate supper quietly. Her mind awhirl, she hoped he was joking about the storm. She'd thought the worst weather was behind them and that her escape was closer.

After supper he stoked the fire and lit his pipe. She sat in the rocker with Socks in her lap and considered another poem.

"Going to read me one tonight?" He blew smoke from his pipe.

"How about you read me a psalm?" She handed him her Bible.

Soon his deep voice echoed in the cabin: "Make a joyful noise to the Lord . . ." He finished the verse, cracked the knee he complained of, walked to the corner, and opened the contraption. Beautifully fashioned from the repurposed crib railings, the contrivance resembled a giant slingshot, a sort of hammock laid out on crisscrossed beams. He sat on the cot and slid off his boots.

"What are you doing?" Her heart beat wildly in her chest.

"It's too cold for me to sleep in the barn anymore," he said.

"But you've slept in the barn all this time. What's different now?"

He peered at the door. "I've got my reasons."

"What are they?"

He eyed her, then looked down and unbuttoned his shirt. "I wanna make sure you're safe. That incident this morning really scared me. If anything happened to you, I'd never forgive myself."

She didn't know whether it was because of what he'd said or the sight of his bare, muscular chest, but she felt her face blush hot.

Except for his long john bottoms, he removed the rest of his clothes and folded them neatly on the floor beside the cot. "Nighty-night." He tossed two blankets, one at a time, over his body and closed his eyes.

After pulling off her own boots, Sally Sue scooped up Socks and got under the covers, fully dressed. She held the cat in her arms and petted her. Sally Sue had always been curious to see what a man's body looked like without clothes. It wasn't as bad as her mother had said.

With Cliff nearby, she felt protected from whatever might come flying through the door. It should have been easy to fall asleep, but the thought of him so close made her lower belly tingle in a strange way, and she shamefully imagined what it might feel like to have him lying next to her in the big bed, in the smooth sheets, touching her body.

34

Anne could do it. She'd show Priscilla and even Karl that she was capable of establishing a space in which all the little artists felt safe and could express themselves creatively. She read her affirmation card and returned it to her backpack. Then she taped the rules-and-consequences chart on the materials shelf.

Usually before the kids arrived, Anne set out everything on the tables, but today she had other plans. The students ran into the room and milled around. One of the twins pushed Penny. She yelped and ran to Anne.

"Teddy, stop." Anne kept her voice calm and was proud of herself for being able to finally tell the boys apart.

She put her arms around Penny and whispered in her ear, "I'm hoping this will stop, but I'll need your help. They're trying to get your attention. Ignore them as much as you can. Can you do that?"

Penny sniffed and found her seat next to Cindy.

"Where's all the art stuff?" Tommy asked.

"You'll see."

"Where's the music?"

"Later, Tommy." Anne clapped her hands, waiting for all to echo her rhythm and be seated.

She pointed at the chart and sang, "*Dat-da-da-daaaa*. We now have rules."

"What!" Tommy yelled.

Anne ignored him, put her hand on rule number one, and read, "Follow the rules. Everyone, repeat after me." She read it again: "Follow the rules."

Most of the students followed her cue.

"Let's practice. Fold your hands."

The students folded their hands.

"Stomp your feet." She allowed some noise to happen, then raised her hand and put the other on her lips.

They raised their hands and quieted down.

"Stand," she ordered.

The students stood.

"Sit."

The students all sat.

Anne pointed to the chart again. "Number two: Raise your hand before speaking or leaving your seat." She planned to loosen up on this one later, but for now she'd remain consistent.

Tommy's hand shot up.

"Yes?" Anne asked.

"May I get a drink?"

"Yes, you may."

On his way back from the drinking fountain, he crossed behind her and gave Penny a noogie. She closed her eyes tightly, folded her hands, and didn't react to him. Anne didn't say a word, either, but wrote his name on the whiteboard, which made Tommy smile.

She stared at him. "Rule number three: Keep your hands to yourself. And number four: Respect your classmates and your teacher. What are some examples of how you might do that?"

Penny raised her hand. "Say something nice to them."

"Yes, good. Look at your tablemate and give them a compliment."

After two minutes of chaotic noise, Anne raised her hand until all the students raised theirs, even the twins.

"Good. Here are the consequences: every time you don't follow a rule, I'll put your name on the board; each time you break a rule after that, you'll get a check mark by your name."

Across the table, the twins frowned.

"Here are the consequences." She put her hand on the chart and read, "First time is a warning. Second time is the sit-out zone." She pulled a chair to the back of the room and sat in it. "And I'll set the timer for five minutes."

She walked back to the tables. "Third time, I'll e-mail your parents."

"Our mom won't like that very much," Teddy said.

"That's the point. Did you raise your hand to speak?" Anne walked nonchalantly to the whiteboard and wrote his name under his brother's.

"Who's ready to follow the rules and do some art?" she asked with a smile.

They all raised their hands. She handed out paper and markers.

"Copy the chart neatly, and decorate it creatively. You'll take it home to share with your parents and bring it back, signed, next Saturday. If not, I'll e-mail them the plan."

Wide-eyed, the twins looked at each other and got started along with the group.

She took a jar from her backpack and held it up. "You're all following the rules so well right now, I'm putting a gem in this jar." She dropped in a green floral piece. "When it's full, we'll have a pizza party."

The students applauded, and she added another gem.

At the end of class, the students walked out nicely, carrying the rules.

Exhausted but smiling, she sat in the sit-out chair. She'd done it. It was going to be easy from now on.

Ten business days had passed since she and Fay had ordered the DNA kit, and it still hadn't arrived. Had it all been a scam? The clock was ticking. At this rate, it would be too late to have an abortion.

Anne examined the e-mail order receipt again and dialed the number. A frazzled-sounding woman answered, and Anne said, "I ordered a kit more than two weeks ago, but it never arrived. I can see that my payment went through." Anne gave her order number and address.

"Just a moment, please."

While Anne waited, a Brahms lullaby played in the background.

The woman had a voice that could cut steel. "Yes, we sent it out a week and a half ago."

"It never came."

"Perhaps it got lost in the mail?"

You think? Anne tried to keep her voice calm. "Please send another one right away. It's an emergency."

"We'll send it out tomorrow. Confirm the address again." Anne repeated it for the second time and hung up.

She checked her social media. It seemed like everyone she knew was having a baby. Chrissy in New York was having her third. Every other day, her friend Kristen posted another adorable shot of her "little man." Even Prince Harry and Meghan Markle had welcomed their first with a plethora of photos. If she had this baby, would she get in on the act too?

Two days later, Anne spied a cardboard envelope squished into her mailbox.

RETURN SERVICE REQUESTED was printed in huge block letters on the outside, along with a return address in Ohio.

Mrs. Landenheim came out of her apartment, holding the black kitten in her arms, and eyed the envelope surreptitiously.

Anne hid it behind her back and stroked the kitty behind the ears. "You are so adorable."

"How are you today, Anne?"

She didn't need this busybody asking questions. Also, she seemed to remember something on the lease about no dogs or children.

"Good. I'm in the middle of something. See you later." She ran up the stairs, sat on the daybed, and further inspected the envelope.

Baby-blue dots connected by lines, like in a high school science textbook, decorated the front and extended onto the back in a zigzaggy helix motif.

"Alexa, play Carlos Nakai." Anne needed some relaxing music to help calm her.

"Music by R. Carlos Nakai," Alexa said.

"Thank you," Anne said, as Native American flute music began to play.

With trembling hands, she opened the envelope, dumped the contents on the bed, and read the directions.

First, she'd have to fill out the form on each envelope and collect four DNA samples for each person tested. She counted out the swabs in their sealed wrappers. To gather samples, a person will rub swabs for thirty seconds from inside the person's cheeks. Put them in the prepaid return mailers and mail. She'd need to be careful because insufficient DNA collected may require recollection.

Sounded easy enough, except it didn't say anything about how to ask possible fathers for samples. She examined the materials again. There was only one prepaid return mail envelope. How could she have been so stupid to get into this predicament? she asked herself, for the fifty billionth time. She was in a pickle and craving them. Maybe she could just have the baby on her own and not even involve either one of them.

Fay was right; Anne needed to find out who the father was. The thought of seeing Barnaby made her skin crawl, so she resolved to contact Sergio and composed a text: *Hi Sergio. I'm pregnant and need a DNA sample from you because you might be the father.* That would be so cold. She erased it. It would be better to tell him face-to-face. Maybe she should wait until tomorrow. No, she had to get it over with.

She took a deep breath and FaceTimed him.

"Hi, Bigfoot. I'm on my way into a meeting. What's up?"

Seeing his handsome face always made her heart twirl. She felt light-headed and just couldn't tell him. "I just wanted to say hi."

"Want to come out next weekend? I'll get tickets to—"

"I'm way too busy."

"Sorry, I've gotta run. Love you. Call you later."

He'd said he loved her. She lay back on the daybed and remembered their last night together. No way could she tell him she'd slept with someone else and that she might not keep the baby. Now she needed to backtrack and go to plan B. She'd have to spill all to Barnaby and get a DNA sample.

She shuddered, imagining sharing custody with him, her baby crawling all over his filthy apartment. When she told him the situation, he might glom onto her and want to be involved. Judging from his living conditions, she suspected his financial support would be zilch, even though she'd never accept it anyway.

Did she even need to tell him? Maybe she could snag a DNA sample without his knowing. Maybe from his hairbrush? That wouldn't work. He was bald. His toothbrush? She'd have to get into his apartment somehow. Was getting a sample without permission even legal?

She scrolled down, found his old Facebook friend request, clicked it, and sent him a message: *Hey, Barn. How are you?*

He got back to her right away. *Who is this?*

That didn't bother her. After all, it had been two months.

Anne: *We met at Rhinestone Ruby's a few months ago.*

Barn: *Oh, yeah. Didn't recognize your art photo. You were the great dancer, LOL, in the green outfit.*

Anne: *Wanna get together?*

Barn: *Sure. How about Ruby's?*

That was the last place she wanted to go.

Anne: *Do you know Coffee Cup Café on Sutter?*

35

The next afternoon, Barnaby waved at her from a table in the middle of the café. "Annie, I'm over here."

She hated when anyone but family called her that.

"Want anything?" Anne mouthed to him and pointed at the barista.

Barnaby raised his cup and shook his head. He could have waited and offered to buy her something, or at least stand with her while they ordered together.

She got a mocha, wound her way through the crowded space, and sat down.

"Annie, you look g—" He pulled back the hand he'd put on her shoulder. "You look different in the light."

What was that supposed to mean? Mr. Wanna-be-Cowboy, not looking so handsome in the light either. "So do you."

Instead of a cowboy hat, he wore a stained Dallas baseball cap, and had grown a mangy goatee. "Where've you been? I was afraid it was a one-night stand." He laughed like a neighing horse.

She tried to laugh too—unsuccessfully. "I've been busy. And you?"

His bloodshot eyes moved to her getting-larger-by-the-minute pregnancy cleavage. "I haven't seen you at Ruby's lately."

She zipped her sweatshirt closed and felt for the swabs wrapped carefully in her pocket. "I know. How've you been?" she asked.

"Groovy. I've been liking your Instagram posts. Have you been seeing mine?" he asked.

She shook her head. Did he just say groovy?

"They're getting a lot of attention. My LPPs have gone up. The photo of me in my chaps got one twenty-five."

She had no idea what he was talking about. "What?"

"Likes per post."

"Oh." She licked the whipped cream off her mocha and took a sip. The warmth of the drink seemed to help settle her stomach.

"Yeah, I'm crushing it." He did an arm pump.

His eyes followed a girl of about twenty, wearing plenty of makeup and tight lululemon yoga pants, as she walked by and sat at a table next to them.

How could Anne ever have slept with this repugnant guy? And how could she tell him now that she might be carrying his child? Suddenly, she felt queasy. "Excuse me."

She ran to the restroom and threw up. She rinsed her mouth in the sink and stared at herself in the mirror. Her pale face accentuated raccoon-like dark circles under her eyes.

What now? Maybe she could tell him she'd found out she had an STD and needed a sample, just to be sure she hadn't given it to him. No, that was lame. It was always best to tell the truth, so she'd do just that.

When she came out of the restroom, Barnaby was chatting up the lululemon girl.

Anne wandered back to the table and sat down. "Sorry."

"You look horrible."

"I'm not feeling well. I think I'm coming down with something." She clutched a tissue from her backpack and blew her nose.

"I'd better go." He stood.

"I thought we might have a chat."

"Some other time. I'll message you."

"But . . ."

He turned and slunk out.

What a jerk. He hadn't even thrown away his cup. A teenage worker with a buzz cut and bad zits came by with a trash bag and reached for it.

Anne wiggled her hands over it. "Wait! I'm saving cups to use in art projects."

"Whatever." The boy shrugged and walked away.

With a fresh napkin, she carefully slipped Barnaby's cup into her backpack.

Later, at home, she put on surgical gloves she had for working with toxic art materials, ripped open the sealed paper covering the Q-tips, and extracted them. Hoping this would work, she ran the first one carefully along the coffee cup rim and placed it inside the sample envelope. She repeated the process three more times.

She closed her eyes and prayed: *Please, God, don't let him be the father.*

The tiny print at the bottom of the sample envelope was so small she could barely make it out, but it seemed to be some kind of disclaimer saying that she'd read, understood, and agreed to the terms and conditions. There wasn't a space to sign it, though—just some information to fill in. So she wouldn't be doing anything illegal, would she?

The form asked for first and last names, and birthday. She realized she didn't even know Barnaby's last name. She could probably find it on Facebook, but she didn't want to have his name on her baby's birth certificate anyway. She scribbled in "Barnaby Cowboy" and a birth date. "Alleged father" was one of the boxes to tick. *"Alleged"*—such an intense word. She checked it and the box for Caucasian, then slid the forms and samples inside the first-class return package and sealed it securely.

She called a Lyft and rushed to the post office before it closed.

Tomorrow she'd have the blood sample drawn and sent directly to the DNA company. If Barnaby was the father, her decision would be easier.

On pins and needles, she checked for online results several times a day. She worked at the museum on Wednesday and Saturday, did her yoga practice, and added more paint to the Southwest sky piece. Sometimes the best way to dispel her anxiety was to just lie on the daybed, play soft music, and rub her belly.

A week later, she still had no DNA results. Darn it!

She studied the sky piece sitting on the easel and felt the canvas needed something more. She gathered the pile of printed nature photos from her Southwest trip, sat at the kitchen table, and cut around the images—deer, boulders, ponderosa pine, oak, meadow. She carried the canvas to the table, laid it flat, and adhered the photos on top of the sky in a collage. Afterward, she washed her hands and took a nap.

When she got up, she logged back in to the paternity-testing site. Finally, there was a response. *We're sorry, but no DNA results were able to be determined from your recent sample.*

Oh my God! She had known it was a long shot, but she had hoped upon hope it would work.

Anne texted Fay: *SOS*

Fay called back right away. "What's up?"

"No DNA found on the cup. What do I do next?" Anne knew the answer but didn't want to hear it. She looked at the sky piece, wishing she were back in peaceful northern Arizona.

"Bloody hell. I'm sorry. You go to Barnaby again, or Sergio, and get a real sample."

"I guess I'll ask Sergio." They hadn't spoken in a few weeks. He'd sent her a few funny gifs and texted, but she'd been avoiding a full conversation. Was there a way she could tell him without revealing the whole truth?

She hung up the phone, picked up her journal, and started writing:

How have you been feeling? I've got the Ebola virus. You know how contagious it is. You should get tested too. I have the chicken flu, rotgut, scurvy, the heebie-jeebies.

Maybe she could send him an anonymous letter, as if it were from the DNA company.

Dear Sir:
Due to unforeseen circumstances, a sample of your DNA is requested.

Anne crossed out "requested" and wrote:

Urgently needed. Read the directions below and submit back to us in the addressed envelope. Have a good day.

Nope—she crossed out that last sentence.

Best regards,
Dr. Daniel No-Nonsense Andrews, DNA

She was losing it. No way Sergio would send his DNA to some crank letter.

She swallowed and called him, trying to keep the panic out of her voice. "I have good news and bad news."

"What?"

"I'm pregnant."

He laughed. "You're kidding."

"No."

"I'm FaceTiming you."

"No, no, I'm not decent." She didn't want to see his face when she told him.

"I've seen you indecent before! Come on—this is too important."

She answered his call.

His blurry face came into view. "But it was only that one night."

"That's all it takes."

"But still." He raised his voice. His face showed disbelief.

She felt like he'd thrown a can of paint on her. "Don't worry. I'm thinking of having an abortion anyway."

He raised his voice even louder. "You can't make that decision. I'm part of this too!"

"That's where the bad news comes in." She brushed the hair out of her eyes.

"That's not the bad news?"

"No."

"What?"

There might have been a thousand things she could have said to smooth over the shock, but she couldn't think of any. She turned her face from the screen. "I need a DNA sample from you."

"What? Why?"

She turned back to the screen; she couldn't get any more words out and just stared at him.

"You've been with someone else." He looked like she'd slapped him.

"Are you saying you've never been with anyone else?" Anne asked.

"I'm not saying that . . ."

"Double standard?"

He winced. "It just drives me crazy to think of you with another man."

"How do you think it makes me feel to know you've been with someone else too?"

His voice softened. "I'm sorry. I'm just surprised. You must have been with him close to the time I was there. When are you due?"

"Mid-January."

"But I'm scheduled for a ski vacation in St. Moritz then."

"Boo-hoo. How shallow."

He hung his head. "Sorry."

"Will you take the test?"

"Of course. What do I need to do?"

"I'll have a kit mailed to you. All you do is scrape four Q-tips inside your cheek and send them back to the lab. I'll check the results online and let you know. I'm so sorry."

He smiled. "No, I'm sorry to have overreacted. You're the one going through this."

"Thanks." He was so sweet.

"I love you," he said.

"I love you too."

She ordered the kit to be sent to him. If it was his baby, she'd need to keep it.

Anne played the waiting game again. Sergio called every day, and she kept checking for the test results.

Finally, a week later, the fifth time she checked that day, she got a message from the DNA company. She paused and put her hand on her stomach. *God, please let this be Sergio's.* She inhaled and clicked the link.

36

Relief washed over Anne. Now she knew for sure she would keep the baby, but she needed to speak with Sergio before she made her final decision.

She FaceTimed him. "Ready?"

"No matter what, I'm behind you."

That was exactly what she'd longed to hear; she took a deep breath, let it out and read, "DNA results confirm Sergio Parmeggianno is the father."

He didn't even smile. "I know it wasn't planned, but we'll work it out." His voice was flat. "You can move to New York and live in the condo. I'll hire an au pair."

Anne had been afraid of this. Would he even propose again? She glanced at the engagement ring on the altar and then back at him. "Hold your horses."

"What? You aren't still thinking of having an abortion, are you? Don't I have prenatal paternal rights?"

"Of course you do. I just don't want to move to New York. I tried before, and it didn't work, remember?"

"How could I forget? But everything's different now, and we still love each other, don't we?"

Anne hoped the baby would have his dark brown eyes. "Of course. But just because you're the father doesn't mean I've changed my mind about New York, or even about whether we should get back together." She couldn't do that East Coast–West Coast back-and-forth thing again, especially with a baby.

"But I'll need to be part of your lives. A child needs a father." She'd never heard him whine before, and it wasn't pretty.

"You can. You have a right to, but I also have a right to stay here in San Francisco. Besides, if I moved there, you'd be gone most of the time for work, anyway."

"You can't raise a baby there alone."

"I won't be. I have a support system." She smiled—a confident front.

He squinted. "I'll come to town soon, and we'll talk it out further. Please consider moving here."

"Okay. I'll think about it."

"Please do. *Arrivederci*."

The call ended. What a mess. He might be right that it made more sense for her to move there.

She stepped through the kitchen door and out onto the deck. The fall sky was foggy and gray. Her residency started next week. She was excited about her project but had a lot of trepidation concerning Karl. Outside her Michigan bedroom window, the maple leaves had probably turned and started to drift toward the ground.

Time to break the news to her mom, but Anne didn't want to crush her heart like those fallen leaves. She'd be hurt Anne was having a baby without being married. In small-town Oscoda, rumors flew fast as wildfire, and Anne didn't want her mom to be embarrassed, either. It would be best to tell her with the whole family around for moral support.

Back inside Anne texted her cousin Pootie: *I've got news. Need favor, have Brian hook up a computer to Mom's TV so we can Skype all at once.*

Of course, Anne's phone rang right away. Pootie would try to get the news out of her. Knowing her, Anne figured Pootie might even guess the moment she heard Anne's voice, then blab it all around town.

Anne let it ring through, then checked Pootie's voice mail. "What's up, buttercup? Call me right away."

Anne ignored the message. After a few minutes, Pootie texted again:

Are you pregnant?

Anne lied: *No.*

Pootie: *Cancer.*

Anne: NO.

Pootie: *Really getting married this time?*

Anne: *No. Just set up the call, and I'll tell you all then.*

Pootie: *Tell me now.*

Anne: Just set it up for 6:30 your time.

Later that afternoon, she brushed her hair, put it up in a scrunchie, and added Avon lipstick. She set up her laptop, held her lucky key in her hand, and dialed the number.

On the plaid couch, Baby Brian perched on Pootie's lap. "Hi, Annie!" he squealed, and waved.

Anne waved back. He sure had grown since the last time she'd seen him, a few months earlier. Aunt Tootie sat beside Pootie, and Big Brian stood behind her in his heating-and-air-conditioning company's T-shirt.

"Mom, where are you? Move over so I can see you!" Anne yelled.

Her mom moved closer to Tootie. "Can you see me now? What's going on?"

It felt comforting to see her. She'd curled her hair and had put on full makeup. "Yes." Anne hesitated and put a hand on her stomach. "I'm having a baby."

The whole family clapped and hollered, including Baby Brian.

Her mom had the biggest smile she'd ever seen. "That's wonderful, dear. I didn't know you were back with Sergio. When're you getting married?"

"We're not. He's staying in New York."

"I don't understand. If you're broken up, how did . . ." Her mom paused. "Are you not getting along?"

"We're great friends"— Friends with benefits?—"and are in contact all the time. We'll probably coparent or something. Sorry to disappoint you again." Her mother had been so disheartened when Anne had left Michigan and never moved back.

Aunt Tootie hooted, "Don't fret. Your mother never tied the knot with your father, either."

"What?" Anne put her hand to her chest.

Her mom pouted at her not-quite-sister-in-law. "In my heart, we were married. The wedding was planned for when he returned from overseas. He just never came back was all." Her mom wept, and Tootie handed her a tissue.

"Why did you lie to me all this time?" Anne reached for a Kleenex too.

"Times were different then. A woman was disgraced if she had a baby out of wedlock, so I added the wedding band on my finger with the engagement ring your father had given me, and I never looked back."

"I'm the only other one in town who knew," Aunt Tootie said. "We pretended they'd had a quick ceremony before he left."

"I can't believe it." Anne felt her mouth gaping.

"Nowadays, plenty of women have babies without a husband. I raised you okay, didn't I?"

Anne wished she could reach through the screen and give her mother a big hug. "Yes, you did. You were—you are—the best mom ever."

"I always meant to tell you, but the moment just never seemed right."

"What about Sergio? Did you miss your chance to marry him?" Baby Brian wiggled on Pootie's lap, and she handed him over to Tootie.

"Not really. It's complicated." Anne didn't feel like explaining it all to them. They probably wouldn't understand, anyway.

"When are you due?" Tootie asked.

"Mid-January."

"I'll book a flight right away." Her mom smiled.

"You mean you'll come out here for the birth?"

"Of course I will!"

Anne felt relief for the second time that day. "Mom, that means the world to me. I know how you hate to travel."

"I won't miss the birth of my grandchild."

Tootie put an arm around her and asked Anne, "What do you plan to do? You can't raise a child out there all alone."

Anne didn't like the way everyone kept saying she was alone. "I'm not sure."

Her mom's eyes lit up. "Move home, and we'll all raise her together."

"I don't think so." Anne didn't want to move there any more than she wanted to move to New York.

"It'll be so much fun."

"Over and out." Anne said goodbye.

Small-town Michigan had been a great place to grow up and continued to be a good place to raise children. What if her mother's suggestion wasn't the worst idea after all?

The next afternoon, the buzzer rang. Anne spoke into the intercom. "Yes."

"UPS delivery."

She ran down the stairs, and the man handed her a big box addressed to Bigfoot. It reminded her of the time Sergio had sent her the Ferragamos right after they'd met. He could be so romantic. He must be feeling bad about his reaction. Going up the stairs, she gently pushed Thai out of the way and pictured stylish maternity clothes or sweet baby outfits.

In the apartment she pried the package open with scissors. Inside were three jars labeled *GIVE, SAVE, SPEND* in Sergio's all-caps writing. What the heck? She sifted through the box and at the bottom found a thin paperback book, *The Opposite of Spoiled: Raising Kids Who Are Grounded, Generous, and Smart About Money*. The cover had a photo of jars with labels like the ones he'd sent.

She tried not to cry. Was this some kind of joke? Was he alluding to the fact that she'd never been good with money?

She texted Sergio: *I got the package. Thank you. I think?*

Sergio: *The author is from the* New York Times. *It's based on research. The hottest new thing.*

Anne: *But the baby won't even be getting an allowance for years yet.*

Sergio: *I know, but it's never too early to start planning.*

Anne didn't reply. She tossed the book across the room, picked up one of the jars to smash in the sink, and paused. What a disaster it would be to clean up. She put the jar back in the box. Sergio didn't have a clue what she was dealing with here. She never wanted to see him again.

37

In the morning, sun streamed through the window, waking Sally Sue. She heard a rustling and quickly rolled over. Cliff, in dungarees and boots, stood shirtless in front of the looking glass. The cabin was warm, even though he hadn't lit a fire. The blankets and long johns were folded neatly on the cot.

His back muscles rippled as he dipped a bristle brush in the water bowl, twisted it in a mug, and swirled the lather on his cheeks in a figure-eight pattern up his sideburns and down his neck. Pursing his lips, he slid foam across his upper lip too. The scent of nutmeg, orange, and anise filled the air.

"Morning glory." He caught her watching him in the mirror.

"Morning." She sat up with a yawn, pulled the blankets up to her chin, and glanced at her clothes piled on the floor. Oh. She'd taken them off again in the night. She'd really need to cease that bad habit now.

Cliff's razor seemed sharp as he moved it across the foam; one false move, and it could kill him. She should have had the urge to jump out of bed and give it a try. Instead, she continued to admire his face as it reappeared, smooth and fresh, from under the froth.

"Gonna teach me to shoot today?" she asked.

"You're not very patient, are you?" He wiped his face with a cloth.

"Not really." Her ma could vouch for that. Always telling her it was unladylike to be in such a hurry. If only she could see Sally Sue now, bare in a bed, watching a shirtless man shave. She'd certainly say this was unladylike also.

"Please."

He set a cup and a plate on a tray, poured coffee into the cup and added sugar, and placed a fresh muffin on the plate. He carried the tray over and put it next to her on the bed.

How delightful. She wondered if husbands brought breakfast to their wives like this. She'd never seen her father do it, though.

"Okeydoke, Miss Smoky. Get dressed, and we'll see what we can do before the storm comes."

Outside the window, the sky was pristine blue.

She laughed. "Where're your big blizzard clouds?"

"Like I said, patience isn't your strong suit." He cracked a knee for effect, donned his shirt, grabbed the rifle, and trudged to the door. "Come on out when you're ready."

She munched down the muffin, gulped the coffee, threw on her men's clothes, brushed her teeth, ran to the privy, and hurried back to the front of the cabin. Cowboy hat on his head, Cliff circled the round pen, placing empty bottles on fence posts. The bright sun hurt her eyes, so she ran inside and got her bonnet, then joined him in the pen.

He handed her a rifle that was smaller than the one in the cabin. "This one'll be better for you."

This gun might not have been as big, but it sure felt heavy.

He picked up another one and demonstrated. "Put your right foot back, point your left toward the target, and extend the rifle straight in front of you and hold tightly. Balance the stock like this: Upturn your palm; use your fingers to create a V with your other hand. Seat the stock of your gun in the other hand, halfway between the barrel and the trigger."

Could it be any more complicated? She copied his stance and struggled to follow his directions, keeping her expression nonchalant to hide her frustration from him.

He tapped her hand. "Hold closer to the trigger guard so you don't strain your muscles."

That was easier.

"Pull into your shoulder pocket, drop your cheek to the rifle, let your head fall gently over the butt, and align your eye here. Breathe normally and fire after exhaling." With a loud blast, he hit a glass bottle and it broke into smithereens. The smell of gunpowder filled the air.

Her palms flew to her ears; she leaned over and felt as if she might faint. Memories of the other bandit's bloodcurdling scream, the bank guard dying, and the gun at her chest swirled in her mind.

Cliff knelt down, reached for her hand, and said softly, "Are you okay? I know it's loud." His kind eyes shone blue as the sky. "Now you try."

This couldn't be the same man as the murderer. He'd changed. Her heart beat wildly. She breathed again, stood erect, selected one of his rum bottles, and peered forward. "I can't see anything."

"Try shutting an eye."

She closed one. "That's better." Instead of nodding, she held her neck position. If she lost it, she'd never find it again.

"Inhale, let it out, pause, and pull the trigger."

She did as he said, the bullet flew into the sky above the bottles, and her arm jerked back. Ouch.

"Try it again."

She repeated the stance, aiming and shooting, but wasn't able to hit a target. "Darn it all."

"Don't worry—it takes time. Now, you've gotta shoot from every possible position."

"There's more?"

"Standing is the hardest. You've almost got that down. There's also kneeling, sitting, and lying down."

He showed her all those stances. She rolled around on the ground until her body got used to moving from position to position. He was right—practicing in a lower position made it much easier to keep her balance.

The sun directly overhead, he said, "Let's stop for the day."

"Not until I hit a target."

"Aren't you tired?"

"No, sir." She shook her head. "I'm not giving up until I've hit a bottle."

"I felt the same way on my first day shooting." He paused, with a far-off look in his eyes. "Now that you have the positions down, don't think about what you're doing—feel the inhale, pause, exhale, and shoot."

She pushed the bonnet back from her eyes, knelt down into position, and followed his suggestion. The first bullet grazed the railing, the second got stuck on a pole right above the mark, but the third shattered the bottle.

"Yahoo! You did it!" Cliff cried, grinning.

Sally Sue had never felt happier in her life.

"I see we didn't get that storm yet."

He glanced out the window. "Not yet, but it's coming. Want to shoot some more today?"

She could barely get out of bed, her body was aching so badly, but even so her fingers itched to get back out there. She practiced an hour or so not hitting a thing but took it easy the rest of the day.

That night after supper, to implement part two of her plan, she started in on Cliff. "Will you teach me to ride?"

He looked at her as if she was daft. "No."

"Why not? I promise I won't run away. What if you're out hunting, or whatever you do when you're gone, and another feral man or Indians come and I need to get away? Or there's a forest fire? Or you get sick and I need to get a doctor? Or—"

"Stop." He held up his hand. "I'll think about it."

After breakfast the next morning, he said, "Okay, girl. Let's do it."

"You mean you're gonna teach me to ride? You're just the most wonderful man in the whole world." Did she really just say that?

He grinned. "I think you're pretty wonderful too."

She blushed.

Even though Sally Sue's body was still a bit sore, her heart felt light when she stepped outside, in her men's clothes and sunbonnet, and Cliff led the pinto from the pasture to the round pen. She leaned on the fence railing.

Cliff whispered in the pinto's ear and let him loose. "Hey! Hey!" Cliff called, then chased the horse in a circle, gently slapping its flanks with a small crop.

Clouds blew in off the peaks and gathered overhead. With his strong body, he continued to urge the horse clockwise and counterclockwise around the pen. She hadn't believed he'd ever really teach her to ride, and now that it was going to happen, her hands began to shake. The pinto wasn't as big as other horses, but even so, he seemed like a giant to her. What if he didn't like her and bucked her off, or, worse yet, escaped from the pen and shot off like a bullet from her gun?

Clouds above Cliff parted, and a shimmering ray of sunlight hit his frame, magnifying his strong, graceful motions. He appeared to be wading through water, like Poseidon, ruler of the sea and horses. She should be ashamed of comparing him to a Greek god and reminded herself that, like Zeus, Cliff also could stir up fury at any time.

Cliff stopped, walked to his canteen on the post beside her, and took a swig. The pinto continued to jog around the pen.

"Do you think he has a name?" Sally Sue asked.

"Name? I don't know. Maybe he had one before."

"Shouldn't we give him one? Your horse also?"

"I don't see why not. How about Murgatroyd and Matilda?" Cliff wiped sweat from his brow with his kerchief and tied it back around his neck.

"How about Petey and Sweetie?"

"Too girlie. Let's name the red one Roan."

Sally Sue admired the white diamond design on the horse's head.

"Okay. And this fellow is Scout." She hoped this one would be able to scout his way off the ranch with her on his back. If only Cliff knew what she was thinking. "Can we get started now?"

"Sure." He got a saddle from the barn. Sally Sue followed him through the open gate, making sure to close it securely behind her. He harnessed Scout and saddled him up.

"First, pet him like this." Cliff stroked Scout's neck.

Sally Sue reached out to tickle Scout's nose, trying to keep her hands from shaking noticeably. He turned his head and snipped at her fingers. She jumped back.

"Horses see from the side, so stand there and keep your hand open. Try again, with a strong caress." Cliff showed her. "Good boy, Scout."

"Good boy." Sally Sue rubbed Scout's neck.

"Try his ears. Let him get to know you."

She stroked his ears.

"Hop up on the railing like this." Cliff demonstrated. "Lift your leg up here, like this, and you're on." Cliff slid onto Scout's back and sat erect, then slid off again.

That looked easy enough. Sally Sue climbed the railing, held on to a post, and lifted her right leg, but no matter how hard she tried, Scout slid away from her. "Darn it all."

"I guess you're kinda puny." Cliff grinned.

She tried not to let that remark get to her.

"Try this." He hopped on the fence again. "Put your belly here, and glide your leg over him like this."

She put her stomach on Scout, but he darted away, and Sally Sue flew off him to the other side and fell on her behind with a thump.

Obviously holding in a laugh, Cliff took her elbow and helped her up. "Darlin', you're gonna have some bruises tomorrow. Let's give it a go another day."

"I'm doing it today if it kills me." She paused and looked at him, but the meaning of those words was lost on him.

"You're as stubborn as a mare in heat."

"What?" she asked.

"Never mind."

She climbed the fence again and this time succeeded.

Cliff readjusted the stirrups to fit her feet, clucked his tongue, and walked Scout around the pen.

Heart racing, hunched over, Sally Sue hung on for dear life.

"Now, sit up straight and use your legs to hug his flanks."

She sat up and tried to keep her balance. "Like this?"

"You've got it." Cliff led them around the pen. "That's good. Now, firmly stroke his neck and say, 'Good boy.'"

Sally Sue reached out her hand and petted below Scout's mane. "Good boy."

The gait bumpy, she didn't like it much, but if she was ever going to get away, she'd better master this. She held her balance, listened to Cliff's advice, and kept at it.

"You're a natural. Tomorrow I'll teach you to lope, as long as the weather holds."

She climbed down off the railing with a laugh, even though the clouds above had darkened.

38

Cliff had been right. That evening, a cold mist blew in over the meadow. He led the horses to the barn and stocked the firewood. Shivering at bedtime, Sally Sue laid another blanket on the bed and curled up with Socks. A raucous rumbling, followed by flashes of bright light, woke her in the dark. Rain pummeled the tin roof like acorns, then turned to a quiet snow that drifted outside the window.

In the morning, she relaxed on the pillow and watched the snow with gratitude. It would give her sore body a chance to recover. She waited for Cliff's "I told you so," but it never came. He wasn't one to gloat.

He brought her flapjacks and a cup of coffee, and held up the rum bottle from the mantel. "Want some?"

"Isn't it a bit early for that?"

"Thought it might make you feel better is all."

"What do you mean?" she asked nonchalantly. "I'm fine."

"Suit yourself."

As soon as he went out to feed the horses, she hobbled to the mantel, grasped the rum, and poured some in her coffee. She might need to drink more of this in the future. She was determined to become an expert rider and hightail it out of there like that mountain man on his mule as soon as possible.

The blizzard took over the ranch for five days and made trudging to the outhouse and back almost impossible. "I promise this is the last storm of the year. Spring will be here before we know it," Cliff said. He'd go in and out to feed the horses and bring in more wood, then rush back to sit by the fire and smoke his pipe. They had begun to act like an old married couple. They bickered about his tracking in slush and whose turn it was to clean up the dishes or put another log on the fire. Even the smell of his pipe tobacco and the way he nagged her to read her poems annoyed her. Instead, she suggested they memorize some psalms and began reciting them to each other.

He put up the wooden rods he'd whittled, and they finally hung the curtains. "These are the downright best-looking ones I've ever seen," he said. As he began to close them, she told him not to—she liked to feel close to the weather and to see nature outside.

At night, primal murmurings echoed from the cot and crescendoed to a sharp pitch, then grew quiet. She imagined him beside her in the bed, where she could inhale his earthy scent, feel his rough hands on her body. When awake, Sally Sue fought those notions. She'd need to stay alert in case his mood shifted and he again became that man who'd held a gun to her chest. But in her dreams, which never lied, desires for him floated in and out of her mind like flickering flames, cool and then hot.

The dreams whispered to her, *Let go. Let go. You can trust him.*

Several days later, the storm subsided and gave way to a radiant sky. Sally Sue woke to birdsong and stepped outside. The smell of sage was in the air. Snow still graced the peaks, but at the ranch below it had melted, and her icy heart along with it. The pond thawed. The ducks were back. Soon she'd be able to ride again.

Cliff poked his head inside the cabin. "I'm off."

"Where're you going?" She followed him outside to Roan, tied up to a fence post.

"Just off." He tacked up his horse and climbed on.

"When're you coming back?" She sounded like her nagging mother.

"Stay close." He stared at her for a moment, then trotted away up the hill.

This was her chance. As soon as he was out of sight, she set to searching for the money again. She'd find it, mount Scout, and take the road out of here. She'd leave the horse in Flagstaff, hitch a ride on a train or a stagecoach, and finally go back home.

She searched in the privy and stomped under the big oak to feel for loose holes in the muddy ground. Even though it was forbidden, she climbed into the barn loft, pitchforked the hay, and looked in every nook and cranny, but to no avail. She couldn't go without any money.

As night fell, Socks in her arms, she stepped outside and watched for Roan to appear, fire red in the moonlight. Why hadn't Cliff returned before nightfall, as promised? Had he lied so she wouldn't try to venture away? Was he sleeping under the stars on the nearby ranch that Mack had mentioned was looking for hands? Or perhaps he'd slipped into town to whoop it up with the girl in that green corset. Sally Sue felt a twinge of silly jealousy. Or—her heart sped up—Mack had caught Cliff. He was locked up in jail and getting ready for the gallows. The poster had said DEAD OR ALIVE.

The full moon appeared, so near she wanted to reach up and touch it. A smattering of stars blinked around it. Eerie shadows began to cover the moon. The mesmerizing whiteness receded in a crescent of darkness that gradually increased until a red glow alight with fire covered the entire orb, the sky around it a canopy of midnight blue. Then, curve by curve, the moon slowly returned to its former white glow.

Her skin prickled and Socks's head popped up as a far-off coyote howled, a snarly, strangled cat sound ensued, and screams followed. Two months earlier, these sounds would have terrified Sally Sue, but now they intrigued her into thoughts of what might have happened. It was all nature's way.

She went back inside, got in bed, and tucked Socks beside her. This missing Cliff reminded her of when her father had left. She couldn't breathe and imagined never seeing him again. She thought of Cliff's teasing grin, the curve of his strong shoulders when he groomed the horses. Slowly, she had begun to get used to their life together: She no longer flinched when he came near, no longer expected his compliments to be mocking, relished their quiet evenings by the crackling fire as he whittled curtain rods or braided leather reins and she sewed or tatted, Socks sleeping on the floor between them.

She could barely sleep that night without his soft breathing coming from the cot.

The next day, he still hadn't returned. The weather had grown warm, and there wasn't a cloud in the sky. She hoped spring was finally on the way. As she walked onto the meadow, a bevy of quail whirred and scattered from the bushes, and flew away. A red-tailed hawk circled over the pond.

A hefty stag came down the hill. He halted and, although he was still far away, fixed his gaze on her and twitched his elliptical ears beside his six-point-antlered head. Behind him the boulders seemed to move, but as she watched, she saw that it was only more deer, a dozen or so. They traveled toward the pond, drank, and nibbled the grass.

Spellbound, she watched the two young bucks tangle antlers and push against each other in a tug-of-war. They pulled apart and with a crashing sound continued to spar. Mama Doe stared at Sally Sue, then rounded up her family and moved on.

She rushed back to the cabin, itching to write another poem:

Deer

I saw a dozen
this morning
as they crossed
the meadow
under the oaks
to browse on
green grass.

Pair of baby
bucks practiced
sparring, their
twiglike antlers
twisted together
back and forth
in a waltz.

Spotting me,
Mama Doe
froze, circled
her family,
led them away
with a high
hop up the hill.

She stopped, put down the pen. These words didn't rhyme, but she didn't care—that was just the way they came out.

Scout must be hungry. She climbed the loft, forked down hay, and brushed his hair until it shone. She struggled to get the bit into his mouth and had to use all her muscles to heft the saddle onto his back. She hopped on him and kept at it until she mastered mounting him and riding around the pen.

The next day, she gathered her courage and rode him out onto the meadow. She practiced shooting her gun. She rolled up the hooked rug, laid it on a fence railing, and beat it clean. Opening the trunk, she pulled out the green satin. She thought about the saloon girl's outfit and began to dream about what she could make with the fabric and how it would feel on her skin. She wrote poetry and ate leftovers for supper. By nightfall, Cliff still hadn't returned.

He didn't return and didn't return. Determined to shoot as well as Annie Oakley, she practiced for hours, breaking many bottles. She rode daily until her body merged with Scout's rhythms while he trotted, loped, and galloped. After the fifth day, she could have easily kept going, but didn't. She had to wait to make sure Cliff returned safely.

Nights were lonely and dark. It was now too warm to make a fire, so she lit the lantern and wrote more poems.

One night she took out the green fabric again, held it up to her body, and considered her options in the mirror. There wasn't nearly enough to make a dress or a top and skirt. Instead, she devised a design that just might suffice, cut the material, and started sewing a sort of frock.

She had another poem dashing through her head but had run out of stationery. She grabbed her Bible and turned to the 23rd Psalm—her favorite. She dipped her pen in ink, and from her heart to her hand, words spilled onto the Bible's margin.

Where are you?

Sunset blushes
mountainside
deep pink.
Where are you?

Stars dot dark
velvet sky,
silver sliver
moon rocks like
an empty cradle.
Where are you?

Crickets sing to
welcome night,
owl calls echo,
a coyote wails,
loneliness hovers.

Free to finally go,
but do I want to, though?

39

After Labor Day three weeks later, the first day of residency arrived. Now that Anne was in her second trimester, her belly bulged, but, fortunately, the nausea had passed. To greet museum guests, she should dress more professionally. She opened the closet door and smiled. Maybe she should let out the back strings on the corset and wear that. She donned soon-to-be-too-tight pants and a tentlike top. She folded an old blue dress shirt of Sergio's she'd brought back from New York into her backpack, brushed her hair, and pulled it back with a headband.

Her phone pinged with a text from him—*Bigfoot, good luck today!* —along with a gif of a cool Obama in sunglasses that said, *You got this!* He really knew how to make her smile.

Since the finance-jar incident, he'd checked in daily and sent presents that totally made up for that denigration—sweet gifts like a *100,000 Baby Names* book, a rattle charm for her bracelet, and fuzzy slippers that she loved. Her favorite, though, was the miniature fedora just like Sergio's own. The card had said, *Because it's gonna be a boy.*

Even though they weren't back together, she was lucky her baby would have such a thoughtful father. She didn't argue with him, even though she was certain it was a girl. The eighteen-week sonogram appointment wasn't for another three weeks, and Anne couldn't wait to confirm her sex.

With a sigh, she reread the e-mail Priscilla had sent over the night before: *Shared Residency Guidelines from Dr. Priscilla Preston*. Oh, for Pete's sake.

1. *Anne will be on the right side and Karl on the left.*
2. *Arrive thirty minutes before museum opens.*
3. *Assist each other as needed.*
4. *Materials are to be kept in an orderly fashion.*

That last one was such a dig. Why was Priscilla so horrible to her? Even though at first the discipline plan had been hard to establish, the Saturday group was humming along nicely. Even the twins were behaving. Plus the kiddos seemed happy, and their skills were improving. As much joy as their progress brought Anne, nothing seemed to impress Priscilla.

Just the other day, she'd come in to observe, clipboard in hand and scowl on her face. Spa music was playing. All students were on task, adorning cigar boxes. Anne called them "gawdy boxes" because every inch was extravagantly covered with found objects. The kids and even their parents said this was one of the best projects ever. Still, Priscilla left a note saying the room was a messy disgrace. Hello lady, that was how creativity was done. Clearly, Priscilla had never created anything of substance in her life.

Anne put on her wingtips, tossed on a sweater, picked up her backpack, and ran down the stairs. She certainly couldn't be late today. She hoped all would go well. At least the fall sky was clear.

She hiked down California Street with her hands on her stomach. She needed to make a firm plan for the future. Come mid-January, her responsibilities would shift. She could barely take care of herself, and the thought of taking care of a baby, too, overwhelmed her.

She didn't know how much longer she'd be able to hide her

pregnancy from the museum staff. Firing her or taking away the residency was probably illegal, but even so, Priscilla would look for any excuse to disparage her.

And how would she ever pay for day care? If she moved to New York, Sergio would take care of them. And if she moved home to Michigan, her family would help. Neither of these options appealed to her. But her apartment was so small. Maybe she should let Sergio buy a San Francisco condo where they could all live. But they weren't together anymore.

Their chemistry made it impossible for her to resist him, and if he started seeing someone else in front of her, she would be devastated. Worse yet, she couldn't imagine what it would be like to have him in the next bedroom, doing it with another woman while she and the baby were trying to sleep.

And what kind of mother would she be? Her mom had loved her unconditionally. But would Anne have that kind of devotion and patience? Plus, she'd need to make more money. Her Gallery Noir sales were inconsistent. Maybe she should get a second job. But if she worked more hours, when would she have time to be with the baby?

She didn't want to go back to valet parking or gallery sitting. Maybe after she completed the residency, she could add on another class at the museum. Maybe observers during the residency would like what she was doing and would want to sign up themselves or their children for more classes with her.

But without Priscilla's blessing, that wasn't going to happen.

Perhaps Anne should double down and create more pieces to sell. She could find another gallery, but far enough away not to compete with the Noir. If she started an online account, she'd need to manage the site and wrap and ship purchases. Many of her pieces with found objects and trays were fragile and heavy and would cost a fortune to mail. One artist she'd known sold a lot of work on Etsy but didn't make a profit because of all the costs involved.

So many maybes. How was Anne going to manage it all?

Even though she arrived at the museum in the nick of time, Karl wasn't there yet. What a relief. She could get her bearings before she had to deal with him.

"Ready, Freddy?" She patted the life-size concrete buck she'd bought on sale at a nursery for twenty-five dollars. When she'd told them what she was going to do with the deer, they had even agreed to deliver it to the museum for free. Still, it hadn't been easy. It had taken three men with a dolly to get it here. At least the studio was on the ground floor.

Anne put on Sergio's discarded shirt as an artist smock and rolled up the sleeves. She hoped it would bring her luck and scanned the space, five times bigger than her whole apartment. It would still have been a dream to have even half this much space in which to do her art. She lit a gardenia votive candle, played Enya on her phone, and connected it to the Bluetooth speaker Sergio had recently sent her.

"Hello." Scruffy in a knit hat, plaid shirt, and unshaven face, Karl rolled in a giant log on a dolly. "Can you help unload this sucker?" The log was as tall as he was.

She wasn't supposed to lift anything heavy.

"Of course." Since she didn't want the museum to find out she was pregnant, she needed to follow Priscilla's rules and get along with him no matter what. She trudged over, bent her knees and helped him move the log into a metal trash barrel.

"I'll be right back." Without even saying thanks, he rolled the dolly out of the studio.

She lined up her art materials on a shelf: chipped plates, old tiles, rags, cutting board, paper bags, hammers. On the floor she put a big bucket, thinset, and a mixing drill.

Karl returned with a chain saw. A frickin' chain saw! Then he turned on some awful rap full blast on his phone that drowned out Enya.

Anne walked over to his side of the room and pantomimed turning it down, but he shrugged. She returned to her side, opened a paper bag on her cutting board, put a plate inside and broke it with a hammer, and emptied the shards into a box on the counter. She put a tile into the bag and broke it. She put another plate into the bag and broke it.

Karl turned up his music even louder, causing a horrible tinny sound. He donned goggles, plugged in the chain saw, and revved it up. Sparks flew as he cut into the wood, the noise as loud as a helicopter. Sawdust flew across the room into Anne's hair and sifted into her materials. Dear God, how was this whole arrangement going to work?

Priscilla teetered in on high heels, wearing a leopard-print miniskirt. Her hair had been cut in a punk rock style and was dyed platinum blonde. What a ridiculous transformation. She stared at Karl with a gaga look on her face. What was going on with these two? Did Priscilla have a crush on him or something?

A docent escorted in a group of gallery guests. Priscilla didn't even notice that they put their hands over their ears and ran out. The cacophony battered Anne's brain. *I will get along with him. I will get along with him.* She put her earbuds in, connected them to her phone, and tried to put it in her back pocket, but it wouldn't go in, so she slid it into a shirt pocket. She turned on some Indian flute music and bashed plates in bags.

She poured thinset into the bucket and poured water on top. She needed to plug in the mixing drill, so she crossed the space where Karl was manhandling the chain saw and motioned that she needed to access the outlet. He ignored her, so she pulled the chain saw cord from its socket and the saw lost power.

He turned off his music and yelled, "What happened?"

Priscilla's heels clicked on the floor as she walked toward them.

"My project is pretty cool, isn't it?" Karl asked her.

"Oh, yes." She shot him a big smile. "It's the bomb."

It certainly was as loud as one. Was Priscilla deaf?

"Obviously, sharing the studio isn't going to work." Anne kept her voice calm.

"What do you suggest?" Priscilla twirled a pen.

Anne looked out the sliding glass doors. "How about if he works out on the patio?"

"How about if you work out there?" Karl sneered at her.

"That's a good idea. Anne, move your things outside, and we'll send guests to you."

You kidding me? She glared at Karl, stared aghast at Priscilla, and set her eyes on the concrete stag. How was she supposed to move such a heavy object outside on her own?

40

Three weeks later, Anne lay down on the examination table, curled onto her side, and fell asleep. The door opening woke her.

Lori stepped inside. “Hi, Anne. It’s good to see you. How’re you feeling?”

Anne sat up with a yawn. “Pretty good. I’m just so tired all the time.”

The midwife put a hand on Anne’s knee and looked at her with kind eyes. “That’s to be expected. Have you been taking your supplements?”

“Yes.”

“Any more nausea?” Lori wrote in the chart.

“Nope, thank God.”

“Have you had anything to drink in the last twelve hours?”

“Only vodka,” Anne joked.

“Very funny. Ready?”

“Yep.” Anne lay back down. Please be a girl.

“This will be cold.” Lori lifted Anne’s shirt and spread gooey gel on Anne’s stomach. “Now, this won’t hurt, but you might feel some pressure. Ready?”

Anne braced herself. Lori began to move the wand over the bump. It didn’t hurt, but it was cold.

Ba-bump, ba-bump, ba-bump. The heartbeat was loud and clear. There really was a baby in there. “Sounds like it’s playing the drum solo for the long version of ‘In-A-Gadda-Da-Vida.’”

"Haven't heard that one before." Lori laughed as she continued to move the wand and turned the screen so Anne could see it. "Congratulations. You have a big, healthy baby in there."

Such a surreal feeling to see in black and white something growing inside her, an actual human, sucking its thumb and wiggling, that she couldn't even sense. Anne had already loved her so much, but seeing the ultrasound intensified those feelings and she started to weep. "I'm sorry."

"Nothing to be sorry for." Lori handed her a tissue. "Most women cry seeing their baby for the first time."

Anne blew her nose and stared at the image. "What's the verdict? Is it a boy or a girl?"

"It appears to be a girl." Lori pointed at the screen.

A girl! Anne felt as if she were riding in a hot-air balloon up in a big blue sky. No, a pink sunset.

"It's a pretty clear view, but you never know for sure."

"Soon you'll start to feel her kick. I recommend you count the flutterings," Lori added. She gave Anne a pamphlet with information on how to do so. "Take care of yourself and the baby. Keep your stress to a minimum."

Lori printed a picture and handed it to Anne. "Check in at the desk as you leave to schedule your next appointment. Keep up the good work."

Once she was outside, Anne looked at the ultrasound photo and beamed. At home, she made a copy of it, a blurry image of the baby inside a cave, and sat at the kitchenette table. She ripped out magazine pages to make a collage for Sergio. She would surprise him with it when he came to visit next week.

Her phone buzzed.

"How was the appointment? Did you find out the baby's sex?"

Anne had planned to surprise her mom with a collage too, but she couldn't help herself. "It's a girl!"

"That's wonderful. I'm so happy." Her mom's voice broke.

"Me too." Anne reached for a tissue.

"Has she started to kick?"

"No."

"Really? Are you sure? By this point in my pregnancy, you were."

Suddenly terrified, Anne put her hand on her stomach. "I'm sure she will soon. The midwife said it won't be for a while."

"Have you thought more about moving here?" her mother asked.

Anne sighed. "Your house is a two-bedroom. There's not enough space."

"If you take down the art-making card table, you'll have plenty of room for the both of you."

"Where would I do my work, then?"

"I'll park on the street, and you can use the garage."

Her mom must not remember Anne had tried that before. With those concrete floors, it was too cold to work in there during winter, even with a space heater.

"I know we don't have a fancy museum in Oscoda, but you can teach at Crafts and Such on Main Street. I'll cut back on my Avon parties and help watch the baby for you."

The idea of being in that small house in that small town made Anne feel claustrophobic. "Mom, that would be such an imposition on you." Her mother loved those parties.

"Oh, no. I'd love to spend time with my grandbaby."

Anne finished the call and cut around a magazine photo of a baby girl with a Pebbles Flintstone hairstyle with a pink bow.

Her phone buzzed with a text from Dottie, her former best friend from college. *Annie, I miss you. Can we talk?*

Anne's heart sank. She never wanted to speak to Dottie again. She'd erased Dottie from her life a few years earlier, after she'd flown all the way to New York to celebrate Dottie's solo art show, only to discover that her friend had completely changed and treated Anne like muck. Ugly tattoos covered Dottie's body, she wore her hair in a Mohawk, and she lived in a filthy loft apartment. She'd even changed her name and insisted on being called Dorothea. She smoked weed and stayed out all night the night of her opening, even though she knew Anne was waiting for her at the loft.

Dottie texted again: *Please FaceTime me.*

Maybe she had cancer. What if she died and Anne saw it on Instagram and felt guilty for not replying? She dialed her. "Hi, Dorothea."

"It's Dottie again."

On Anne's screen, it looked like traces of the old Dottie had come back. Her hair had grown out and was cut in a simple bob, and her nose ring was gone. "Hello, Dottie."

"I'm so, so, so sorry for the way I treated you. Will you ever be able to forgive me?" Dottie began to cry.

"Are you okay?"

"I am now. I've missed you so. Things got out of control, and I ended up in the hospital."

"What?"

"I OD'd on heroin." Dottie reached for a tissue.

"Oh." Anne put her hand on her chest. She'd been afraid something horrible might happen to her friend. Maybe if she'd told Dottie her concerns when she'd been there, that wouldn't have happened, or perhaps she should have contacted Dottie's parents about doing an intervention.

"I could have died. My parents took me home and put me in rehab. They've forgiven my meanness. Will you?"

"Of course." Anne wished her friend was there so she could hold her.

"I love you." Dottie blew her a kiss, like they used to do in college.

"I love you too."

They both sniffled a bit; then Dottie asked, "What've you been up to?"

"I'm teaching at the Museum of Modern Art here."

Dottie raised her eyebrows. "I could never do that. Kids or adults?"

"Both."

"Are you still doing art? Do you have gallery representation?"

"Yes, Gallery Noir. I had a solo show there a while ago."

"I wish I'd been there." Dottie paused. "I miss you. Will you come visit soon? I'll pay your way."

Anne thought of all the times she'd been in New York with Sergio and tempted to call Dottie, but her feelings had been too hurt.

"This isn't the best time for me to travel." She raised her shirt and moved the phone to show Dottie her belly.

"What, what are you showing me?"

"I'm going to have a baby girl."

"You're preggers? Did you get married without me?"

"Not married."

"Who's the father?"

"Sergio. Remember him? I met him at your art show."

"I know him. Just saw him the other night."

"You did? Where?"

"At a gallery opening."

"Did you talk to him?" Anne asked.

"No, he was with some woman."

Anne felt a twinge in her chest. Ridiculous. She had no right to be angry or jealous.

"What did she look like?"

Dottie hesitated. "Gorgeous. She had a great body and short, dark hair. But not as gorgeous as you."

"Oh, yeah. I'm so gorgeous." Anne moved the phone to her stomach again.

"I'm sure she's just a friend. When are you due?"

"Mid-January."

"Are you moving home to your mom?"

"No!"

"How are you going to do it alone? Why don't I come help you take care of her? I've been thinking of moving anyway."

"You have? That would be fantastic." Anne wasn't sure that was such a good idea.

"Yes, we could be roomies again."

Maybe that was the answer to the day care conundrum. Dottie could move in and help with the baby. They could get an apartment together, just like old times.

41

Still working on the patio seven weeks into the residency, the longest seven weeks of her life, Anne patted the stag on the head. "Morning, Freddy. I hope you had a good night's rest."

She lifted the tarps off her art supplies, but fog had seeped into everything. At first, she'd tried to carry the materials inside and out after each session, but it required too much energy. She had needed five staff members to help her carry Freddy out here.

Karl hadn't arrived yet. This was no surprise. Often he was late, and some days he didn't show up at all. At least she could get started in peace—or what passed as peace, given her location. Traffic whizzed by, and a helicopter flew overhead. She huddled in her oversize sweater and sweatpants and began mixing thinset. At least the weather would keep it moist, and there was a power source out here. So much for the stress-free life Lori had recommended.

The project wasn't as far along as she had thought it would be. No museum guests had found their way to the patio, let alone participated in the artmaking. On the two days it had stormed, she hadn't been able to work outside at all.

Her Saturday kiddos met her here for their class. She posted the rules and consequences and warned them that on the second consequence, they wouldn't get to participate in the project at all.

She had the students line up on the ground. The twins took turns breaking dishes and tiles in paper bags and dumped the shards into boxes. That kept them out of trouble. Penny, as her assistant, carried the boxes to each student as they picked a piece. One at a time, each child spread thinset with a spatula, like icing a cupcake, on their piece and adhered it to the dear deer.

She had the smaller kids place their pieces on Freddy's hooves and the taller ones, on the head. They did a pretty good job, but when they were finished, she sometimes had to take off one or two, lather them up again, and stick them back on to make sure they'd stay.

Alone now, she'd better do the underside while she still could get down on the concrete. She slithered as best she could under the deer, slathered thinset on a piece of broken tile, and stuck it underneath. She knew all spaces should be covered in a professional manner, even if they weren't visible. She'd saved the six-point antlers for last. It would be tedious work because they'd need such small pieces.

The music cranked up from inside, and the chain saw too. Darn it all. She hadn't closed the sliding door. She put on a few more pieces, until she couldn't take it anymore and rolled out from under the deer. Getting up off the ground was hard, so she crawled to the door, reached up, closed it, and returned to the deer.

A few minutes later, the door opened.

"Anne, what are you doing out here?" Mr. Willingsby bent down to see her.

She scooted out and tried to stand.

"Here, let me help you." He reached for her.

She put out her right hand, covered in thinset, gave him her left hand, and let him guide her up.

"It's too noisy in there, and sawdust gets stuck in everything."

She gestured through the sliding glass door at Karl going at it inside.

"Wouldn't it make more sense for him to be the one outside?"

She shrugged and resisted the urge to complain. In the glass door, her frizzy hair resembled a tumbleweed and she wished she had on something more presentable, but none of her clothes were comfortable anymore.

"I've been out of town. How long has this been going on?" Mr. Willingsby asked.

"Seven weeks, since the start."

He sighed. "Let me see what you're working on."

"This is Freddy." She patted the stag's head.

Mr. Willingsby imitated her enthusiastically. "Hi, Freddy. I suppose you're named after Fredricka."

"Oh, no. I didn't even make that connection. I hope she's not offended. She came by the other day, but she didn't say anything."

"It's perfect. I'm sure she's flattered."

"Do you want to put some tesserae on him?" Anne asked.

"What?"

"Tesserae are pieces of a mosaic. It's one of our young-artist vocabulary words."

"Sure." He took the box of shards she handed him.

"Pick one."

He chose a blue-and-white one. Anne buttered it with thinset, and he stuck it to Freddy's back.

"That sure felt good." He put on a few more pieces.

She gave him a Handi Wipe. He cleaned his hands and glanced again at Karl working in the studio.

"You're doing a great job, considering the circumstances." Mr. Willingsby shook his head and left.

A week later, Karl began being nicer to her. He made sure the patio door was closed before he revved up his chain saw, and he kept the music lower. One afternoon when rain was predicted, he even helped her tarp the deer and her art supplies. He hadn't said anything, but maybe he'd noticed her baby bump and realized she was pregnant.

A week later, he had skipped several days of work in a row. Not that Anne had missed his noisy presence, but she did start to worry. It was time to inform Priscilla about the baby anyway, so Anne wandered down to her office.

How odd. Mr. Willingsby sat at Priscilla's desk, studying the computer. The printer churned out pages.

Anne knocked on the doorjamb. "Where's Priscilla?"

Mr. Willingsby looked up at Anne and waved her in. "Take a seat."

She slid into a chair.

"Priscilla has taken a leave of absence."

"Is she sick?"

"I don't think so."

"Is Karl okay? He hasn't been in for a few days."

"I know." Mr. Willingsby put his fingers in a triangle under his chin.

Anne waited for him to go on.

"Is he sick?"

"No."

"Did he take a vacation?"

"Not really." Mr. Willingsby shook his head.

She didn't want to sound nosy but couldn't help herself. "Where is he, then?"

"It's a personnel matter that I can't discuss." Mr. Willingsby's eyes returned to the computer screen.

Anne sat back in the chair and stared at him.

"Anything else?" he asked.

"When will he return?"

"Let's just say you can move into the studio space now."

"Whoa!" She resisted the urge to do a fist pump. "Thank you."

"I'm sorry you've had to work outside all this time."

"It's been rough."

"For the time being, you'll report directly to me."

"I'm pregnant," Anne blurted out.

"I know." He raised his eyebrows.

"You do?"

"Yes. I've known since the first day I met you at the interview."

"Don't worry—the residency will be over before the baby comes."

"I'm not worried." He had such a kind smile. "Let me know if you need help moving your things inside."

"Thanks."

Anne grabbed her backpack, hurried outside, and dialed Fay. "Oh my God. Something crazy is going on at the museum."

"What?"

Anne relayed to Fay her conversation with Mr. Willingsby.

"Blimey."

"You haven't heard anything?" Anne asked.

"Not yet. You know me, though—I'll ask around and get the scoop."

"I have no doubt." Anne couldn't wait to find out what was happening.

42

"Darn it all." She tried to pull on her favorite sweats, but she couldn't even get them up over her belly. A shift with a baggy sweater over it would have to do.

Neither her sneakers nor her wingtips would go on over her swollen feet, either. They were bigger and uglier than ever. No way could she even get into her silver shoes. When Sergio saw her engorged feet, he'd really tease her about them. She decided to just get it over with, so she texted him a photo. She slid on flip-flops and studied her ensemble, if you could call it that, in the mirror. At least as an artist she could get away with dressing funkily for work, but this was absurd.

On her computer, she scrolled in search of maternity clothes. There were so many cute styles. The boho floral top was to die for; she clicked through. Yowza—$300. She could probably wear it even after the baby was born. No, no. She needed to conserve her finances now more than ever.

After work, even if she didn't have much energy, she had to go thrifting. It would be a challenge to shop without being lured into buying a found object. Since she'd decided to keep the baby, she'd promised not to buy any more art materials. She needed to make way for her daughter in her life, physically and financially, and anything else for the museum, she had to pay for out of her own pocket.

She climbed onto her daybed, picked up her journal, and composed an affirmation: *I will not buy any more found objects.*

She crossed it out. She needed to write it in a positive way, without the word "not." She tried again: *I will choose not to pick up . . .*

No. She crossed that out also.

I will keep my hands off found objects while in the thrift shop.

She rewrote it on an index card, slipped it into her backpack, and raced off to work.

She still hadn't heard anything about what had happened to Priscilla and Karl. At this point, she didn't care, because having the entire studio to produce in had been heavenly. Museum guests had been coming in and having fun adding pieces to Freddy, and he was getting covered all over.

By the time work was over, her back and swollen feet hurt. She ordered a Lyft, removed her affirmation card, and read it silently, over and over.

I will keep my hands off found objects while in the thrift shop.

The Lyft dropped her off in front of her favorite thrift shop, Rescued Relics. Anne stepped inside and paused to get her bearings. Even though she hadn't been there for ages, they still hadn't fixed the blinking fluorescent lights.

The shop was stuffed with toys, household goods, and clothes. It was the same store where she'd bought Sylvia's black velvet coat. Was that only five years ago?

How much Anne's life had changed since then. Her art career had taken off, she'd been to Europe, she'd even fallen in love for real, and she felt more confident about herself. And now she was having a baby.

The same clerk with the beehive hairdo sat behind the counter, working on an earring display and snapping her gum. "Hi, doll."

"Do you have maternity clothes?" Anne asked.

The clerk eyed her. "Not separated. Try women's large, or even the men's." She pointed toward the back of the shop.

Even though Anne wasn't going to get much, she grabbed a basket anyway and started down the aisle. She'd promised Sergio she wouldn't buy anything used for the baby, but that knit hat shaped like a daisy with the yellow sweater to match was adorable. Anne tossed them both in the basket. She'd wash them several times, and Sergio would never know the difference.

As she passed the knickknack shelf, she kept her eyes focused forward, repeating, *I will keep my hands off found objects.*

Her peripheral vision caught a ceramic cowgirl, but Anne walked right by. See, she could obey her affirmation.

In the back of the shop she flipped through the size XXL tops. An oriole orange one seemed big enough. She pulled it out and held it up to her in a mirror. The ghastly color clashed with her auburn hair. She laughed at a hideous black-and-white butterfly smock with pearls sewn on that reminded her of something Moira from the hilarious TV series *Schitt's Creek* would wear. A humongous black velour top caught Anne's eye. Black made you look smaller. She pulled off her sweater, took the velour from the hanger, and tried it on. She swam in it, but she'd be able to wear it for the rest of her pregnancy, and it would be cozy to do her art in forever.

In men's shirts, she picked out a few that would work for her: a chambray dress shirt, a Pendleton plaid, and even a floral Robert Graham, like the guy on *Modern Family* wore. The shirts were all plenty big. She could just roll up the sleeves. No need to try them on. She tossed them in the basket.

She saved the worst for last. Solid black would be best. She found a pair of sweatpants with an elastic drawstring. That would be convenient.

Pushing the basket past the knickknack shelf, she made it safely to the checkout counter and got in line behind three people ahead of her. Waiting her turn, she spun a hat rack display of scarves.

"Well, I'll be." She reached for a green feather boa, the exact color of the corset. She threw it around her neck. How serendipitous. Would she ever get to wear that outfit again? It would take forever to lose her baby weight.

The woman in front of her dumped coins from a paper bag onto the counter's glass top. The beehived clerk helped count them into stacks and plunked the woman's toaster into the sack.

A baggie of watches under the counter caught Anne's eye. The bag even had a red sale dot on it, which meant 50 percent off. She bent down to take a closer look. She loved to put watches in her mosaics. People didn't wear watches much anymore; they just checked their cell phones. Maybe used watches would be easier to come by.

"Would you like to take a look?" The clerk snapped her gum and slid the baggie onto the counter.

"Thirty dollars is a bit high." Anne leaned over and tried to see the watches.

The clerk opened it for her and dumped the watches on a tray. "Go ahead and pick out the ones you want. We'll make a deal."

"I'd better not." *I will keep my hands off found objects.*

"Come on. Choose at least one."

It wouldn't hurt just to look. Anne riffled through the tray—sports, white rhinestone, some with broken bands, some that appeared brand-new.

"No way." She picked up one with a yellow Tweety bird on the face and pink numbers. This was too perfect. She would wear it when she drove her Karmann Ghia.

"I'll take this one." Wishing she could have bought the whole kit and caboodle, she strapped the watch onto her wrist and piled the rest of her choices onto the counter.

When she arrived back at her apartment, Mrs. Landenheim

stepped into the foyer with the black-and-white kitty in her arms.

Anne hid the bag behind her and stroked the kitten's soft back. "You've sure grown since last time I saw you." She didn't want nosy Mrs. Landenheim going through her purchases. Since she wouldn't let Anne have a dog, she certainly wouldn't be happy about a baby living in the apartments.

Even though it was early evening, Mrs. Landenheim still had her curlers in. "Isn't Zorra the cutest thing you've ever seen?"

Sounded like a burlesque dancer. "Zorra?"

"It's feminine for Zorro."

"Clever."

Thai wound around Anne's ankles and mewed loudly.

"Okay, I'll give you some love too." Anne crouched carefully, almost tipped over, and patted the Siamese. Thai snarled and skittered away.

"Did you hear Val's moving?" Mrs. Landenheim asked.

"No. I'm sorry." Anne stood back up. She would miss his nightly warm-ups floating up to her from the apartment below before he left for his performance in *Beach Blanket Babylon.*

"Don't be. He got a part in a TV series."

"Really? Which one?"

"*Crazy Ex-Boyfriend.* He's playing the boyfriend."

Anne hoped someone else artsy would move in. Maybe Dottie could rent it if she really did come out. But housing costs had increased so much, only a techie could probably afford to live here now. Maybe Mrs. Landenheim would give Dottie a break on the rent.

"Ray Ray is taking me to Vegas for a few days soon."

"For an Elvis wedding?"

"Maybe." Mrs. Landenheim raised her eyebrows. "Would you feed the cats for me?"

"Sure." It would be good practice for a baby.

"You won't need to poop-scoop or anything. We'll only be gone two nights."

That was good, because Anne had heard somewhere that cat litter was unhealthy for pregnant women. She nodded.

"Really?" Mrs. Landenheim pushed open her door. "Come on in, and I'll show you what to do."

Having never been inside, Anne had always been curious, and followed her neighbor. The apartment smelled of cat. A forest of philodendrons hung from macramé baskets. The sofa and love seat were covered with plush purple and pink pillows. And on every flat surface were Siamese-cat ceramics that would be great in mosaics.

"Here's the kibble." Mrs. Landenheim opened a cupboard and filled two bowls. "You have to use separate bowls, or Thai goes nuts. Tap the water bowls too."

"What've you got in the bag? Let me see." Mrs. Landenheim held out her hand, fingers polished pearl pink.

Oh, well, I'll have to tell her sometime. Anne sighed, pulled out the velour top, and handed it to her landlady.

"It's a little big, isn't it?" Mrs. Landenheim had a confused look on her face.

"Not in my condition." Anne stared at her flip-flops. She didn't want to see Mrs. Landenheim's reaction.

"You're having a baby?" She put a hand on Anne's stomach. "That's sure gonna change things around here."

Anne wasn't sure what her landlady meant and didn't want to ask.

43

The next evening, all the way to the restaurant, Sergio tried to convince Anne of all the reasons she should move to New York: his place was bigger, better private schools, near Central Park.

Jam-packed Jardinière was filled with tony patrons. Even though Sergio had made a reservation, they still had to wait for a table in the noisy, boiling bar. Anne tugged off her black velvet coat. Underneath, her *Modern Family* shirt and black pants seemed to be okay, but she could only get her feet into the Uggs she'd bought in a size bigger than what she usually wore. Sergio was probably mortified, but he hadn't said anything.

After twenty minutes, they followed the hostess up the stairs to a lovely loft table overlooking the downstairs bar. Once they were seated, Anne told Sergio about the odd happenings at the museum. "Fay wouldn't say on the phone what she's found out. After you leave for the airport tomorrow, I'm meeting her for coffee so she can tell me all about it."

"Can't wait to hear. Why don't you come to New York and stay for a while?"

Anne blurted out, "Won't it be crowded with your gorgeous, dark-haired woman?" She'd promised not to say anything but couldn't hold it back.

"Who?"

"You know who I'm talking about. Dottie saw you with a girl at an art show, and she wouldn't make something like that up." Anne kept her voice calm, like she'd been practicing with the students.

"Probably Bella. She came for a visit."

"Your sister?"

"Yes. Short, dark hair."

"But she has long hair."

"She cut it."

Anne remembered another time Bella had visited Sergio. At first, she'd thought he had a new girlfriend.

"I'm sorry." She hung her head.

He took her hands in his. "*Cara mia*. There's no need. I'm sorry it's taken me so long to get out here to see you. Work has been crazy busy." He glanced down at her stomach for the twentieth time. "I'm sorry about the way I acted when you first told me about the baby."

"I know. You've said that before. All's forgiven."

"I'm *estatico* now."

Hearing him say he was happy about the baby made her feel like he'd spewed a mouthful of diamonds at her, or the twinkle lights strung across the restaurant's ceiling.

Anne paused, took the collage from the silver tote he'd sent her, and slid it across the table to him. "It's a girl."

"*Meraviglioso*."

"Isn't it *meravigliosa* if it's a girl?"

Sergio laughed. "Pink champagne's in order here." He glanced at the wine list and waved at the waiter. "Do you have the pink Veuve Clicquot?"

"I'll send over the sommelier."

The sommelier came by with a draped cloth over her arm. "What may I get you?"

"None for me, thanks."

"What's wrong?" Sergio asked.

"It's not good for the baby."

"But it's a special occasion. Pregnant women drink wine all the time in Italy."

"My midwife did say an occasional sip was fine."

"I'll get it right away." The sommelier left.

Sergio sat back with a smile. "What shall we name her? How about Patricia Parmeggianno? I like the alliteration."

She squinted. "I'm not sure." She hadn't told him yet she'd decided not to give the baby his last name. It would take forever for her to learn how to spell it. McFarland had been hard enough when she was young.

He took a roll from the basket, buttered it, and placed it on Anne's bread plate. "Madison?"

"That's a helicopter parent's name. I'm going to raise her to be an independent woman. If you want a city name, how about San Francisco or Nob Hill, near where she was conceived?"

They laughed loudly. The couple at the next table turned around and glared at them. The sommelier brought the ice bucket, popped the cork with a flourish, and poured champagne into each flute.

Sergio clinked his glass with Anne's. "To her."

They each took a sip. The bubbles popped in Anne's nose.

"How about Bella, after your sister?" Anne ate a roll.

Sergio studied the menu. "Maybe."

"How about Prudence, after my cousin Pootie, or Trudy, after Aunt Tootie?"

"Oh, sure." He kept studying the menu.

"Princess Genevieve Labrador?" Anne offered.

"We're naming a girl, not a dog."

Their waiter came over.

Sergio began, "We'll each have a gem salad. She'll have the halibut, and I'll have short ribs." He tilted down the menu. "Do you want oysters?"

"They're off-limits for pregnant women."

"Really?" He raised his eyebrows at her. "Chocolate panna cotta?"

She smiled seductively. A pregnant woman's libido was supposed to increase in the third trimester. She wasn't quite there yet, but still . . .

"Okay. Chocolate it is. That'll be all," he told the waiter. "How about a chef's name? Wolfgang?"

"Like you said, we're naming a girl. Julia?"

"Musicians: Beyoncé, Madonna, Fergie. Cher?" He drank more of the champagne.

Anne started singing, "Love child . . ." She thought about Cher's wild costumes. The Native American one was Anne's favorite.

"Would you like another glass?" Sergio reached for the bottle.

"I shouldn't." She picked up her water goblet and tilted it toward him. "To the baby."

"Hey, I've got it. Since we met in a gallery and you're an artist, how about an artist's name?"

Anne squinted, thinking. "Frida, Georgia, Cindy."

"Who's Cindy?"

"You know, Cindy Sherman. That cool photographer who dresses up in different personas and does self-portraits."

"Hmm."

"Let's noodle on it for a while." In her heart, Anne had a secret name that she wasn't ready to share yet.

Their salads arrived, and they both dug in.

"So, what's the plan?" Sergio asked.

"I'm going to work at the museum and do my art."

"Please come to New York, and let's be a family."

What a broken record. She wished that were possible. "We'll still be a family, but, as I've said, New York didn't work before."

He looked deeply into her eyes. "But now everything's changed."

"I'll consider it." He was probably right. A big condominium with a nanny was tempting. She still wasn't sure. She'd never thought she'd consider living in New York again. Plus, she didn't want to get her heart broken like before. For the baby's sake, though, she should probably give it a try. Even though she had grown up without a father, she'd always wished she'd had one.

He leaned toward her and took her hands again. "Let me make an honest woman of you."

"Are you saying I'm not honest?"

"Well? There was some confusion at the beginning of all this. But let's get married."

"What? When?" Here we go again.

"Now. Let's fly to Vegas. Tonight."

Oh, and maybe we'll run into Ray Ray and Mrs. Landenheim at the Elvis chapel. "Don't be ridiculous. Why so fast?"

"To get you settled. You need to decorate the nursery, hire a nanny."

"If I were to move, it wouldn't be until after the baby was born."

"How come?"

"I like my midwife, and Fay is going to be my coach."

He got a sad puppy-dog look on his face. "Don't you want me to be?"

"You don't even live here."

"I'll stay with you, and Fay can be backup if I'm traveling for work."

That wasn't a practical situation. "Remember when I cut my finger being your sous chef and you had to take me to urgent care?"

"That's a night I'll never forget."

She recalled how queasy he'd become at the sight of all that blood—he had practically fainted when the wound was being stitched.

"Okay. I'll think about all these options."

"*Magnifico.*" He paused. "How about Portia Parmeggianno?"

If they couldn't even agree on a name, how would they raise their daughter together?

44

After Sergio left for his flight the next morning, Anne tried to go back to sleep, but her stomach felt like it had fish swimming around in it. Could it have been all that rich food at dinner? She put her hand where she had experienced the movement and felt one again. She waited and felt another one. The baby was doing the bossa nova. She wished Sergio were still here with her.

Anne's phone buzzed. "Hi, Fay. I had the best time last night."

"That's good. So did I."

"You did?"

"Diana's here!"

"What?"

"Yes. I went into labor in the middle of the night."

"Is everything okay?"

"Yes. Don't worry."

"Why didn't you call me? I wanted to be there."

"I know. It was the middle of the night, though. You were having your reunion with Sergio, and I didn't want to interrupt. She's so beautiful."

"I can't wait to see her. I'm on my way."

"No, no! Please wait. They're releasing me soon. I'll call you when I get home."

The next day, George called and told her Mother and Baby were doing fine but needed some time to recuperate.

"Are you sure they're okay?"

"Yes. Fay will call you later."

"Send me photos."

Anne didn't make it over to Bay Breeze for another week.

"Blimey! Look at you!" Fay gave Anne a kiss as Anne bent down to see the baby.

"Yeah, look at Shamu. I can't believe I still have ten weeks to blow." Anne sat on the step stool in the kitchen.

"Here. I just finished feeding her." Fay passed Diana to Anne.

"What a cutie-patootie!" She ran her hand over the baby's peach-fuzz head and her adorable floral onesie.

"She'll be here before you know it. Coffee or tea?"

"Herbal tea. I've already had my two hundred milligrams of caffeine for the day."

Fay put the kettle on to boil.

Diana was so tiny and fragile. Anne couldn't wait to hold her own daughter. "Are you feeling okay now?"

"Almost fit as a fiddle." Fay yawned.

"Okay! What've you found out?"

Fay chopped mushrooms on the island. "Let me fix brunch, and then I'll tell you all I know."

"Come on." Anne groaned.

"I can't cook and talk at the same time. Besides, I want to see your face when I tell you."

"Can I help?"

"You are, by holding Diana."

Diana whined. Anne cradled Diana in her arms and rocked her until she quieted and fell back to sleep.

"Thanks for being my coach."

"I'm honored. I love you, and I'm up on just what to do."

Paul ambled in, pushing his walker, and kissed Anne on the cheek. "You look stunning."

"Yeah, right. Isn't Diana adorable?"

"That she is." He leaned over and kissed the baby's forehead.

"Remember when you showed me how to toss pasta on the ceiling to make sure it was finished?"

He chuckled. "I sure do."

George came in the back door and let Lucky off his leash. The dog scurried around the kitchen, yapping.

Diana woke again, with a wail.

"Naptime for you, princess." George reached for Diana.

"Bye, cutie." Anne handed her to him. "I'll see you again before I go."

Paul scooted toward his room. "Naptime for me too. See you soon."

Fay whispered, "He's doing pretty well, just sleeps a lot."

Anne frowned. She should visit more often. "Okay, spill it about Karl!"

"Hold your knickers. Let me get the omelet going. Gather some mint in the garden."

Tottering down the stairs reminded Anne of the times she'd picked basil, tomatoes, peppers, and other fresh produce from Sylvia's garden to make spaghetti. What an overgrown mess now. Worse than her own. Sylvia would be so disappointed. The herbs had all gone to seed. Anne tugged out a few sprigs of mint and carried them back inside.

"Fay, the garden's a mess." Anne rinsed the mint in the sink. "Don't the gardeners still come?"

"They come weekly, but all they do is mow and blow." Fay put a fruit salad in front of Anne and flipped over the omelet.

Anne cut up the mint with scissors and sprinkled it over the salad. "Maybe after my little one's born, I'll come help rejuvenate it."

Anne put the salad bowl on the table and opened her napkin on her lap.

Fay joined her, carrying over omelet-filled Haviland plates. "What's your plan?"

"My head's spinning with the options. I feel like a hamster on a treadmill. I just want to stay in my studio apartment." Anne bit into her salad.

"That's not realistic. It's too small. Don't you think? What do Sergio and your mom say?"

"They both say I should be with family and claim they're the best option. Sergio even proposed again to me last night. But I really want to stay in San Francisco."

"Move in here with us. The place is huge, and we're family also."

"You've already got your hands full."

"You wouldn't be in our hands. Your hands would be another set to help."

"Let me think about it." Anne loved the idea, but she couldn't impose. "Okay—Karl and Priscilla!"

"Ready? It's as juicy as that salad."

"Who did you talk to?"

"Fredricka. But I didn't hear it from her, and you didn't hear it from me. Word is, Priscilla and Karl were caught together at the Ritz-Carlton in Palm Springs."

"What do you mean, 'caught together'?"

"Caught, as in caught with their pants down." Fay paused and raised her eyebrows. "By his wife."

Anne had a hard time holding back a smile. "Go on."

"I don't have all the nitty-gritty, but she does know that Wifey is a big-time attorney."

"She is? When I was seeing him, he told me he couldn't leave her because she didn't have any job skills."

"She suspected something was going on. He told her the museum was paying for a business trip."

"He's not the brightest bulb in the chandelier."

"Let's hope she won't need to give him anything. He might even be able to get alimony from her."

"How did Fredricka get so much detailed information?"

"From a mutual friend. Apparently, Priscilla had been using the museum's credit card for hotels, expensive dinners, et cetera. So, bye-bye, Priscilla and Karl."

Anne couldn't believe it.

45

A week later, on a warm evening, pink shadowed the mountains and the sun began its slow descent over the hill. Sally Sue ran out into the meadow with relief as Cliff rode down the slope toward her on Roan. His shoulders slumped, but when he saw her, he sat up straight and gave her an enthusiastic wave.

"I've been so worried." Sally Sue couldn't help herself. "Wherever have you been?"

"On the range." Cliff gave her a weary smile within his unshaven face. His clothes were filthy, saddlebags jam-packed. He struggled to get down off Roan. "I'm a bit light-headed." He limped toward her and started to fall.

"Careful." She caught him in her arms and guided him inside, where she helped him to sit on a kitchen chair.

Socks scurried over. Sally Sue lifted her up into Cliff's lap. He stroked the kitten's back.

"What's wrong with you?" Sally Sue asked him.

He removed his hat and pushed back his hair, revealing a deep gash on his forehead. One of his eyes was black and blue, bloodied, and swollen shut.

"Oh, my stars and garters. What happened to you?" she gasped.

"It's nothing."

"Have you been at the saloon, fighting over a girl?" Sally Sue tried to tease.

"Maybe."

She felt another sprig of jealousy. It wilted when he didn't laugh at her joke.

Had he been in a fight? Robbed another bank? Shot and killed another man? She glanced at the gun in his holster. "What happened?" She doubted he'd tell her the truth.

"Got into a scuffle with a grizzly bear."

She was right he wasn't going to tell her the truth. If it had been a grizzly, he would be dead, or at least have more lacerations.

"Really, what happened?"

Cliff tried to smile but winced instead. "Got into a tussle with a cowboy."

"What?"

"Yep. You know how they spell 'cowboy' don't you? 'O-p-i-n-i-o-n.'"

That was a hoot.

"I went to that ranch, looking for work. The foreman didn't like the way I swung my lasso. He said I should do it overhanded, but I always have more luck doing it underhanded."

"Are you lying?"

"I'm not telling you a thumper. It's the God's awful truth."

"Sounds like you didn't get the work."

"Nope."

"Do you really need a job anyway?"

"Every man needs to work."

With a straight face, she said, "As Mama used to say, idleness is the devil's workshop."

"Then I'd better find some work, and fast."

"Yes, you'd better."

She touched his wound gently. "It might need stitches."

He pulled away. "Don't bother. It'll be fine."

"But it might become infected."

He pulled a flask from his coat pocket and took a swig. "Okay. Do what you like."

She grabbed her sewing kit and a cotton remnant from her pile. Standing before him, she seized his flask, poured alcohol on the cloth, and dabbed the lesion.

"Ouch!" He jerked away.

"Don't be a baby." She held his stubbled chin and lightly cleaned his eye and the wound.

She couldn't see to thread a needle, so she lit a lantern and had him hold it up. Her hands shook. She'd never done this before, only watched Doc Mackenzie stitch up her finger when she'd cut it chopping carrots. Even then, she could hardly bear to look.

Feeling queasy, she placed her hand tenderly on Cliff's forehead. "Keep steady, now." She inhaled and let it out. "Ready?"

"Yes, ma'am."

She gritted her teeth, drove the needle into Cliff's skin, pushed it through, and pulled the thread. She kept going until she'd made five neat stitches. While she worked, he flinched only once. As she snipped off the thread's end, relief flooded her and she collapsed next to him on a chair. "I'm glad that's over."

"You and me both." He closed his eyes.

"Come on." She grasped his elbow, helped him up, led him to the cot, and pulled off his boots.

"It feels good to be home," he said, and soon fell to snoring.

She stared at him. Now that she knew he was okay, and given his weakened state, this was her best chance to find the money and scurry away. Outside, she climbed the fence railing and flipped open the saddlebag on Roan's back.

"What're you doin'?" Cliff bellowed from the doorway.

Her heart leaped into her throat. "You shouldn't be up. I'm just gonna let Roan graze in the pasture with Scout."

Cliff hobbled toward her, clutched the bags, and stumbled inside.

Sally Sue used all her strength to take off Roan's saddle. She returned to the cabin. Arms crossed, she plunked down in the rocker and moved to and fro to dispel her frustration. How was she ever going to find the money and get away?

Before she got in bed, she wiped the perspiration from Cliff's brow. He had tucked the saddlebags between the cot and the wall. She'd be unable to get to them without waking him.

Overnight, Cliff's wound festered and became red and raw.

"Does it hurt much?" She tilted his head sideways to inspect it.

He took a swig from his flask. "Nah. Only feels like someone threw a pine cone at it."

She doubted that very much and reached for the flask. "Here, I'm going to clean it again."

"Let it scar over." His voice was gruff. "Just slap a little honey on it."

Was he teasing her? "Really?"

"Yep."

She got the honey from the cupboard. It reminded her of Elvira, that strange woman the first day in Flagstaff. Hadn't she said something about honey? "Honey in every pot," or something like that? Sally Sue carefully spooned some over Cliff's eye.

A few days later, Cliff's wound began to heal, but he continued to sleep late.

White clouds parted like saloon doors to reveal chartreuse mountaintops, the snowy peaks now gone. Under the turquoise sky, a joyful explosion of wildflowers dotted the meadow. A quail shook his topnotch plume as his family bobbed and skittered behind him. A turkey hen, red waddle hanging off her chin above a long, curved neck, zigzagged her drooping body along the meadow toward the pond.

A white-tailed doe and her twin white-speckled yearlings nibbled green fodder that had magically sprouted overnight. The doe's ears perked up; she turned toward and stared at Sally Sue as if she knew Sally Sue was there. Then, suddenly, she sprang away, her babies following on spindly legs.

Spring had arrived, and with it, Sally Sue's sadness had begun to abate. At home she'd never paid much attention to nature, but here the graceful beauty of the peaks and sweeping meadow filled her heart with newfound vigor. She'd thought she'd miss the springtime hustle-bustle of the city, but the surrounding quiet here was so peaceful, and she felt freer here than in Missouri.

A stream had begun to flow and gurgle into the gulley behind the big oak beyond the cabin. Birch trees, sycamores, and cedars had sprouted leaves. From the giant oaks' cupped leaves, tendrils twirled down like cherubs' curls. The beauty of the ranch filled her with awe and gratitude for God.

Sally Sue's chest felt hollow, eggshell thin, ready to crack and break as she realized the paths were clear. It would be difficult to leave all this budding nature, especially after the hard winter she'd endured. But she needed to depart soon, before she changed her mind or Cliff snapped again.

But once she got off the ranch, she would have no idea which way to go. She wandered to the pond with a bucket, singing her favorite hymn aloud: "All things bright and beautiful. All creatures great and small . . ." She'd sung it in church her whole life but had never truly listened to the words until today.

Maybe if she asked nicely, Cliff would take her to church in town and she could memorize the way.

Later that evening, she sat at the table while he finished the supper dishes, the cabin aglow with candles and lantern light. Crickets whirred a constant cadence.

Cliff dried his hands and joined her at the table. Daily doses of honey had helped heal his lesion. She'd soon remove the stitches.

She got up enough gumption to broach the subject. "Don't you think Sheriff Mack will wonder if he never sees me in town?"

"Why should he?"

She tried a different tactic. "Now that the weather's clear, don't you think it's time to go back to church?"

"Church." He scoffed. "I don't go to church."

"Why not?" she asked.

"Don't believe in God."

"What?" She'd never heard anyone admit that before.

"If you'd seen the horrible acts I've witnessed, you'd agree."

"Like what?" Maybe this was a clue to why he'd robbed the bank. He'd never really answered her questions and got angry every time she even came close to talking about it.

"Like . . ." He paused.

"What?"

"Never you mind." He looked away.

She leaned across the table and put her hand on his arm. "I'd like to go to church anyway."

He pulled away and crossed his arms. "We'll see," he said.

She could tell that meant no.

He put his hands back on the table, and his eyes softened. "Sally Sue, you're a mighty fine woman."

She felt herself blush as a whisper of desire clung to her—a desire to touch his hand, his cheek, the back of his hair where it kissed the nape of his neck. She shuddered. How could she be so angry at him one minute and feel this way about him the next? This man who kidnapped her, kept her, wouldn't let her go. A bank robber, a killer.

As if he could read her mind, he slid his hand across the table toward her, the gnarled scars of a life deeply lived evident on his fingers. She reached out her hand and clasped his, unable to resist his touch a moment longer. The thought of those large hands on her body frightened but also thrilled her imagination. What might happen in the big bed with him next to her at night, or maybe during an afternoon with the spring sun shining through the window?

She caught herself, withdrew her hand from his, and stood. "It's getting late."

Next Sunday, come hell or high water, she'd set out for church if she had to, even if it made him angry. At least she'd asked him first.

46

Sunday morning, Cliff still asleep on the cot, Sally Sue quickly and quietly dressed in her travel suit—stains, flat bustle, and all—and tied her bonnet beneath her chin. As the sun peeked over the mountains, feathery pink clouds hovered in the sky. She marched out to the pasture, haltered Scout, and led him to the fence railing. Saddling him up, she slid her rifle onto his side, climbed on his back, and headed up the road toward town. Would she be able to find the way?

She looked behind her to make sure Cliff wasn't following and kneed Scout into a lope. Water gushed under the bridge as they crossed it. A mile or so out, Scout settled into a steady pace twisting along the trail. Blue lupine adorned grasshopper-green grasses, and giant ponderosa pines shaded her way, giving off an intoxicating scent.

After a while, Scout's pace slowed, his neck filled with foamy sweat, and he began to pant. A river rippled in a ravine below the road, and she turned the reins and walked down the slope toward it. She dismounted on a tree stump, scooped water into her cupped hands, and offered the horse a drink. He lapped it up like there was no tomorrow, and then she sipped some herself.

She led him back up the slope and onto the road again and continued down it. After that long ride, it had felt good to stretch her legs. At a clearing, they came to a crossroads. Should they go left or go right? She tried to find the sun to help her get a sense of direction, but clouds covered the sky.

A woman's voice called from behind a creosote bush, "I've been waiting for you."

Sally Sue pulled her rifle off Scout and raised it.

Underneath a calico bonnet, a woman stepped from behind the bush, staring with deep-set eyes. "Hey, now. Put that thing down." She walked toward Sally Sue and gently pointed the gun's barrel toward the ground. "Don't you remember me? I'm the one Mr. Bjork shucked off the hotel porch."

"Elvira?"

"Yes."

"Thanks for the tea. You also said something about honey. What was it, again?"

"There's honey in every heart. I hope you found it." Elvira put a hand on Sally Sue's shoulder. "Whatcha doin' out here all alone?"

To be in the presence of another woman after all this time brought a sense of calm to Sally Sue. "I've been . . ." For some reason, she didn't want to say "kidnapped," so she chose "passing winter on a nearby ranch."

"That's what I heard." Elvira paused, as if she could tell Sally Sue had more to tell. "Where're you off to now?"

"Church. Which road takes me to Flagstaff?"

Elvira pointed up the road that curved around a boulder. "I'm heading that way myself. I'll show you." She stroked Scout's nose.

"That's mighty kind of you." Sally Sue slid the gun back onto Scout, took his reins, and fell into step beside Elvira.

Comforted to walk beside this odd woman, Sally Sue etched in her mind the outcropping of boulders and big oak that stood by the side at the split, so when the time came, she'd be able to find her way.

However, they barely got around the bend when the sound of

horse hooves pounded on the road behind them. Sally Sue aimed the rifle toward the sound as Cliff, Roan, and the buckboard appeared around a bend.

"Whoa." He held up his hand. "Put that gun down, darlin'. It's only me."

Elvira mouthed to Sally Sue, *Honey*.

"Where're you goin'?" He gave Elvira his friendliest-man-in-the-world grin.

"I'm going to church is all." Sally Sue lowered the gun.

"Scout appears tuckered out." Cliff climbed down from the buckboard and took the horse's reins. "Let's go together. Ma'am, want a ride?"

A gunshot rang out from a copse of trees above them on a hill. In a flash, Sally Sue swung her gun and pointed it toward where the shot had come from.

As another bullet flew toward them, Cliff quickly released Scout's reins, unhooked Roan from the buckboard, and slapped their rumps. "Git!"

Both horses whinnied, leaped, and ran off.

The women helped Cliff tilt the buckboard on its side. He pushed them behind it. "Stay down. I'll take care of this."

He skittered back, pulled his pistol from his holster, and shot into the copse of trees. Another shot reverberated, this time closer.

A man's voice called, "I know who you are. I'm gonna collect that bounty." A bullet whizzed over their heads, and a volley of gunfire ensued.

The women huddled behind the buckboard. Were they going to die?

It grew quiet, and Cliff joined them. Sally Sue rose, but he reached out and shook his head.

Another shot rang out. Cliff loaded, stood, and pulled the trigger, but the gun jammed. As he tried again and again, the shots from the hill grew louder, but his pistol still wouldn't shoot. Sally Sue crawled on her stomach to where her rifle had fallen. She jumped up, took aim, and focused until a figure sprang out from behind a boulder. She pretended it was a bottle, held steady, inhaled, exhaled, and pulled the trigger.

The man screamed.

Her body shook. She sat next to Cliff and Elvira until her heartbeat began to ebb. She couldn't believe she'd really shot at a man and hoped she hadn't killed him.

Cliff held out his hand, and they waited a few minutes. "Okay." He rose. "We should be safe now."

Sally Sue helped Elvira up as he walked toward the mounded heap on the hill. "Stay back," he told the women.

They followed him up the slope anyway. Cliff rolled over the body, and Elvira gasped. The scruffy man, in dirty buckskin, stared with open eyes. Blood seeped from a bullet hole that passed clean through the hat still on his head.

"Looks like his soul has passed," Cliff said.

"If he had one." Elvira smirked.

Sally Sue turned her head away from the second dead body she'd ever seen, only this one, she'd killed. "Cliff, it's that mountain man who came to the cabin."

"And he was also my husband." Elvira closed his eyes with a swipe.

"I'm sorry." Sally Sue took Elvira's hand.

"Don't be. He deserted me long ago. You done the world a favor. He was mean as a rabid dog—wild, wily, a scalawag, a scavenger. He deserved to die." She looked at Sally Sue. "No sweet honey in him."

"Guess I ought to bury him," Cliff offered.

"Don't bother." Elvira growled. "Let the coyotes pick at him. Besides, Sheriff's been after him for ages. He might wanna see the body."

"You sure?" Sally Sue couldn't imagine leaving someone out here like that, even a scalawag. "Let's at least say a few words."

Elvira nodded.

Cliff joined Sally Sue in the recitation of the 23rd Psalm: "The lord is my shepherd. I shall not want . . ."

As they walked back down the hill, Elvira asked, "Still offering to drop me off in town?"

"Sure can." Cliff smiled sadly at her.

They pulled the buckboard upright. Cliff whistled for the horses and hooked them up.

"You go to church with your gal, and I'll tell the sheriff what's what," Elvira said.

Cliff cleared his throat. "Are you sure? Shouldn't I go with you?"

"Nah. I can handle it."

"Wanna ride up front with my hubby?" Sally Sue asked Elvira.

"No, I'll hunker down in the back." Elvira stuck her hand out, and Cliff boosted her up.

"I'm going to ride back here to comfort our friend. She's just become a widow, after all." Sally Sue hopped in beside Elvira, settled in, and patted her hand. Even though he'd been a despicable scoundrel, Sally Sue felt horrible about killing him.

47

Sorry for your troubles." Sally Sue put her arm around Elvira.

"Me too."

Cliff clucked, and the buckboard began to bump along.

"Children?" Sally Sue asked.

"I had five. They all passed. One at a time. Last one died this winter. Ran out of vittles. I did my best to feed them." Elvira sniffled.

Sally Sue handed her a hanky from her pocket. "I'm sure you did."

Elvira dabbed her eyes and blew her nose. "Worked my tail off. Sold herbs, did mending, even worked as a cattle-ranch hand."

"You did?" Imagine that, a woman working with livestock.

"Still do, but only during roundup season. It's gonna be different this year, on account there's a warrant out for Mr. Brigham Young's arrest. He was forced to sell his shares and hastily exit the territory."

"Why?"

"He's one of those Mormon polygamists. Maybe now that my husband's dead, I can track down Mr. Young and get him to wed me as one of his sister-wives. He takes real good care of them."

"You'd do that?"

Elvira cackled.

They passed an oak grove. A herd of sheep grazed in a nearby meadow. Sally Sue thought she'd rather have sheep than cows on the ranch, as long as they didn't have vermin.

"What did you do on the ranch?" Sally Sue asked.

"Castratin'."

"What?" Sally Sue stared at her.

"Yep, been asked to do it for another outfit this season. They've got one hundred seventy head at the Arizona Cattle Company, and branding time's coming up. I'm the best around here, with small hands perfectly suited for the duty." Elvira wiggled her fingers.

She raised her voice: "I grip those balls, slice 'em off, toss 'em in a bucket. When boiled over a hot fire, they make good eatin'."

Cliff turned around and gave her a smile. Sally Sue imagined holding a pair of bloody, hairy testicles in each palm. She should have been aghast but instead was spellbound.

Elvira studied Sally Sue's hands. "Yours are perfect. Maybe I could teach you. My joint swelling has been kicking in. I don't know how many more years I'll be able to do it—rolling on the ground, wrestling around with them young bulls. Yep, yours are perfect for the task. Want to be my protégée?" She pronounced it with a hard "g." "Money's purty good." She grinned. "I've got special tools to use. No one but me is allowed to touch them. I'll pass them on to you."

Sally Sue would like to make money. That wasn't her cup of tea, though.

Canvas tents and shabby shacks dotted a hillside beside a mill next to a quiet lumberyard. A little while later, they passed the downtrodden ranch where they'd picked up the horses and buckboard. The windmill was lying on the ground.

As they drove into Flagstaff, Sally Sue's heart raced with excitement. It had been months since she'd been around folks. The town seemed deserted, though. No one strolled or rode horses down the street, no hussies preened, no one swept the hotel porch, no fights today.

Cliff steered the team behind the church, where horses were lined up. He climbed down, proffered his hand to Elvira, and helped her out of the cart.

"Thank you kindly. After service, come on over and say howdy to the sheriff."

"Sure thing." Cliff saluted her and watched her hobble away. "She's a weird bird."

"Yep." Sally Sue hopped out of the buckboard, ignoring the hand he held out to her.

He tilted his head at the church. "Go on in. I'll wait for you."

On the church steps, she tried unsuccessfully to brush the dirt off her suit. As she entered, a portly, ginger-haired pastor led the congregation in reciting the Lord's Prayer. The McMillans and their son Isaiah sat in a front pew with Mr. Ivry from the hotel. Men in clean shirts with combed hair and hats in hand were spread throughout the congregation. Instead of their colorful getups, the saloon girls, sitting in a row, wore modest Sunday best in pastels, with beribboned bonnets to match.

Sally Sue stepped into an empty pew in the back row, opened a hymnal, and joined in to sing "Onward, Christian Soldiers."

Afterwards, the congregation sat and the pastor began to read the scripture from Matthew. "'You shall not murder; and whoever murders will be liable to judgment.'"

Sally Sue's hands flew to her chest. Had he chosen this passage just for her?

He smoothed down the edges of his black shawl over his white robe and began his sermon. "Flagstaff ruffians, we've been overrun by sinners." As he spoke, his Adam's apple bobbed up and down. "Those among you who sin will be liable to the hellfires of damnation." The pastor's gaze scanned the congregation and landed on her. A chill went up her spine.

During the sacraments, as the pastor held up a cup and said,

"This is the blood . . . ," she closed her eyes and could see the blood seeping through that hat and the man she'd killed, his dead eyes staring at her, then the body of the bank guard Cliff had murdered. Was she no better than Cliff? No, he'd done something against the law, she'd just been trying to protect herself and the others. Maybe there was no difference. He was trying to protect himself too.

A commotion in a front pew broke her reverie. Isaiah's head popped up, and he made a run for it down the aisle. As he passed, she seized him by the hand, pulled him next to her, and held him close.

"Hello, pitty."

She put a finger to her lips and whispered, "Hello, Isaiah. Shh."

Danica stepped into the aisle. Sally Sue waved that she had him, and Danica sat back down.

Isaiah pointed to her bonnet. Sally Sue removed it and set it on his lap, and he fiddled with the flowers.

At the end of the service, the pastor walked solemnly down the aisle and the congregation followed.

Sally Sue led Isaiah out of the pew and out the door. Cliff was nowhere to be seen.

The pastor shook her hand. "Welcome. New in town?"

She considered telling him she was in trouble, but even though she hadn't seen him, she sensed Cliff watching nearby.

"There you are." Mrs. McMillan, braided hair on her head, knelt and grabbed Isaiah's elbow. "Naughty boy. Sorry if he's been a bother."

"Not at all. He's a good boy."

Mrs. McMillan laughed. "Usually." She kissed him on the forehead and let him run off to his father, talking with a group of men nearby.

"It's nice to see you. I'm glad you made it through the winter okay. We were worried about you folks."

"We were very comfortable. Thank you." Sally Sue swallowed the lie.

"Want to join us for supper?" Mrs. McMillan asked.

"Better not. My husband will be here soon to fetch me." She looked up and down the street.

"Of course you'd both be welcome."

"I'll ask him."

Did she dare go to the jailhouse and talk to Mack? She took a step that way, then heard a whistle from behind an ash tree and saw Cliff gesturing for her to come to him.

The horses trotted along as they rode home in silence toward the homestead. That was fine with her, because she didn't feel much like talking. It had been one of the worst days of her life.

Just over the bridge, Cliff stopped the wagon. A midnight-blue canopy covered the ranch in the moonless night, and crickets chanted their evensong. An owl hooted, and its mate answered.

Cliff turned toward her with soft eyes. "Sally Sue, I don't know what I'd do if I lost you."

Captivated by his words, she forgot herself and let his hand touch her cheek. Her face grew warm, and for a moment, just a moment, she wished he'd kiss her. But then she pulled away. If he thought she'd ever let him kiss her, he had another thing coming.

When they arrived at the cabin, she ran to the privy and stayed there until she was sure he had fallen asleep. How could she even consider letting this bank-robbing kidnapper get so close? She realized again, for at least the hundredth time, that he could get close to her anytime he wanted. She resolved to do something drastic before he lost his patience or she lost her resolve.

48

In the morning, Sally Sue found a straw cowgirl's hat at the foot of her bed. She scrambled into the nightgown she had tossed on the floor. Hat on her head, she looked in the mirror. The wide brim would keep the sun out of her eyes.

Her mind flew back to the previous day. So much had happened. Even though she'd shot a man, she didn't look like a killer. That poor Elvira. Sally Sue had been in town, she'd been to church, she'd been told by Cliff he didn't want to live without her. Sorry, buddy, but you'll have to soon.

She smiled at him as he came inside. Long ago, she'd given up worrying about his seeing her in the nightgown. Too much trouble to be modest in these close quarters.

"Thanks for the hat." She tilted her head up toward him, and it fell off. She plopped it back on.

He shrugged. "Why're you thanking me? I have no idea where it came from."

"Thank you, whoever snuck in here and brought this to me."

"Now that the weather's cleared, it's time to start our garden."

She'd never planted before. Even though there had been space in their yard, Mama had refused. Said it would be too much work, so they traded laundry washing for fruits and vegetables.

Sally Sue didn't feel like getting dressed. She put her boots on and, still wearing her nightgown, followed Cliff outside to stunning blue skies. The mama deer and her twins grazed in the field. She glanced up at Sally Sue and Cliff; used to them, she didn't pay them any mind. The twins had grown stronger by the day.

Beside the cabin in the garden patch, with strong arms, Cliff chopped the hoe in a rhythmic motion, releasing flaxen weeds from the hard dirt and flinging them aside. It seemed easy.

He handed her the rusty tool. "Your turn."

She grasped the hoe and hacked at a clump, but it wouldn't budge.

"Give it some elbow grease." Cliff swung his arms to demonstrate.

She tried again with all her might, to no avail.

His warm body close to hers, his arms encircling her from behind, he put his hands over hers and moved them firmly onto the wooden handle. "Hold it like this. Now pull back." He guided her hands up. "Think of someone or something that makes you angry."

That should be easy. She swung, but the force didn't have much gumption. At the moment, she hadn't been able to conjure up any anger toward him.

"Try again," Cliff encouraged. "Get furious."

Surprised that her mama came to mind, Sally Sue attacked the weeds and they began to give way. She felt a powerful sense of accomplishment.

"Good job. Keep at it. I'm going to work the horses."

She continued to hoe until the warm breeze picked up. A blue jay flew onto the barn roof and hopped up to its twirling weather vane. North faced south, east faced west, the four direction points rearranged.

A gale blew off her hat, and she chased it across the meadow.

"Dang it!" she yelled, frightening the doe and her babies, who hopped up and bounded away. She scooped up the hat and stomped into the cabin.

With her sewing scissors, she poked a hole on either side of the brim, draped a remnant from the trunk across it, and wove it into each hole, pulling it through. She stuck the hat back on her head and tied it under her chin, the silk smooth.

"That oughta teach you," she said, and went back outside, where Cliff was brushing Roan in the round pen. "Hey, boy. I know you're shedding."

Hat snug on her head, dust blowing around her, she worked the soil until her arms grew tired, and then she tossed the hoe on the ground, bent over, and began to tug weeds out by hand. When there were no more, she stood back to admire her work. Gratification filled her senses like she'd never felt before, as she imagined the future plot yielding tall corn stalks, green rutabagas, and plump tomatoes. She could see herself as she cut them up, added them to a stew, and stirred them in the cauldron.

"Take a taste," she'd say to Cliff, holding a full spoon out to him.

"Delicious!" he'd say.

She knew he'd meant more than the stew and shook the fantasy away. That day would never come, because she'd be gone by the time any vegetables they ever planted were ripe. With renewed energy, she tilled the ground. Before she keeled over from exhaustion, Cliff steered a wheelbarrow toward her.

"Look at all you've done. Let's celebrate. Put your hoe down, and let's have a hoedown tonight."

"What?"

"Let's have ourselves a hoedown. A dance. You're from Missouri. You never heard of one of those?"

"Mister, of course I have." She smiled at his enthusiasm, even though she was so tuckered out, she didn't think she'd be able to walk to the cabin, let alone dance.

Inside, she knew she should start fixing supper. She'd just take a little rest first. She plopped on the bed and promptly fell to napping.

She awoke to a dove cooing. The setting sun cast a warm glow across the peaks. She'd slept too long and arose with renewed vigor.

Still in her dirt-stained nightgown, she didn't want to don the filthy men's clothes and had a hankering to wear something fresh and feminine. She pulled the red dress from the trunk.

She laid the dress on the bed, stepped out of her nightgown, and rinsed herself at the washstand. The cool water was invigorating. She donned the dress, tugging the puffed sleeves up to hide her shoulders and cleavage. She brushed her hair, now grown to her shoulders, and pulled it into an updo like she'd seen the saloon gals wear. It felt good after all that hard work.

After she finished fixing supper, she opened the door and called, "Come and get it, or I'll feed it to the hogs."

Cliff came in, carrying an armful of sage, the blossoms deep blue. He arranged them in a large canister and set it on the mantel beside the Indian items.

"Lovely," she said.

He studied her. "You're the lovely one."

She felt her face redden and suddenly felt shy. He must have dunked his head in the horse trough to wash up. He was looking mighty fine. His slicked-back hair and smooth-shaven face shone in the fading light. He had also donned a clean denim shirt.

"Smells good," he said. He lit the candles in the chandelier and sat at the table.

"Dig in." She served them and sat down too.

He put the spoon in his mouth, and closed his eyes while he chewed. "Ooh-whee, this stew is tasty. You've become quite the cook, Sally Sue." He ate another spoonful.

She smiled at the compliment. She'd been working on it. Some day she might even become as good a cook as he was. She'd grown to enjoy it—chopping, mixing, and stirring. Even though she liked it, though, she didn't want to have to do it every night. She was lucky because Cliff traded off making meals with her. What would those complaining housewife biddies in Missouri say about that?

After supper, she gazed at his handsome face and imagined what it might have been like if their beginnings had been different—no bank robbery, no dead men, no kidnapping. Maybe he'd be her beau and then her husband and they'd have a normal life, with children. They'd live near Mama, go to church, and have Sunday afternoon suppers together. No, she wouldn't like that at all. She scrunched up her nose.

"Does your nose itch?" Cliff asked.

She scratched it.

"You know what that means, don't you?" He grinned.

"No, what?"

"Means you're gonna kiss a fool."

"I guess it means I'm gonna kiss you, then." She put a hand over her mouth. Did she just say that? That reply had just leaped out like a frog.

He laughed so hard, she thought he might get apoplexy. "Sally Sue, you're a hoot. Let's get this hoedown going."

They stacked the dishes in the washbasin. He carried the table to the side of the room, arranged a chair in the middle, and proffered his hand. Nervous, she giggled and sat.

"Ready?"

"Sure."

He stood before her. "I sure wish I had my banjo."

"You don't play the banjo."

"Yes, I do. I promise I'll get one and play for you someday." With gusto, his deep voice filling the cabin, he began to sing "She'll Be Coming 'Round the Mountain"—the same song he'd sung that first night on the way to the homestead.

She clapped and sang along to the first verse.

On the second verse, he said, "Dance around me like I'm a mountain."

As he continued to sing, she galloped around him in circles, holding the edges of her dress's hem. He sang very fast on the last stanza, and she had a hard time keeping up with him, but she managed. Out of breath and laughing, she fell into the chair.

Next, he serenaded her, pronouncing every word in a twangy, exaggerated fashion:

Oh my darling, oh my darling
Oh my darling, Clementine
You are lost and gone forever
Dreadful sorry, Clementine

She was surprised he knew the words to all five verses. "Why do you think all the good songs are written about women?" she asked.

"Because you're the fairer sex. Any requests?"

"'Oh! Susanna'?"

He stomped his boots on the wood floor in time. "*Oh! Susanna, oh don't you cry for me* . . . Come on, Sally Sue, give it your all."

She couldn't resist—she sang full out, hit a high soprano C with perfect pitch and then a low C, like she'd done at home in choir. No warbling in between.

Cliff yelled, "You can sure sing, girl. Dance, Sally Sue, dance!"

They danced around each other, her skirt twirling at her ankles as she spun around and around. His muscular body shook and wiggled. She copied his movements, the merriment exhilarating. At the end of the song, she sat again.

Then he was quite clever, making up his own impromptu words:

Oh! Sally Sue, oh won't you cry for me
for I've brought you to Arizonee
with a banjo on my knee.

He extended his arms toward her and began to hum the "Blue Danube Waltz." The notes flew straight into her heart like arrows. She shouldn't let him hold her; she stepped back.

His eyes glowed deep blue—the color of the Danube, or maybe even the Pacific. Her body tingled for his touch. When he reached toward her, she allowed him to clasp her hand in his and guide the other around his firm waist.

As they hummed in unison, he led her in circles around the cabin, keeping them in a continuous rhythm. The intoxicating scent of sage filled the air. Candles sent dreamy shadows as they shimmered above them.

She shouldn't let him hold her so tight, but she couldn't pull back. She leaned into him and felt the strength of his body against hers.

At the end of the song, he whispered in her ear, "Ah, Sally Sue."

When she looked up at him, he leaned down and kissed her. For a moment she hesitated, until a spark flickered and ignited inside her body and she returned his kiss with deep longing—a longing filled with sorrow for her own mixed-up feelings for him: fear, hatred, admiration, maybe even love.

He abruptly shook his head and stepped back. "I'm sorry. I didn't mean to be disrespectful."

In a daze, she stared up at him.

"You're just so beautiful is all." He turned away. "I'll be in the barn."

Sally Sue wanted to grab his arm and pull him to her again. Instead, she curtsied as if it had been any old town-hall dance. "Thank you for the hoedown."

He closed the door on his way out. She removed the red dress and crawled into bed. Her mind relived the kiss over and over again. It took her ages to fall asleep.

In the night, a dream aroused her. Cliff was beside her in the big bed, his kisses plum soft, hers back juicy-sweet. Candles flickered like stars. The ceiling opened; they rotated, levitated together, into a blue velvet sky. Soft breezes twirled and swirled their bodies in circles toward the heavens. Even though she knew it was a dream, she held on to him for dear life, wanting God to make this bliss, not a sin, but real and divine.

49

Mid-November, two months before her due date, Anne could barely fit out the door to her deck. Even so, she was feeling pretty good. Clouds hovered above. Just like in Sylvia's garden, the mint had taken over Anne's own garden. She peeked underneath the mint in search of fall strawberries, but there weren't any. The antioxidant blueberries she had planted a few months earlier for healthy smoothies had never taken hold.

A big surprise was the volunteer blackberry bush. Its prickly leaves curled up; the stems twisted under and over each other, spreading out like giants' hands. A ripe berry sprang off into her fingers, and she plopped it in her mouth. Delicious.

She filled an empty pot with the blackberries. There were tons of them. Maybe she'd even make jam. She could watch a YouTube video to figure out how. Wait. Was she becoming domestic now? Inside, she rinsed her hands and the berries, made a smoothie, and put the extra in the fridge.

The residency had ended a few days before. The Freddy project had become a hit; museum visitors had lined up to adhere pieces. Mr. Willingsby had insisted the buck stay on display at least through the holidays and maybe longer. Anne could now concentrate on adding to her art inventory before the baby came. Her mom wanted her to go home for Thanksgiving, but Anne didn't want to fly back in her condition and had decided to spend the holiday at Bay Breeze. She would see her mother when she came for the baby's birth.

Scanning the knickknack shelf, Anne's eyes landed on a Lladró-like Madonna. If it were authentic, she couldn't have bought it for only a dollar.

She held it up to her stomach and said to the baby, "This is *Our Lady of the Garden*."

She glued the statue in the center of a silver tray ready on the table and slipped a toy tea-set plate behind her head for a halo. She selected and added a ceramic Scottie dog, a rabbit, and a snail at the lady's feet and two angels above her shoulders. In and out, Anne breathed, getting into the zone.

She dumped found objects from a baggie onto the table and searched for assorted flower earrings and brooches. She removed their backs and placed them all over the tray, then added broken dishes and florist gems throughout the empty spaces. When the pieces dried, she'd squish glue in the cracks and sprinkle in seed beads.

Waddling down the stairs, she unlocked Mrs. Landenheim's door. Thai meowed and ran to his bowl. There was no sign of the kitty.

"Zorra," Anne called, filling the food and water bowls.

She followed the sound of soft mewing to the bedroom. Anne carefully crawled down and peeked under the bed. "Zorra, there you are."

The kitty wouldn't come, so Anne grasped a hanger from the floor nearby and gently coaxed Zorra to her. Anne held her on her lap and caressed her. "You're okay, sweetie. You must be lonely."

Anne got up with Zorra in her arms and went down to the kitchen. Thai was eating from the kitty's bowl. "Scat!" Anne shouted.

Thai hissed. Anne swept up the bowl and carried Zorra and the bowl up to her own apartment. Zorra jumped on Anne's bed.

"You rest now, sweetie." Anne stroked her back until Zorra fell asleep.

Anne moved *Our Lady of the Garden* to the counter, placed the finally clean hubcap on the kitchen table, and sorted through her found treasures for the right focal point, searching with her heart and not her mind. Settling on a turquoise-haired doll, she glued it in the hubcap's center.

Since the hubcap was round like the sun, she wanted to create a sense of sunrays. She encircled the doll with a conch belt and glued down the pieces. On top of those, she added stars she had made at a clay workshop, and blue florist gems. For reflection, she added rectangular mirrors, and for inspiration, she glued word magnets on top of them: *breathe, happy, honey, alluring, flame, compassion, star, light*.

She added colorful bottle caps she'd collected from the Flagstaff bed-and-breakfast. Then dumped out *milagros* she'd purchased at El Santuario de Chimayó, north of Santa Fe, onto a tray, and the tiny vial of holy dirt fell out too. She thought about her visit to the National Historic Landmark pilgrimage site.

The sanctuary there was gorgeous, with pointed caps on the towers and a metal pitched roof. Folk art decorated the walls. A separate building displayed photographs, discarded crutches, and testimonials of those who claimed to have been healed. She had knelt down into a round pit and into the vial scraped up dirt believed to have healing powers. Seekers of cures rubbed themselves with the dirt. Anne hadn't planned to do that. But life was unpredictable, and she set the vial on the coffee table by the bed.

Breathing deeply, she fastened *milagros* along the hubcap's edge: a head, a heart, eyes, a rose, a leg like the one she'd given Mrs. Landenheim, a key, an angel, a cabin, and more.

Anne stepped back to inspect what she'd done. The combination of color, texture, and repetition was perfect. She eyed the centerpiece doll and said, "You go, girl."

Oh, wait, she had a better title: *You Glow, Girl!* If that wasn't a positive affirmation for her daughter, she didn't know what was.

She picked up Zorra and put her in front of the bowl, where the kitty nibbled a few bites. Anne picked out a bowl from her art stash, filled it with water, and put it in front of Zorra, who lapped it right up.

Anne carried her back to the daybed and cuddled her until they fell asleep. Thai's scratching outside on the door woke Anne up. Zorra slept at her feet. Anne rolled over onto her back, propped herself up on some pillows, and picked up the vial, ignoring that bully until he gave up.

She spun the vial in her fingers, pulled up her shirt, popped off the vial's top, poured the dirt onto her giant belly, and caressed it in. "Here's to a healthy, happy baby."

She opened her journal to the chart where she'd been recording kick counts for week twenty-eight and added, *Thursday, 9:00 p.m.*

She lay on her left side, bare feet resting on Zorra, set her phone's stopwatch, and put her hand on her stomach. "Come on, sweetheart, you can do it." Anne closed her eyes and waited. Soon the flutterings in her stomach began, feeling like Calder's *Flea Circus*, which she'd seen at the Whitney. With a contented smile and love, she patiently counted ten kicks, marking an X on the chart after each one. If this wasn't heaven, she didn't know what was.

50

At dusk six weeks later, Anne dragged herself to the bay-window table at the Coffee Cup Café. She'd been up off and on all night with some kind of false labor and planned to order a Lyft. But because it was New Year's Eve, the cost had been prohibitive. She'd thought about canceling on Fay but wanted to see her friend, so she'd put up her umbrella and hailed a cab.

The baby wasn't due for another two weeks. She felt the cramp again, but this time it was in her back. She held on to the edge of her chair until the pain passed.

A couple at a nearby table held hands and smooched. The woman seemed a lot younger than the tuxedoed man, but it was hard to tell. Given his dark Groucho Marx eyebrows, Anne expected him to hold a cigar to his mouth and crack a joke at any moment. Another gentleman, in a red bow tie and sport coat, typed on an iPad.

Anne waved at Fay as she walked in, wearing a purple pageboy and a smashing silver jumpsuit. She wandered over through the crowded café. "Hey, mate. Did you order?"

"Sorry. Too beat. Would you please get me some water?"

"I've got you, sister." Fay put her hand on Anne's shoulder and got in line.

Anne felt a cramp again, put her head on the table, and closed her eyes until it passed. At the table behind her, she overheard some women talking.

"When are you due?"

"Six months."

"Have you fixed up the nursery yet?"

"Oh, yes—it's green and orange. No pink for my girl. It's all about owls. She's going to be wise. Maybe a scientist or doctor or something."

Anne's daughter would be whatever she wanted to be. But she would wear a lot of pink. She thought about her apartment. Where was she going to put the bassinet George was bringing over from Bay Breeze? Diana had already graduated to a larger crib. She'd better straighten up her place tonight to make room.

"Here you go." Fay handed Anne a glass of water.

Thanks for meeting me. New Year's Eve and all."

"No problem; it's on my way home from work anyway. How're you feeling?"

Anne groaned. "I'm glad Sergio and my mom are coming in next week. I'm done being alone for a while. I can't believe I still have another two weeks to go."

"She'll be here before you know it."

Anne felt another twinge and leaned over.

"What's wrong?" Fay put her hand on Anne's arm.

"Give me a moment." She tried to catch her breath.

Fay eyed her, then added cream to her tea and stirred.

"Something's wrong." Anne stood, and a pool of liquid spilled down her legs and over her flip-flops.

"Blimey! Your water broke."

The man in the bow tie and the teens and women at the table behind them stared. Fay grabbed Anne's backpack and escorted her to the sidewalk. Standing under the café awning, trying to get a Lyft in the rain, was a nightmare.

Finally, a clunky van pulled up to the curb. "Are you Lyle?" Fay asked.

"Yep."

She helped Anne get in and climbed beside her.

The van swam slowly back into the dense Sutter Street traffic.

Fay called the hospital. "I'm with Anne McFarland. Her water just broke, and we're on our way there."

Anne moaned as another contraction hit her.

Fay grasped Anne's hands. "Look at me and breathe." She exhaled short gusts. *Breathe, breathe, pant, pant.*

Anne joined in, and soon the pain subsided. "Gawd, Fay, you sounded like a monkey."

"Can you drive any faster?" Fay yelled at the driver. "For bloody sake, I might be delivering the baby right here."

Lyle turned around with wide eyes, revved the engine, and sped up. "Don't be having a rug-burn baby in the back of my Chevy!"

"Get my phone," Anne cried.

Fay rustled in the backpack. Anne seized it from her, found the phone and punched a number. "Mom! My water broke, and I'm on my way to the hospital."

"But, dear, I'm not even there yet."

"I know. Change your flight ASAP. Come now!"

Anne hung up and punched again. "Sergio! You're gonna be a daddy sooner than later."

She screamed as another contraction hit, and she handed her phone to Fay. Lyle turned up his music.

"Oh my God. Anne, Anne!" Sergio was yelling.

"Hi, Sergio, it's Fay. We're on our way to the hospital. Call you later."

"Take a left here, beside the carpark," Fay hollered.

Lyle flew into the hospital's emergency lane and screeched to a stop.

"Where's the bloody wheelchair?" Fay hollered.

Lyle honked his horn. "Okay! Get out!"

Fay helped Anne down out of the van.

"Thanks for taking Lyft," Lyle yelled, and sped away.

Fay guided Anne to the entrance as an orderly rushed out the door with a wheelchair.

Anne woke up groggy, as if she'd slept forever. The last she remembered was holding the gooey-faced doll right after the birth. She opened her eyes and tried to sit up.

"Where's the baby? Is she okay?"

"She's just fine. The pediatrician said she's perfect. See?" Fay put the lavender-scented bundle in Anne's arms. She gazed at the little miracle.

"Drink some water?" Fay held up a straw in a plastic cup, and Anne took a sip.

"You're the best friend ever." Anne smiled at Fay.

Paul hobbled in on his walker with an IT'S A GIRL mylar balloon tied to it. He leaned over and kissed Anne and then the baby on their foreheads. "What a cutie." He chuckled.

George handed her a bouquet of pink roses. "Congratulations!"

"I'll put them in a vase." Fay picked up the flowers.

"Have you decided on a name yet?" Paul asked.

Anne scanned the faces of her San Francisco friends. Her eyes landed back on Paul and teared up as she said, "Sylvia. I want to call her Sylvia."

Paul's blue eyes filled with tears too. "She'd like that. How about Sylvie for short?"

"Ideal." Anne brushed her fingers across the baby's peach-fuzz hair.

Paul touched Sylvie's tiny hand. "I wish she was here to meet her namesake and enjoy this moment."

Anne looked up to the ceiling. "She is. I know she is."

51

How could anything be so beautiful? Anne rocked her three-day-old baby, ran a finger over Sylvie's soft cheeks, finished nursing, and moved her onto her shoulder.

Anne's apartment felt even smaller than usual; besides the art materials, it was crammed with a secondhand rocking chair, the bassinet, and a futon rolled out on the floor, where her mom had slept last night after flying in on a red-eye.

She came out of the bathroom wearing Anne's kimono and drying her hair with a towel. "I brought some more gifts. Do you want them now?"

The door buzzer rang.

"Later. That's probably Sergio. Please buzz him up." Anne couldn't wait for him to see the baby.

"How?" her mom asked.

"Push that button by the door."

"Well, I'll be." She pressed it, grabbed some clothes from her giant suitcase on the floor beside the futon, and headed toward the bathroom. "I'd better make myself decent."

"Where is she?" Sergio bounded through the door, put his bags down, and tossed his fedora on the top of the fridge.

"Hello to you too." Despite all their spats and separations, seeing him always made her heart full. No matter what, she'd love him forever.

He redid his ponytail and kissed her cheeks. She was a god-awful mess. In the mirror that morning, her hair had been a frizzy jumble, her unibrow had grown back in, and mascara had smeared her eyes. She had on sweatpants and a humungous SUPER MOTHER T-shirt her mom had given her that morning. She was so tired and happy that she didn't care. The two people—no, three people—she loved most in the world were here with her.

Sergio stared at the baby and watched as Anne patted Sylvie on the back.

Her mother exited the bathroom in a pink velour sweatsuit, her wet hair up in a scrunchie, and full makeup. Sergio hugged and kissed her.

"Congratulations to us!" she said. "Want a pop?"

He didn't understand her mom's joke. "Want to hold her?" Anne offered.

He removed his leather coat, put it on the back of a kitchen chair, sat down, and reached out his arms. When Anne placed the baby in them, his face lit up, but then Sylvie howled.

He held the baby toward Anne again.

"Try jiggling her up and down."

"Like this." Her mom crossed her arms and wiggled them.

He jiggled Sylvie, but she kept crying.

"Sing to her." Anne loved it when he sang.

"Alexa, play '*O sole mio*,'" he commanded.

He started singing along with Pavarotti, and Sylvie quieted down.

He will be a good father after all. Anne moved to the daybed, picked up a scrunchie from the coffee table, and put her hair up. After the song, Sylvie howled again, this time with a high screech.

With a scared look, Sergio tried to hand her back to Anne, but her mom swooped in and expertly rocked the baby in the chair until she settled again. "Look at those long fingers and toes," she said, bouncing Sylvie's feet. "These are enormous for a baby's. She'll grow into them like a puppy. She's going to be tall like you, Anne."

"Maybe she'll be a model," Sergio said.

"Or a ballerina," her mom offered.

"She's got the wardrobe for it." Anne found the pink tutu Sergio had sent after he'd found out the baby was a girl. Anne put it on her head and wiggled it. "She'll wear pink but will be whatever she wants to be. I'll make certain of that."

Sergio walked over and pulled a box from his bag and gave it to her. "Speaking of pink . . . Open, *amore mio*."

She tore into the wrapped box and held up a miniature hat with a scarf to match.

"There's more; look under the tissue paper," Sergio said.

She lifted a pair of booties in the air. "These are adorable."

"I designed them myself."

Anne handed them to her mom, who read the label: LITTLE FOOT BOOTIES.

Sergio and Anne laughed.

"What's so funny?" her mom asked.

"It's a private joke. Sergio calls me Bigfoot, so it's a take-off on that."

"You've always been so sensitive about your feet."

"I know, but I'm over it now." Anne and Sergio gazed at each other.

"That's nice, dear. Do you want to hold her again, Sergio? Let's lower our voices. She's asleep."

"Alexa, off," Sergio said, and traded places with her mom, who gently put the baby in his arms. "*Bellissima bambina*," he whispered.

Anne's mother handed her wrapped items from her suitcase. Quietly, Anne opened each one individually. Everything was pink: onesies, bibs, socks, footed pajamas. There was also Avon's Calming Lavender lotion and baby wash and shampoo. Anne opened the lotion, squirted some into her hand, and rubbed it in. Sylvia's scent.

"I'm glad you wanted to name her Sylvia." Sergio rocked the tiny baby, who fit snugly in his arms. "What about her middle name?"

Anne picked up her journal. "How about after your grandmother? Nonna."

"Sylvia Nonna McFarland?" her mother asked.

"No, Mom, *nonna* means 'grandmother' in Italian."

"Nonna's name is Maria."

Anne wrote, *Sylvia Maria McFarland.* "That's beautiful, and visually appealing."

"Like her." He looked back at his daughter. "Oh, she's smiling at me."

Anne exchanged knowing glances with her mom.

Sergio's nose wrinkled. "PU. I think she needs changing." He held her toward Anne, and her mom came to the rescue again.

"I'll do the honors. Come on, you cutie-patootie." She spread a receiving blanket on the kitchenette table and laid Sylvie down.

"But that's where we eat," Sergio complained.

Her mom shrugged. "There's no room in here for a changing table."

"I'll be so glad when you move to New York with me." He sat on the bed next to Anne and put his arm around her.

"They're not moving to New York; they're coming to Michigan," Anne's mother said.

Anne froze for a moment and made a split-second decision. Even though she hated to break both their hearts, she announced, "I've decided to stay here."

Sergio moved his arm and stared at her. "I thought . . . She's my baby."

"And she's my grandbaby." Anne's mom picked up Sylvie and carried her to the rocker.

"Yes, she is. And you are both welcome to visit whenever you wish, but I'm staying here."

"It's too small," Sergio said.

"I don't care. My life is here. Our life is here." Anne took the baby from her mom and sat back on the bed.

"Can I at least get a bigger place for you and Sylvie?" Sergio asked. "Then I can stay with you when I come to visit."

"That's not appropriate. We're not together anymore."

"You seem to be together to me." Her mom pursed her lips.

"I want to be independent. I'm staying here, and that's that. I'll have plenty of help."

"Who?" her mother asked.

"Mrs. Landenheim has offered to watch her when I'm at the museum."

"Mrs. Landenheim! That old bat." Sergio raised his voice.

"Shh!" Anne put a finger to her lips and pointed at the baby. "I thought you liked her."

"I do. Not to help raise my child, though. She'll have the baby in curlers and lipstick before she even turns one."

Anne couldn't help but laugh. "That's funny."

"Your landlady? Is it fitting to mix renting with day care?"

"It'll be convenient. It'll be fine." Anne shrugged. "Besides, Dottie's coming in a few weeks and is considering moving out here to help."

"Dottie?" Sergio stood. "A drug addict?"

"You know how undependable she's always been." Her mom raised her usually calm voice.

"She's changed. I told you, she went to rehab and apologized."

"That girl's a piece of work." Sergio shook his head.

"Also, Fay told me I can drop off Sylvie at Bay Breeze anytime, if need be."

"Won't she have her hands full with her own baby?" Sergio seemed to be looking for any reason to complain.

"She said the more the merrier. George helps out there too." Anne didn't want to tell them he was Mr. Mom when Fay was at the gallery. "Don't worry—we'll be fine."

The baby was so sweet, it would be easy, she hoped.

52

Outside in the pitch darkness, a siren wailed, the dog in the building next door howled, and Sylvie started to bawl. Exhausted and bleary-eyed, Anne started crying as well. She pulled the baby into bed with her and tried to feed her. However, Sylvie continued to shriek. Anne changed her diaper and rocked her until the baby's brown eyes, just like Sergio's, blinked closed. Anne ran a hand over the soft, dark hair. Only a month old, Sylvia was starting to look like Sergio.

Anne couldn't stop crying. She was in love more than ever with Sylvie. What was wrong with her, then? She should be happy. Could she be sleep deprived or have postpartum depression, or did she just miss her mom? She had slept on the futon for two weeks while Sergio had stayed at the Mark Hopkins, come down to the apartment every morning, and stayed into the evenings.

She had been relieved to see them go, eager to begin a life of motherhood on her own. Now, she would give anything to have them back. She missed her mom changing the baby and rocking her, trips to the Laundromat, and her mother's cheery disposition. She missed Sergio's help, especially his frittatas, mochas, and opera singing. If her mother hadn't been there, Anne wondered if he would have tried to stay with her and how that might have worked out.

At times, though, he got on her nerves, constantly picking up after them, trying to keep the apartment neat and tidy. He didn't say anything about it, but she could tell the mess drove him crazy. What would he be like when Sylvie threw toys all over the floor?

When he left, she'd been sure she'd made the right decision; now, she wondered whether she had. Maybe she should have taken him up on his offer to get them a bigger place, and perhaps even a nanny. She really wanted to be independent. Before the baby was born, she'd thought her life was complicated. Now, it was just plain ridiculous—the stink of dirty diapers, laundry piled up, sleepless nights. She looked forward to going back to work next week and having Dottie come help.

Anne tried to set Sylvie back in the bassinet, but she screamed. The new guy in Val's apartment below banged on his ceiling. "Knock it off up there."

"Sorry!" Anne yelled down to him, and returned to the rocker. Many experts recommended letting an infant cry it out. Living in an apartment like this meant that didn't work. A crying baby wasn't fair to the neighbors; plus, Sylvia's wails broke her heart.

"Hush, little baby, don't say a word. Papa's gonna buy . . ." Anne sang to Sylvie through the screams until they both dozed off.

Anne woke when the sun began to fill the room. Where was Mrs. Landenheim? This wasn't the first time she'd overslept. She was supposed to be here at six o'clock to watch the baby while Anne took a shower, ate breakfast, and did some chores.

She texted her: *Where are you?*

Anne waited a few minutes, but Mrs. Landenheim hadn't replied. She couldn't stand her grungy body any longer, so she put Sylvie in her bassinet and climbed into the shower with tears streaming down her face.

Out of the shower, Sylvie bawling again, Anne threw on sweats and pulled her wet hair into a scrunchie. Frantically, she checked her phone. Still no word from Mrs. Landenheim. Anne hoped she was okay.

With the baby in one arm, she opened the refrigerator with the other: a black banana, two olives in a jar, a cardboard piece of pizza. Sergio had stocked up before he'd left, but by now everything had run out. Old Mother Hubbard scrounged in her cupboard, but nothing was there. She climbed out onto the deck, but there weren't any berries in the garden. She located the Chips Ahoy from the freezer, where she'd hidden them from herself, and ate a few. She'd go back to eating healthfully tomorrow and planned to go to the grocery store and do laundry while Mrs. Landenheim watched Sylvie.

Anne called her landlady because she still hadn't responded to the text.

After the fifth ring, she answered.

"When are you coming up?" Anne asked.

"Sorry, no can do."

"What do you mean?" Anne tried hard not to scream. "Are you sick?"

"No, no. Ray Ray has whisked me off to Napa. We're staying at Calistoga Spa Hot Springs."

Anne pictured the former gallery owner and Mrs. Landenheim wallowing in the mud baths, and it wasn't pretty.

"Please feed the cats."

Crying, Anne hung up. When Mrs. Landenheim had offered to provide childcare, Anne had thought she would be more dependable. At least Dottie would be here soon.

Anne breathed in and out and gazed at her Southwest cloud collage. "Serenity now!" she called.

She couldn't get Sylvie to stop crying, no matter what she did. "Alexa, play '*O sole mio*,'" she commanded, as she put Sylvie back in the bassinet and let her cry.

Anne wrote with a Sharpie on three stickies—*I am independent; I am calm; I am happy*—and stuck them on her bathroom mirror.

Anne's phone chimed with a text from Dottie: *Call me.*

Speak of the devil. As soon as Sylvie fell asleep, Anne tiptoed into the bathroom, closed the door, and called her friend.

"How's it going?" Dottie asked.

"It'll be fine as soon as you're here. I can't wait for you to see the baby. What time do you get in?"

"About that. I can't come just yet."

"What? Why not?" Anne held back the panic rising from her stomach to her throat.

"I've been invited on a ski trip."

"But you don't even ski."

"I've always wanted to learn." Dottie whined, "How could I say no?"

"You could say no because your dear friend needs you."

"It's Switzerland. You know I've dreamed of going to Europe. You should be happy for me to have the opportunity for a free vacation."

Happy for you. Girl! Right after I slap you! Anne felt as if she'd taken a bullet to the chest as she remembered that Sergio was also going to St. Moritz. Was that too much of a coincidence?

"Who are you going with?"

"Some guy I saw at a gallery event."

Anne waited. "What's his name?"

"You don't know him. I'll come visit another time."

Anne tried to keep the rage out of her voice. "The ticket is non-transferable."

"I'll pay you back. I'm not sure when. I need to make some money first."

"I thought your art was selling well." After all, Dottie had made $10,000 at her solo show a few years back.

"Sure, but I've decided to go in a different direction. I'm thinking of hosting a podcast where people send me a topic and I talk about it for twelve minutes off the top of my head, without doing any research, and then I research and talk for another twelve minutes. Don't you think it's a fantastic idea?"

No. "Sure. Sounds lucrative." Anne nodded.

"I also might go back to school to get a certificate in museum studies to learn how to become a curator. I'd be good at telling people where to put their artwork. Don't you think?"

Yes, if you planned to hang everything upside down.

Sylvie wailed.

"Bye," Anne blubbered, and hung up.

She wanted to call her mom, who'd tried to warn her about Dottie, but Anne hadn't listened. At least her mother wasn't the type to ever say "I told you so."

Anne picked up Sylvie and sat in the rocker. If she was going to be independent, she'd better start now. She loaded Sylvie in the front pack, put on a giant down coat, zipped it up to the baby's head, and placed the pink cap on her. Anne ran down the stairs, fed the cats without even saying hello, and dashed across the street to the grocery. Filling the cart, she bounced Sylvie until she quieted. Back at her apartment, Anne seized an armload of dirty clothes, ran back down the stairs, and tossed them into the cart. Back upstairs, she drank a glass of water and repeated up and down two times more with dirty clothes, her coin jar, and laundry detergent.

Amid all the motion, Sylvie had fallen asleep in the front pack. From all of this running around, Anne would lose her baby weight soon. She started pushing the cart up California Street toward the Laundromat and ran into Mata. She hadn't seen her for months.

"Missy! Has it really come to this? You're homeless now too?"

Anne burst into tears. "I can't keep up with it all!"

"Now, now. It'll be okay. What's this?" Mata asked, pointing to the bulge under Anne's coat.

Anne unzipped it and turned the baby's little head to the side.

Mata's eyes grew wide. "What a living doll!"

Sylvie shrieked.

"Better call in the reinforcements."

Anne jiggled Sylvie up and down. "I'm trying to be independent."

"It's time to ask for help. Don't you have that one friend you can always count on?"

Anne dried her eyes and pushed the cart up the rest of the way to the empty Laundromat. She filled all the washers, added coins, and turned on the machines. Sylvie started crying again. Arms tired, Anne let the baby hang in the front pack, hopping up and down until Sylvie quieted.

Sergio called on FaceTime. She considered not picking up, and besides, the washers and dryers were noisy. But she decided she needed to confront him about Dottie.

"Ciao, bella."

"Ciao." Anne moved the phone so he could see Sylvie.

"She's growing fast."

"She'll be playing basketball before we know it." Anne paused. "When're you going to St. Moritz?"

"St. Moritz? What do you mean?"

"Your ski trip."

"I decided to come out and see you and Sylvie instead."

"So, you're not with Dottie?"

"Dottie? What are you talking about? Of course not."

"Oh, I didn't know."

"I'm going to search for a condo to buy so I can stay in it when I come to visit."

Did that mean he'd be out here all the time? Anne had mixed feelings about that. "With all the techies, that would be so expensive."

"Staying in a hotel all the time would be expensive also."

She finished the laundry and returned home with three armloads of folded clothes to carry up. Sylvie started shrieking again.

Anne changed her, she tried unsuccessfully to feed her, she rocked her. She couldn't stand it anymore. Mata was right; there was a friend Anne could always count on.

She typed, *SOS!* And pressed SEND.

53

Cliff touched her shoulder. "Morning, glory. Or should I say afternoon?" His voice teased her, as if he not only remembered the kiss, but knew about her dream as well.

Bright sunlight streamed into the cabin. Outside, a mourning dove cooed. Sally Sue rolled over and hid her blushing face. After tilling the soil, after the hoedown, after the kiss, after the dream, she wanted him. She wanted him more than anything she'd ever wanted in her life.

"I'm off to work the horses." His boots clomped to the door.

Today, no matter what, she needed to find a way to hightail it away from here before he kissed her again. If not, she was afraid of what might happen.

At the window, she watched a buck wander toward the pond. Gray clouds swooned in across the turquoise sky. Oak trees formed black silhouettes below. Far off, thunder boomed.

Outside, she paused as a tom turkey swaggered down the meadow, warbling. His red waddle and snood shook. A hen hunkered in the grass, ignoring the tom's wooing. Sally Sue hoped she'd reciprocate soon.

She climbed down to the ravine behind the cabin. She scooped fresh water into a bucket that flowed below the rocks under a willow tree. As she walked back to the cabin, she saw the tom's feathers quivering with desire.

Cliff haltered Roan and led her to the round pen. He brushed her back, saddled her up, and got on, his tall, straight body erect. Sally Sue longed for him again as he rode up the path beside the meadow. Clouds rolled overhead and the sky darkened, foretelling rain. She'd better stay.

Heat penetrated the cabin. She opened the trunk and pulled out the green dress from the trunk, laid it on the bed, and fingered the black lace. She poured the cool water into the bowl and washed her hands and face with lavender soap. Using a rag, she scrubbed sticky perspiration from the rest of her body.

Just then, lightning lit the sky and thunder boomed. Rain began to batter the roof. She held the frock up to her in the looking glass and had no choice but to do what she had to do.

She slipped off her nightgown, pulled the frock's straps over her arms, and tied the bows tight at her waist. The flimflam man's black lace fanned across the top of the bodice, exposing the tops of her breasts. She'd repurposed her travel suit's bustle, plumping it as much as possible to accentuate her derriere. She shook it like that tom. The bottom of the frock hit the tops of her knees.

The door opened. Cliff slipped inside with the rough earth smell of his body—horse, hay, loam—and she turned to him. His hair and clothes were wet with rain. Her heart raced as she moved toward him, the satin rustling between her legs.

She liked it when he put a hand on the back of her neck and traced his fingers between her breasts. She liked it when he gazed into her eyes, pulled her close, and kissed her. He tasted of honey and sage. She touched the cleft of his chin and couldn't help but kiss him back, forgetting her upbringing, herself. This was the kind of kiss no one ever wanted to end—full of heart, heat, and desire.

She pushed him onto the bed, unbuttoned his shirt, slid it off. She untied her dress, let it fall to the ground. Rain continued to pound on the roof. He moved his hand onto her thighs. She moved on top of him and had no idea what to do next, but in the throes of their rocking, slow heat, she ached for him. The thing she'd been warned about most. The thing she wanted most.

Her instincts overpowered her. She lost sense of time and place, ran her fingers through the back of his damp hair, touched the small of his back. Those steel-blue eyes, now sky blue, gazed into hers until the very end, the connection divine.

Afterward, she wanted to stay that way forever, floating in his arms. She rolled beside him and watched him sleep, a slight smile on his face, his muscled chest moving up and down. She wanted to put her hand there gently to wake him for more.

Instead, she ran outside. The rain had ceased; the sun was warm on her bare skin.

"Hallelujah!" she yelled. She should have been saddened by her innocence lost; instead, she twirled around, the soil soft beneath her feet. The mystery now over, she just looked forward to doing it again.

Her mother had always told her, "Your womanhood is your main asset. Only bad women like sex." Pastor Grimes spoke of the sins of the flesh. Instead of guilt, Sally Sue felt free. If it felt so good, why would God consider it a sin?

And what about love? She could hear Elvira say, "There's honey in every pot."

Yes, Cliff was filled with honey, but he could also be hot as those red peppers. Could you love and hate someone at the same time? Mama had told her a wife's duty was to submit to her husband. If Sally Sue was married to Cliff, and even if she wasn't, she would consider it not submittal but rapture. She thought about all the nice things Cliff had done for her: taught her to cook, shoot, ride.

She looked forward to seeing their garden grow, to picking the vegetables and eating them for supper. Long afternoons on the porch he planned to build, just talking. And—she smiled—more afternoon dalliances. Evenings with singing, dancing, and then more luscious lovemaking. Living here in all this beauty with him for the rest of her days would be miraculous.

Overhead, a hawk circled. Purple shadows shifted in the faraway sky. The storm had moved on. In the west, lightning flashed and thunder boomed. Her mind flashed to the robbery, the man's scream, the gun on her chest. Cliff was an outlaw, wanted dead or alive. Maybe her mama was right, and all men were evil. How could she have coupled with a man like him and have these thoughts?

54

Sally Sue quickly and quietly donned the red dress and slipped out to the barn. Inside, Scout whinnied beneath her loving hands as she stroked his neck. "Hush."

He calmed under her touch. She haltered and saddled him up. She'd ride to town, borrow money from the McMillans, leave Scout with them, and hop a train back to Missouri.

A day moon rose over the edge of the mountain as Sally Sue began her escape. She glanced back at the cabin and dug her heels into Scout's flanks. He whinnied and ambled out the dirt path toward the bridge.

Past it, she whispered, "Gentle moon, lead the way." Salty tears choked her voice. "Away from him."

On the other side of the bridge and out of sight, she clucked and kicked her heels into Scout's flanks. "Good boy. Let's go."

Sally Sue leaned forward, and Scout began to lope. After a few strides, she fell into Scout's rhythm and became one with him. Ponderosa pines lined the road like sentinels guarding their way.

Before a bend in the road, she stopped. She thought she heard Roan's hooves behind them, so she encouraged Scout to pick up the pace. Soon they were flying along, Scout a Pegasus. They followed the curves and continued on the road, this way and that, until, exhausted, Scout slowed to a walk.

They passed the crop of boulders where Elvira's revolting husband had been killed. Had a coyote, wolves, or vultures picked away at his mangy body? Had Elvira told the sheriff what had happened? The wind whooshed, and clouds swirled above, covering the moon. Sally Sue shivered—she didn't believe in ghosts—but even so, she encouraged Scout to split into a gallop.

At the lumber camp, she paused to catch her breath. A scarlet sunset filled the windy sky. She kept going, and after a while, from a rise, she spotted the town lights below.

Entering Flagstaff, she passed the church and headed toward the mercantile. As they drew closer, her eyes began to water and sting. A strong gale blew sticky moths that landed in her hair and on her arms, smelling of soot. This was not moths, but ash. A flickering light rose and lit up the dark night sky.

In shock, she held Scout's reins tight as the hussies and men ran from the saloon across the road. Crackling sounds echoed, more voices called, and folks started to pass buckets from the well, dousing flames.

In horror, Sally Sue watched a spark fly across the street to the mercantile eaves, and the roof quickly caught on fire. She imagined fabric ribbon, lace, hats, shoes igniting, guns and tools melting.

"Is the family inside?" she shouted.

No one heard her.

She leaped off Scout, ran toward the mercantile, and shoved the door open.

As her boots crossed the threshold, Cliff, seemingly out of nowhere, pulled her back by her arm. "Sally Sue, there you are." He dashed into the burning building. "Get back. Leave it to me."

Coughing and trying to inhale, she staggered over to the hotel porch, catty-corner from the mercantile. It felt like an eternity until he ran out of the building with the boy Isaiah in his arms.

"Mama, Mama!" Isaiah cried.

Sally Sue dashed toward Cliff. He handed the boy to her. "Move him to safety."

Cliff raced back into the inferno. She returned to the hotel, sat on the wooden steps, and shifted the sweet boy onto her lap. Soot tears streaked his cheeks.

She cooed, wiped his face with her handkerchief, and held him close to her chest, not wanting him to see the mercantile ablaze. Her eyes focused on the wooden structure in hopes Isaiah's parents would escape the building with Cliff. *Please, God, protect them*, she prayed.

A crashing sound came as the roof caved in. It seemed like hours but was probably only a minute by the time Cliff lumbered into sight and collapsed in the doorway.

Sheriff Mack and the blacksmith reached Cliff as the whole mercantile gave way behind him. One picked up his arms, the other his feet, as they carried him to the hotel and laid him near her on the porch. Then they ran back to help put out the flames.

She sat Isaiah down on a step, slid over to Cliff, and put his head in her lap. "Breathe, please, breathe."

She wasn't sure if her eyes were teary from the smoke-filled air or from a deep longing and love for this man—the man she'd wanted to get away from all this time.

His eyes opened, and they blinked at her with a smile that said so much.

She ran her fingers along his forehead scar where she'd stitched the lesion.

Then his eyes closed for the last time.

She held him close, her heart tugged with grief, and she cried, "Cliff, don't go! Come back to me."

55

A spark flew toward the church steeple but disappeared as it blew out. Isaiah reached for her hand and moved close to her. The fire burned down to its last embers. The livery, saloon, and mercantile were all destroyed. Fortunately, the flames hadn't spread farther or jumped across to the north side of the street.

Elvira sat beside Sally Sue and wiped her cheeks with a cloth. "Turns out there was honey in that heart."

"You were right."

"It's a miracle God saved you." Elvira put her hand on Isaiah's back.

"God saved me?" he asked.

Mr. Bjork came out of the hotel and walked toward them with an armload of blankets. Elvira stood up and backed away.

"Wait." He handed her a blanket.

"Thank you, Mr. Bjork." Elvira accepted it, spread it over Cliff's body, sat again, and put her hand on Sally Sue's shoulder.

"I'm sorry, ma'am." Mr. Bjork gave Sally Sue a blanket too.

"Thank you kindly," Sally Sue said, pulling Isaiah onto her lap and covering them both.

"The poor lad." Mr. Bjork looked at Isaiah.

The boy coughed and began to cry. Sally Sue hummed a lullaby to him softly. He put his thumb in his mouth and quieted.

"You go home now, Elvira." He gave her a blanket and said to Sally Sue, "Come on in, ma'am, before others descend on me."

"Much obliged. I haven't any money."

"At times like this, money doesn't matter. My workers will care for your horses."

Sally Sue followed Mr. Bjork upstairs to a small room at the end of a hallway, carrying the boy in her arms, and laid him on the bed. She poured water from the pitcher into the bowl on the washstand.

Isaiah squirmed while she removed his soot-filled clothes and cleaned him as best she could. She tucked him in bed and hummed to him. He turned over and sighed, then stuck his thumb back in his mouth. Soon his eyes closed, and his breathing grew soft and shallow.

In a split second, both of their lives had changed forever. Her love for and with Cliff, which she hadn't even known was there, was now gone. And what would become of Isaiah? Her heart shifted, and a yearning tugged on it. She didn't want to part with him. Maybe she could take him with her back to Missouri, but without a husband or even a pretend one, she knew Flagstaff would probably never let her keep him.

She rinsed his clothes in the washbasin, squeezed them out, and hung them up to dry. Could she steal out of town with him? What would she do for money? She could tell Mack who Cliff was and collect the dead-or-alive bounty. He'd start asking questions, though, and she didn't want to share details of their life together. It was too private.

Maybe it was best not to tell anyone and to let Cliff rest in peace. Memories of their time together would be precious to her forever. She would make certain he had a decent Christian burial. Even if he didn't believe, his body needed to go back to the earth with dignity.

Outside in the hallway, voices chattered and doors slammed. Isaiah coughed and woke up teary-eyed. She sat on the bed's edge and rocked him back and forth until he fell asleep again.

She pulled off her boots, and in her soot-covered dress, she curled up beside him. "Sweet boy," she whispered. "Sweet, sweet boy."

She closed her eyes and drifted off to sleep.

The next morning, a loud knock woke her. "Sheriff's downstairs and wants to see you."

A hazy eastern sun shone through the lace curtains. Her throat ached, and her eyes still watered.

"I'll be right down," she called.

Isaiah coughed and rolled over, fast asleep. Sally Sue pulled her boots back on, picked up Isaiah, and descended the stairs.

Vittles filled the dining room table, where Mr. Bjork was serving folks biscuits, flapjacks, and eggs. Men in filthy clothes stood around, eating. The saloon girls, with flattened hair and smeared makeup, looked like any ordinary women fallen on hard times.

"What do you think started it?" the redhead from the saloon asked.

"I think lightning." The livery owner spooned honey on a biscuit.

"Is this the end of Flagstaff? No one's gonna want to move here now." The redhead sighed.

"That's not true. We're resilient. I'm going to rebuild in brick starting next week." His voice was firm. "I'm going to propose a law that every new building in town should only be stone or brick," he continued.

Several people nodded in agreement. Sally Sue agreed.

The redhead smiled at her kindly, with sad eyes. "Sorry about Mr. Cliff, ma'am."

"Thanks." Sally Sue wondered again if he had frequented the saloon on any of those nights away.

"Step outside, please." Sheriff Mack looked like he hadn't slept for weeks. The redhead opened her arms, and Sally Sue put Isaiah in them.

The porch was covered in ash an inch thick. The smoke-laden air was stifling. Sally Sue coughed.

The sheriff held his hat in his hands. "I'm sorry about your husband."

She lowered her eyes.

"Thanks for caring for the young one last night."

"I was happy to. What's to become of him?"

"No next of kin that I know of," the sheriff whispered, and looked at the door.

"Won't someone from the church take him in?"

"Everyone's got troubles now. If a decent family doesn't step up, we'll have to take him to the orphanage in Prescott."

Her stomach lurched. "I've heard they're horrible: gruel for food, cramped dormitories, even beatings." She just couldn't let that happen. She'd find a way to care for him, even if she had to become a hootchy-cootchy girl.

"Can't be helped."

"How about if he stays with me?" Sally Sue offered.

"You know I can't do that, ma'am. As much as I'd like to, you're alone now, without a man to take care of even you."

Sally Sue thought fast and swallowed. "He's so distressed. How about if I take him out to the cabin for a good night's rest and return him to you in the morning? I'll make arrangements for my husband's burial then."

Mack handed her a fat envelope. "This is for you from Cliff. He had me hold it in the safe for you, in case anything happened, since a few months after you arrived."

She slid the envelope into her pocket.

"I reckon the homestead is yours now." He held up a piece of paper. "Here's the deed. Want me to keep it safe for you?"

"Yes, thank you."

"He was a good man. He sure loved you."

"What makes you say that?"

"He said sometimes you could be ornery, but still you were the best little wife a man could ever have. This is also for you." He handed her a heavy pouch that shook with metal. It must have been filled with coins. "Do you want me to hold the cash and these for you too?"

She paused. "No, sir. Thank you. I'll take them."

Isaiah ran out the door past her and stopped in the middle of the road, staring at the devoured mercantile. "Where's Mama?" he cried.

Sally Sue knelt down and held his hands. "Your mama's in heaven now."

"Heaven?" His big blue eyes blinked back tears.

"Papa?"

"Papa too. They're together in heaven."

She led him back toward Mack. "Let's go talk to the nice sheriff."

Isaiah wiggled and pulled his hand away. "Where's Mama?" he asked again.

"In heaven." She put her arm around Isaiah. "Please, Sheriff, he's so confused. Let me take him to the homestead for a night."

"I reckon that wouldn't hurt anything. I'll see you tomorrow."

Sally Sue held Isaiah in front of her on Scout's back as they rode at a gentle pace on the trail toward the homestead.

When they arrived at the cabin, she climbed down and lifted Isaiah to the ground. Socks mewed and greeted them at the door. "Kitty!" With delight, Isaiah bent down and petted her.

It was the bright hour when sunlight filled the cabin, sinking into the floorboards, and warmth began to rise.

He coughed. "Mama."

Sally Sue cuddled him onto her lap in the rocker. "It's me, Sally Sue."

He whined, "Mama."

"Bye, Baby Bunting, Daddy's gone a-hunting." She rocked him until he fell asleep and tucked him under a blanket on the cot. Cliff's blanket, Cliff's cot. Her heart ached. She stepped over the green dress she'd let fall on the floor and crawled into bed. Had that been only yesterday?

Propping up her pillow behind her, she pulled the envelope from her pocket, opened it, and shook out the contents. A handful of cash fell out, along with a letter. She felt a twinge in her chest as she counted the bills. Even from the grave, he was taking care of her.

She unfolded the letter and read:

Darlin',

If you're reading this, I'm a goner. Your caring presence has forced me to realize what's important in life. I'm not a bad man, as I said, but I had been painted into a corner and couldn't get out of the past without stomping tracks all over, hurtin' others along the way. I'm sorry you were one of them. Enjoy your freedom. Thank you for your kindness, which I never deserved.

Always, C

Caring and kindness? Tears sprang to her eyes for all the times she'd been surly to him. He hadn't had any idea how much she had hated him. He'd told Mack she could be ornery, but that wasn't even the half of it. Cliff had been the caring and kind one, and she'd been too stubborn and hateful to even take notice. At least not until the end.

She read the epistle again, lay down, and closed her eyes. Cliff's scent wafted from the empty pillow beside her. She picked it up, pressed it to her nose, and inhaled the deep, musty aroma of him, letting it fill her senses, memorizing it. She wrapped the pillow in her arms, rolled over, and wept uncontrollably. He'd had lots of honey in his heart.

"'Ally." Isaiah patted her hand. "You okay?"

"Yes, dear one." She lifted him up, held him close beside her. He just couldn't go to an orphanage.

As much as she had grown to love the ranch, she wouldn't be able to stay here without Cliff. Sure, she could take care of herself without him, though it wouldn't be worth it. Besides, the missing him would be too much.

Sally Sue wiped a tear from her eye and cuddled Isaiah, certain what she had to do. She would miss the turkeys, deer, owls, horses, and even frogs. The magnificent meadow and pond. She wouldn't get to see the garden grow or what the ranch looked like in the fall, as the aspens turned golden.

She'd saddle up Scout. At the crossroads she'd go right, instead of left, avoiding Flagstaff, and head on to the next town. They'd take the train back to Missouri, where Mama would help her raise the boy. Sally Sue would tell everyone she'd become a widow whose husband had died in a fire and left her his child. Everyone would be convinced.

56

Grass tickled Sally Sue's ankles through her wool stockings as she strolled between windswept dunes toward the sound of pounding waves.

A gull squealed and flew overhead.

"Birdie." Isaiah ran down the path toward it. "Big birdie."

Basket on one arm and a satchel on the other, she followed him. A miraculous view took her breath away. Not another person was in sight. The coastline seemed to go on forever and disappear around a bend. Offshore swells rolled toward the beach and roared as they smashed onto the dark sand.

"Look!" Isaiah yelled, then raced toward the mighty Pacific.

"Isaiah, come back!" she called into her cupped hands, right before he darted into the water.

He turned around. She motioned for him, and he dashed back to her.

"You're such a good boy." She gave him an enormous hug, and he squeezed her back. "Let's at least take off our shoes."

She laid her shawl on the sheltered edge of a sand dune, sat, and patted the shawl beside her. "Sit down."

"Yes, ma'am."

She removed her shoes and stockings. "Now you."

He took off his shoes and socks and set them aside. He mimicked her with a giggle as she wiggled her toes in the warm sand.

Socks mewed from inside the basket. Isaiah opened it. The kitty poked her head up.

"We need to let her out for a moment." Sally Sue lifted Socks out and kept a close eye on her. She ran in circles, scratched at the sand, and soon returned to the basket.

Sally Sue rolled up Isaiah's overall legs, and the two of them walked toward the sea. Clasping his hands in front of her, she waded with him into the icy water.

"Brrr," she hollered.

"Bwrrr," Isaiah hollered.

She pulled him up and over ripples that grazed her knees. She picked him up in her arms and waded out farther and dunked them both in. He started to cry, so she splashed back to the beach and shook her body like a dog to make him laugh. It worked; he giggled again.

They sat on the shawl to dry in the sun. She kissed him, smelling the salty sea on his cheek, and ran her fingers through his blond locks. The sun reflected off them, and his blue eyes sparkled. He leaped up, shot down toward the water again, and inspected its edge. Leaning down, he reached for something and scurried back to her. He opened his hand and held up his prize. "Look!"

"Shell." She accepted it from him and ran her fingers over the white ridges. She'd never seen a real one before, only in picture books. She handed it back to him.

"Pitty."

"Yes. It is very pretty."

He stuck it in his pocket and curled up beside her. She looked out at the ocean. It had come to her at the train station that she couldn't take him back to a life with her ma. Impulsively, she had bought tickets to the Pacific and a new life.

She removed her blouse, down to her undergarments, and let the velvety sunshine caress her bare shoulders, reminding her of

Cliff's warm touch. The touch she'd never feel again. She remembered his arm around her shoulder, warming her on their first ride to the homestead on that cold winter's night. His deep voice, booming out songs to keep the boredom at bay. His kindness and concern for her in his ever-changing blue eyes.

She'd done everything she could to get away from him and hadn't let his actions melt her resolve to hate him. She'd stayed alert and interpreted his actions as devious, ready to trick her like a shape-shifting coyote throwing his voice to trap her in his snare.

But his kindness toward her had been sincere after all, and she regretted all those months she'd fought the urge to let go, lean into him, and accept the love he offered. Now it was too late. The memories of their short time together would be with her eternally. She'd move forward in her life, keep hold of that one afternoon of bliss in her heart forever.

She gazed out at the vast blue ocean. Clouds billowed over it. She'd come to the end of this part of her journey and would stay for a while and a day. She wasn't going to have the normal life she had thought she wanted. God had given her Isaiah, which was worth so much more. She didn't know what her future held. As with the Pacific, she couldn't see to the other side.

57

Outside the window, early March breezes had pushed the morning fog away to reveal blue skies. A month after Anne's meltdown, her heart and mind were now clear as that sky. She sat in the rocker with her tiny, two-month-old miracle, Sylvie, in her arms. No, she was a big miracle. Anne couldn't believe she'd ever considered not having her. This was what God had planned for them.

She looked up at the mosaic hanging on the nursery wall and said, "You glow, girl!"

The path wouldn't be easy, but she'd move forward in a life filled with love. She sighed and smoothed down Sylvie's curls, which had begun to grow out in all directions. Turned out Sylvie had inherited not only Anne's big feet, but her wild hair as well. Her big brown eyes and long lashes were totally Sergio's.

It felt so good to be settled in a real home. They'd visit her childhood home at least once a year. She hoped Sylvie would like to fish there, too, someday, beside the purple hyacinth, pussy willows, and water lilies. The quiet watch for a great blue heron to fly overhead, a tug on the line, or a thunderstorm to erupt with passion in a world full of wonder.

Anne put Sylvie in the bassinet and cranked the forest-animal musical mobile over her head, and she soon fell asleep. It had taken some hard convincing to get Anne to move to Bay Breeze, but when Paul had told her Sylvia would want it that way, that clinched it. Moving into the mansion had felt like a fairy tale come true. At first,

Anne continued to see Sylvia around every corner, but soon even those feelings were comforting.

Fay came into the nursery with Diana in her arms. "You'll never believe—"

"Shh. I just put Sylvie down," Anne whispered, with a finger to her lips.

"Sorry." Fay set Diana in her own crib, tossed a blanket over her, and kissed her forehead. "Beddy-bye, baby."

They would raise the girls together as sisters—an untraditional family, but a family, nonetheless.

The women snuck next door to the guest room, which had become Anne's room. Boxes were still piled in a corner, and the bed was unmade.

Fay gasped. "Blimey, girl. You've been here all this time, and you haven't even finished unpacking."

"I've been overwhelmed getting Sylvie settled and going back and forth to the museum and all, but I'm ready to start tackling my room today." Anne gathered up a pile of clothes on top of a box.

Her phone rang.

"Sorry. It's the museum. I should take it."

"Hope they aren't letting you go."

"That's not even funny."

"Hi, Anne. This is William Willingsby."

"Yes?"

"We just had a board meeting, and we'd like to offer you the art director job."

"You would?" She couldn't believe what she was hearing and sat on the bed.

"Because of our financial situation, it's only part-time for now, but we hope you'll continue to teach too."

"I'm not qualified." After all, Priscilla had a doctorate and Anne had only a BA. She put the phone on speaker so Fay could also hear.

"You're an accomplished artist, and we like your hands-on and inclusive approach. I know you have a new responsibility at home, but we'd love for you to take over. We feel you have a good sense of what it would take to build a vibrant educational outreach program."

Anne's heart zigzagged with joy.

"That sounds wonderful. I'll need to check about childcare. I think I can work it out."

Fay nodded and did a happy dance.

"Come on in tomorrow, and let's talk about it. You don't need to decide right away. I'm hoping you can start soon, because I have to get back to my own life."

Anne hung up.

Fay hugged her. "I'm so proud of you! Of course we'll work out childcare."

She checked her phone. "I need to get to work soon, but I'll help you get started first." Fay began to fold a sweater rumpled on the dresser.

Anne shooed her out. "No, no. I'll do it. I promise. You go to work."

"Thanks for watching Paul and the girls this evening so we can have a date night."

Anne walked her to the top of the stairs. "It's the least I can do."

"Maybe you'll putter in your studio a bit today too. Cheerio," Fay said, as she traipsed down the stairs.

"Maybe." Anne dragged a box filled with shoes into the walk-in closet. She'd never dreamed of having a closet this big. She pulled out the silver shoes, held them to the overhead light, and admired the sparkles. She remembered the first time she'd seen them, in the New York antique shop. They truly turned out to be magic. She slid them onto the built-in shoe rack and slipped the Ferragamos beside them. Too big to fit on the rack, she put her cowgirl boots on the floor underneath.

After she finished unpacking all her shoes, she returned to the bed and looped the green boa over the corset outfit hanger, in hopes she'd be able to fit into it again to entice another man someday. Maybe it would be Sergio; then again, maybe not. She hung it in the closet with a smile. She and Sergio would be seeing each other often enough, whenever he came to see the baby and stayed in his condo here. So who knew?

She unpacked the green lace cocktail dress she'd worn the first night she met him and hung it in the closet. Collecting the black coat from the bed, she touched the snowflake pin and ran her hand along the smooth velvet. She held it up to her nose and imagined for a moment she caught a whiff of gardenia, then hung it in the closet too.

Opening another box, she saw the finance jars Sergio had sent. A good mother would actually use these to teach a daughter how to be financially responsible. Perhaps Anne could even use them to keep her own finances on track and set a good example for Sylvie. She lined them up on the dresser: *SAVE*, *SPEND*, *GIVE AWAY*.

She peeked at the girls in the nursery, both still sleeping peacefully, and made her way upstairs to the spacious attic that was now her studio. She twirled around like Julie Andrews on that mountaintop in *The Sound of Music* as bright sun streamed through the casement windows. Anne opened one and let the salty, cool breeze float inside. The bay below sparkled in the beauty of the day.

Anne pulled the lucky key from her jeans pocket, put it on her altar, fingered her father's dog tags, and rubbed the Buddha's belly.

"Thank you for all my blessings." She stared up at the ceiling and promised to write them down in her journal before the day was done.

Fay had surprised Anne by having shelving installed in the studio, and together the women had placed knickknacks on them, sorted the found objects into plastic bins, and loaded them neatly onto the shelves. Chipped and broken dishes were stacked there as well. Four six-foot tables had just been delivered. She placed them in the room's center and positioned oilcloth covers on top. A dream-come-true studio all Anne's own.

Fay had lined up all the finished and someday-to-be-finished pieces around the space. Anne curled up on the daybed, resting on a far wall, and listed them in her journal:

Southwest Sky Collage
Hugs and Kisses Washboard
Things People Pray For (with Lady of Guadalupe)
Cast-Away Stones
Our Lady of the Garden

She paused and added, *You Glow, Girl! (Would put "NFS" on it.)*

Without realizing it, she had intuitively made many pieces with female figures as focal points. She could combine the whole series to express the theme: female empowerment. Her fingers itched to add more to the collection.

These past months had been the longest period since she'd worked on her own. Uncertain where to start, she moved to her altar, rang the Tibetan chimes, lit a gardenia candle, and closed her eyes. She saw herself in the green lace corset and scrolled through her photos from the Southwest print until she found the one Lola had taken of her at the resale boutique. Anne printed it out, cut around it, and adhered it to the sky collage with a smile.

Inspired to keep going, she intuitively selected a ceramic statue of a girl wearing a headscarf. Anne glued it in the center of an antique oval tray, carried over her container of shells and one with pearls, and began to glue them around the girl. She added two fish chopstick holders she'd bought on sale in Chinatown, and blue-and-white dishes. She added *Sally Sells Seashells by the Seashore* to the list of pieces in her journal, sat on the daybed, and kept writing:

Gratitude for All My Blessings

Sylvie

Mom

Pootie

Tootie

Michigan nature

Sergio

Paul

Fay

George

San Francisco

Bay Breeze

Art

Sylvia

And the list could go on and on and on.

ACKNOWLEDGMENTS

First, I want to thank the San Diego Writers, Ink community for nurturing me through all these years while I created this trilogy, especially Executive Director Kristen Fogle for her dedicated leadership, and Nicole Vollrath for the prompt that started this novel's train on its tracks.

Brooke Warner, Crystal Patriarche, Samantha Strom, and my She Writes Press sisters, I so appreciate your wholehearted support and guidance. Enchantress Julie Metz, your book covers are more beautiful than anything I could ever have dreamed. Jordyn Smiley, thank you for the gorgeous green lace corset design and construction. I can't wait to wear it! A shout-out to my editors Tracy Jones, Judy Reeves, and Annie Tucker for your enthusiasm and much-needed keen eyes. Jen Coburn, publicist extraordinaire, your humor, perseverance, and positive attitude are never-ending. Thank you to all independent bookstores for supporting readers and writers, particularly La Playa Books, The Book Catapult, and Warwick's. And to Zorro the tuxedo cat, thank you for your wondrous surprise visits to my garden.

My sincere gratitude goes to these dear inspirational women who have been a gift to me: Jill Crusey, Minna Lopez, Susan Rapp, Tania Pryputniewicz, Paula Herring, Tinsley Correa, Dottie Laub, Leigh Akin, Tanya Peters, Rebecca Chaama, Debra Bandera, Leslie Meads, Lynn Cooper, Lisa Hampton, Banoo, Karen Begin, Meline Cox, Marti Hess, Lisa Laube, Carol Leimbach, Patti Wassem, Pat Fitzmorris, Holly Foster, Sandy Baine, and Stephanie Tsuruda.

I'm eternally grateful to my siblings Todd Greentree, Sandy Greenbaum, and Leslie Zwail for your love and encouragement.

Gratitude to Phil Johnson and Seth Krosner for always believing and being there for me. To my Westminster family, especially Tom Haine, Megan Cochran, and of course my soul brother Corey Pahanish, I thank our blessed stars for bringing us together.

A special thank-you goes to my readers—because of you I keep writing.

ABOUT THE AUTHOR

photo credit: Chris Loomis

JILL G. HALL is the author of a dual-timeline trilogy about women searching for their place in the world, connected by vintage finds. The first of the series, *The Black Velvet Coat,* was an International Book Award Finalist, and the second, *The Silver Shoes*, was a Distinguished Favorite in the NYC Big Book Awards. Her poems have appeared in a variety of publications, including *A Year in Ink, The Avocet,* and *Wild Women, Wild Voices.* Hall is an instructor at San Diego Writers, Ink, as well as a seasoned presenter at readings and community events. Her career as a public-school educator spanned over twenty years. She holds a doctorate from Northern Arizona University in Flagstaff. In addition to writing, she practices yoga, gardens, and fashions whimsical mosaics using found objects. On her blog, *Crealivity*, she shares her poetry and musings about the art of practicing a creative lifestyle. Learn more at www.jillghall.com.

SELECTED TITLES FROM SHE WRITES PRESS

She Writes Press is an independent publishing company founded to serve women writers everywhere. Visit us at www.shewritespress.com.

The Black Velvet Coat by Jill G. Hall. $16.95, 978-1-63152-009-9. When the current owner of a black velvet coat—a San Francisco artist in search of inspiration—and the original owner, a 1960s heiress who fled her affluent life fifty years earlier, cross paths, their lives are forever changed . . . for the better.

The Silver Shoes by Jill G. Hall. $16.95, 978-1-63152-353-3. Distracted by a cross-country romance, San Francisco artist Anne McFarland worries that she has veered from her creative path. Almost ninety years earlier, Clair Deveraux, a sheltered 1929 New York debutante, becomes entangled in the burlesque world in an effort to save her family and herself after the stock market crash. Ultimately, these two very different women living in very different eras attain true fulfillment—with some help from the same pair of silver shoes.

Portrait of a Woman in White by Susan Winkler. $16.95, 978-1-938314-83-4. When the Nazis steal a Matisse portrait from the eccentric, art-loving Rosenswigs, the Parisian family is thrust into the tumult of war and separation, their fates intertwined with that of their beloved portrait.

The Great Bravura by Jill Dearman. $16.95, 978-1-63152-989-4. Who killed Susie—or did she actually disappear? The Great Bravura, a dashing lesbian magician living in a fantastical and noirish 1947 New York City, must solve this mystery—before she goes to the electric chair.

Beautiful Garbage by Jill DiDonato. $16.95, 978-1-938314-01-8. Talented but troubled young artist Jodi Plum leaves suburbia for the excitement of the city—and is soon swept up in the sexual politics and downtown art scene of 1980s New York.

Start With the Backbeat by Garinè B. Isassi. $16.95, 978-1-63152-041-9. When post-punk rocker Jill Dodge finally gets the promotion she's been waiting for in the spring of 1989, she finds herself in the middle of a race to find a gritty urban rapper for her New York record label.